G

5 MINUTES TO DIE

RJ PATTERSON

AETHON THRILLS

aethonbooks.com

5 MINUTES TO DIE
©2024 RJ PATTERSON

ALSO IN THE SERIES

GARRETT KNOX

5 Minutes to Die
Terminal Threat

Check out the entire here! (Tap or scan)

For Brian Courteau

CHAPTER ONE

Bitterroot National Forest | Montana

Garrett Knox spun on the gravelly trail in the direction of the panicked scream. It had been a while since he'd heard a sound so desperate, so terrified. Reacting to the cries for help, he hustled past the three hikers behind him, all with their backs plastered against the rock face on the narrow path overlooking Blodgett Canyon. Then he heard more shouts for help, this time more frantic than the last.

Forty feet below, Carley Whitmire, a member of the Challenger Camp team, dangled tenuously from a tree branch jutting out of the mountain. Her backpack had snagged on the limb, though Knox could tell immediately that it wouldn't hold Carley for long, especially with the way she was kicking her feet and yelling for help. She also had a stiff June breeze to contend with.

Knox ripped his pack off his back as he knelt and formulated a plan. He scrambled into a prone position, his feet buttressing up against the mountain.

"Just relax, Carley," he said, his hands cupped around the sides of his mouth. "I'm gonna get you up here. Don't worry."

Allison Matthews, Knox's colleague at the camp for teenagers and official leader of the hike, picked her way along the path, maneuvering around the entire hiking contingent. Eight hikers in all, including Knox and Matthews, had completed about three-fourths of the nearly 13-mile hike to Blodgett Lake. Allison gasped as she peered over the edge at Carley.

"How did that happen?" Allison asked.

"How did what happen?" Knox asked. "A limb snagging Carley? Or her falling off the edge?"

Allison shook her head.

"You got a plan?" she asked.

"Of course."

Using the survival skills Knox had learned while serving as a Ranger in the U.S. Army, he scanned the area behind him and located a pine tree growing in the middle of the trail. He secured a rope around the trunk and then tied the other end around his waist as a makeshift harness. At age thirty-five, he maintained his buff physique from his days in the military. The mindset he'd adopted as a Ranger kicked in naturally in an emergency situation.

"You sure you wanna do this?" Allison asked. "We can wait for search and rescue."

"There isn't time," Knox said, as he removed his lucky coin from his pocket and kissed it before yanking on the rope and rappelling down to Carley. "But call them now, in case we need them. We have no idea what kind of shape she's going to be in when I get her back up here."

Knox had only known Carley for three days, a newcomer to Challenger Camp who seemed determined to use the experience to help her overcome some of her greatest fears, with height being chief among them.

"Just look at me, Carley," Knox said, as he eased down the mountain.

Carley looked up, her face streaked with mascara.

"I thought we said no makeup for a week," Knox said, trying to distract her.

"Do I look that bad?"

"Raccoon eyes times ten," he said.

A faint smile spread across her lips as she sniffled and then glanced down again.

"Eyes up here," Knox said, his hands burning as they slid down the rope.

As he neared Carley, he felt the line go taut while still ten feet above her. He swore softly through gritted teeth. A sloping rock face full of boulders and scree lay about fifty feet below her. If she survived a fall, she was almost certain to slide into the canyon if she didn't get clobbered first by rolling rocks. The hypotheticals seemed nearly endless, so many variables to take into account, yet only two outcomes that mattered—death or survival.

As Knox surveyed the area around him, he swallowed hard. A bead of sweat trickled down his nose.

"How you doing, Carley?" he asked.

"Would it qualify as a dad joke if I said I was just hangin' in there?" she asked.

Knox smiled. Carley had calmed down, her sharp wit and sense of humor fully functional in the direst of circumstances. It was a good sign.

"Search and rescue are on the way," Allison announced from the ledge.

He glanced at Allison and gave her a thumbs-up before looking at Carley.

"Did you hear that?" he asked. "We've got a search-and-rescue team coming our way. Probably a half-hour or so away. Think you can *hang in there* for that long?"

"Don't steal my jokes, Knox," she said.

"I never steal dad jokes. All mine are Knox Knox jokes."

"That's really bad," she said. "If I have to hear any more of those, I might just jump to spare myself the torture."

Knox thought for a moment. His original plan had been to rappel down to Carley and coach her on how to use the rope to ascend. He also considered the possibility that the rest of the team could pull her up, but Knox was concerned about the amount of weight on the rope as it slid across jagged rocks. Because it wouldn't have just been

Carley they were pulling up—they would've been pulling him up as well. The last thing he wanted was to endanger anyone else on the team.

He closed his eyes and took a deep breath. The sweet scent of Douglas firs wafted through the air, a pleasant aroma standing in stark contrast to the heightened sense of anxiety hovering over them. But he'd been here before.

Don't overthink it. You already know what to do.

He looked down at his left leg, a high-tech prosthetic which served as an ever-present reminder of his inability to resist helping others in need. Then he looked at the strap on Carley's backpack that had snagged on the tree limb. It started to sag and appeared like it might give way at any moment.

"Carley, do you think you can reach up and wrap your arms around that limb?" he asked.

"Of course," she said. "You're looking at Snow Valley's top gymnast. Gotta be able to pull yourself up for the uneven bars."

"Great," he said, forcing a smile. "Just make it quick, okay?"

Carley extended her arms over her head and grabbed the limb. She pulled herself up and slung her arms over it.

"Feel good?" he asked.

"Depends on how long I have to stay like this," she said.

Knox looked up at the ledge. "Allie, got an ETA on search and rescue?"

"They should be about twenty minutes out," Allison said.

He shifted his focus back to Carley. "Think you can hold on for another ten minutes or so?"

"I heard Allison," Carley said. "She said *twenty* minutes."

"Just trying to keep you focused on small increments," he said.

Before she could respond, Knox cringed as he heard a sickening sound. The limb creaked as it bent, this time unable to withstand the weight placed on it any longer.

A snap echoed off the mountain followed by an even more horrific scream than Carley had unleashed minutes earlier.

She only fell about ten feet before landing on the loose rock along the steep pitch of the mountainside. But it didn't stop her momentum. She slammed into several boulders, somehow avoiding a direct hit to her head, then spun sideways and slid off the edge.

Knox craned his neck to see what he could just beyond the lip. From his perspective, there appeared to be a sheer drop down into the canyon. There was no way she could survive such a fall. The canyon floor was at least five hundred feet below where they were, though Knox couldn't actually see straight down to the ground—and neither could Allison, from up above.

He wanted to talk with Allison, see if there was something else he could do. But she was too busy calming the other campers, freaking out over the potential loss of their new friend.

Knox sighed, immediately second-guessing his decision to ask Carley to take hold of the limb. Her pack dangled too tenuously, with the end of it struggling to maintain her weight. But he stopped his mental spiral, something he'd been trained to do in the fog of war.

Stay focused, Knox.

As he pondered how to proceed—or if there was anything for him to do—he heard a faint sound, a cry for help.

"Carley?" he asked aloud to himself before shouting her name.

"I'm down here," she yelled.

He strained to hear.

"What's going on?"

"I'm wedged between two rocks, but I'm not sure how much longer I can hold it."

Knox knew Carley wouldn't be able to hold on for more than a few minutes. He needed to secure her before the search-and-rescue team arrived.

"Allison, you still there?" he called out.

She poked her head over the edge. "Is that—"

"Yeah," he said. "She's still alive, stuck between two rocks. But she needs help."

"What can you do now from there?"

"Nothing," Knox said, "which is why I need you to cut me loose."

"Are you insane?"

Knox didn't answer her question. "Just cut the damn rope."

"What do you think you're going to do?"

"The only thing I can do—try to help Carley," Knox said.

"But, Knox—"

"Don't argue with me. I know what I'm doing. Cut the rope now or I might not have time to help her."

Allison set her jaw and shook her head before disappearing from view. Then a few seconds later, she called out to him.

"Ready?" she asked.

"Yeah," Knox said as he clung to the side of the mountain, toes and fingers gripping whatever notches he could find.

"Good luck."

The rope that had been suspending Knox above the branch gave way. Knox didn't move as the rope snaked past him. Waiting until it was dangling beneath him, Knox eased down the rock, carefully placing his footholds.

Then a slip.

He scrambled to get his foot back into place before continuing.

After descending about ten feet, nearly even with the spot where Carley had been hanging, his foothold broke off, sending him skidding down the wall and into the slope.

Rolling, twisting, turning. Knox's shoulder banged into a boulder, his momentum swinging his legs around the rock. Scree cascaded around him as he continued to slide. Briefly orienting himself, he looked down and couldn't see anything but the canyon floor below.

And he couldn't stop either. Slipping, spinning, grabbing. He needed something to slow him down—and quickly—before he flew over the edge. Using his feet, he pushed off a small rock, propelling himself to one side before latching onto a boulder and halting his death slide.

Panting, Knox sat up, bracing himself with the large rock that was about the size of a medicine ball. Careful not to dislodge it, he eased around it and crab crawled closer to the edge.

"Carley," he called out, "are you still there?"

"Still here," she said, her voice quivering. "But I'm starting to slip."

He peeked over the side and saw Carley about fifteen feet below, bracing herself between two large outcroppings, arms and legs extended as far as she could reach. Her right foot slipped against the side of the rock before she repositioned it.

"Just don't move," he said.

"I'm trying."

Knox scanned the area and found a lip on the ledge. He kicked at it to make sure it was solid. It didn't budge. He wedged his feet against it before gathering the loose rope and easing it over the side.

"Carley, I'm sending down a rope. Do you think you can hold on?"

"Yeah."

Knox lowered the rope to her waist level.

"Just grab on," he said. "I'll pull you up."

Carley wrapped her right hand around the rope just as her foot slipped again. She scrambled to regain her footing, but she couldn't. The sudden jerk pulled Knox forward. He slid a few inches toward the ledge before he stopped himself. With Carley swinging beneath him, her movements pulled him slightly from side to side.

"Settle down, Carley. Stay as still as possible."

But she didn't. And then her other foot slipped, leaving her swaying as she tried to reach up with her left and wrap it around the rope. Her first attempt failed, resulting in her looking down again and heightening her already hysterical state.

"Carley, I need you to look at me," Knox said. "Focus on my eyes."

Instead of following his instructions, she lunged again for the rope with her left hand, this time wrapping her fingers tightly around the line. But the sudden jolt caused Knox's foot to slip.

And then he went over the edge.

As Knox tumbled, Carley's weight accelerated his descent. But with the rope secured around his midsection, he remained somewhat upright, which was what he needed to prevent a fatal fall to the canyon floor.

Plummeting between the two rocks where Carley had been just moments earlier, Knox spread his legs and used his feet to grind against the mountain face until he came to a stop just a couple of feet before the outcroppings ended.

Carley screamed below him, her arms and legs flailing wildly.

"Carley, I need you to stay calm," he said. "If you keep this up, I might not be able to hold us. Now just take a deep breath and focus."

After a few seconds of panic, she calmed down as much as could be expected. The swinging stopped and Knox exhaled. His arms burned as more sweat beaded up on his face, his fingers sensing every bump and nodule. While he was in excellent shape, he wasn't sure how long he could hold on. It wasn't like wedging himself against a rock with a person suspended from a rope beneath him was in his training regimen.

Knox could feel his heart thumping as if it was trying to escape from his chest. A sense of dread washed over him. He knew it all too well, the screams that preceded it too. Death was at the door—and she had a battering ram.

Then he felt something else thumping in his chest, but it was different.

A helicopter whomped in the distance.

Just hold on.

Knox's hand slipped and then he readjusted it. The attachments on his prosthetic leg dug into his skin as the weight of Carley and the gravity of the moment combined to create a pressure so intense that he wasn't sure how much longer he could endure it.

Just as he thought he was about to give way, the rescue chopper appeared from around the rock and navigated closely to them. Moments later, a man rappelled down, moving straight for Carley. He hooked her into his harness and then ascended.

The sudden release of her weight relaxed Knox.

I can do this.

After she was returned safely to the helicopter, the man rappelled again, this time to retrieve Knox. He didn't fully exhale until he was strapped into the helicopter in the backseat. Two members of the team tended to Carley's injuries. Another tried to look at Knox's scrapes, but he waved him off.

"Take care of her first," he said.

Knox looked at his leg. This time, he'd managed to do what he couldn't do before.

He looked at Carley, tousled her hair, and winked. Between grimaces, she offered a weak smile in return.

"You're gonna be all right, kid," he said.

She looked down at her leg, which was bruised and swollen.

"They think it's broken," she said.

"Could've been a lot worse," Knox said. "But I'm impressed that you braced yourself with a broken leg. I've known grown men who would melt down over something like that."

"Grown men who were Army Rangers?"

Knox chuckled. "I'm glad to see you've got your sense of humor back so quickly."

She smiled, this time more genuinely.

"Thanks," she said.

Knox scooted back in his seat and closed his eyes. He jammed his hand into his pocket and felt for his lucky coin.

"There you are," he said, as he held it up and inspected it. "You never disappoint."

When the chopper landed, Knox waited until everyone was off except the pilot before exiting. He trudged across the helipad at the private airfield and found camp manager Guy Valentine, with a furrowed brow, leaning up against his truck. He rushed over to Knox as soon as the two men locked eyes.

"Are you all right, Knox?" Guy asked.

"I'm alive," Knox said. "And that's about the extent of it."

"What the hell happened out there today?"

Knox bit his lip and slowly shook his head.

"Sometimes, things just don't go how you expect," he said. "It was just a routine hike, one we've done dozens of times with hundreds of kids. And never once did we have any problems, not even as much as a slip on the trail, at least not where it was this smooth. Narrow? Yes. But not a flat section like that. I don't know how Carley did it, but I'm just glad she's all right."

"We all are," Guy said as he ushered Knox into the truck.

Once they were both inside, Guy ignited the engine with the twist of his key.

"That should've been me up there on the mountain today," Guy said. "I know you're my boss and all, but—"

"But what, Guy? You think you would've been able to help Carley? You're a good twenty pounds overweight and you would've been able to hold her about as well as you hold your liquor, which, it should go without saying, isn't very good."

"I know, I know, but If I had been up on time—"

"But you weren't, Guy," Knox said. "You were hung over. You might have plenty of guilt right now, but you need to forget about that and just be thankful I haven't fired you already."

Guy sighed. "It's just that—"

"What, Guy? Spit it out."

"Oh, never mind."

Knox winced as he rolled down his window, cranking it down for some of nature's air conditioning, the only kind in the F-150 with a rusting tailgate and flaking white paint.

Neither man spoke as they rumbled back to Challenger Camp. As they entered under the camp gateway sign, Knox shifted in his seat.

"We need to talk later," he said.

"About what?" Guy asked, fumbling for a cigarette.

"About a lot of things," Knox said. "I'm actually glad you didn't make it today. I don't think things would've turned out as well as they did if you'd been there instead of me."

"Probably not," Guy conceded. "Look, I'm sorry about everything. I—I know I shouldn't have been drinking again. But I always do around the anniversary of Ellen's—of Ellen's—"

Knox patted Guy on the shoulder. "I understand. We'll deal with it—together. Okay?"

Guy nodded as he drove the truck over the washboard dirt road leading up to the camp.

As they rounded the corner and the camp's administrative building came into view, Knox saw a dark SUV parked near the front. He pointed at the vehicle.

"Was that SUV there when you left to come to get me?" Knox asked.

"Why? Were you expecting someone?"

"Answer the question, Guy."

"Yeah, it was there."

Knox cracked his knuckles. "Did you speak to anyone?"

"That's what I wanted to tell you earlier. There's someone who stopped by to see you. I didn't know who it was, but he said he would wait for you."

Knox immediately glanced down at the federal license plate beneath the SUV's bumper. He cursed and opened the door a few seconds before Guy came to a stop.

"Is everything okay?" Guy asked.

Knox waved dismissively at him before striding up to the vehicle. The tinted window behind the driver's side lowered. A man who appeared to be in his fifties with a bald head and a salt-and-pepper goatee locked eyes with Knox.

"Theodore Garrett Knox?" the man asked.

Knox scowled. He hadn't heard anyone utter his full name in years, so much so that he'd almost forgotten what it sounded like. His mother said it often, usually said with an irritated shout after he'd gotten into some kind of mischief. Yet, now, the name seemed so strange and foreign. It was a relic of his past life.

"Who's asking?" Knox said.

The man eased his hand out of the open window, offering it to Knox, who shook it while still unsure about the man's identity.

"I'm Colonel Julius Ballard, the President of National Security Affairs. We need to talk."

"About what?"

"A special mission."

"You can forget about it," Knox said. "In case you didn't get the memo, I'm retired. Been that way for a while now."

Ballard didn't flinch. "This has to do with your old unit. And I think you're gonna want to hear this. Get in."

Knox hesitated and then walked around to the other side of the SUV and climbed in.

CHAPTER TWO

Hamilton, Montana

Knox held open the door to Bitter Root Brewery for Ballard, gesturing for him to enter the pub. A perky hostess clutching a pair of menus grinned as she locked eyes with Knox.

"Back so soon?" she asked.

"My friend here just asked me to take him to the best beer joint in Hamilton," Knox said.

"Wasn't a difficult choice for you, was it?" she asked.

Knox sucked in a quick breath through his teeth.

"Higherground Brewing wasn't open, so—"

She playfully hit him with the menus and shook her head.

"I swear, Knox, one day you're gonna be serious with me and I'm not gonna believe you."

Knox didn't crack a smile.

"Who says I'm not?"

She rolled her eyes and led them to a table in the back corner of the dining area before doling out the menus.

"Misty will be your server tonight," she said. "You two gentlemen enjoy your evening. And Knox?"

"Yeah?" he said, looking up from his menu.

"You behave," she said, wagging her finger at him.

Knox sighed as she walked off.

"That's Polly Dixon," he said. "She'd flirt with Sasquatch if she thought he'd buy her dinner."

"She seemed kind of sweet on you," Ballard said.

"That's Hamilton for you," Knox said. "The women here don't really have quality men to choose from. Aside from a few scientist nerds working at the town's research facilities, Hamilton's short on men blessed with upward mobility. Like most small towns, it's kind of a crap shoot after a handful of prime bachelors."

"And are you a prime bachelor?"

"Maybe among the town's amputees," Knox said.

"Is there a sizable population of amputee men?"

"More than you might think. A mistake or two while working on heavy farm machinery will leave you scouring a field for a finger or a toe before you know it. But I know you didn't come here to talk about that. I think you said you need me for some job, right?"

Misty bounced over to their table and took drink orders before disappearing around the corner.

Ballard ran his hand over the top of his smooth head before shifting in his seat. He glanced around the room before leaning in close.

"Look, sorry about not being more upfront with you about this, but I really do need your help."

"I'm sure there are more qualified people out there."

"Maybe, but not many qualified people who get what we're about," Ballard said, gesturing rapidly between Knox and himself.

Knox furrowed his brow. "We?"

Ballard rolled up his right sleeve, revealing a tattoo of a skull wearing a beret with swords crossed in the background. Beneath the image was the inscription, "Rangers, lead the way!"

"Were you in the seventy-fifth?" Knox asked.

"First Battalion," Ballard said, pausing a beat before continuing, "just like you."

Knox pushed up his sleeve, revealing a nearly identical tattoo.

"So, what's this really all about?" he asked.

Ballard scanned the room one final time before lowering his gruff voice.

"I'm surprised you don't already know," Ballard said. "I thought you would've kept up with military news, especially given how you have so many friends still active."

Misty came up to the table and clunked a pair of mugs teeming with foam in front of the two men before quickly dashing off to other customers.

"Take a look around, Colonel. Does it look like I'm trying to stay on top of current events, living in a place like this? I came here to disappear, live my life in peace."

"I guess that much was obvious, based on how long it took me to find you," Ballard said.

Knox wrapped a hand around his mug and took a long pull. He set it down on the table and leaned forward.

"Can you speed this up?" he asked. "I really do want to get back to my campers."

Ballard rubbed his forehead and sighed.

"The long and the short of it is the President for National Security Affairs has the power to deploy certain assets to assist in the process of keeping this country safe from attacks, both foreign and domestic. I'm here to recruit you for a single mission concerning one of your former colleagues, a Frederico Garcia."

Knox nodded. "We called him Rico."

"And you know this individual well?"

Knox wasn't sure how much he wanted to reveal to Ballard, especially given that he acted like everything he was doing was highly secretive. While Knox didn't have all night, he wanted to squeeze more information out of Ballard before agreeing to anything.

"Rico's a good man—at least he was when I knew him. The dude could survive in the wilderness for a month with a toothpick. He could also hack his way the most technologically advanced firewalls any cyber security system could construct. And he'd give you the shirt off his back if you needed it. But serving as long as he had has a way of changing a man."

"Then I'm afraid he's served too long, that is, if the reports we have are accurate," Ballard said.

"What reports?"

Ballard took a sip of his beer and then continued.

"Military brass sent a unit to the Congo to investigate the ambush of five Army Rangers. At the time, Rico was working as a private security contractor for Aspen Mining, a global behemoth in the mining industry located in Angola. Next thing we know, everyone in the unit is dead."

"And you have proof that Rico did this?"

Ballard nodded. "Ballistics match the kind of gun Aspen issued him, according to one of the Rangers we sent to investigate the site."

"And you're sure it was Rico? This doesn't make any sense."

"Well, aside from ballistics, we also have airport security footage of Rico flying into the Congo a couple of days before the Rangers were slaughtered," Ballard said, before taking another sip of his beer. "But as for why he would do something like this, turns out that the mining company was expanding into the Congo and started engaging in some shady business practices, taking shortcuts that put natives at risk. They'd secured the rights to a very lucrative mine and stood to lose hundreds of millions of dollars if it got shut down. That Ranger unit was on a routine mission when they stumbled on the atrocities happening there at the hands of Aspen Mining. The unit was gathering evidence to give to the proper authorities. Eventually, Aspen resold the land before what they were doing became public. Not long after that, Rico left the company and tried to disappear."

"But you have evidence of what Aspen was doing?"

Ballard shook his head. "Unfortunately, Rico has all possible evidence. Maybe he disposed of it along with the bodies—we don't know. We just know it's gone."

Knox stroked his chin, his eyes shifting upward, staring at the ceiling fan rotating slowly overhead.

"So, let me get this straight," he said. "You have no irrefutable proof that Rico did anything. You're simply accusing him based on circumstantial evidence."

"*Strong* circumstantial evidence," Ballard said. "Rico was the only member of the security team who would've been capable of killing those Rangers. They were all gunned down, according to reports we've received. And the only thing that makes sense is that Rico killed them. How else would you explain someone getting the jump on a unit of Army Rangers?"

"I'd have to think about it, but I'm sure there are other plausible explanations."

Ballard, in the middle of a long sip, shook his head.

"*Plausible* is the key word there. And I can assure you that there aren't any."

"So, what's the assignment?"

"Rico needs to be handled."

"You want me to—" Knox leaned in close and then looked around the brewery. "You want me to *kill* Rico?"

Ballard drew in a long breath. "Rico knows how dangerous this mine is—and he killed every American soldier who knew about it, all to protect his employer. That was obviously a red flag."

"But Rico's not there anymore?"

Ballard nodded. "Yeah, but he still has the evidence, footage of the alleged crimes. We want him handled. We also want you to get the evidence. Aspen Mining has some loose ties to Russia and China, so we want what our Rangers found to use as leverage."

"You didn't answer my question—you want me to *kill* Rico?"

"Yes," Ballard said. "I want you to kill Rico. He's become more than just a fly in the ointment as we're pursuing the truth in the Congo. So, what do you say? Will you help us?"

Knox took a long pull on his drink, draining the last drop of his beer. He smacked his lips and slammed the mug on the table.

"I think I'm good," Knox said. "You're gonna need to find someone else to take up your crusade."

"You can't be serious," Ballard said.

"Do I look like I'm joking?" Knox asked.

Knox picked up his water glass and finished it before asking for the check. They both slowly rose once the bill had been paid and walked toward the front door.

"I know you want to figure out what's going on," Ballard said. "Based on everything I read about your relationship with Rico, this situation is personal."

"*You* need some answers," Knox corrected. "Rico's life decisions aren't my concern at this point. He's a grown man and does as he pleases. Why he does it? I'm not sure that's my place to inquire, especially as long as innocent people aren't getting hurt."

"Those Rangers were innocent."

"This all seems a little sketchy to me, Colonel," Knox said. "Based on everything you've told me, there's a lot of gray area here. And, as you know since you've scoured my record, you know that I don't do gray. It's black-and-white or nothing at all. I'm not one to pass judgment."

Ballard cracked his knuckles.

"Are you sure you don't want to help me? This could be big— and your country really needs you."

"So do my campers," Knox said. "And if it's all the same to you, I'd rather just be left alone. I'm honored that you think I could help, but you'll have to find someone else."

Ballard, resigned to Knox's rejection, gestured toward his SUV. Knox climbed in and they rode back to Challenger Camp in silence.

As soon as they pulled up to the compound's main building, Ballard directed the driver to put the vehicle into park.

"Are you sure you're not the least bit interested in avenging the other Rangers' death? Yes, we need some answers, but we also need closure. And making sure Rico gets what he deserves would go a long way in making that happen."

"Sorry, not interested," Knox said.

"Not interested? Or not willing?"

"You have your job to do. I have mine."

"The only difference is, my friends aren't dying," Ballard said. "But yours are."

Knox unlocked the door and climbed out. He leaned into the open window.

"Good luck, Colonel," he said. "I hope you find what you're looking for and that you can bring closure to this in some other way."

Guy poked his head around the corner and shouted at Knox.

"We have a stall over here that needs cleaning," Guy said.

Knox slapped the side of the car.

"*Duty* calls," Knox said.

"Your dad jokes are atrocious," Ballard said.

"I'm not sure I'd say that if you actually got my joke," Knox said with a wink.

"If you reconsider, please give me a call," Ballard said as he handed Knox a business card.

"Don't hold your breath."

"You're just going to scrape by at this camp, year after year, crossing your fingers and hoping you can pay your bills?"

"Pretty much," Knox said with a curt nod.

"You didn't even let me tell you how much I'm authorized to pay you. It's enough to pay off your loans on this place—even the shady one."

Knox forced a smile. "You certainly did your homework, Colonel. Sorry you wasted your time."

He backed away from Ballard's vehicle, keeping his eyes focused on the business card in his hand. The painful meeting was over. Knox had survived—and he was going back to his camp. Though he couldn't help but feel a twinge of regret, due to the mystery of why Rico would be targeting fellow Rangers. And with Challenger Camp struggling financially, he knew the money would've been nice, too.

He looked up at Allison, whose gentle smile made him dismiss those feelings—if only for the moment.

CHAPTER THREE

Hamilton, Montana

"What was that all about?" Allison asked as she nodded toward Ballard's vehicle speeding away down the dirt drive, leaving a dusty contrail. "We were wondering what had happened to you after we got back."

"How's Carley?" Knox asked, ignoring her question.

"She's gonna make it with just a broken leg and some scrapes and bruises, thanks to you and that search-and-rescue team," Allison said.

"That's good to hear. Is she back at the camp yet?"

"Guy's bringing her back now. But I asked you about that SUV. You gonna tell me what's going on?"

Knox snatched a gravel rake and entered the stall, getting to work without saying a word.

"Why are you ignoring me?" she asked, her head tilted to one side.

Knox stopped and sighed. He rested his hands on the end of the handle and turned his attention to Allison.

"It's nothing, really," he said. "Just part of my old life in the military."

"You want to talk about it?"

He stared off in the distance, thinking for a moment before responding.

"Not really. What are you always telling me? 'What's in the past needs to stay in the past' or something like that, right?"

"Well, yeah, but—"

"Seriously, it's not a big deal. Just a former colleague who wanted to see if I could help him with something he's working on."

"And could you?"

"I don't think so," Knox said. "Besides, I've got more important issues here with this camp."

He eyed her carefully, hoping his answer satisfied her curiosity. She resumed raking without saying a word. For a moment, he thought he'd given her the answer she needed. But Allison wasn't easily placated.

"You don't miss it?" she asked.

"I suppose there are days that I miss it," he said.

Allison leaned her shovel against the stall and walked up to Knox, putting both hands on his shoulders.

"I think you miss it more than you're willing to admit," she said. "What you did out there today on the mountain for Carley—it was both amazing and insane. It takes a special kind of person to not only take a risk like that, but pull it off."

Knox looked at the ground, uncomfortable with Allison heaping praise on him.

"I mean it," she said. "When I watched you rush to help Carley, I knew it was special. You're a real American—."

"Don't say it," he interrupted. "I just did what anyone would've done in that situation."

Allison removed her hands from Knox and then wagged her index finger.

"I don't believe that for one second. Most people are hardwired for self-preservation. But not you. You're a little different."

Knox glanced at his prosthetic leg.

"I won't disagree with you there," he said. "Most people have two legs."

She chuckled and shook her head.

"Joke about it all you want, but I know the truth about you. If you'd been looking out for just yourself that day, you'd probably still have both legs. Yet, here you are, years later, a man who clearly hasn't learned from the past—and, in this case, that's a good thing."

Knox resumed raking.

"We need to get moving if we're going to have time for the ceremony tonight," he said.

Allison joined him in cleaning the stall.

"We're not done with this conversation," she said.

Knox had grown fond of Allison, both as a colleague and as a friend. But she was like a dog with a bone when it came to trying to get him to confess his true feelings. And he knew she was right. He missed the military, but he wasn't exactly elite forces material after losing his leg, even if there wasn't much he couldn't do as a result of losing it. However, he'd found a new purpose in life with Camp Challenger and he was determined to enjoy it—as long as he could keep the doors open.

His phone buzzed with a message, snapping him right back into the reality of the harsh world that existed, even out in the hinterlands of Montana.

"What is it?" Allison asked, her eyes studying his fallen face.

"It's nothing," he said. "Let's just get this cleaned up as quickly as possible."

He pocketed his phone.

I'll have to deal with that later.

Later that evening, Knox gathered around the firepit with all the campers, as well as Allison and Guy. Even Carley, with her leg in a cast and bandages on her arms, sat on a large rock to join the group. She drew sympathetic looks from her fellow campers, peppering her with questions about what it was like to cheat death.

Allison led a Camp Challenger tradition—one she conceived

during her first year working there—called The Hot Seat. One by one, campers took turns sitting in an Adirondack chair across from their peers where they voiced character traits they liked about the occupant. This ritual strengthened budding relationships and left everyone with a positive feeling about not only the camp, but also about the people they shared their time with.

Knox loved the exercise—except when Allison started coaxing him to sit in the seat at the end of every camp. And he wasn't looking forward to his time in the hot seat. He preferred to hang back in the shadows and watch her work her magic with the campers. She was incredible—smart, easy-going, never-mind her drop-dead gorgeous looks. But Knox had yet to take the plunge and define their relationship. He knew it could get messy, which was the last thing he wanted on his little sliver of paradise. For the time being, he just wanted everything to stay as it was so he could revel in the moment.

As the night went on, he wondered if Allison was going to force him to face the campers and listen to them heap praise on him. Of all the times he'd been subjected to her torturous tradition, this was the one he wanted to slink off into the darkness the most. But Allison wasn't about to let him off so easily.

"Last but not least, it's Knox's turn," she said, gesturing toward the chair. "I think today's hero deserves to hear what we think about his actions this week, and on the mountain when he saved Carley."

"Really?" Knox asked, as he stood.

"Of course," she said. "You have a seat there and I need to run and go get something."

Knox sighed and shuffled to the chair, easing into it and leaning back as Allison scrambled to her feet and darted off into the night.

The campers took the moment to discuss how much the camp had changed them and what they would take from it moving forward. This was the part Knox enjoyed. Listening to others discuss how the rigors of working on the ranch as well as facing challenging obstacles and fears would prepare them for other formidable tasks in the future. Knox started to relax, soaking in the fruit of his labor. But he didn't care what they talked about—as long as it wasn't about him.

After ten minutes had passed, he checked his watch, starting to wonder what happened to Allison. With the fire pit situated near the edge of a wooded area, the women's cabin was only about thirty meters away beneath the shadows of the trees. In daylight, she would've been easy to spot, but at night he could barely make out a silhouette of the structure.

Knox sat up, straining to hear any activity in the woods over the chatter around the fire.

"Has anyone seen Allison?" he asked. "I thought she said she forgot something in the cabin, but this is taking a long time."

"I saw her go into the cabin," one of the girls said.

"Well, I'm going to check on her," Knox said.

"Don't do that," Carley said. "You might ruin the surprise."

"The surprise?" Knox asked. "Do you know what this was all about?"

Carley nodded. "I'm not supposed to tell you, though."

"Okay," he said, "keep it to yourself. But I'm going to find out what's going on. You guys keep talking about how you're going to change the world."

Knox marched toward the women's cabin and eased open the screen door.

"Allison, are you in here?" he asked as he flipped on the light.

He scanned the room but didn't see anything that appeared out of place. The bathroom door was shut and he strode over to it and knocked.

"Did you fall in?"

No response.

"Allison, this isn't funny. We're all waiting for you."

He noticed a small wrapped box on the foot of Allison's bed with a card attached, his name scrawled on it in her handwriting. He picked up the box and shook it before putting it back down.

"This has to be what she came back to get," he said to himself. "So, where'd she go?"

He headed toward the back of the cabin and opened the backdoor. Stepping onto the porch, he squinted, straining to see into the darkness. Aside from nature's nightly orchestra from crickets, frogs, and owls, Knox didn't hear as much as a left rustle on the still summer evening.

As he eased forward, he heard another sound behind him, a familiar one that made him sick to his stomach.

Click.

Knox raised his hands and slowly turned around.

"That's right," an armed man said, his gun trained on Knox. "Nice and easy. We don't want any trouble, Mr. Knox."

"Where's Allison?" Knox asked.

"She's safe and unharmed—for the time being," the man said.

"What do you want?"

"I like you," the man said with a grin. "You get straight to the point."

"I'm not interested in dragging this out—whatever *this* is—any longer than we have to."

The man spat to the side and set his jaw.

"You owe my boss some money—a lot of money. And if you don't pay him back in full within twenty-four hours, your little friend is going to pay a steep price."

"I'll get you your money, but leave Allison out of this," Knox said.

"Of course," the man said. "I won't lay a finger on her. But I'm going to keep her around as insurance that you're going to do what you just said you're going to do. Understand?"

"Please understand that I'm going to find you one day—and you're going to wish you never knew me," Knox said.

The man chuckled as he stepped out of the shadows, revealing his hulking frame. Knox was no pushover as a six-foot-four-inch man, checking in at two-hundred-twenty pounds. All muscle—except for the carbon fiber and titanium comprising his prosthetic leg. But this man was a different breed, the kind of guy who looked like he moonlighted as a wrestler for the WWE on the weekends. He wore a black t-shirt with the sleeves cut off, revealing a tattoo of a skull and crossbones with the name "Tiny" etched beneath it.

"You talk big for man with just one leg," Tiny said.

"Just trying to even the odds for you," Knox said. "Now, when and where do you want to meet for the money?"

Tiny gave Knox the details and then slipped back into the woods.

Knox had hoped this day would never come back to haunt him. He'd borrowed money from a loan shark in Vegas named Mr. Giovani when no bank would finance his dream camp. He'd paid back most of what he'd borrowed within the first year, but then stopped making payments when he started struggling to bring in enough campers. He owed half a million dollars and some interest, but he had counted on Mr. Giovani being unable to find him. It had taken him two years to track down Knox, but it had finally happened.

And Knox couldn't help but note what a strange coincidence it was that Col. Ballard approached him about working for his organization in exchange for paying off the camp loan on the same day that Mr. Giovani's thugs found him.

After returning to the campfire and telling the others that Allison had a personal emergency to tend to, Knox fished out of his pocket Ballard's card and dialed his number.

"You finally come to your senses?" Ballard asked.

"In a roundabout way," Knox said. "Turns out the man I secured a loan from for this camp paid me a visit tonight and wants his money now. You wouldn't happen to know anything about that, would you?"

"Knox, there are lines I would never cross—and that's one of them," Ballard said. "But fortunately for you, I've got your money. Just tell me where to meet you and I'll drop it by."

The next morning after Knox waved good-bye to all the campers, he drove out to a remote trail to make the exchange. He lugged a backpack stuffed with cash along with a pair of water bottles affixed to the side. Tiny met him along with two other men, all armed. But Allison wasn't anywhere to be seen.

"Where is she?" Knox asked as he approached Tiny.

"Settle down," Tiny said. "You'll see her soon enough."

Knox memorized the faces of the three men present, taking mental pictures of them. He had plans for them, plans they wouldn't appreciate. But not today. Today was about retrieving the person who meant the most to him in the world, even if he hadn't fully expressed it to her. He'd avenge their actions some other time. At the moment, all he wanted was to have her back, safe and free from the men who inflicted untold emotional damage on her sweet and innocent soul.

"Where is she?" Knox asked again in a measured tone.

"Let me see the money," Tiny said.

Knox removed the water bottles from the backpack before tossing it to Tiny. He caught it and handed it to the other two men to count. After ten minutes of silence, they both looked at Tiny and nodded knowingly. He pulled out a radio and then called a man, telling him something in a hushed tone.

"There's a man heading down the trail about a mile from here," Tiny began. "You should meet him about halfway. He's wearing a red cap and a green t-shirt. He'll give you the keys to the woman's handcuffs."

"If you're lying to me, I swear I'll—"

"No, no, no," Tiny said, wagging his finger. "Don't make idle threats. It's not a good look."

Knox glared at the beast.

"I don't make threats, Mr. Tiny. I only make promises."

"Tough talk for a man who hid in the mountains after failing to pay his bills and folded like a cheap suit when pressed to pay up."

Knox marched up the path, putting his shoulder into Tiny's and knocking the hulking man back a couple of steps.

"Good luck, Mr. Knox," Tiny said. "Don't let the bears catch you."

Knox hustled along the path before he met the man just as Tiny had described. Red cap, green shirt. The man dangled the keys from his fingertips before tossing them to Knox without breaking stride.

Knox sprinted up the path, hurdling downed trees and jumping over rocks and trickling streams. A few minutes later, he found Allison, fastened to a tree with handcuffs and a gag in her mouth. Her eyes widened once she locked eyes with Knox. He rushed over to her and quickly released her.

She hugged him tightly, tears already flowing. Knox had been on a few dates with Allison and was seeing if there was any potential for a long-term relationship. He couldn't deny that this ordeal had made him believe that there was. Maybe it was just the trauma playing tricks on his mind, but he wanted to continue to pursue what they had. If there hadn't been any real spark, he was sure he wouldn't have felt this strongly about her being in such danger.

"It's gonna be all right," Knox said, refusing to let go.

"I thought they were going to kill me," she said. "Those men—they were horrible."

"Did they touch you?" he asked as he drew back.

She shook her head. "No, but they threatened to do things to me, things I don't want to even mention. Will you please tell me what the hell is going on? I feel like I'm in the middle of some mystery and nobody's telling me anything. First, the man who took you to dinner yesterday and now this."

"I'll explain everything along the way," Knox said as he offered his hand. "But before I do that, I need to ask you a question."

"What is it?"

"Do you think you and Guy can handle the last session or two of the summer?" he asked.

"Why? Where are you going?"

"I've got some business I need to take care of."

"Does it have to do with those monsters?"

Knox shrugged. "Sort of. I'll tell you everything you want to know. No more secrets, I swear."

She locked eyes with him.

"No more secrets."

When Knox and Allison returned to camp, he felt relieved, not only because she was safe again but also because he'd finally told someone. Unburdening himself like that lightened his step, even though nothing had changed. He was still shouldering an enormous amount of weight, making him question his life choices. He'd never been good with money, which wasn't a problem when he couldn't ever spend it, while slogging through jungles and deserts hunting government-sanctioned targets. But he'd screwed up, surrendered to desperation, falling prey to the ever-present predator—a Vegas loan shark. Now, he'd pay more than just interest. He'd have to do something for Col. Ballard, likely more than the initial offer. And Knox wasn't sure exactly what that entailed. He just knew it wouldn't be pleasant.

Knox retreated to his office to call Col. Ballard.

"How'd it go?" he asked.

"It's done," Knox said. "So, I guess I'm all yours now."

"Look, I'm sorry it had to happen like this, but I do appreciate your willingness to help me out, to help out your country."

"With all due respect, sir, I don't want any of your platitudes. I just want to get the job done."

"A man of action," Ballard said. "That's why I pursued you for this job. We're going to get along just fine. Now, meet me at the airfield tomorrow at 0500 hours . You'll be briefed then."

Knox acknowledged the directive and then hung up.

What have I gotten myself into?

CHAPTER FOUR

Washington, D.C

Mark Moore descended the steps of the Capitol before stopping in front of the lectern. He resisted the urge to loosen his tie. The dog days of August were still two months away , but the combination of humidity and heat made an early appearance. Of all the differences the U.S. senator from California had to adjust to upon moving to Washington, the humidity was the most difficult.

Sweat beaded up on his forehead as he turned and looked at his wife, Ashley. The former Miss Iowa dabbed his forehead with a handkerchief.

"Are you going to be able to do this?" she asked.

Moore stared solemnly at her before glancing at the press corps that had gathered nearby. Then he nodded.

"Just don't leave my side," Moore said. "And I'm not just talking about today."

"Of course not," she said as she squeezed his hand. "You know I'll always stand with you."

"Thanks," Moore said before turning toward the press.

Moore's press secretary gave a brief introduction before turning the proceedings over to the senator.

Standing against the backdrop of the Capitol, banners detailing the importance of mental health hung behind him.

"As many of you know, Ashley and I have a story that's sadly not all that unique in this country," Moore began. "We thought we knew our son, that he was stable and sound. But we found out in the most painstaking sort of way that he was battling demons none of us could see. And the tragedy that we've all endured is something I wouldn't wish on anyone, though I know hundreds of thousands of Americans have grappled with the loss of someone they love due to mental health struggles. And while nothing we do will ever bring back our beloved Chase, my hope is that this new bill that we just passed will save other families from suffering the same heartache we've had to endure."

Moore outlined the new Congressional Act for Mental Health, a bill that funded local and state governments to provide more resources to help those dealing with mental health-related issues. As he spoke about his son Chase, Moore couldn't suppress his tears. Ashley stepped forward a couple of times, placing a hand on his shoulder and whispering words of encouragement to him.

Due to the public nature of Moore's position in the senate, Chase's story dominated the headlines a year earlier. He was serving with the Peace Corps in the Congo when he wrote in his journal that he was ravaged by despair over the situation of the people there and felt everything else in his life was hopeless. As a virus worked its way through the village that he was helping, Chase watched a handful of people succumb to a rare disease. According to Moore, his son didn't know how to process all of the tragedy he witnessed, and ultimately decided he couldn't bear it any more before killing himself.

Moore took off several months to deal with the grief, angering many in his political party. His absence resulted in his party's inability to pass a handful of important bills. But Moore stood his ground, chastising them for not responding with empathy. As a result of Moore's leadership on the issue, he rode a wave of unlikely bipartisan support, quickly rising to national prominence. And that meant more opportunities to share Chase's story and other important lessons they'd learned with popular media outlets.

On this day, Moore's press secretary arranged an interview with Erica Everhart, a bulldog of a journalist. Erica also had a brother who'd committed suicide, shocking his entire family. Since then, mental health awareness had evolved into her personal crusade, along with her other reporting duties. She seized every opportunity to discuss this topic with government leaders, pestering Moore's press secretary for an interview mere minutes after she announced the press conference.

Following the press conference, Erica and Moore retreated to senator's office in the Capitol to discuss the topic.

In the corner, Erica took a seat across from the small sofa where Ashley held Moore's hand while they sat cozily.

"That was a great speech out there today," Erica said as she tucked blonde tendrils behind her ears. "As you know, I share in the pain of losing a loved one this way."

Moore nodded knowingly. He'd always remained guarded about Chase's death, even as he spoke publicly about it. A member of the Senate Intelligence Committee, Moore claimed he was watching via video feed when a special forces team dealt with the unrest stirred up by a burgeoning terrorist group in the Congo the day his son died. The Congolese government asked for U.S. assistance to squelch the group before it took control of the region. With U.S. soldiers infiltrating the area, they stumbled into the village that Chase had been serving in with the Peace Corps. According to Moore, the video feed flickered and then went out for fifteen minutes. When it returned, footage showed Chase slumped against the outside of a hut, a gun dangling from his hand as he lay dead.

But Moore didn't want to share that with anyone, a horrifying moment that had remained unknown to everyone, except for those in that room. He felt like it would've sensationalized his son's death.

Moore shared a few new revelations with Erica, all related to items discovered in Chase's journal. According to what he'd written, Chase had been struggling with depression for several years. Due to

Moore's position as a senator, Chase felt pressure to put a good foot forward all the time, as he understood his every move would be broadcast or written about by the press. He went to the Congo to escape, to do something good with his life, where the stigma of being a senator's son couldn't follow him. But depression clung to him, eventually having its way with him.

During the interview, Moore expressed his regret about how he parented Chase. As a busy senator, Moore admitted that his relationship with his son often took a back seat to his political aspirations, something that he wished he could go back and change. But all he could do was look forward and do better.

When the interview concluded, Erica thanked Moore and Ashley before rushing away to write her story.

Once the door shut behind her, Ashley looked at her husband.

"How are you holding up, honey?"

Moore leaned forward and buried his head in his hands. She put her hand on his back and rubbed.

"I know this isn't easy for you, but I think you did a great job," she said. "I'll never get over losing Chase, but helping others identify potential issues early deadens the pain a little for me."

Moore leaned back and sighed.

"I'll be fine," he said. "Talking about it always takes a little bit out of me."

He leaned over and gave her a kiss.

"See you tonight around seven?" he said.

"I'll be there," she said. "I'm making my family's famous baked ziti dish, so you won't want to be late."

Moore forced a smile. "I wouldn't dream of it."

Later that light after dinner, Moore retreated to his study. He read a few online articles about the bill that he helped pass along with coverage of his press conference. All of it was positive, casting him in a favorable light.

He opened the bottom drawer of his desk and pulled out his secret stash of bourbon. Ashley had made him swear he wouldn't touch alcohol any more, after his drinking problem nearly cost them their marriage ten years earlier. He'd managed to get his drinking under control, though he kept some around for those weak moments.

His decision to keep a little bottle went against everything he'd learned in Alcoholics Anonymous. Moore justified it by saying that he wasn't *really* an alcoholic. And according to everything he'd read, he didn't fit the typical definition. Ashley had wanted him to quit drinking mostly because he turned into a monster after a couple or three shots, often raging around the house looking for anyone to lash out at. But once he realized what harm he was doing with such behavior, he changed his ways and his drinking habits. If he did decide to imbibe, he swore to only do it late at night, just before bed, or when Ashley was out of town.

Moore glanced at the clock ticking on the far wall.

Nine o'clock.

He still had two hours before his usual bedtime, a much earlier time to sneak a drink. And Ashley wasn't out of town either.

But it had been a challenging day, and he needed something to take the edge off. Talking about Chase was never easy.

His hands shook as he poured the glass. After returning the bottle to its secret location, he took a sip and then leaned back in his chair, eyes closed, enjoying the sensation of the alcohol working its magic on his mind. He'd gotten so caught up in the moment that he didn't even hear Ashley's footsteps coming from down the hall.

"Mark, what the hell are you doing?" Ashley said, her voice startling him.

He sat up, eyes bulging as he realized he'd been caught red-handed. An inquisition was sure to follow. But Ashley simply sighed and shook her head.

"I'm sorry, baby," he said. "It was a rough day and—"

She held up her hand and turned her head away. He stopped before slinking back in his chair. Ashley disappeared down the hall without another word spoken.

"I'll be joining you in a minute," he called after her.

"Don't bother," she said.

Another wave of guilt washed over Moore. Awash in wave after wave of guilt that had crashed on him today, he wondered why he hadn't drowned yet.

He opened his top drawer and stared at the loaded pistol on top of a stack of papers. His eyes lingered on the weapon longer than they should have before a text message on his phone buzzed, snapping him back to reality.

He picked it up and read it:

It was all for naught

Moore furrowed his brow as he read the message, sent from an unknown number.

It was all for naught? What does that even mean?

He fired off a response:

Who is this?

Moore smiled faintly, remembering how Chase had jokingly chastised his father for writing out the full text phrase that the kids shortened to "who dis?". But after a few minutes with no reply, Moore wasn't laughing.

He wanted to know who sent the message. And he also wanted to know what it meant: What was all for naught?

He shuffled upstairs to his bedroom, wondering if Ashley would forgive him one day when the truth finally came out.

CHAPTER FIVE

Hamilton, Montana

As Knox trudged up the steps of the Bombadier Global 8000 jet, he peered over the top of his sunglasses, rucksack slung over his shoulder. He rarely slept well the night before a flight, always anxious about missing it. But this time, he didn't sleep well for other reasons.

Despite Col. Ballard's promise to hire a private security force to help with the camp while Knox was away, he wasn't comfortable with any of it. In fact, Knox wasn't sure who he despised more—Mr. Giovani's goons or Col. Ballard. Knox hoped repaying the loan would satisfy Giovani, but Ballard demanded something else, something more. And Knox still wasn't convinced that Ballard hadn't alerted Giovani to his location, something Knox had managed to keep a secret for several years. The coincidence was difficult to ignore.

Ballard sat in the chair closest to the entrance, a faint grin spreading across his lips.

"How'd you sleep?" he asked.

Knox grunted and headed toward a nearby empty seat.

"That good, huh?" Ballard asked.

Knox waved him off without saying a word before sitting down. Ballard leaned forward and handed Knox a cup of coffee.

"Rio Jolt," Ballard said. "I've heard it's your favorite."

"It's in my top three."

Knox accepted the drink and placed it in the cup holder on the arm of his chair. He let out a breath as he leaned back. After a few moments of silence, he sipped his coffee before resuming his inquisition.

"So, just to be clear, you didn't make contact with Giovani before you came to visit me?" he asked.

Ballard shook his head. "I understand why you might think that, given the timing of everything, but I swear to you that I didn't tell him anything."

"But you did talk to him?" Knox asked.

"Didn't do that either. All I did was a little snooping to find out if there was any way we could mutually help each other. I help you pay off the loan.you help me with this rogue Ranger."

Knox gave Ballard a sharp side eye.

"You don't have to believe me," Ballard said, "but I do need you to trust me if we're going to work together."

Knox took another sip of his drink.

"The only way I'm going to trust you is if you're honest with me. Understand?"

"Of course," Ballard said.

The engine spun up as the co-pilot secured the door.

"Ready, gentlemen?"

Knox and Ballard both nodded. Neither said a word until they were airborne.

"So, where are we headed?" Knox asked. "You can at least tell me that now, can't you?"

"I suppose so."

"Well?" Knox said, his patience already wearing thin with Ballard.

"We're flying into Belem, Brazil," Ballard said.

"The Amazon?"

"Well, technically, Belem isn't in the Amazon."

Knox shook his head.

"Unbelievable," he said. "You're sending me into the Amazon after I land, aren't you?"

"There's still time to back out," Ballard said. "I mean, it won't be pretty—and the IRS might scrutinize your camp's non-profit status—but you're free to go anytime you wish."

Knox huffed. "You know I'm not exactly fond of the jungle?"

"I didn't see anything about it in your file," Ballard said. "Besides, it doesn't matter anyway. It's where Rico is. If there's another way, I'm open to hearing your ideas."

"This is ridiculous," Knox said as he subtly shook his head and closed his eyes. "Of all the people you could get to do this mission, you chose me."

"All I know is that, according to your file, you're one of the toughest SOBs we have—and your mission completion rate is unprecedented."

"You don't have to butter me up," Knox said. "You've literally got me caged in a little tin box thirty thousand feet in the air. It's not like I can back out now."

"With all your impressive skills, I wouldn't be surprised if you figured out a way to do so," Ballard said. "But I'm not buttering you up. I'm just being honest with you, which is what you asked me to do. Besides, if I told you where I wanted to send you, would you have volunteered so quickly?"

"Probably not."

"Well, my job was to recruit the best person for this mission. And I sure as hell wouldn't lead with a deal-breaker."

"Fair enough," Knox said. "Just don't think you're gonna get a second mission out of me."

"One's all I need," Ballard said.

After the jet touched down in Belem,, Knox followed Ballard down the steps and over to a small desk in the back corner of a private hangar. A woman wearing aviator sunglasses and a green military jumpsuit leaned back in a chair, her feet propped up on the desk. She was sucking on a lollipop, her face stoic as they approached. As they drew closer, she subtly shook her head.

"Seriously, Colonel," the woman said as she stood, "this is who you want me to fly?"

Ballard shrugged. "If you'd rather drive him into the jungle, I'm fine with that."

She rolled her eyes. "Hours with him on the back of my bike? I don't think so."

"Makes no difference to me. You just have to get him there."

As Knox drew closer, Makenzie smiled wryly before walking over to him and giving him a hug.

"Scraping the bottom of the barrel for help these days, I see," she said.

"It certainly seems that way, Makenzie," Knox said as he drew back. "I mean, they're asking you to fly me. But don't worry—I've got my own parachute this time."

Ballard tilted his head to one side.

"Knox, Captain Hall—sounds like you two are more than well acquainted with one another, so I'll leave you to it," he said. "Knox, you know what to do. Just stay in touch and let me know once you've taken care of Rico and secured the footage."

"Of course, sir."

Knox waited until Ballard returned to his jet before saying a word.

"You all right?" Makenzie asked.

Knox took a deep breath before settling into Makenzie's chair behind the desk. He hadn't thought about her in several years. After all they went through in the jungle, he couldn't forget her. But it was a time in his life—a moment, if he was being precise—that he wished he could eliminate from his memory forever. Yet, he knew that would never happen. He lived with the repercussions of that trip every day.

However, none of his reservations about the mission were related to Makenzie Hall. He was actually glad to see her, though not under these circumstances.

"I've been better," he finally said.

"Did you ever get that dream camp of yours off the ground?" she asked.

"In a manner of speaking."

"But you just couldn't stay away from this life, could you?"

Knox pulled his lucky coin out of his pocket and flipped it into the air. He caught it and repeated the motion several times before responding.

"I can promise you that I wouldn't be here unless I absolutely had to be."

"That doesn't sound like the Knox I know."

"I'm still the same man—just not all that excited about being coerced into doing favors for some pretentious Washington bureaucrat."

"Nobody does anything for Ballard unless he has you over a barrel. So, what's this mission of yours?"

Knox stared outside as a plane zipped along the runway.

"He wants me to kill Rico."

Makenzie's eyes widened.

"Holy hell. Are you serious?"

"I wish I wasn't."

"Ballard was adamant that if I didn't do this, more innocent people would die."

"Because of Rico?"

Knox nodded. "Apparently, Rico is taking out members of my old unit one by one."

"And nobody knows why?"

"Ballard gave me a reason, but I'm not sure I believe him."

"So you're not going to kill him, are you?"

"If what Ballard says is true, I don't think I'll hesitate. But everything I've heard from Ballard seems inconsistent with the Rico I know. I want to talk with him first, feel him out and see if he's turned into the monster Ballard is accusing him of being."

"How do you think that'll work out for you?"

"There's only one way to find out," Knox said with a shrug.

The next morning, Knox strode into the hangar, a cup of coffee in one hand, a small white box in the other. With his rucksack slung over his shoulder, he approached Makenzie. Her feet were propped up on the desk, her eyes closed. He playfully knocked her legs off the desk, startling her awake.

"Geez, Knox," she said. "A *good morning* would've worked."

He tossed the box on the desk in front of her.

"Consider this my peace offering," he said.

"Is this what I think it is?" she asked, pointing at the box. "I swear, Knox, if you found a way to make your famous biscuits here, I—"

"Before you get too excited, I made them before I left," he said. "Always gotta be prepared."

"But the box?"

"I picked one up at a store yesterday on my way to the hotel," he said. "Got a small container of my famous jam too."

Makenzie opened the box and a smile spread across her face.

"This makes up for all the bad dad jokes I had to endure last time," she said.

He wagged a finger.

"Don't get too excited," he said. "We've got a three-hour flight ahead of us. I've got some new jokes I want to try out on you."

She rolled her eyes. "Did you bring your parachute?"

"Always, when I'm flying with you."

Makenzie punched him in the arm. "Grab your gear and let's go."

"Wait, did you sleep here last night?"

She didn't stop, continuing toward the plane.

"Hurry up, Knox," she said, ignoring his question. "We're burning daylight."

They loaded up and prepared for the 400-mile flight into the heart of the Amazon jungle. According to the coordinates Ballard provided, Makenzie needed to land the plane on a remote airstrip along the Iriri River, where Knox would hike ten miles over some mountainous terrain to reach Rico's location. The simple flight plan included a stop halfway to refuel.

"You ready?" Makenzie asked as she ran through her pre-flight checklist.

"Let's do it."

Once they were in the air, Makenzie and Knox used the opportunity to catch up. They discussed their personal lives, Knox sharing about his camp and Makenzie about her burgeoning jungle pilot venture. She had a wealthy financier who bought a small fleet and employed several other pilots. He was rich but stingy, promising her a greater share of the profits after he paid off all the debt he owed on the planes. However, as much as she wanted to get away from the American military machine, she confessed that CIA missions comprised most of her business, flying over locations of suspected drug kingpins and clandestine manufacturing facilities.

After a few minutes of silence, Makenzie spoke.

"Look, I know we joke about it all the time, but I'm really sorry about what happened with—you know—"

Knox flipped his lucky coin as he stared out across the horizon.

"My leg?" he asked. "It's okay to talk about it. It's a part of me now. And, yes, before you say anything, I'm well aware of the irony in my statement."

Makenzie smiled.

Oh, that smile.

Knox didn't realize how much he'd missed Makenzie and her friendship. He hadn't seen her since that day five years ago. He hadn't wanted to visit because it was too painful to think about, at least in the initial aftermath, partially because he blamed her for what happened. That wasn't fair, he'd later realized, and he forgave her for something she didn't need to be forgiven for.

"You ever talk to the family of that kid?" she asked.

Knox shook his head. He'd moved on from the consequences of that day, of the reality of losing part of his leg. But there were some things that were still too painful to talk about.

"How's your dad doing?" Knox asked.

"Dr. Hall is just fine," she said, dropping the topic of Knox's incident. "Saving the world with his chemistry genius. He even accepted an invitation to present at Pittcon this year. Guess his celebrity has finally caught up with him and now people are expecting him to talk about his genius."

"He doesn't like that, does he?"

"Not any more than he likes the fact that I'm still flying airplanes and not working in the chemistry field."

Knox chuckled. "Still having a hard time that his daughter was blackballed from attending just about every college with a decent chemistry program?"

"He's never going to forgive me for that. But he should—he's the one who taught me how to make bombs in the first place. It's not my fault that Jennifer Oldham decided to rat me out for having a bomb in my backpack at my middle school. Can you blame me for thinking it would win my school's science fair? I never intended to blow up the school, like Jennifer said."

"Sometimes I think you'd be better off working in the field of chemistry," Knox said. "And then we go over the details of that story —and I think that it's probably best that you're not anywhere near a lab."

Makenzie glared at him.

"I'm still your pilot," she said. "And I can hear you."

Knox laughed. "How much farther before we refuel?"

"A half-hour," she said, her jaw still set.

~

Makenzie announced they were about ten minutes out from the airstrip when she pushed a button to activate the wheels for the Cub's float wheels. A mechanized whine followed. She tapped the button again, but got the same result.

"I don't like the sound of that," Knox said.

"That makes two of us."

She leaned forward in her seat, straining to see the wheels nestled beneath the float.

"Can you see the wheels under the float?"

Knox furrowed his brow and scooted to the edge of his seat.

"I can see the one on the left, but not the right."

"Are you sure?" she asked.

"Yeah—and I think I've got a pretty good view of both of them."

Makenzie swore softly.

"Now what?" Knox asked.

"I hope you were serious about having the parachute of yours," she said, "because you're gonna need it."

CHAPTER SIX

Along the Iriri River | Brazil

Rico Garcia slid his right hand along the roughhewn axe handle as he drew it over his head. He stared at the target before driving the sharp edge through the center and splitting the piece of wood. Dabbing his brow with his forearm, he smiled, proud of the growing pile at his feet. Chopping trees to survive wasn't his ideal lifestyle, but he wasn't going to complain.

At least I'm alive.

"*¿Cómo estás?*" came a woman's voice from behind him.

He turned and looked at Maria standing on the porch and leaning against the post. She brushed her curly brown hair out of her face and smiled, her short dress flowing in the breeze. Rico had to admit that he was more than just alive. Having Maria by his side certified that he wasn't just alive—he was lucky, too.

"*Bien,*" Rico grunted as he waved.

"*La cena es lista*," she said.

Rico drew the axe back and smashed another log before answering.

"Estaré allí en un minuto," he said.

I'll be there in a minute.

He'd worked up an appetite chopping all the wood he'd collected and was more than ready to scarf down another one of Maria's delicious meals. While he would've preferred to heat their oven by other methods—less strenuous ways—he knew he would balloon to fifty pounds overweight in a matter of months with the way Maria cooked. As a result, he decided not to complain about the hard work.

He split a few more pieces of wood before jamming his axe head into a log and rushing up the steps to his house. He washed up before sitting down to devour Maria's cooking.

"Will you help clean after dinner?" she asked in English.

"Well done," Rico said, a smile easing across his face as he pulled back a chair and took a seat at the table.

"Really?" she asked. "Am I getting it right?"

"You're doing fantastic, Maria."

She slid a plate loaded with a burrito in front of him.

"Enjoy," she said, her voice almost melodic.

"Thank you," Rico said.

Rico discussed with Maria a few of the chores he needed to finish up after dinner. Then he paused.

"Do you hear that?" he asked as he pointed to his ear.

"*¿Que?*" she asked, her brow furrowed.

Rico crept over toward the front window, grabbing the binoculars out of the end table drawer. He eased the drapes over just far enough so he could peer through the glasses at the area surrounding his house.

Dirt bikes whined in the distance, though not the kind he was used to hearing. These were different, smooth sound, foreign sounding, standing in stark contrast to the ones he usually heard puttering around the gulch.

Rico's cinder block house sat on a knob overlooking a dry gulch. The small village a couple of miles away consisted of dirt roads and no stoplights. A generator purchased from a California billionaire looking for a tax write-off created a buzz among the residents as well as opportunity for enterprising businessmen. Even without paved roads, the generator provided enough power for the two hundred or so residents living nearby. Lights along with cell phones and televisions sucked up most of the energy.

But with technological advancement and legitimate business also came illegal activity. A drug lord named Chefe Silva from a neighboring territory had sent several of his men to investigate the village's potential. However, a month ago Rico provoked Silva by killing one of his minions, who had been trying to take advantage of a woman behind a bar. That made Rico a marked man, though he'd managed to avoid the wrath of Silva—until now.

If there was any question about whether Rico had misread the situation, a bullet ripped through the window and shattered the glass. Shards tinkled against the floor, forcing Rico away from the window. Maria shrieked behind him.

"Stay down," Rico said as he belly crawled toward his room to get his rifle and pistol.

Bullets peppered the house as Rico made his way back to the living room.

"Lock yourself in our room," he said to Maria.

Rico used the barrel of his rifle to clear out the glass in one of the broken window panes and started firing. He counted four motorcycles, but wasn't sure that was all of them. As he scanned the area, searching for flashes, he noticed one man perched in a tree. Rico sighted him in and shot the man in the head, sending him crashing to the ground with a thud. Angered by seeing one of their colleagues killed, two of the men jumped on their motorcycles and advanced on Rico's property while another laid down cover.

The two attackers split up, increasing the degree of difficulty for Rico in defending his home.

"What's happening?" asked Maria, who hadn't complied with his request.

"What are you still doing out here?" Rico said. "Get back in our bedroom."

"I want to know what's going on

"I killed one man, but at least three are left," he said. "Maybe more. Now go."

Maria finally left for their bedroom.

Then Rico took aim at the man on the motorcycle approaching the front, zigging and zagging as he rendered Rico's efforts to stop him futile. Rico quit firing until the man got off his bike in order to avoid wasting precious ammunition. But Rico's plans changed when he heard a loud thump coming from the back of the house followed by a crash—and then a scream.

Rico rushed toward his room and found two men with Maria, one with his arm around her and pressing a knife to her throat, the other with his gun trained on Rico.

"Put down your gun," one of the men said in Portuguese.

As Rico slowly squatted to place his rifle on the floor, he held out his free hand in a gesture of surrender. Maria locked eyes with him and nodded knowingly. She squirmed and grunted, trying to break free of the man's grip. Her reaction drew both men's attention for just a second, which was all Rico needed. He reached behind his back and pulled out his pistol, taking aim at the gunman next to Maria. Rico squeezed off a shot, hitting the man in the head. The man holding Maria gripped her tighter as he glared at Rico.

"Chefe doesn't like that you've killed some of his men," the man said. "He wanted me to send you a message."

Before the man even twitched, Maria drove a knife through his back. He staggered back, releasing Maria.

"Behind you," she said.

Rico whirled to find another man wielding a gun rushing toward him and dove to the floor. Rolling to the side, Rico scrambled behind the couch and laid prone. As soon as he saw the man's feet, Rico fired a shot, hitting the man in the shins. He instinctively reached for the wound as he collapsed to the ground. Then Rico squeezed off two more shots, one hitting the man in the back and the second one ripping through the back of his head.

"Is that all of them?" Maria asked.

Rico crawled over to the window and watched another gunman crank his motorcycle before tearing out down the hillside. With a sigh, Rico, still clutching his gun, slumped against the wall.

"He's getting away," she said. "He's going to come back."

"He's too far off, and it wouldn't be wise for me to go after him."

"So, we're just going to sit here and wait for him?"

"Hardly. Once that man reaches Chefe with the news, he'll assemble a new team and send a new wave of hostiles back. It's never going to end. But we have a few hours to pack before we leave."

She nodded as she scanned the bodies strewn across the floor.

"And what are we going to do with all these bodies?" she asked. "We don't want Chefe and the police after us."

Rico smiled. "I've already thought of something. Go get some rope from the shed and we'll take care of it right now."

Rico picked up the man by the couch and lugged him outside while Maria got the rope. He transported the other two bodies from inside the outside to the back. He found the other man on the edge of the woods and then worked with Maria to rope together all the bodies. Then he attached the rope to his dirt bike and rumbled down to the edge of the river.

A large crocodile nestled in the mud didn't move as they approached, catching the day's waning rays of sunlight.

"Fernando," Rico said as he carted the first body down to the riverbank, "have I got a treat for you."

He heaved the first body into the water, resulting in a big splash that rocked the banks of the calm section of the river. One by one, Rico and Maria flung the bodies into the Iriri, leading to a feeding frenzy with Fernando and the other crocodiles in the area.

Rico stood a safe distance away on the back as he watched the reptiles tear the men apart.

"Let's go," Maria said.

Rico didn't move.

"Come on," she said. "We need to go."

"I need to see this," Rico said. "They almost killed you."

"And Chefe is going to send his men back to kill us both. You said it yourself. We need to start packing."

Rico sighed and walked back to his bike. Maria straddled the seat behind him, clinging to him as he rode up the hill back toward their house.

"You all right?" Rico asked after he stopped near their porch and dismounted.

Maria nodded. "I'm angry, but I'll be fine."

"You going to be okay leaving this place?"

"When you don't have a choice, you have to make peace with whatever you do," she said. "But it's temporary. I'm going to kill Chefe."

Rico smiled. "You look more beautiful than ever when you talk like that, honey."

She winked at him as she hustled up the back steps.

Once they were inside, they re-heated their dinner and ate. When they finished, Rico encouraged Maria to pack.

Rico went outside and gathered a few of the logs he'd split from earlier that afternoon. He dumped them on the front porch and then paused when he thought he heard something. Holding his breath, he froze and listened hard. Footsteps and the breaking of branches in the woods nearby.

He eased inside and locked the door.

"Maria," he said, "you need to go now. I think they're almost here."

"But I'm not done packing."

"It's just stuff," he said. "You need to go now."

"Without you?"

"Just meet me at our rendezvous point, okay?"

She didn't respond.

"Maria, I need to know that you're with me and you understand."

"I don't want to leave you," she said.

"I understand, but the next group of men Chefe sends aren't going to be as easy to take out, and there will be more of them."

"All the more reason that I stay with you."

Rico closed his eyes and pinched the bridge of his nose.

"I don't want to argue with you about this. I just know what they're going to do to you if you're here."

"Without me, you don't stand a chance—and you know that."

"Please, honey, you have to trust me. If I can take out two dozen Taliban fighters in Afghanistan, I'm capable of handling whatever Chefe sends our way. But, just in case they somehow get the jump on me, I'm begging you — please go before something unspeakable happens to you. I'd never forgive myself."

Maria sighed and then gave him a hug.

"Good luck," she said. "Promise me you'll see me soon."

"Promise," he said, holding up his hand as if he was pledging. "Very soon."

She toted her bag out to the truck and ignited the engine before driving away. Once her taillights disappeared through the trees, Rico rushed back inside and gathered all his guns.

CHAPTER SEVEN

Washington, D.C

Senator Mark Moore folded his arms and leaned back in his chair as he listened to the briefing on the latest substantial threat to the American public. Port security searched a Japanese freighter in San Francisco and somehow missed a North Korean scientist, who had several dozen vials of a virus. Hours after disembarking from the vessel, a tip to an FBI hotline alerted the bureau to the man's presence, presumably by the Japanese captain after the scientist didn't complete the rest of his promised payment. Meanwhile, CDC officials had yet to determine the nature of the virus, but their initial inspection suspected that it was a new deadly and highly contagious one.

The ranking member of the senate intelligence committee slammed his fist on the table and swore to take action. Moore understood his colleague's frustration. They spent hours discussing how the Department of Homeland Security could shore up its ability to stop enemies from infiltrating U.S. soil through ports of entry—and none of their ideas had been implemented, leading to another near disaster.

But Moore didn't display the same kind of ire. The curious text message he received consumed his thoughts, distracting him from anything that was happening in the moment.

It *was all for naught.*

Moore remained perplexed about the meaning of the haunting text. He'd never told anyone—not even Ashley—why he'd pushed and cajoled Chase into entering the Peace Corps. After watching previous presidents endure the embarrassment of their children, Moore sought to control every aspect of Chase's life. And in the areas he knew he couldn't control, he worked hard to instill in Chase strong character and virtue, so much so that he'd been approached by several publishers to write about his parenting tactics. But Moore declined, partially out of the fear that one day Chase could decide to publicly sow his wild oats, and partially out of guilt. While the results looked impressive—and they were—Moore harbored an ulterior motive: he wanted everything to be perfect for his presidential run one day. He wanted a perfect family with a sterling image of him as both a husband and a father. If Chase looked good, that would make Moore look good. He also couldn't deny that Chase's death made voters view him in a sympathetic light, which also piled on guilt.

I should've never arranged for him to go into the Peace Corps.

Despite his regret, he couldn't change anything about Chase's fate. And even though no one knew his internal struggle, Moore couldn't shake how the words *It was all for naught* spoke to his guilt.

But what else was for naught?

His inability to discern the meaning ate at him, like an inability to remember a once-familiar name. It was going to bug him until he figured it out.

Once the meeting concluded, Moore left the Capitol, descending the front steps only to find a pack of reporters. They swarmed around him, shoving microphones into his face as bright lights from cameras blinded his vision.

"Senator Moore, can you tell us how the Senate Intelligence Committee plans to respond to the report of a foiled North Korean bioterrorism attack?"

"What does this say about U.S. relations with North Korea?"

Always one to soak up attention from the press, Moore declined to comment.

"We don't discuss committee meetings publicly," he said. "Thank you."

He pushed his way through the crowd before finally emerging when one of the reporters noticed another committee member and rushed toward him.

Once Moore reached his car, he drove to CIA headquarters in Langley, stopping only for a quick visit to an upscale tobacco shop. Serving on the intelligence committee gave him some extra privileges, one being unfettered access to Langley. He flashed his credentials and went through a brief security check before winding his way down several corridors and reaching the office of chief analyst Victor Perryman.

Moore knocked on the door, but didn't wait for anyone to respond before entering. Perryman looked up, wide eyed.

"Mark, isn't this a surprise, Perryman said.

"A pleasant one, I hope."

Perryman shrugged. "Depends on why you're here and what you want."

"Why do you always think I want something?"

"You didn't just stop by to deliver a gift, did you?"

Moore grinned and reached inside his coat pocket, producing a leather humidor large enough for two cigars. He offered it to Perryman.

"What's this?" Perryman asked as he took the humidor.

"I think you know what it is."

"What's inside will let me know just how badly you want something."

Perryman slid the cover off the top and tugged one of the cigars out high enough to read the label.

"A Montecristo," he said, his eyebrows arched. "Not bad, though I think you know by now that Fuente Fuente Opus X is my favorite."

"They were out," Moore said.

"So, this is a spur-of-the-moment request?"

Moore sighed. "Okay, okay. Guilty as charged."

Perryman smiled. "I'm just messing with you, Mark. You know I'd do anything for you."

"Then I can take back those Montecristos?"

"Let me rephrase that—you know I'd do anything for you *as long as I get good cigars in return.* Yes, I know. I'm shallow. So sue me. Now, what've you got?"

"Thanks, Vic," Moore said as he reached into his coat pocket again, this time producing a mobile phone. "I'm trying to track where a text message originated from on this cell phone."

"Is this *your* burner?"

"I didn't say it was even my phone," Moore said. "I just received this strange message and I want to know who sent it."

"Okay, let me see what I can find out," Perryman said. "Are you going to leave this with me?"

"I'd rather not."

"Doesn't matter to me. I just need to download the data. Is that okay?"

"Yes, but please delete it once you're finished. There might be some state secrets on that the phone's owner wouldn't want getting out."

"Of course," Perryman said. "I'll be discreet. Just give me a couple of minutes to get the data I need."

Perryman plugged a cord into the phone and then pecked on his keyboard. Once he had what he needed, he pointed at the screen, which displayed the text messages in an organized list.

"Just to be clear, is this the one you want me to trace?" Perryman asked, pointing at the screen.

Moore nodded. "That's it."

"Perfect," Perryman said as he unplugged the phone and handed it back to Moore. "I'll call you as soon as I find something."

"Thanks again. I owe you one."

Perryman waved dismissively. "Nah. You brought me two Montecristos, which for how easy this job is means we're square."

Moore pocketed the cell phone and left the office. As he drove home, he tried to think about anything but the message. He turned on the radio, listening to an anchor on a news talk program speculate about the next presidential election cycle. Moore's name was mentioned, bringing a faint smile to his face. But as he realized a potential dream of his was within reach, his thoughts drifted back to the message.

Does somebody know something? How could they?

He decided it was impossible and tried to move on. But he couldn't, instead left to drum his fingers on the steering wheel as he awaited Perryman's call. Fortunately, Moore didn't have to wait long.

He picked up his phone as it buzzed with a call from the CIA analyst.

"You figure it out already?" Moore asked.

"Not exactly," Perryman said. "I was able to trace the phone number that the text message was linked to."

"And?"

"It's associated with a pre-paid phone."

"A burner? Figures."

"However, it's not all bad news," Perryman said. "I was at least able to determine where the text message originated from the moment it was sent."

"And where was that?"

"This is the part you need to be sitting down for—or your friend whose cell phone that belongs to."

"Spit it out, Vic."

"The message was sent from the West Wing of the White House."

Moore swore softly, thanked Perryman, and then ended the call.

While Moore still wasn't sure what it all meant, his pulse quickened. Someone at the very least knew the number to his burner—and they were trying to send him a message—even if he wasn't sure what it was they were exactly trying to convey.

Moore remained determined to find out *who* and *what*—and *why*.

CHAPTER EIGHT

Iriri River | Brazil

Knox grabbed his parachute and cinched the straps on the parachute and stuffed what extra supplies he could into his rucksack. He then peered out the window at the jungle canopy below.

"Can't you just land this thing on the river?" he asked.

"There isn't a stretch long enough," Makenzie said. "I'd be skimming across the water and we'd slam into a tree, never mind that this part of the river is very shallow."

"What about upstream?"

Makenzie shook her head, her pony tail whipping back and forth.

"It's probably about fifty miles before I'd find a section of the Iriri suitable for putting this girl down. And I can promise you that you don't want to try and make a fifty-mile trek in the jungle with only what you've got in your pack."

Knox leaned back in his seat as Makenzie pulled back on the stick, taking the plane to an altitude fit for jumping.

"I certainly didn't think I'd have to make a jump today when I woke up," he said.

"Never make those assumptions when you're flying in the jungle."

Makenzie climbed higher before leveling off.

"Do you see that sharp bend right there?" she asked.

"Yeah."

"That's your target," she said. "It's only about two hundred meters east of the landing strip, so that should help you get your bearings based on the original coordinates we had."

"And what are you going to do?" he asked.

"I'll figure something out," she said. "You know how to reach me. I'll get back home and get this fixed—and hopefully before you'll need an extraction. Good luck."

She gestured toward her door, the only one in her Super Piper Cub. Then she explained how she wanted him to climb over her before jumping out.

Knox remained frozen, his mind whirring in search of other options. He couldn't think of any.

"Are you sure this is going to work?" he asked.

She nodded. "As long as you don't forget to pull the rip cord."

Knox gave her a sarcastic smile before bracing himself as he stepped over her. Seconds later, he launched himself headlong out of the plane and over the jungle.

Knox stumbled once his feet touched the jungle floor. He fell and rolled before bouncing upright again, his parachute cords wrapped around him in a tangled mess. After he caught his breath, he cut himself free and gathered his chute. It didn't take long before he was surrounded by several natives. But the natives had evolved, something he learned on his last fateful trip to the Amazon.

A half-dozen men wearing loin cloths surrounded him. But instead of toting spears, they were armed with cell phones, evidence of technology's relentless march on the world. One of the men chattered rapidly on his phone, while the others discussed something as they pointed at Knox.

Knox broke into a smile as he looked at the men, hoping to put them at ease. While he was prepared to take out Rico if necessary, Knox understood he couldn't fight off an entire Amazon tribe. He scanned the area, searching for a way to communicate that he didn't pose a threat to them.

He slowly knelt and picked up a stick. Wiping away the debris from a small section in front of him, he sketched out a picture of himself driving a dirt bike.

"Bike," Knox said as he pantomimed riding one. "I need one."

The man on the phone ended his call at looked at Knox.

"You're American?" the man asked.

Knox nodded, surprised to hear the man speak English.

"Well, why didn't you say so?"

Knox drew back, wide-eyed, still stunned into silence.

"What's the matter? Never heard a *savage* speak English before?"

"Who *are* you?"

"I think the real question is who are *you*? After all, this is our land and you just fell from the sky here."

"Garrett Knox," he said offering his hand.

The man looked at it and scowled.

"You clearly don't know the customs of the Mebengokre people —or as your people like to call us, the Kayapo. To offer your hand is a great insult."

"Oh, I'm sorry, I—"

All the men started to laugh.

"I'm joking with you," the man said before grabbing Knox's hand and shaking. "I'm Damiana. Nice to meet you. But in all seriousness, we need to know your business here."

"I'm looking for a friend."

"And does this friend have a name?"

"Rico, though he might go by something different here," Knox said.

Damiana looked at his fellow tribesman and held a brief discussion in their native tongue.

"We know him, but we must warn you that he is a marked man," Damiana said.

"Someone is after him?"

"Chefe has put a bounty on his head," Damiana said. "He has killed too many of his men and disrupted his supply chain."

"Supply chain?"

"Drugs," Damiana said. "Surely, you've heard of that where you're from."

Knox smiled, taken aback not only by Damiana's command of the English language but also his sense of humor.

"I'm all too aware," Knox said. "That's just a little surprising based on what I've heard about Rico."

"We don't know much about him, but he keeps to himself and lives near a village not far from here."

"I have coordinates for his house."

Damiana wagged his finger. "It's not easy to get to his place, but if you do, you're going to need a dirt bike."

"Do you have one I can borrow?" Knox asked.

"What do I look like? An Enterprise agent?"

"I have money."

Damiana laughed. "In that case, I have a whole fleet of dirt bikes, though all but one are checked out right now. Hopefully the one we have will meet your needs."

Knox cocked his head to one side, trying to suppress a smile.

"How long were you in the U.S.?" he asked.

"Long enough to earn degrees in business and ecology from UCLA," Damiana said. "Now let's get you on your way."

After receiving a map and directions along with instructions on how to use the bike Damiana described as finicky", Knox left the natives. Despite landing somewhat close to the coordinates Ballard had given him, Knox needed nearly an hour to reach Rico.

Once Knox drew close to Rico's house, he surveyed the area. He realized Rico had been intentional about the location he picked for his home. Set atop a knoll, the property was well positioned for Rico to discourage any unwelcome guests. While the trees provided good cover, Knox also considered them as a way to reach the house undetected. He figured they were his best option once he noticed the discreet perimeter alarm, creating a buffer zone of two hundred meters. No matter how fast he could move on foot, that would be plenty of time for Rico to get the jump on him.

Knox dug a grappling hook out of his rucksack and attached it to a rope. He whipped it around before hurling it toward the lowest hanging branch of a ramón tree. After pulling himself up, he ascended over a hundred feet up into the canopy, using his hook to extend his reach in spots where the limbs weren't as sturdy.

As he moved closer to the house, Knox reached a section of the trees that required a rope. However, the branch his hook landed on was weaker than he suspected. The limb bent and then snapped, sending Knox plummeting toward the ground. He saw a limb approaching and reached for it. The branch smacked against his chest before nestling beneath his armpits. As the momentum swung Knox, he locked his hands together, stabilizing his position. Once he stopped moving, he caught his breath and assessed his situation. He'd fallen about fifty feet and was dangling above nothing. If he'd missed, he would've hit the ground, all but ending his mission, if not his life.

Knox pulled himself up onto the branch and picked his way through the rest of the canopy leading up to Rico's house. And then Knox saw his target.

Rico knelt next to a stack of logs about twelve feet in length and tied twine around them at various points. Knox noticed the pistol tucked in the back of Rico's pants, the only weapon visible on him.

Knox descended to the jungle floor and crept closer, careful not to alert Rico. But despite Knox's best efforts to move quietly, Rico stopped and slowly scanned the area behind him, as if he heard something.

Knox ducked behind a log and didn't move for a half-minute until he heard Rico resuming his task. Then Knox continued to the house, remaining out of sight as he dashed from tree to tree for cover. When he was within twenty feet, he emerged from behind a tree, his gun trained in front of him. Rico was bent over tying a knot when Knox announced himself.

"Put your hands where I can see them," Knox said.

Rico complied, slowly raising his hands in the air.

"I know that voice," he said.

"You sure do," Knox said. "And if you don't want it to be the last one you hear, turn around and don't make any sudden movements."

Rico obeyed, shuffling his feet until he came face to face with Knox.

"Knox, what the hell are you doing here?"

"We need to talk."

CHAPTER NINE

Washington, D.C

Col. Julius Ballard stood on the balcony of the posh event center and overlooked the city. As the bustling of the nation's capital waned, Ballard took a drag on his cigarette and exhaled, avoiding the pretentious crowd inside gathered for a senator's fundraiser. He stood near the railing, wondering if he'd done enough to snuff out the threat posed by the sixth Ranger. A slap on the back jolted him out of his contemplative state.

"Staying away from the cameras again?" asked Randall Helton, a senator from Illinois and Ballard's longtime friend.

"I don't want to break any of them," Ballard quipped, as he ran his hand along the top of his bald head.

"Scars on your forehead are popular these days. You've heard of Harry Potter, haven't you?"

Ballard grunted. "If only I could wave a wand and get rid of half of these people."

"And this is why you never entered politics."

Ballard took another long drag on his cigarette. "It takes a special type of breed to put up with these bloodsuckers funding your political aspirations, just so they can demand a *favor* in the future. Sorry, it's not for me."

Helton placed his hands on the railing and looked out across the cityscape.

"Not everyone has a stomach for it, but someone's got to do it. Then again, not everyone has the stomach for the kind of business you conduct."

Ballard nodded. "I guess I just prefer the shadows over the limelight."

"And if we didn't have people like you—"

Helton let his words hang as the two men watched the first lights of the city start to blink on.

"You raising a ton of cash in there?" Ballard asked, changing the subject.

"Not as much as I'd like, but enough to secure another six years in the senate. But that's not why I came out here."

"You need a cigarette?" Ballard asked. "I thought you'd given that up."

"No cigarettes for me. But I was wondering how things were going with the rogue Ranger."

"I've got someone handling it," Ballard said.

"Better than the last guy?"

"The best. Took me a while to track him down, but I found him."

"And he took the assignment willingly?"

"He was in the same unit as the sixth Ranger, at one point."

Helton drew in a deep breath and then exhaled.

"Well, keep me posted. I'll rest a lot easier once I know that guy is six feet under instead of taking out some of our best soldiers."

"Of course," Ballard said.

Helton moved away, his voice booming as he glad-handed more donors on the balcony behind Ballard.

The colonel dropped what was left of his dwindling cigarette and extinguished it beneath his foot. A tap on his shoulder made him turn around again.

"Sir," a young man said, "I have a message for you."

He handed Ballard a small slip of paper.

Ballard read the note and then pocketed it.

This isn't going to be as easy as I thought, he mused to himself.

He fished his phone out of his pocket and placed a call.

CHAPTER TEN

Washington, D.C

Elliot Schwartz licked his thumb and flipped a page of the thick document on top of his desk. As the president's chief of staff, Schwartz refused to let his boss get caught signing anything without being able to brief him on every significant term in the agreement. His attention to detail often frustrated the president, but it also rescued him from embarrassment on more than one occasion. Schwartz squinted as he re-read one line before highlighting it in yellow and then circling it with a red pen, his system for determining how to address concerns with President Lewis. This particular marking would result in a lengthy discussion.

A knock at the door broke Schwartz's concentration. He looked up and then checked his watch. The past hour had ticked by so quickly he'd almost forgotten about the impromptu meeting he'd scheduled with Mark Moore.

Schwartz gave permission for his assistant to open the door. She poked her head inside and announced Moore's presence.

"Send him in," Schwartz said.

He gathered the loose papers on his desk and stacked them neatly, separating them into two piles before leaning back in his chair.

Pulling a stress ball out of his top drawer, he squeezed it as Moore entered the office. Schwartz pointed at the seat across from his desk as he studied Moore.

Schwartz served as Moore's first campaign manager during his first run at the senate seat. Moore lost, but the race was much closer than anyone anticipated. The lessons from that failed bid had endeared the two men to each other, despite the disappointing outcome. It had only taken a series of missteps by the incumbent during the following term before Moore was able to handily win on his second run. In the years since, Schwartz and Moore had both navigated Washington's cut-throat environment, unafraid to get the proverbial blood on their hands. But Moore didn't have his confident air, today. He slumped into the chair, his crisp appearance replaced with tousled hair, a half-tucked shirt, loosened tie, and a tattered file folder.

"Mark, what's going on?" Schwartz asked. "You don't look like yourself."

"I've lost some sleep over this, and I'm hoping you can help me."

"Sure," Schwartz said, scooting forward in his chair. "What have you got?"

Moore pushed the folder across the desk.

"I received a text message on a burner phone I have. I printed out the message along with some other details I learned."

Schwartz scanned the pages, seeing the message *It was all for naught* along with cell phone data and the geolocation of the phone that sent the text.

"What's got you so rattled?" he asked.

"First of all, who has my cell phone number?" Moore asked. "I don't think more than a handful of people know it."

"Maybe it's a wrong-number text."

Moore scowled as he leaned forward. "Who sent just one random, cryptic message like that? No, this was intentional."

"Have you asked everybody on the short list of those who have this number?"

"I'm starting with you," Moore said.

"Well, I would never do anything like this."

"I wouldn't think so, but I had to ask, because this happened on the anniversary of Chase's death. I mean, how cruel can a person be?"

Schwartz pushed the papers back across his desk.

"Maybe somebody's just pranking you."

"It's not a funny prank," Moore said. "But as you can see from that document, the text originated from somewhere within the West Wing of the White House."

"Anyone else in the White House know this number?"

Moore shook his head.

"Well, that's strange," Schwartz said. "I wish I could help you with this, but I wouldn't worry about it. What could it mean, anyway? The link to Chase's death could just be a coincidence."

"No, clearly someone is trying to send me a message."

"What good is a message if you can't figure out what it means?"

Moore sighed and sat back.

"I think we both know how much is at stake. If someone knows something or even *thinks* they know something—"

"Look, if you're worried about The Consortium, don't. We're all unified around you."

"Are you sure?"

Schwartz nodded. "I wouldn't lie to you about that. We're only as effective as we are trusting in one another. And I know trust is a scarce commodity in this city, but you don't have anything to worry about. You'll see. But leave that file with me, and I'll do some digging on my own and see what I can come up with. I might have access to some resources that you don't."

Moore flicked the folder back toward Schwartz.

"Okay, just let me know as soon as you hear something. Even if it's a mistake, it makes me jumpy."

Moore stood and pushed his chair back toward the desk.

"The minute I hear something, I'll let you know," Schwartz said.

Once Moore left the room, Schwartz reached into his desk and pulled out his burner cell phone and checked the number against the one on the document. He didn't need to check, but he did it anyway. The tech guru Moore had used was good; number belonged to Schwartz.

The message had done exactly as Schwartz had intended. He wanted to see how Moore would react—and the fact that he was jumpy made Schwartz concerned. If Moore couldn't handle a little heat from a random cell phone, how could he be entrusted with weighty secrets when the pressure was on?

Schwartz decided to let the senator twist a little bit longer to see how it played out before he reported back to the rest of the group. But the initial signs weren't promising.

And there was only one way The Consortium dealt with a weak link.

CHAPTER ELEVEN

Along the Iriri River | Brazil

Knox kept his gun trained on Rico, marching him up the steps of his house and inside to the kitchen table. Rico slowly turned around, his hands still raised.

"This isn't necessary," Rico said.

"I'll be the one who makes that determination," Knox said, as he eased the door shut and locked it.

Rico sighed and shook his head. "I don't know what's—"

"Is anyone else here?" Knox asked.

"Not right now," Rico said.

"Are you expecting someone?"

"In a manner of speaking, yes."

"What's that supposed to mean?" Knox asked.

"Someone will be arriving here soon, but they're not exactly invited guests. Kind of like you, right now."

"Put your hands down," Knox said, gesturing with his gun. "Just keep them where I can see them, and no sudden movements."

Rico complied, placing his hands on the table.

"You mind telling me what this is all about?"

"Why don't we start with you telling me why you're living in the middle of the Amazon, and why I've been tasked with hunting you down and killing you," Knox said.

"Honestly, we don't have that long."

"Give me the abridged version," Knox said, pulling out one of the kitchen chairs and easing into it about ten feet from Rico.

"I don't know, Knox. You'll have to forgive me for being less than forthcoming. I'm sure you'd be the same way if your own government was trying to murder you."

"All I want you to do is tell me why I shouldn't kill you. It shouldn't be that hard if you're innocent."

"*Innocent* is such a loaded word."

"It's not really. Not in the context I'm using it," Knox said, glancing at his watch. "Now, I don't have that much time, so I'd appreciate it if you'd just get on with it."

Rico shook his head.

"The fact that someone within the U.S. government went through all the trouble of sending you here to find me—and, presumably, kill me—ought to be enough of a red flag to you. They didn't ask you to arrest me, did they? They just wanted you to dispose of my body in some untraceable method. Am I right?"

Knox pulled his lucky coin out of his pocket and flipped it into the air. It hit the table, spinning around for a few seconds before the speed slowed and it rattled. He slapped the coin, stopped its movement. Then Knox picked it up, holding it so Rico could see.

"You see what's on this?" Knox asked.

Rico nodded.

"Even after leaving the Rangers a few years ago, that image and those words remind me what kind of man I need to be every day," Knox said. "And from what I understand, you seem to have lost your way."

"Things aren't always as they seem," Rico said.

Knox held his hand up as he heard the clattering of an engine outside. He darted over to the window and eased back the drapes, peeking outside. A woman clutching a gun walked toward the front porch.

"Is that who you were expecting?" Knox asked.

"Maria! Damnit, I told her to leave."

"You know her?"

"It's my fiancee."

"Your fiancee?" Knox asked. "We *do* have a lot to discuss. But first things first—"

A bullet shattered the window where Knox had just been standing. As shards tinkled to the floor, Knox dove down. Rico flipped over the table and ducked behind it. Knox crawled over to him.

"What'd you do to piss off your wife like that?" he asked.

"She's not the one shooting," Rico said.

"What have you got yourself into?"

"Like I said earlier, it's a long story. But if you want to hear it, I'm gonna need your help."

Knox reached into his pocket and felt for the coin. He ran his fingers along the edges of the debossed skull and beret as well as the lettering of the Rangers' motto: *Rangers, lead the way!*

"I intend to hear all about it," he said. "Now, where's your weapon?"

"So you trust me now?"

"For the time being," Knox said. "We need each other."

"Just like old times," Rico said, before scurrying across the room on all fours and grabbing one of the weapons he'd collected and placed on the couch. He retrieved a pistol and checked for ammo. Satisfied that he had enough, he hustled back over to Knox.

"Who are these guys?" Knox asked. "Please tell me you didn't piss off some drug cartel."

"Okay, I won't. Who would you like for me to have pissed off?"

Knox's eyes widened as more bullets whizzed through the shattered window at the front of the house.

"You pissed off a drug cartel, didn't you?"

Rico raised up and fired a few shots in the direction of the attackers before crouching behind the table again.

"It's not like I had much of a choice," he said. "They're the ones who instigated this whole thing."

More bullets. Chunks of the walls peppered the floor. Gun smoke wafted through the room, creating a thick ribbon of haze that hovered throughout the entire house.

"Rico," a woman called through one of the windows around the side of the house, "you in there?"

"Yes, but I told you to leave. Why did you come back?"

"Who's in there with you?" she asked, ignoring his question. "I don't trust him, whoever he is."

"Get outta here now," Rico said.

"And leave you to fend for yourself?" she said. "Not a chance."

More gunshots popped off before a resounding thud landed on the side of the porch. The ensuing scream from Rico rattled Knox, making him wonder what his rogue colleague might do next. Turn on Knox in rage? Run through the front door firing his weapon until he was riddled with holes?

"Maria!" Rico shouted. "Maria!"

She didn't respond.

Knox hunched over as he dashed over to the window. Maria's body laid limp, blood pooling around her head, a gaping wound in her forehead.

Knox saw his former colleague's face turning a hue of dark red. Rico stood to run for the door before Knox dove near after him, taking him down. Rico grimaced as he slammed against the wall and toppled to the floor.

More bullets peppered the wall in front of them, dust and particles of wood and sheet rock trickling from above.

"You're going to get yourself killed," Knox said.

Rico's eyes narrowed.

"Why do you care?" he asked. "Weren't you sent here to kill me?"

Rico bolted toward the door again, but Knox grabbed Rico's legs and yanked him back. Knox put his forearm into Rico's chest, pinning him to the floor.

"I came here to get answers," Knox said, through gritted teeth. "And I'm not about to let you die because you've lost your mind."

Rico looked away, still seething. Knox snatched a fistful of Rico's shirt and pulled, lifting him just off the ground.

"If you want revenge, let's do it together—and let's do it the right way."

Rico took a deep breath and then closed his eyes.

"Are you thinking Khyber Pass?" he asked.

"They don't know I'm here yet," Knox said as he let Rico up off the floor.

"Khyber Pass it is."

The two men scrambled to opposite sides of the house before Rico opened fire first. The combatants outside responded, unleashing a hail of bullets on his position. Meanwhile, Knox peered through the other window and counted the muzzle flashes he saw in varying positions.

"We've got four hostiles," Knox shouted.

"Copy that."

Rico waited for a brief reprieve before firing back. Once the shooting recommenced, Knox slipped out the back door. He spotted one of the attackers coming around the corner and felled him with a double tap.

Three remaining.

Knox hoped he hadn't miscounted.

He crouched low as he rushed toward the woods, gliding back toward the front porch, putting the hostiles between him and the house.

Rico continued firing, though his objective was to hold their attention. And he'd managed to do that so well that Knox hit all three men from behind before they had a chance to react. They all dropped where they stood. Knox scanned the area once more. Satisfied that he'd taken them all out, he walked toward the house.

"Well, that worked out better than Khyber Pass," Knox said.

Then Rico stuck his head out of the window, his gun trained in front of him.

Knox gasped before cocking his head to one side. He slowly raised his hands.

"Seriously, Rico. After what I just did for you?"

Rico squeezed off a couple of shots. Knox winced, bracing for the shot. But instead, he just heard the thud of a man falling to the ground behind him. Knox turned around to see the dead man lying face down in the dirt.

"Thanks, Rico."

But Rico was gone. Knox turned to see his former colleague rushing out the front door and cradling Maria's lifeless body.

"Bastards," Rico said, before unleashing a scream of agony, which quickly morphed into agonized tears.

Knox knelt next to Rico, placing a hand on his back.

"I'm so sorry," Knox said.

"Why did they have to kill her? Why?" Rico said, his emotions bubbling over and spilling out in a sorrowful stream of consciousness. "I should've discouraged her thirst for revenge. I should've stayed with her. If I hadn't, she'd still be alive right now. Why did I do that? Why? Why?"

Knox put his arm around Rico's shoulder and then patted him on the back.

"It's not your fault. You didn't do this."

Rico's anguish oscillated between raw anger, with him slamming his fist onto the porch. to looking skyward to unleash a guttural shout and uncontrolled crying. With all the time Knox had spent in battle, he'd seen this kind of emotion before, felt it himself too. He knew Rico needed space—and time, too, though Knox wasn't sure he had as much of the latter.

In the distance, gunshots rang out.

"You hear that?" Knox asked.

Rico took a deep breath and then exhaled quickly. He nodded slowly as he eased to his feet. Bending over with his hands on his knees, Rico convulsed as he sobbed some more. Then he wiped his eyes with his hands before his gaze met Knox's.

"We need to go," Rico said, his voice more calm and composed. "Chefe, the leader of this cartel, will gut us all if he finds out we just killed the men he sent here."

More gunshots. Knox looked skyward and then back at Rico.

"We don't have time to bury these bodies."

"Who said anything about burying them?" Rico asked.

A few minutes later, the two former Rangers were hauling all the dead bodies down to a swampy area in the woods just off the river.

"So, we're just going to hide these in the weeds here?" Knox asked.

Rico shook his head.

"Fernando," Rico said. "Have I got another feast for you."

Knox twitched and jumped back a few feet when he saw a large crocodile slither off the opposite bank and plunge into the water. Fernando's eyes were positioned just above the rippling waves as it swam toward the Rangers.

Rico backed up, clutching the feet of one of the dead men.

"Come on, Knox," he said. "Fernando's hungry. And he can pretty much eat whatever he wants."

They launched the body into the water, slapping hard against the surface. Seconds later, Fernando tore into the flesh, ripping the dead body apart and devouring it. Other crocodiles on the opposite bank eased into the water and joined the feeding frenzy.

"Good idea, Rico, but are you sure those crocs are going to eat all of these men?"

Rico stopped and studied Knox, glancing at his leg.

"Oh, man, I'm so sorry. I almost forgot."

Knox waved lazily at him. "Don't worry about it. It's in the past and I—"

"You know I wasn't thinking."

"It's okay, Rico. Let's just hurry up so we can get out of here before Chefe sends more men back. I'm not sure I have another gunfight in me."

"You always have another gunfight in you."

Once all the bodies had been dumped into the swamp, Knox and Rico raced back up the hill to the house, grabbed some essentials, threw them into Rico's truck and ignited the engine. It sputtered for a moment before roaring to life. Rico tapped the accelerator pedal a couple of times before putting the vehicle in gear and lurching forward.

But before they'd left the property, Knox grabbed a handful of Rico's shirt.

"We need to go back," Knox said.

"Seriously? More of Chefe's men will be here soon."

"No," Knox said. "There's something we need to do first."

CHAPTER TWELVE

Washington, D.C

Erica Everhart clicked the down arrow on her keyboard, scrolling through her emails. Most of the time, her messages consisted of a combination of readers who either hated her most recent story or wanted her phone number. Waking up to such negativity each day had made her consider waiting until noon to sift through her inbox. But such an approach in her profession wasn't plausible. The news waited for no one. And if she opted not to pursue a legitimate story sent to her, she would later regret it, mostly likely as the target of her editor's frustration.

But today was different, and different in so many ways.

For starters, Erica's inbox contained an unusually high number of complimentary emails regarding her latest article about Senator Moore and his son's death. And instead of people asking for her cell number, they were giving her theirs, requesting a call from her to discuss their experience with the Peace Corps.

Most of the time, Erica would reflect on why her writing made such an impact on her readers. Then, she would move on to the new article that her editor needed by six o'clock that evening. But something caused her to linger, to mull over her story a little longer.

Why did Chase kill himself? Did he get infected with the virus, too?

The latter question was one she should've asked Senator Moore when she sat down with him. He told her that she could call him back any time if she had any follow-up questions that she needed answers to, though she knew he didn't likely mean indefinitely. But the only way to find out was to ask him. Erica jotted down a few questions in her notebook before focusing on her piece due that evening, one regarding the demand for more security at the Capitol. While her editor claimed that this story would be of interest to the Post's readers, she doubted it would draw even a small fraction of the attention garnered from another article about Senator Moore's son. But she didn't have that kind of power. Her editor wanted what he asked for, nothing more and nothing less.

Erica shuffled some papers on her desk, and was looking for the Capitol security chief's phone number when her computer dinged with the arrival of a new email. She sighed, half expecting it to be another solicitation to purchase an extended warranty for her car or a questionnaire to find out if she could join in a large lawsuit if she drank water at Camp LeJeune. But the subject line arrested her attention: *there's Moore to the story.*

Clever. Okay, I'll bite.

Erica clicked on the subject header, opening up a new email from a man named Jared Norton.

Hello, Erica. I read your article in The Washington Post about Chase Moore. And I hate to tell you this, but you're missing the big story with this one.

Erica furrowed her brow.

I'm missing the big story. Okay, Mr. Jared Norton, what am I missing?

Erica leaned back in her chair and thought for a moment, wishing Jared had been forthcoming with any information he had. She often received messages from conspiracy theorists, clamoring for her to pursue some of the most ridiculous theories out there. Everything ranging from the moon landing being faked to *JFK never being assassinated.* No idea was too absurd to be propagated by the readers who flooded her inbox with ideas they likely found while scrolling through some random chatroom that attracted like-minded conspiracy theorists.

However, this email seemed different, piquing her curiosity.

I have to think like a conspiracy theorist. And if I am, what exactly could I be missing?

Then a nagging question returned to her. She searched for the number of the Peace Corps headquarters online and hesitated before calling. It could be nothing—or it could be something. Either way, she now had a question that she hadn't asked Senator Moore, not that it hadn't occurred to her. At the time of her meeting, asking the question seemed a little tasteless, or at the very least, the kind she should wait to ask at the end of her interview, so she had everything she needed in case the question rankled the person. But now she wanted to know, wondering if that would help her understand what the big story was—if there even was one.

She glanced at her inbox. The message on top from her editor all but flashed at her. But the whole Capitol security story bored her. But a story about Senator Moore's dead son would prove far more exciting and interesting to write—and would be to her readers, too, if her hunch was right. Putting aside her reservations, Erica dialed the number for the Peace Corps.

A pleasant woman answered the phone and quickly directed Erica to the media relations department. A few seconds later, a young woman answered the phone. She listened patiently to Erica's request before answering.

"So, let me get this straight, you want to know *how* Senator Moore's son died?" the woman asked.

"Yes," Erica said. "Do you have any documentation on that?"

"Not exactly. What did you say you needed this for?"

"I'm writing a follow-up on Chase's death from the story I wrote a few days ago, about the bill Senator Moore drafted and just passed," Erica said. "I now want to cover Chase's story with a little more depth."

"I'm not sure I—"

"Look, I'm just trying to help. If just one person decides not to commit suicide after reading this story, then it's worth it. It's just a detail regarding Chase, so it's not essential. But it does at least let readers know I've done my homework. I want to get every little detail right."

"Aren't you a breath of fresh air among your kind?" the woman quipped. "Now, I can't tell you any of that information in any official capacity, mostly because I don't know it. But there is someone who served with Chase's team in the Congo, who might be more privy to those details than I am. And he just so happens to be serving here at HQ now. Just remember that what he tells you comes from a fellow Corps member, not an official statement from our office."

"Of course," Erica said.

"All right. Now that we understand each other, let me patch you through to Hayes Collins."

The line clicked and went quiet before it clicked again.

"This is Hayes," said a young man, his voice scratchy and deep.

Erica introduced herself before getting straight to her question.

"I just want to let you know upfront if this is uncomfortable for you, just let me know at any point and I'll stop with the questions," she said.

"What exactly do you want to know?" he asked.

"I want to know about Chase Moore."

There was a long pause, so much so that Erica wondered if Collins had hung up on her.

"Hayes? You still there?"

"Yeah, I'm here," he said, followed by a sigh. "What exactly do you want to know?"

"Do you know how he died?"

"Nobody does," Collins said, "But if I had to guess, I'd say he probably shot himself."

That makes sense, since Senator Moore is a big advocate for gun control.

"But that's just a guess?" she asked again. "It's not something you've heard, is it?"

"No. But why do you want to know this anyway? It seems a little morbid."

"It is, I agree. But details matter to readers. It lets them know that you're knowledgeable about the topic."

Collins grunted or laughed. Erica couldn't decipher which one it was.

"Is everything all right?" she asked.

"If you were so knowledgeable, you would've never written an article without mentioning that he was there by himself, at the very end," Collins said.

"What do you mean?"

"I mean, he was supposed to come back with the rest of us, but the Corps wanted him to stay," Collins said.

"Is that unusual?"

"It's certainly not something I've ever seen. We never want to leave any member of the Corps alone in the field. It's against our policy."

"Yet Chase Moore was left alone. Any ideas as to why that is?"

"It's always been a head-scratcher for me."

Erica paused for a moment, considering if she wanted to extract more information out of Collins before getting to the crux of her reason for calling. She decided to gather more details from Collins, starting with his background and his experience with the Peace Corps in the Congo. Once she was satisfied, she returned to the discussion about Chase being left alone.

"So, in your opinion, do you think leaving Chase alone had anything to do with his death?" she asked.

Collins waited a beat before answering.

"I'm not sure it'd be fair to answer that, but it does make you wonder."

"Did he seem suicidal when you left him there?"

"Honestly, no. He sent me a text about how he'd seen some things that he wished he could unsee, but that was about it."

"And you showed that to the police?"

"Nobody ever asked to see it," Collins said. "We all just assumed what they said about him was true. However, I think I would like to get some closure. A few answers would go a long way in helping answer that for me and the others."

"The others?"

"Yeah, the rest of us who were serving with Chase. We all loved him. He was a fun-loving guy. Wicked good looks, and very smooth with the ladies. It was hard to hate on him."

Collins' voice took on a tone of sadness as he finished.

"And now, he's gone," he said.

"Look here," Erica said. "I'll make a deal with you, Hayes. You help me out—and don't tell anyone you're talking with me—and I'll do my best to get the answers you want, so you can get the closure you need. Sound good?"

"Sounds reasonable," Collins said.

Erica thanked him again before ending the call. She tossed her cell phone on her desk and leaned back in her chair, interlocking her fingers behind her head. Looking skyward, she closed her eyes and took a deep breath.

She would write the Capitol security story by noon. But in the afternoon, she was going to dig into Chase Moore's death. Her curiosity heightened, she smiled.

Maybe this won't be such a boring day after all.

Erica made quick work of her story, filing it with her editor just a shade past 12:30 p.m. Then she dialed Senator Moore's number.

He picked up on the second ring, opening up by thanking her for the article she wrote about his bill. But his mood soured when she asked him about his son.

"I hate to do this to you, Senator," Erica said, "but I'd like to ask you a few more questions about Chase."

"Now's really not a good time."

"Can I call you about it tomorrow?"

"I don't think so," Moore said. "I'm sure you understand just how painful this is for me and my family. But thank you again for all your previous work. I must be going."

Before she could say anything else, Moore ended the call.

Erica scratched down a few notes in her moleskin, now more determined than ever to find out what really happened to Chase Moore.

CHAPTER THIRTEEN

Washington, D.C

Colonel Julius Ballard slid into the plush blue bench in the L'Ardente dining room and rested his elbows on the table. He pushed his short sleeve up his arm, exposing his tattoo. The waiter raised an eyebrow as he looked at the design.

"A little tame for body art, isn't it?" the waiter asked, placing a menu in front of Ballard.

"Oh, this?" Ballard asked, pointing at his skull-and-beret tattoo. "Like most tats, it's meaningful to me—and that's all I care about."

The waiter tugged his long white sleeve up his arm, revealing his own design just above his wrist of a colorful demon with red horns and a lightning bolt in one hand and a severed head of a goat in the other.

"Now, *that* is a tattoo," Ballard said. "Did you design that one yourself?"

The waiter nodded proudly.

"I belong to a society of graphic artists here in the city that service tattoo parlors," he said. "My design is widely distributed, and was the most requested design from our society last year."

"And yet you're still working here?"

"Just trying to save up enough to buy my own studio," the waiter said, as he placed a glass of ice water in front of Ballard. "What about you? Did you design that yourself?"

Ballard didn't want to embarrass the man for not recognizing the Ranger tattoo, nor did he want the man thinking they were about to become best friends over a conversation regarding body art.

"Designing tattoos isn't my thing," Ballard said, with a faint smile.

The waiter scurried off, not to be seen again until Ballard's lunch partner took a seat across the table.

Senator Mark Moore scooted his chair forward and then stroked his chin as he scanned the restaurant.

"Has anyone here approached you yet?" Moore asked, still glancing around.

"Nobody recognizes me when I'm not wearing a suit," Ballard said. "Just had a short conversation with our waiter about tattoos. The guy was clueless about the Rangers' tattoo. Wanted to know if I designed it myself."

"He's just angling for a big tip," Moore said. "I'm not sure you could even draw a stick figure version of that."

"Maybe not, but I could kill you with a couple of sticks, even dull ones. It'd take long for you to die, but it might be more fun to watch you bleed out."

"Has anyone ever told you that you're a sick bastard?" Moore asked.

"That was my nickname in the Rangers for a while—Sick Bastard. Guess *bastard* sounds close to *Ballard*."

"And they gave you a new nickname?"

Ballard nodded.

"They called me Nero."

Moore shook his head. "How big of an asshole do you have to be to get nicknames like that?"

"A big one," Ballard said, forcing a smile. "But I didn't invite you to lunch today because I wanted to discuss how ruthless I am. We've long since established that fact."

Moore looked up to find the waiter hovering over him, requesting a drink order. Moore said water would be fine, sending the waiter heading for the kitchen again.

"What's so urgent, Nero?"

Ballard held up his hands.

"Before we get started, I wanted to ask you how you were doing with your son. I know the anniversary of his passing was just a few days ago, and I didn't get to talk with you about it."

"I'm fine," Moore said.

Ballard arched an eyebrow.

"No, really, Colonel. I'm fine."

"It's okay if you're not," Ballard said. "I know something like that has a way of sticking with you and—"

"I may not have been a war hero like you, but I've dealt with more than my fair share of loss in my lifetime. And while Ashley and I are still processing Chase's death, I promise you that we're handling it as good as could be expected, maybe even better."

"If you need anything, or ever want to talk, just let me know."

Moore squinted and shook his head as he studied Ballard.

"Caring about someone isn't exactly the kind of thing Nero would do."

"We haven't gotten to the real reason I wanted to talk with you today," Ballard said.

Before he could continue, the tattooed waiter returned. He suggested a few items and took their orders before leaving.

Moore leaned in close and spoke in a hushed tone.

"You do realize that everything he recommended was among the most expensive items on the menu. He's just trying to bilk you for a good tip."

"This lunch is going on my expense account," Ballard said. "What he doesn't realize is that the American taxpayers—himself included—are the ones actually paying for this meal."

Moore chuckled and shook his head.

"Always ready for a witty retort, aren't you?"

"Can't miss any opportunities," Ballard said.

"So, what did you want to know?"

Ballard glanced around the room, then clicked a small device in his pocket, one designed to create interference in case anyone utilized a digital device to listen to their conversation.

"Are you still in touch with The Cleaner?"

"The *Cleaner* Cleaner?" Moore asked.

"Is there more than one?"

"Are you talking about the former CIA operative?"

Ballard nodded.

"Yes," Moore said. "But he only helps us out when everything has gone wrong."

Ballard rubbed his bicep, moving up and down across the skull-and-beret tattoo. But he didn't say anything, instead fixing his gaze on the breadbasket in front of his plate.

"Did something go wrong, Colonel?" Moore asked, through clenched teeth.

"Not yet, but it's always good to be prepared."

"Are you sure something's gone wrong?"

"Not yet, but it appears to be headed that way," Ballard said. "And the last thing I want is for any of us to catch any of the blow-back that might come, should everything fall apart."

"I don't like the sound of that," Moore said, his voice staying muted, but his pitch rising an octave. "You do realize I'm contemplating a presidential run, don't you?"

"Just calm down, Mark. Everything's under control. I'm simply developing a mitigation plan in case things go wrong. If so, you wouldn't be affected by it at all. Understand?"

"Want to tell me what's going on?"

"Like I said, it's nothing you need to worry yourself with," Ballard said. "That's why I get paid the big bucks."

Moore sighed and took a sip of his water.

"So, will you?" Ballard asked.

"Will I what?"

"Set up a meeting for me with The Cleaner?"

Moore nodded reluctantly.

"Good," Ballard said, patting Moore on the arm. "Don't you worry. I—I mean, The Cleaner — will take care of everything."

Moore put his hands up, palms out in a move suggesting he didn't want to hear anything else.

"Not another word. I need plausible deniability."

"Understood," Ballard said.

"And what about the other thing?" Moore asked.

Ballard smiled. "It's coming together quite nicely. It's only a matter of time now."

CHAPTER FOURTEEN

Iriri River | Brazil

"I need a picture of you—dead," Knox said, as Rico wheeled the truck back around toward the house.

The pair wasted no time in creating a plausible scene. Rico sprawled out on the porch next to a pool of blood left by Maria. Knox wasn't sure how Rico would handle seeing her body again, but he seemed focused on the task at hand, operating with a high level of combat urgency.

Once they were both in the truck, Knox holstered his weapon.

"Is this truck going to get us where we need to go?" he asked.

"Depends on your plan for getting back to civilization. There are some navigable roads, but we won't get that far, not without drawing Chefe's attention, anyway. But I know you didn't come out here without a plan for getting home."

"We need to get about fifty miles upriver."

Rico, in the midst of a thousand-yard stare, pursed his lips and nodded his head.

"I think we can do that."

He downshifted and whipped around a corner, kicking up a cloud of dust. The tires slid across the dirt before Rico straightened the wheel.

"Buckle up," Rico said. "We've got the bumpiest ride you've ever been on up ahead."

Knox shook his head.

"There's no way this was like the time we were in the Patagonias."

Rico arched his eyebrows and smiled.

"You'll see."

Seconds later, a teeth-rattling bump tossed Knox around in his seat. Then they ascended over a rise, only to be jolted again once they hit a dip at the bottom of a hill. Knox's head bumped against the truck's ceiling.

"Okay, I stand corrected," Knox said, as he pulled out his lucky coin and kissed it.

After a few minutes, Knox turned to Rico.

"So, let's talk. I'm obviously not itching to kill you. But I just need to know what's going on."

"Once you start down this rabbit hole, there's only one way out for you," Rico said. "Are you sure you still want to know?"

"Rabbit holes and foxholes—you know I love them both. So, why don't you start by telling me what happened in Congo," Knox said.

Rico nodded. "Of course—and it's a good thing you're already sitting down."

While Knox realized he likely wasn't going to get every question answered about what happened in the Congo, he suspected Ballard had misinterpreted Rico's action, at best—or he was being set up, at worst. The knee-jerk reaction by Ballard to eliminate Rico without taking the time to find out the truth bothered Knox. He wasn't one to cast stones at anyone for making snap judgments, because it was something he'd done regularly while in the throes of war. But this wasn't war. Ballard had plenty of time to gather intel and determine if Rico had truly gone rogue, or if other factors played a role in what happened.

Had Knox been sent on a fact-finding mission, he wouldn't have hesitated to let Ballard know everything. But that wasn't the case. Ballard expressed his expectation for the mission—Knox needed to kill Rico. And if Knox didn't, he couldn't be sure that Ballard wouldn't exact revenge on him for not upholding his end of the deal.

"I'm really sorry I have to make you do this," Knox said.

"Better than you putting a bullet in my head," Rico said, with a shrug.

Knox decided to take a different approach to his uncomfortable interrogation.

"So, why didn't I kill you back there?" Knox asked.

Rico shrugged. "I'm the best spades partner you've ever had?"

"Seriously," Knox said. "Why didn't I pull the trigger?"

"That's only a question you can answer."

"But you know why, don't you?"

Rico downshifted, slowing down to take a nearly one-hundred-eighty degree turn. The engine whined as he jammed his foot onto the accelerator pedal.

"I might know why," Rico finally said.

"And?"

"Because they wanted me to do the same thing they're asking you to do."

"Which was?"

"Kill an innocent man—an innocent American soldier, no less—without any evidence."

"That's what this is all about?"

"It's about a cover-up, one our own government is wanting us to help them facilitate," Rico said, as he took another corner. "But here's the thing about a cover-up—it only works when everyone's compliant. And right now, there are a lot of leaky holes in this ship that they're trying to plug."

"But you killed an Army Ranger unit."

Rico took his hand off the stick shift and then shook his head.

"I was just following orders," he said. "I'd been told that this unit had murdered an entire village, and they needed justice meted out."

"So you just killed them all?"

"Not all of them," Rico said. "I let one of the Rangers go. You know him—Kevin Canfield."

"Wait. Chaos?"

"*Chaos* Canfield, the one and only," Rico said. "He had supposedly killed an entire village in the Congo, but that's not the story he told me. While I was working for Aspen Mining in Angola, someone presumably from the CIA approached me about taking care of a little matter, accusing the unit of going rogue—and that Chaos was the ringleader."

"That's plausible. He was always a little different."

Rico nodded as he slowed down and rumbled over a small stream cutting across the dirt road.

"That's putting it nicely. I always thought that if anyone in our unit had the capacity to go rogue, it was Chaos. According to my contact, Chaos had orchestrated an elaborate plot to wipe out a village that was threatening to stop the government from shutting down an illegal mining operation that was selling diamonds on the black market."

"Still plausible."

"I know," Rico said. "But it's all bullshit. I went to the Congo, where the unit was, and ambushed them, killing everyone except Chaos. He'd managed to escape. But I found him cowering in a cave and decided to give him the common courtesy of a conversation to explain his actions. I felt I owed it to him, after all the time we'd spent together. However, he claimed it was all a lie and that I'd find out soon enough."

"He didn't tell you anything else?" Knox asked.

"He refused, telling me that he didn't want me to get involved."

"And naturally, you couldn't stop there."

"Naturally. So, I pressed him a little, maybe even applied a little pressure, if you know what I mean."

"And?"

"Nothing. He refused to talk. Told me that it was going to get me killed if I didn't just drop it."

"And so you did?"

Rico nodded. "The weight of the guilt made me do it. You don't know how many times I thought about eating my gun in the days after that."

"But you didn't."

"I got over it, sort of—the guilt part, anyway. Probably not fully, but enough that I decided to get on with my life."

"And then you moved to Brazil?"

"I sent the proof-of-death picture in, quit my job and disappeared," Rico said. "I had more than enough money saved up to live in a remote place. I wanted to see the Amazon, met Maria on a tour along the Iriri River, and the rest is history. More so than I'd like for it to be."

Knox stared out at the bumpy terrain, the gnarled contour that was making the truck rattle.

"But five dead Rangers in Africa? That didn't make the news?"

"It did, but it was spread out and buried—and the reports told a different story," Rico said. "Two Rangers were killed in a training exercise, and then two more died in a helicopter crash around the same time. All guys in our unit, too. McGuire, Bellinger, Jones, and Lancer. Then Chaos reportedly died in a single-vehicle accident, careening off the side of a mountain."

Rico glanced at Knox, who stared back, mouth agape.

"Who *allegedly* died in the chopper crash?"

"Jones and Lancer. And the details of the event were scarce, such as who the pilots were or what caused the accident."

"I would've remembered seeing that news, if I didn't live in the Montana wilderness."

"Well, I'm a newshound, and I don't think that had been released to the public yet when the CIA officer approached me."

"So, what'd they promise you if you killed me?"

Knox sighed. "They paid off my ranch loans, one of which I got through a loan shark in Vegas."

"A loan shark? Really, Knox?"

"You know I'm no good with money."

"Yeah, but you sure know how to hang onto a lucky coin."

"I don't feel lucky right now. And if what you're telling me is true, four really good men are dead, compliments of our own government."

Children darted back and forth in front of the vehicle, playing games and laughing. The elder tribesmen clutched spears and glared at Rico and Knox. A couple of the boys eased in front of the truck, tapping the hood and pointing to a souvenir stand.

"Want an authentic gift to bring back from the Amazon?" Rico asked.

"The Amazon has already given me a gift—and it's not one I'm very fond of," Knox said, holding out his prosthetic leg.

Rico shooed the boys away from his truck before resuming their escape.

"So, what now?" Rico asked. "You want to drop this thing? Pretend like it never happened?"

"That'd be the smart thing to do."

"Why do I have the feeling that you're not going to do the smart thing?"

"Because you know me all too well."

Rico tapped on the steering wheel to a beat only he could hear.

"Come on, Knox. This isn't something you should be fooling around with. Think about those kids at that camp. That was your dream. You're just going to throw it all away because you can't leave well enough alone?"

Knox bit his bottom lip and stared out his window.

"You might be able to run away from Chefe, but you can't outrun the long arm of the U.S. federal government. It's stand and fight or be killed. If Ballard isn't convinced you're dead, he'll send someone else after you—and then someone after me, too."

"Knox, you can disappear. In fact, you're as equipped as anyone to do it."

"But I've got those kids at that camp who I care about too much —and Ballard knows that. He visited the camp, so he knows how much it means to me. And if I'm going to be able to keep doing that,

I need to get to the bottom of this. And I need to give them that footage from the Rangers. That was part of the deal."

"Tell him I said the evidence was destroyed before you killed me," Rico said. "Then text back the photo of me dead and go home. I promise to stay hidden, and you can continue to live your life however you wish."

"If only it was that easy," Knox said. "I need to buy some more time in order to find the footage. And I'm gonna do this on my terms. I'm gonna find out what the government was trying to hide in the Congo."

"That's a nice sentiment, but if your friend isn't ready for us when we get up the river, you won't be exposing anyone, except yourself and me to Chefe's goons."

Rico stopped and revved the engine on his truck.

"What's going on?" Knox asked, as he surveyed the road in front of them.

"It's a little bit of a mud pit here. We need to get some momentum to get us across."

"You sure this is a good idea?"

"Better than going back to my house."

Rico stomped on the accelerator as they lurched forward. Knox placed his hands on the dash, bracing himself. As the truck entered the boggy area, it skidded across a few feet. Rico kept on pushing the gas pedal, spinning the wheels. Mud flew in every direction. And with every passing seconds, the tires sunk deeper into the muck.

After a few more seconds, Rico accepted defeat, cursing under his breath and then hitting the steering wheel. He opened his door and peeked out the side.

"How's it look?" Knox asked.

"Like we're in deep shit."

Knox looked around again. A few men emerged from the bushes and stood around the truck, pointing at the tires as the talked among themselves.

"I'm going to call Makenzie, while you figure out a way to get us out of here," Knox said. "I want to make sure she'll be ready for us when we get there."

Knox opened the passenger side door and turned to exit. He put his feet on the chrome runners and leaped over the mud. He landed in a patch of bushes and rolled for a few feet before he stopped. After untangling himself, he got up and dialed Makenzie's number.

While he waited, Knox took a deep breath, drinking in the fresh jungle air. The humidity hung in the air, so thick it was palpable.

The phone rang and rang. Makenzie didn't answer. He dialed the number again. Same result. Knox pulled out his lucky coin and rubbed it before attempting a third time. Still no answer.

He pocketed the coin and then grunted as he trudged back toward the truck.

"What'd she say?" Rico asked.

"Nothing," Knox said. "She wasn't there."

"Looks like we're in even deeper shit than we thought."

Knox forced a smile and then paused. He heard what sounded like a dirt bike engine clattering in the distance.

"Is that—"

"Chefe's men?" Rico asked. He nodded.

CHAPTER FIFTEEN

Washington, D.C

Erica Everhart picked lint off her dress as she sat in the lobby on the seventh floor of the Peace Corps headquarters. Around her, young professionals bustled back and forth between the different office suites, toting files and other reading material. There was a time in her life where she wanted to travel abroad and see the world, put her hands in the dirt and help people in some foreign country. But that was before she nurtured a different passion—a passion for the truth. In an odd way, she had come full circle, though it wasn't anything she would've ever predicted.

Ever since Erica spoke with Hayes Collins, she couldn't stop thinking about what he'd said. Chase Moore had supposedly committed suicide, though nobody had seen the body. And any investigation was cursory at best. Even a first-time detective would've interviewed those closest to Chase.

But why didn't the investigators?

The *why* question always nagged Erica, not in a way that bothered her but in a way that drove her. Her first journalism professor at the University of Missouri, the irascible Dr. Cleveland Youngblood, taught her that curiosity — an endless supply of it — was the most important attribute of a great journalist. Youngblood's tirades over milquetoast articles were legendary among the school's journalism students. He once put his fist through a chalkboard when a senior student turned in an article about a local bar that had been shuttered for serving alcohol to minors—and she didn't make any attempt to interview the owners. He shredded her article in front of the class before tearing into her. Erica didn't require fear of Youngblood's ire to motivate her. Sleepless nights and a cacophony of unanswered questions provided sufficient incentive for her to leave no stone unturned in her pursuit of the story behind the story.

A mousy woman with glasses waddled into the lobby and glanced at her clipboard before speaking.

"Erica Everhart," she said, scanning the room. "Erica Everhart."

Erica stifled a laugh as she looked around at the empty seats in the lobby. There wasn't another person in sight.

"Right here," Erica said, raising her hand and smiling as she sauntered over to the woman.

"Director Mecklenburg will see you now," the woman said. "Follow me."

She led Erica into the executive suite and around the corner. Once they reached an office door displaying a placard with Amanda Mecklenburg's name on it, the assistant knocked and then opened the door.

"Erica Everhart from *The Washington Post* is here to see you, ma'am," the woman said, before turning slowly and shuffling back to her desk.

Director Mecklenburg remained entranced by her work, refusing to even look up. Behind her, Erica could see a healthy slice of Washington's cityscape, with the ATF headquarters below just across the street.

She eased inside, tucking her hair behind her ears. She closed the door and headed toward the chair across from the director's desk.

"Let's leave the door open," Mecklenburg said, pointing at the door with her head down. "I don't like secrets in this office."

Erica walked back over to the door and cracked it.

"All the way," Mecklenburg said, still without looking.

Once Erica complied, Mecklenburg removed her glasses and eased to her feet, steadying herself by leaning on her knuckles. She offered her hand to Erica before the two women shook and sat down.

"I've read your work," Mecklenburg said. "Consider me a fan."

"Thank you, Director."

Mecklenburg waved dismissively. "Oh, call me Brenda, please."

"Okay, Brenda. I appreciate you taking the time to meet with me today."

"Of course," she said. "Your story on Chase Moore is the kind of journalism the world needs. Back in my younger days—you know, the ones when the only place you could get your news was either the six o'clock news or the newspaper—those kinds of stories were the ones that we bonded over around the water cooler."

Erica leaned forward and smiled.

"I appreciate that, Brenda. You have no idea what a compliment that is coming from you. I keep trying to tell people that the reports of journalism's demise has been greatly exaggerated. There's still a handful of journalists out there who care about the truth."

"Well, keep it up. Now, what can I help you with today? I'm afraid that I've been so busy that I didn't get a chance to read up beforehand on the topic of our meeting."

"I wanted to talk about Chase Moore."

Mecklenburg knit her brow before she looked down at her desk. She scooped up her glasses, biting down on the end of one leg.

"What kind of story are you writing about Chase Moore? An in-depth look at his life? His work in the Congo?"

Erica shook her head, her eyes locked on Mecklenburg's, searching for any hint of discomfort.

"Actually, I've got some questions about his death," Erica said.

"Questions? What kind of questions?"

"Like, why didn't anyone interview the people who were with Chase in the Congo? How exactly did he die? Were there any signs that Chase was going to kill himself? Just some basic questions like that."

Mecklenburg's scowl didn't budge.

"You think the family wants you to dredge up those kind of details and share them with the world?"

"Good journalism doesn't always make everyone comfortable," Erica said. "Same professor who taught me to be curious also taught me that."

"Then I'd say you had a journalism professor who failed to understand how to relate to other people."

"If I'm going to tell a story, one that my readers would be eager to hear, then I'm going to tell it right. I'm going to present as many angles as I can be privy to. In other words, I'm going to leave no stone unturned."

"That's a bold pronouncement," Mecklenburg said, as she stooped and picked up her briefcase. "I'm afraid that those are questions I can't help you with today, Miss Everhart."

"*Can't* or *won't?*"

"Does it matter?"

Erica nodded.

"Why? Why does it matter so much to you?" Mecklenburg persisted.

"You would've made a good journalist with that line of questioning," Erica said. "And that's all I'm here trying to do, trying to get some answers as to why nobody seemed to care about Chase Moore. Or figure out why he killed himself, because by all accounts I've gathered, he was a stable young man. Even colleagues in the field with him perceived him as such. Nobody thought he was capable of doing such a thing."

Mecklenburg loaded her briefcase with documents stacked in various spots on her desk, a new singular focus.

"Suicide rarely makes sense," Mecklenburg said. "We want it to make sense, in order to assuage our guilty consciences. But what we really want to do is absolve ourselves from the crime of not caring enough. However, sometimes a person is just ready to leave this earth

—and they want to do it on their terms. And that's how I see Chase Moore. He was just a young man who was affected by what he'd seen working in the bush of Africa and experienced a despair he didn't think he could come back from."

"I'd almost believe you, if those who knew him best parroted what you're saying. But they didn't."

Mecklenburg put the last book in her briefcase with a thud. She closed it and yanked it off the desk. She sighed deeply, and her gaze met Erica's.

"Miss Everhart, I really do appreciate your dogged determination here, but this is one of those times you just need to let it go, if for anything, for the sake of Chase's family. I know Senator Moore personally, and the last thing he wants to do is have his son's death be made a public spectacle."

"He conveyed something very different to me."

"Perhaps you should speak with him again about this, see if he still feels the same way."

"I'd thank you for your time, Director, if you'd been a little more forthcoming," Erica said. "Unfortunately, I now have more questions than answers. And my dogged determination, as you call it, isn't going away any time soon."

"I hope this story is worth your career," Mecklenburg said, "because that's what it's going to cost you."

Erica spun on her heels and headed toward the door. As she reached for the door, she heard Mecklenburg's begin speaking in a hushed tone into her cell phone, though it was loud enough for Erica to hear it.

"We need to meet ASAP," Mecklenburg, said before Erica shut the door.

She hustled out to her car and maneuvered around the parking deck so she could see everyone who exited the building. After a few minutes, Mecklenburg shuffled out, lugging her briefcase. She kept her head down, only looking up as she approached her car. She scanned the parking garage before getting inside.

Safely hidden in the shadows in the back corner of the garage, Erica remained undetected.

Once Mecklenburg ignited her engine, Erica powered on her Tesla and followed the director into Washington's rush hour traffic.

They drove along surface streets for a couple of miles before a driver aggressively stuck the nose of his Prius in front of Erica's vehicle. She tapped the brakes, allowing him to get in. Meanwhile, she kept peering around him, trying to make sure she was still following Mecklenburg. After following her down one street, the man slammed on brakes, catching Erica off guard as she was distracted trying to make sure she was staying with Mecklenburg.

The man jumped out of his car and loosened his tie. Marching around to the back bumper, he inspected the damage and shook his head. He put his hands on his hips and cursed. Then he turned his steely gaze toward Erica, who had remained in the car.

She eased outside, leaning on the top of the door to create a buffer between her and the man.

"What the hell was that?" he said, his hands waving wildly. "Weren't you paying attention?"

"Yeah, but—"

"The judge isn't going to listen to your excuses, lady," he said. "You're toast. Unbelievable."

Then he resumed ranting and cursing at Erica.

She shielded her eyes from the sun, trying to keep an eye on Mecklenburg.

"You're not even paying attention to me now," the man said. "Why would I believe you were paying attention earlier?"

"Just shut up, will ya?" Erica said, her irritation level rising, her eyes still following Mecklenburg.

The man grew more incensed with Erica, shuffling into her line of vision and jumping up and down as he waved his arms. After a few seconds, she lost the director, who vanished into a wave of Washington's endless traffic.

The man put his car in reverse and rammed into Erica's Tesla before speeding away.

Erica sighed as she climbed back into her car. She'd lost Mecklenburg. However, Erica's curiosity only grew.

And she wasn't about to discard the story now. There was definitely something there.

All she needed to do was find the right thread to tug on and unravel it.

CHAPTER SIXTEEN

Washington, D.C

Elliot Schwartz wiped the sweat off his forehead as he dribbled the basketball up the court. Senators he regularly sparred with in the press were both on his team and his opponent's team in this after-work pickup game. He usually owned the court; his team remaining there until he could hardly stand. But this evening, he and his four teammates were facing an unusually large deficit.

Hunched over guarding the ball with his left hand, Schwartz pounded the ball into the court with his right.

Senator Hutchins from Nebraska clapped, demanding the ball. Schwartz wanted to launch it at the loudmouth's face and knock his teeth out, after what he'd said about the president earlier that morning on one of the cable news shows. Instead, Schwartz delivered a perfect bounce pass to Hutchins. With his back to the basket, he spun around and fired a shot off the backboard. The ball hit hard and high, resulting in a bullet of a rebound. Senator Underhill, the diminutive man from Wyoming, snared the ball just off the floor and wove through traffic before laying it off to Senator Nichols, who slammed the ball through the hoop, a dunk that rattled the metal wires holding the backboard suspended just behind the baseline.

"Game," Nichols said, pointing at Schwartz and winking. "Not your night tonight, is it?"

Schwartz wiped more sweat off his forehead and shrugged.

"Can't win 'em all, can you?" he said.

"Not if you're the president," Underhill said, before breaking into an annoying cackle.

Schwartz glared at Underhill.

"I didn't realize it was comedy night at the senate gym," Schwartz said.

"Your play on the court was leaving everyone in stitches," Underhill said. "I've seen senior citizens with better skills than you tonight."

Schwartz lunged toward Underhill and tried to take a swing at him. However, Nichols grabbed Schwartz from behind, preventing a melee from ensuing.

After the two men cooled off, Nichols seized Schwartz by the back of his arm and nudged him to the far corner of the court. Neither man spoke until they were away from the others.

"You want to tell me what the hell is wrong with you tonight?" Nichols said. "It's like you want to fight or something. What gives?"

"Just a rough day at the office," Schwartz said.

"We played hoops a month ago after the president received his worst public approval ratings since he took office—and you didn't act this out of control. So don't act like it's just a bad day. I'd more likely believe you had a good day than a bad one that made you look like you wanted to murder Underhill."

Schwartz leaned against the wall.

"I'm not lying. I just had a bad day, and I'm stressed out. That's all."

"You done spewing all that bullshit? Because I'm not buying it."

"What do you want me to say? Want me to make something up?"

Nichols patted Schwartz on the chest.

"You've been around Washington long enough to know that you can't let what happens in the public arena affect your relationships with everyone on Capitol Hill. Whatever's got your knickers in a knot, get it together, man, okay?"

Schwartz nodded. He rubbed his thumb across his lip, sweeping aside more sweat that had beaded up on his face.

"All right, Nichols," he said. "I'll do better."

"Good. And if you ever want to talk, you know where to find me."

Schwartz headed for the locker room and waved good-bye to his teammates. After a quick shower, he drove home, lost in thought.

He shouldered plenty of guilt for how he handled his business, concluding long ago that it took a strong stomach to take on the tasks that actually changed the world. Status quo had obviously failed—and he didn't intend to work for a president who wasn't serious about putting his stamp on policy. But Schwartz wasn't there for the history book. He was there on his own covert mission, a man who clung to his private principles and sought ways to implement them no matter the cost.

However, he wasn't ready to go bankrupt just yet.

Schwartz smiled as he pulled into his driveway. On the ride home, he'd managed to work through his looming problem, the issue that had distracted him from basketball. Once inside, he fished another burner phone out of his bottom drawer in his office. He still had a use for Senator Moore.

Schwartz pounded out a short text message on his own phone, one he hoped Moore would understand:

Give Joe Garber to your journalist friend. I can give you proof that he was responsible.

He smiled as he pushed the send button. His smile widened seconds later as Moore made a predictable phone call.

"What is this all about?" Moore asked. "The reporter?"

"That's right, Mark. She's not going away until she gets what she came for."

"But Garber? Really? Is that even believable?"

"Make it believable," Schwartz said. "You ought to have no problem selling it. I mean, hell, you managed to sell yourself to voters, which is no small feat."

"Okay, okay," Moore said. "I'll do it if you truly think this is going to get her off our back."

"It solves two problems for us," Schwartz said. "It gets rid of her —and Garber, too."

"What makes you think that?"

"Garber is so predictable. And Everhart's not going to put up with any of his antics. It's going to be beautiful."

"You're that certain?"

"Just make the call and sell it. I'll send you over some good talking points. I know you can do it."

Schwartz ended the call and compiled a few key notes for Moore to share with the pesky reporter. Joe Garber, a liaison with the Pentagon, made the perfect fall guy.

And Schwartz was unflappable in his belief that Garber was not just going to fall, but fall hard.

CHAPTER SEVENTEEN

Iriri River | Brazil

Knox studied the small crowd that had gathered. Men, women, children, dogs—they all slowly surrounded the vehicle. They chattered amongst themselves, pointing at the truck firmly stuck in the mud.

"Do you understand what they're saying?" Knox asked Rico.

"More or less. One of the men is saying that they need to move the truck so their shipment can get through later this afternoon."

"Shipment? Out here?"

"A handful of tribes along the river carve out Brazilian nuts for this online candle company," Rico said. "The buyers think they're saving the environment, but it's just a company filling their coffers with sales from just another product."

"Do the people know this?"

Knox nodded. "They're using the bulk of the money, among other things, to hire a security force to keep illegal gold miners off their land, so they can continue to live off of it."

"So they have a vested interest in getting your truck moved."

Rico nodded. "Problem is, we don't have enough time to get it moved before Chefe's men arrive."

"Then we'll have to make time," Knox said.

"Let me just get out my time-making machine and see what I can whip up," Rico said sarcastically.

"Just hear me out, okay?"

After Knox finished explaining his plan to Rico, they approached several of the men who appeared to be in charge and asked if they would be willing to help. A brief discussion ensued, and the tribesmen agreed.

Knox and Rico hid in a front bedroom in a hut just off the main road, putting them close enough to hear any conversations. Ten minutes later, Chefe's men rumbled into town on their dirt bikes. They all dismounted and drew their weapons when they saw Rico's truck.

The leader of the group scowled as he shouted at the people. After a few awkward moments of silence, one of the tribesmen boldly stepped forward and started speaking.

"What's he saying?" Knox asked.

"Exactly what we told him to," Rico said. "He's showing off the watch and then telling Chefe's men that he traded a canoe for it and that we went downstream."

"Perfect," Knox whispered.

Moments later, Chefe's men wheeled their bike around and headed in the opposite direction.

"Now, that's how you make time," Knox said.

"Well, we're going to need every minute of it to get my truck out of that mud."

When Knox and Rico re-emerged, they wasted no time in working with the tribe to extract the truck from the mud. Knox found some fallen trees from the jungle and showed the other tribesmen how to work the trees under the tires to create traction. After a half-hour of fighting with the barely pliable terrain, they were able to create enough of a surface for the tires to drive over and out of the bog. The people celebrated by whooping and jumping up and down. But once the noise died down, Knox stopped.

"You hear that?" he asked.

"The motorcycles in the distance?"

"Think it's Chefe's men?"

"Gotta be," Rico said.

"How did they—" Knox stopped as he saw a teenaged boy perched high atop a tree and signaling to someone.

"What?" Rico asked.

Knox nodded toward the tree.

"Think he told Chefe's men?" Rico asked.

Knox noticed a small radio clipped to the boy's shorts.

Rico rushed over to some of the tribesmen, who then ordered the boy to the ground. As soon as he reached the jungle floor, he darted off into the woods.

"Let's let them deal with him," Knox said. "We need to get the hell outta here."

The two men hustled over to the truck and waved at the people still milling around the vehicle before driving away. Rico pushed the limits of what the truck could handle along the bumpy road. Overgrown brush scraped the side of the vehicle

It didn't take more than fifteen minutes before a pair of nimble dirt bikes roared up behind the truck.

"Any ideas on how to buy some more time?" Rico asked. "Because we're in short supply of it."

The sound of a gunshot reverberated throughout the truck. Seconds later, the back window shattered after a shot penetrated the truck. Both men crouched low before their eyes met.

"I'm waiting," Rico said.

Knox thought for a few seconds, which felt like minutes as more shots pinged off the back of the truck. His mind whirred with ideas before he settled on one.

"You see that bend up ahead?" Knox asked.

"Yeah."

"I want you to take the corner and then block the road by parking perpendicular."

"And then what?"

"Just follow my lead."

As soon as they rounded the bend, Rico did as instructed. Then Knox scrambled up a small hill with Rico in tow. Knox steadied his breathing as the two dirt bikes rounded the corner. With the truck blocking the roadway, the two bikers slowed before skidding to a stop. As Chefe's men looked around for the truck's occupants, Knox and Rico opened fire, felling both hostiles.

After hurling the bodies into a small gulch, Knox and Rico collected their belongings before cinching them onto the back of the bikes.

"Ready?" Knox asked as he eased behind the truck.

"Just give me a minute," Rico said. "I need to tell this ole girl good-bye."

Knox chuckled and shook his head.

"Let's go."

Rico kissed his hand and then reached inside, slapping the dashboard.

"I'm gonna miss you."

He hustled around to the back of the truck with Knox and the two men shoved the truck down the side of the mountain. The truck bounced, moving up and down with the terrain. Hurdling stumps and fallen trees, the vehicle came to a stop when it slammed into the trunk of a tree.

"I'm so sorry, girl," Rico said.

Knox straddled his bike before ramming the kickstarter down. The engine clattered, then sputtered to life.

"You ready to ride?" Knox asked.

Rico nodded as he hopped onto the other bike and fired up the engine. They rode for a half-hour before they stopped to rest.

"We're moving much quicker now that we have these bikes," Rico said. "When you said the landing strip was fifty miles up the river, I was thinking it'd be at least a two-day trip, but I think we can make it there before nightfall."

"The only problem is our ride out of here."

"You still haven't been able to reach her?" Rico asked.

Knox shook his head. "Let me try her again."

He removed the satellite phone from his rucksack and dialed Makenzie's number. After two rings, she picked up.

"There you are," she said. "I was wondering if you'd disappeared."

"I've been trying to. But we've stumbled into more trouble here."

"You're still the same ole Knox."

"And I might be a dead Knox, if you can't get us out of here. Rico kind of started a feud with the local drug lord, and he's hunting us."

"Hunting you?"

"Yeah, killing a bunch of his men tends to have that kind of effect."

"Where are you?" she asked.

Knox gave her their coordinates.

"That's not too far from me, maybe twenty miles."

"Twenty miles?" he asked.

"Yeah, I was able to connect with one of my buddies who services an airfield for an oil company. There's a lake nearby that I landed on, and he helped me get the tire fixed, so I'm good to go anywhere now."

She gave him her coordinates, which Knox scratched onto a sheet of paper and then handed to Rico.

"We can make this in an hour," he said.

Knox flashed a thumb-up signal.

"Rico says we will be there in an hour."

"I'll be waiting," she said.

Knox ended the call and then looked at Rico.

"You ready to get back at it?"

"Of course, but—"

He paused and stared at the ground.

"What is it, Rico?"

He covered his eyes with his hand and sobbed quietly. Knox climbed off his bike, edging closer to Rico.

"Is it Maria?" Knox asked.

Rico nodded, his eyes clenched shut, tears streaming down his face.

"I warned her not to mess with Chefe and his men," he said. "I told her that we didn't need that kind of trouble. But she refused to stand by and do nothing, especially after Chefe was the one who got her little brother hooked on drugs before he OD'd. She just had to go and report Chefe to the federal police. And it's not like they don't know about Chefe—they just don't care. He's a small fish in a big pond in the middle of nowhere. And some of Chefe's informants in the federal police told him that Maria reported what was happening. When Chefe sent his men to confront her, I killed them. So, Chefe sent more and more of his men. If she'd just listened to me—"

Rico let his words hang in the air, his implications clear.

"She sounds like a strong woman, a good woman," Knox said.

"She was," Rico said. "She was more or less a female version of you, without all the dad jokes."

"It's hard to find the perfect woman," Knox said.

Rico huffed a laugh through his nose, a faint smile spreading across his lips.

"You would've liked her, I know."

"Well, let's honor her today by not letting Chefe win."

Rico leaned against his bike, his arms now crossed over his chest.

"There's one more thing I need to tell you," Rico said.

"Can it wait?"

"No, it can't wait. If something happens to me, you need to know about it."

"What is it?" Knox asked.

"I might have a way to get in touch with Chaos."

Knox's eyes widened.

"And you're just now telling me this?"

"I wasn't sure I could trust you when you first got here."

"But now you can?"

"I think so," Rico said, with a wink.

"Then let's get to some place safe and we can talk about it."

"Just a second," Rico said.

He pulled his cell phone out of his pocket and thumbed a text message before hitting send.

"Now are you ready?" Knox asked.

"Let's ride."

They started their engines and Rico took the lead, navigating Knox to the coordinates Makenzie had given him. When they were within a few miles, Knox's bike sputtered before conking out. He shouted to get Rico's attention, who, upon hearing the cries for help, skidded to a stop and circled back to Knox.

"What's wrong?" Rico asked.

Knox unscrewed the lid to the gas tank and peeked inside.

"Bone dry," he said.

"We've only got about three more miles to go," Rico said. "You can saddle up behind me and we'll be there before you know it."

"Or I can walk."

"There's plenty of room for two grown men on here."

"Just because you can, doesn't mean you should."

Rico shrugged. "So you're going to walk?"

Before Knox could answer, he heard the whine of a dirt bike in the distance, followed by the low rumble of a truck. Then, gunfire.

"Why walk when you can ride?" Knox said.

He slung his leg over the seat behind Rico and held fast to his waist with one hand, while using the other to dig out the satellite phone and call Makenzie.

"Are you at the airfield?" Knox asked, once she answered.

"Just going through my pre-flight checklist here," she said.

"You might want to speed it up," Knox said, as he bounced along the rocky path. "We're coming in hot."

"Hot? What are you talking about?"

"As in, we have some of this drug lord's minions after us."

"How hot do you mean? Like Indiana-Jones-and-the-natives-along-the-river hot?"

"Yes, but with guns."

Makenzie swore. "Okay, I'll do my best to have her ready. Just be ready to climb in quickly so we can get in the air."

Knox pocketed the phone and then held on with both hands. He heard a gunshot, and looked over his shoulder to see a well-worn pickup truck with a machine gun mounted in the bed. Bullets whizzed past them. He turned around a second time, to see a couple of dirt bikes humming along the road and edging closer.

"Makenzie said we better be ready to just climb right in, so we can take off," Knox shouted to Rico.

"Copy that."

Rico rounded a corner and came into a straightaway that led directly to the hangars. Knox spotted Makenzie's plane, the Super Piper Cub's propellors already whirring.

"It's going to be a tight fit in there," Knox said.

"I'm sure you'll manage just fine in the back."

Knox growled while Rico laughed.

Bullets peppered the ground around them as the truck reached the straight section of road at the airfield. It gained on them along the flatter surface.

Knox signaled for her to turn the plane around, making their entry into the aircraft more efficient.

When they reached the area near the hangar, Rico applied the brakes. They stopped and dismounted. They grabbed their packs and then sprinted toward the plane, climbing over Makenzie to get inside. Once they were both in, Makenzie began to taxi down the runway.

The Cub's speed increased with each passing second, but that didn't matter to the truck, as the gunman in the back sprayed bullets across the tarmac, a few shots pinging off the airplane.

Knox craned his neck to look behind them and noticed the truck come to a stop at the end of the runway. The sound of gunfire ceased.

"What's going on?" Makenzie asked.

Knox swore under his breath.

"They've got an RPG."

Makenzie pulled back on the stick, forcing the plane airborne. However, it struggled to climb. As they raced toward the end of the runway, Knox wondered if they could clear the trees, the jungle canopy drawing closer. Behind them, Chefe's goons took aim with a rocket launcher.

"Get ready to bank hard," Knox said.

Knox noticed a flash from the missile launcher.

"Gotta go one way or the other," he said.

Makenzie yanked the stick left, pulling back on it as she gritted her teeth. The pontoons brushed against the top of the trees as the three passengers all leaned left. Knox, fixated on the missile, watched it whiz by the right side of the plane before falling into the jungle and catching fire.

Makenzie circled over the runway as they gained altitude and then leveled out.

"So, boys, where we headed today?" she asked.

"What's the range on this thing?" Rico asked, as he fiddled with his phone.

"You planning on a long trip?"

"Depends on what your definition of a long trip is," Rico said.

"Where are we going?" Knox asked.

Rico smiled as he glanced down at his phone.

"Everyone up for a trip to Fiji?"

CHAPTER EIGHTEEN

Falls Church, Virginia

Julius Ballard leaned against a post at the corner of J.T.'s Good Times Bar and Restaurant on the outskirts of the city limits. Rain pelted the aluminum awning, while water drained over the edge, spattering onto the pavement. The neon sign affixed to the front of the building cast a red glow on the puddles that had quickly formed.

While J.T.'s clientele wasn't exactly the type that would recognize Ballard, he understood the importance of taking precautions. Carelessness in his line of work could result in a quick exit, oftentimes in the form of bullet to the head. He glanced at his watch and then flicked his lighter, holding the flame for ten seconds before igniting the end of his cigarette. The signal wouldn't have been noticeable to anyone, except the person who was looking for it.

Ballard kept his head down before taking a long drag on the cigarette. He didn't look up until he needed to exhale, forcing a plume of smoke upward. After about a minute, a man wearing sunglasses and a baseball cap pulled low across his brow approached Ballard.

"Two roads diverged in a yellow wood," the man said.

"Were they paved or dirt?" Ballard asked.

The man grunted and stuffed his hands into his raincoat.

"Why do you have to ruin such a good poem?" he asked.

"Maybe because I hate Robert Frost."

The man looked over his shoulder.

"Let's make this quick. I wouldn't want anyone to recognize me at a place like this."

"Me either," Ballard said, "which is why I picked it. Trust me when I say this—your identity is safe here."

Ballard took another long drag on his cigarette before handing over an envelope to the man. He slipped his finger beneath the flap before loosening it, taking one more glance around the parking lot before pulling out the document. His eyebrows twitched, presumably from recognition, a gesture so subtle that most people would've missed it. But Ballard didn't miss any details. It's why he was so good at his job.

"Is this going to be a problem for you?" Ballard asked.

"Not at all," the man said as he thumbed through the pages.

"Are you sure? Because if it is—"

"I can handle it."

"My contact warned me that you might have worked with the target in the past and—"

"The past is the past."

"Okay," Ballard said, flicking away his cigarette. "I wouldn't want this to become a problem for you later."

"It won't be a problem, but I do have one question before I accept this job."

"I'm listening."

"If I complete this assignment for you, I believe there's a good chance that it could raise some uncomfortable questions for you."

"That's why you're going to make it look like an accident—or a suicide. Dealer's choice."

"Is this one of your mistakes?" the man asked.

Ballard ran his hand across his bald head and scanned the parking lot before answering.

"If it wasn't, do you think I would've contacted a man known as The Cleaner?"

The man glanced back down at the paper.

"No matter how I complete this task, people are going to wonder."

Ballard chuckled.

"Any time someone in Washington dies, conspiracies blossom like daisies on a grave. But I've got other people to help me with that, maybe a doctor who confirms it was a heart attack nobody could've seen coming, or a first responder who saw your target go for a swim under the moonlight. The resources I possess to craft a believable narrative are nearly endless. So, you just worry about doing your job and I'll worry about the fallout—if there is any."

"As long as I get paid, I don't really care."

"That's not something you need to worry about either," Ballard said. "And now that I think about it, suicide might be the best option here, since the target had some gambling debts and struggled with finances."

"You're the boss," the man said.

"I'll be in touch."

"No," the man said. "No more contact with me until this is over. And when it's over, you'll know it."

With that, The Cleaner shoved the papers back into the packet and walked away.

Ballard lit another cigarette and watched the drunks stumble out of the bar.

Everything is going as planned.

CHAPTER NINETEEN

Maryland | Congressional Country Club

Erica Everhart inspected her golf clubs as she secured them to the back of her cart. She adjusted her visor and pushed her sunglasses up the bridge of her nose. After tying her shoes, she wheeled the cart around and met the starter at the first hole. Placed in a foursome with two Marines and a doctor, she figured she could endure a couple of holes with the strangers before striking off in search of Joe Garber.

Senator Moore had sent her an initial message about Garber, before following up with a more in-depth phone call to discuss the matter. Moore shared how he was still working through proper legal channels to address Garber's egregious actions, but also suggested Erica might be able to expedite the process. Although Moore admitted an article wouldn't give law enforcement exigent circumstance to search Garber's home, it would give a judge solid footing to issue a warrant. Erica had plenty of alleged evidence from Moore regarding Garber's inexcusable actions, but it was nothing more than hearsay. She needed to get Garber to admit as much, but she knew it wouldn't be easy based on her previous interactions with him.

Garber served as a Pentagon liaison, communicating the president's desires and wishes with the country's top military brass. By all accounts, he was a lifelong bureaucrat, charming his way into some of the best unelected jobs in the city. He'd worked with Congressional leaders, lobbyists, and just every alphabet agency at one time or another. It's what made him such a sought-after man. It's also what made him a dangerous man.

Pinning anything on Garber was about as easy as getting spaghetti to stick to a wall bathed in oil. He'd been accused of harassment on multiple occasions, always managing to wriggle free through either a favor from a judge or a political fixer. The rumors of his appetite for women seemed exaggerated, based on Garber's public persona. A widower after his wife died from a bout with breast cancer, he'd remained on Washington's most eligible bachelor list for so long that he'd ascended to the top of it for the past five years. Rich, powerful, and handsome, Garber seemed content with his single life, taking full advantage of it behind the scenes, if the rumors were to be believed.

A year had passed since Garber went to the Congo on behalf of the U.S. military, accompanying the Secretary of Defense on a lengthy diplomatic mission. However, Garber visited several Peace Corps teams there, serving as a morale booster. He even delivered a batch of Ashley Moore's family-famous chocolate chip cookies to Chase a few days before he died while he was by himself. Erica knew the story well, retelling it in her recent article about Senator Moore's new bill that had passed. And there wasn't anything that made her question what else Garber was doing when he visited Chase.

According to Senator Moore, Garber delivered chocolate chip cookies—and a pistol. Possessing a weapon while serving for the Peace Corps was forbidden, and grounds for immediate dismissal and a swift return to the U.S. In Erica's initial interview with the senator, he refused to reveal how Chase died. Now, she understood why. The senator wanted to keep it a secret because having a firearm wasn't allowed. There would be questions as to why he had one. When Moore revealed the sordid details of Chase's last days, he explained that he didn't initially know how Chase obtained a gun. But now he did. Joe Garber provided it.

Garber's actions broke plenty of laws, but proving anything substantial wouldn't be easy. Senator Moore expressed to Erica how he'd like to see Garber charged with manslaughter, on the ground that he'd provided a weapon to a young man struggling with mental issues. But an article revealing what Garber had done might be more than enough to send him slinking out of Washington. At least, that's what Moore said he hoped would happen after giving the information to Erica.

Despite how strong the evidence appeared, Erica knew she was dealing with a politician—and a hurting one at that. She needed to perform due diligence on this potential story just like she did with all the others she covered. It's why she stood in the tee box clutching her driver at the Congressional Country Club, there as a guest of one of Moore's Washington socialite friends.

Erica drew back her club and smashed the ball, sending it straight down the fairway, and outdriving the doctor and one of the Marines.

"She can write and play golf—and look good doing it," the doctor said. "What can't she do?"

"Break up your marriage," Erica said, pointing at the doc's ring. "Sorry, doc, but let's leave my looks out of it. And I promise not to hold yours against you."

The other two Marines laughed, high-fiving each other as they reveled in the doctor getting called out.

"Somebody better straighten up," one of the Marines said.

"It was a compliment," the doctor huffed.

"A gateway compliment," Erica said, as she leaned on her club. "One minute you're making comments about my appearance; three beers later on the back nine, you're getting all grabby with me. I'm just letting you know that this all ends right here. Are we clear?"

"Yes," the doctor mumbled.

Erica tallied a bogey on the first hole and then a double bogey on the second, good enough for second after the first two holes. But she had no intention of sticking around.

"Gentlemen, it's been a pleasure, but I don't feel well," she said, bending over and clutching her stomach. "I'm going to head back to the clubhouse."

After driving in the direction of the clubhouse, she turned and headed straight for the tenth green. She'd received a text message informing her that Joe Garber was about to arrive there as part of a threesome.

When she came to a stop along the cart path of the tenth tee, Garber was jiggling his beer can, checking to see if there was anything left. Satisfied that it was empty, he tossed it into the trash and cracked open another one.

"This ought to be fun," Erica muttered under her breath, as she got out of her cart.

Joe Garber ran his finger back and forth along the gold chain hanging around his neck. He took a long pull on his can of beer before offering Erica a toothy grin.

"Well, well, well, what do we have here?" Garber said. "The best-looking reporter at *The Washington Post*, if you ask me."

"Mr. Garber," Erica said, as she offered her hand. "I see you have room for a fourth. Mind if I join you?"

"Only if you join me in my cart," he said.

She rolled her eyes and snatched a ball out of his cart before marching up to the tee box. She eased the tee into the ground and set the ball on top. Then she launched a missile shot straight down the fairway, outdriving all the men.

"Impressive," Garber said. "But I'm still not letting you join us unless you ride with me."

"Fine," Erica said. "Let me get my clubs."

After she returned with her gear and secured her clubs, Garber stomped on the gas, sending the cart lurching forward along the path. Then Garber swerved onto the fairway and sped toward his ball.

"Now, just because you outdrove me isn't a reason for you to beat your chest," Garber said. "I'm one of the worst golfers you'll ever meet. I'm just out here for the sunshine and the booze—and the cart girl."

"Charming," Erica said.

"Only when I'm sober," Garber said, nudging her with his elbow before coming to a stop.

"Look, Mr. Garber, I'm not here to be eye candy for you," she said, as Garber selected a club and then addressed his ball in the fairway. "I have some serious questions."

He wound up and then unleashed his swing. The ball squirted off the end of his club face, bounding about thirty yards away.

"If I must be interrogated, it might as well be by someone who's so easy on the eyes as yourself."

Erica narrowed her eyes. "Please, Mr. Garber."

"Okay, okay," he said, waving his hands. "Just calm down. I'm just messing with you."

Garber held onto his club as he maneuvered the cart to where his second shot landed.

"Now, what do you want to know?" he asked, as he got out.

"I have a few questions for you about your trip to the Congo a year ago," she said.

"Oh, hell, lady, I can hardly remember what I had for breakfast, much less a trip to Africa a year ago."

He hit the ball again, this time with more loft, but it sliced toward the trees.

"I've heard some serious allegations levied against you, but I wanted to give you a chance first to respond to them," she said. "And based on what I've heard, this trip was memorable."

"So, basically," he said, pausing to guzzle some more beer, "what you're saying is that you've already written a hit piece on me, but you need some quotes to make it look like you did your job as a journalist."

"That's not at all what I'm saying," she said. "But I would like to get you on record responding to what was said about you."

"Oh, whatever. Just ask your damn question."

Garber sat down and pushed the gas pedal, driving straight down the fairway toward Erica's first shot.

"I have it on good authority that while you were visiting Africa with the Secretary of Defense, you gave Chase Moore a gun, the very gun that he shot himself with," she said.

"Where'd you hear that load of bullshit?"

She got out and grabbed her three iron. She hit a laser shot that skipped along the fairway before veering into a sand trap.

"Look," Garber said. "She's human after all."

"Mr. Garber, are you sure you don't remember anything about giving Chase a gun?"

"If I'm not mistaken, it's illegal for Peace Corps members to have weapons while serving on foreign soil. So, why would I give him a gun?"

Erica shrugged as she sat in the cart, and Garber took off again in search of his ball.

"That's what I was hoping you could tell me," she said.

"Whoever told you that was just shoveling some bullshit your way," Garber said.

"So, you didn't visit Chase Moore in the Congo?"

"I did, but I didn't give him a gun. Poor kid was so depressed when I found him there. I tried to cheer him up with some jokes and a few brews, but he was too far gone."

Garber paused and looked down before continuing.

"Too bad what happened to him. He really was a good kid, even if his old man is the biggest horse's ass on Capitol Hill."

Erica jotted down a few notes in her notebook, taking her eyes off Garber.

"Speaking of which," he said, with a chuckle.

She felt a pinch before swatting his hand away.

"Excuse me," she said, glaring at him. "What do you think you're doing?"

Garber drew back and gave her a devilish smile. She stood up and backed away from him.

Then Garber lunged toward her and grabbed a handful of Erica's rear end.

"What the—" she said, swatting at him. "This is inappropriate, sir."

Undaunted, Garber made another pass. Erica dodged to one side and grabbed her nine iron out of her bag. She held it up in her right hand, waving it back and forth.

"I suggest you back away before I'm compelled to use this."

Garber moved toward the cart.

"Hey, now. Let's just calm down here. Even though you're a woman, there's no need to act *this* irrational."

"Stay away, perv."

Garber sat down in his cart as Erica grabbed the rest of her clubs and marched off without another word.

Moments later, Senator Moore's phone buzzed with a text message—and a video.

He shook his head as he watched at the footage.

"I'll be," Moore said. "Schwartz was right. Joe Garber never fails to disappoint."

CHAPTER TWENTY

Nadi, Fiji

Knox stared out the window at the turquoise waters, the reflection of the sun shimmering with the waves. Vacation-goers dotted the white sandy beaches, soaking up rays and basking in the tropical warmth. The harbor below bustled with tourists and natives alike crowding onto a ferry. The plane banked left, giving Knox an even better view of the place many travel writers deemed a paradise.

"Gentlemen, the tower asked me to wait in a holding pattern before landing, so I apologize for the delay," Makenzie said, her voice crackling through the intercom of the Gulfstream G650ER she'd borrowed, as a favor owed to her by the CEO of a Brazilian oil company. She'd flown the man's college-aged son out of the jungle in the middle of the night after an excursion down the Amazon went wrong and he started suffering from sepsis. Makenzie was able to get him to a hospital in time, saving his life, but not before she flew him out of the jungle in the midst of a storm. The CEO told Makenzie she could use his jet whenever she wanted. She'd never taken him up on the offer, until now.

"I'm more upset about the cabin service in this thing," Knox said. "No snacks or drinks."

"Keep it up, and just wait and see how long it takes you to get checked luggage," she said.

Rico sat up in his seat.

"This is one of the best flights I've ever been on," he said.

"Suck-up," Knox said, with a sarcastic sneer.

"All right," Makenzie said. "Settle down. The tower just gave us clearance to land."

Moments later, the tires barked as Makenzie set the plane down at the Nadi International Airport. After a cursory customs inspection, they exited the airport and picked up a rental car before heading straight to the CEO's posh private villa near Natadola Beach.

"You sure know how to pick your sugar daddies," Knox said.

Makenzie laughed.

"If only that were true," she said.

The trio picked their rooms,then regrouped to discuss how they were going to make contact with Chaos. After they finished developing a plan, Makenzie made margaritas for everyone and then sauntered onto the lanai, leaving Knox and Rico alone.

"Think you'll be able to get your life back?" Knox asked, before sipping his drink.

Rico sighed.

"I had a life with Maria," he said.

"I know. But I'm sure you have family back home that you'd want to see now, right?"

"Of course, but it's exhausting trying to live while having to look over your shoulder all the time," Rico said. "Do I wish things had been different? Yes. But I'd already made peace with the fact that my life wasn't going to be some American dream once I understood my own country's government wanted me dead."

"If Ballard had sent anyone else after you, you certainly wouldn't be sitting here right now."

"There's no doubt in my mind that I'd be dead," Rico said. "And I'm not out of the woods yet. Ballard isn't going to let me live if he finds out you didn't kill me. And he won't let you live, either."

"Do you really think Ballard is that corrupt?"

Rico shrugged.

"What's your gut tell you?"

"I think Ballard might be caught in the middle of something," Knox said. "He's probably just following orders, unaware of what's going on. You know what that's like. How many times did we know all the details of our missions? How many times were we blindly following orders? They told us to take out some terrorist living in a cave in Afghanistan, we took him out. For all we know, he could've been Mother Theresa, helping teach young girls to read and providing medicine to dying women. But did we know that? No. We just did as we were told."

"But there's a big difference between being a grunt and being a commander. And we know Ballard isn't a grunt. He's in on everything. I doubt many covert missions are happening without his knowledge."

"You might be right, but he's an Army Ranger," Knox said. "That's not exactly the Ranger way."

"Don't be so naive. Rangers are susceptible to corruption just like anyone else. Give a person enough power and you never know what they'll do with it. Ballard's no different. And look at me. I killed four men from our unit because I believed they were heartless killers. I did exactly what I was *told* they did. And I'm a Ranger."

"Maybe you're right, but I'm having a hard time seeing it. We can't discount the fact that maybe Ballard doesn't know, either."

"You're right, Knox. Maybe Ballard doesn't know a thing. And maybe I'll sprout wings and flitter out onto the lanai."

Knox took another sip from his glass without saying a word.

"Just think about it," Rico said. "And if you go down this route, promise me that you won't quit until you either convince Ballard to expose this, or you expose all the bastards who are behind whatever's really going on here."

Knox looked up, his eyes meeting Rico's.

"Now, that's something I can promise you."

Rico got up and strolled outside to join Makenzie, leaving Knox alone with his thoughts. He didn't like the idea that Ballard had manipulated him into murdering an innocent Ranger, whether Ballard was aware of Rico's innocence or not. But Knox knew Rico was right. Ballard could be corrupt. But Knox didn't want to become guilty of the same thing, accusing someone without all the facts. If Ballard was covering something up, Knox wanted to make sure he could expose every last person who was part of the illegal operation.

Just before sunset, the trio drove to a beach-front bar near Cuvu Beach water and waited to meet Chaos. Knox and Rico retold combat stories about Chaos, including the one that earned him his nickname. He had gone on a legendary rampage while they were pinned down in a mountain village south of Jalalabad near the border of Pakistan. He killed fifteen men in less than five minutes, sending Taliban fighters retreating and allowing their unit to escape. Knox was nursing a bullet wound in his leg and had required medical attention, or else he would've been beside Chaos. But that was the day "Can Man" morphed into "Chaos."

"Sounds like it was a justified nickname change," Makenzie said.

"He would've done anything for his brothers," Rico said. "I still can't believe I trusted my contact, for even a minute, that Chaos did what they said he did."

"Don't live your life in regret," Makenzie said. "We're all guilty of something while blindly following orders."

Moments later, a man approached their table.

"Rico?" the man asked, his eyes scanning back and forth between Rico and Knox.

Rico squinted as he studied the man, who appeared to be a native islander. Dark complexion, even darker hair, and a hulking stature, making him appear imposing.

"Do I know you?" Rico asked.

The man shook his head.

"But you know my friend Kevin Canfield, who asked me to send his regrets that he couldn't meet with you this evening," the man said. "He's a little jumpy after he believes someone tried to kill him today. He said he would meet with you tonight at this address at ten o'clock. Come alone and don't be late."

The man eased a small slip of paper onto the table and slid it to Rico.

Before Rico could ask a question, the man turned and lumbered away. Rico looked at Knox and shook his head.

"If they found out Chaos is still alive, they didn't believe that I killed him," Rico said.

Knox knew where he was going with his line of thinking, and it wasn't good—for either of them.

"If they didn't believe me, what makes you think they're going to believe you?" Rico asked.

Knox steepled his fingers and looked at Rico and then Makenzie.

"Something about this feels off," Knox said.

"You think we're being set up?" Makenzie asked.

"If we are, by who?" Rico asked.

"Let's just be cautious tonight," Knox said.

"Us cautious?" Rico said. "Did you hear what he said? He said for me to come alone."

"You might be meeting Chaos alone, but you're not going by yourself," Knox said. "Makenzie and I will be there as backup in case things go sideways."

"We're just going to talk," Rico said.

"You're the one who just told me that you think there's something nefarious going on," Knox said. "We'll honor Chaos's request, but we're going to be watching you."

A few minutes before ten o'clock, Makenzie eased their rental car to a stop a block from St. Paul's Catholic Church along the Sigatoka River. The cool ocean breeze sweeping inland rustled the leaves in the trees overhead, the water lapping against the rocks along the shores. Knox drew in a long breath of the fresh air as he got out of the car.

"What do you think you're doing?" Rico asked, in a hushed tone.

"I told you that we're going to keep an eye on you," Knox said.

"You'll do it from the car," Rico said. "If you haven't blown this meeting already. If Chaos sees you—"

Knox put his hands in the air in a gesture of surrender.

"Okay, okay. Simmer down. Just be careful, okay?"

"Always," Rico said.

Knox climbed back into the car and watched as Rico headed toward the gate entrance detailed on the slip of paper Chaos's messenger had delivered. The full moon shone brightly overhead, muting the pale street lamp.

"Is he gonna be all right?" Makenzie asked.

"We're about to find out."

Rico had only gone about a hundred feet before Knox noticed the silhouette of a man emerge from the shadows near the church.

"That's him," Knox said.

"You sure?" Makenzie asked.

"I'd know that walk anywhere. His shoulders swing forward, like a man going somewhere with a distinct purpose."

"Let's hope his purpose is to tell us what we need to know in order to get our hands on that evidence."

Knox smiled and patted Makenzie on the knee.

"What's that for?" she asked.

"You're not just along for the ride, are you?"

"I want to nail these bastards to the wall, expose them for everybody to see how corrupt they are," she said. "And I'm with you until this is finished."

"I wouldn't hold it against you if you returned to your job."

"In for a penny, in for a pound," she said.

Knox turned his focus back toward Rico, who shook hands with Chaos. The two men didn't speak for more than a minute before they parted ways with another handshake. However, Rico hadn't walked more than a few steps before Chaos slumped to the ground.

"What the—" Knox said.

Rico spun around and saw what had happened before taking off and running back toward the car. Knox opened the car door and stood. He peered back at the scene, beckoning Rico to run faster.

Makenzie started the engine as Knox opened the back passenger side door. Both men scrambled back inside before she stomped on the accelerator. The tires barked and rubber burned. Seconds later, Makenzie zoomed along the narrow and winding road, chattering nervously.

"What happened? What'd he say? Is he dead?" she asked, in rapid fire succession.

"What the hell was that?" Knox asked.

Rico shook his head.

"I don't know, but he's dead," Rico said. "That was the work of a professional. Straight double tap."

"Damn," Knox said. "I didn't hear a gunshot."

"I have to stop this trend of everyone around me getting shot," Rico said. "I'm already tired of it."

"I didn't see anyone either," Knox said.

"They had to know we were going to meet," Rico said.

"But how?" Makenzie asked.

"I don't know," Rico said. "Maybe they just followed Chaos. If he thought somebody was trying to kill him earlier today, it's obvious that his suspicions were right."

Makenzie whipped the wheel left, sending her and her passengers leaning to their right. She straightened out the vehicle and then pressed hard on the accelerator again.

"What did he tell you?" she asked.

"He told me he sent a note to his brother with instructions on how to retrieve the evidence," Rico said. "He's a missionary in South Africa. Didn't say where exactly, but Chaos hadn't talked to him in months. Then he gave me a coded message that he said his brother would understand, for some reason he didn't get the first one he sent him. He was going to tell me more, but got jumpy and said we needed to split."

Makenzie applied the brakes, sending them skidding to a stop at a traffic light.

"We need to go back," Knox said.

"Go back? Are you out of your mind?" Rico said.

"What if Chaos isn't dead?" Knox said. "What if this was some sort of a setup, a way to get us to go to South Africa?"

"You're taking this 'trusting no one' to another level," Rico said. "You're not even believing a dead guy, someone you watched as his brains were blown out of the side of his head."

"Not anymore," Knox said. "There's definitely something going on. I'm surprised they didn't target you after you turned around."

"I guess I'm lucky."

"Which makes twice in the past few days. But you can't avoid being in the crosshairs much longer. It's going to catch up with you soon, at this pace."

"That's why I'm out after this," Rico said.

"We'll discuss that later, but I'm serious, Makenzie. We need to go back."

She performed a U-turn and drove back to the scene of the shooting. Chaos's body still laid sprawled on the pathway leading up to the church. Knox rushed over to his former colleague's body and knelt, checking for a pulse. There wasn't one.

"Damn," Knox said. "He's gone."

Rico hustled up behind Knox.

"What'd you expect?"

"I don't know. I'm just suspicious of everyone."

"We call the police to report this—anonymously," Rico said. "And then we need to get the hell off this island."

"Agreed."

They both walked briskly back to the car.

"Now do you believe me about Ballard?" Rico asked.

Knox cocked his head to one side and sighed.

"There are plenty of red flags at this point, for sure. But if there's one thing I do know, it's that whatever happened in the Congo is bigger than either of us thought."

CHAPTER TWENTY-ONE

Washington, D.C

Elliot Schwartz leaned against the Capitol Building's parapet, his back turned to it. Jackson Miller and Randy Carmen, two of Washington's more powerful environmental lobbyists, chatted with Schwartz about their ideas for a bill to create more wildlife protection in national parks. Then the conversation drifted toward their upcoming fishing trip along the Conway River in Shenandoah National Park.

"Are you sure you're going to be able to get away this time?" Miller asked. "Because last time, you were there all of two hours before you had to go back to Washington."

"Barring some world catastrophe, I'll be there," Schwartz said. "The president will be on vacation with his family, so it's going to have to be a very big deal for him to cut that short and call me back in."

"Well, I have to warn you that the cabin we're staying in doesn't have great cell reception," Carmen said.

"Then I'd say my odds of being able to get away and stay away just went up to about a hundred percent," Schwartz said, as he slapped Carmen on the shoulder. "This is why we put you in charge of our accommodations. You know how to pick 'em."

"I do what I can," Carmen said. "Besides, I need to be somewhere remote where those nuts can't find me. Did you know someone threw a brick through my front window with a note on it the other day, threatening me if I didn't stop?"

"Did they catch who did it?" Miller asked.

Carmen shook his head. "Got away clean. But it's got my family on edge. Gloria's taking our son to her mom's for the weekend, so if anything happens, we won't be there."

"Well, if any of those psychos try to find you in the woods, they'll wish they hadn't," Schwartz said.

After a brief discussion of what new fishing tackle they were planning on bringing, Schwartz excused himself, spotting Senator Moore plodding up the steps.

"Hey, Mark," Schwartz said as he approached. "How are you doing?"

"I've been better."

"Well, I've got some news that might turn your day around."

"I'm not sure that's possible."

"I'm still going to try," Schwartz said. "I just found out that Joe Garber is resigning—and I wanted to tell you before you heard it on the news."

Moore stopped as he reached the top of the steps. A faint smile spread across his lips.

"Really? Joe 'Grabby Hands' Garber is leaving Washington?"

"I'm not sure if he's leaving, but he is resigning. Apparently that incident at the golf course yesterday proved to be the last straw."

"That's because the world finally got to see what we've been seeing him do for years," Moore said. "How did you get that footage anyway?"

Schwartz put an index finger to his lips.

"A good magician never reveals his secrets. Snaring Garber in a trap like that, though, was easy. All you have to do is find the right bait. And let me tell you, Erica Everhart is the perfect bait for just about anyone, but especially for Garber. There wasn't a snowball's chance in hell he wouldn't try to get his hands all over her, if he thought he was in a private setting."

Moore nodded and smiled, but said nothing as he looked past Schwartz, quiet and lost in a thousand-yard stare.

"Mark, what are you thinking?"

Moore waited a beat before answering.

"I'm just not sure this is going to make Erica drop the story."

"Who cares how she tackles Garber's resignation?" Schwartz said. "But she will drop *the* story, the one we don't want anyone to know."

"But if she keeps digging—"

"She won't," Schwartz said. "At least, she better not. And it's your job to make sure she drops it."

"You're insane if you think I can control her."

"Everybody has their buttons. You just have to find the right ones for her. Or just give her a better story. You've been around Washington long enough to know whose closet holds skeletons that will pique her interest."

Moore sighed.

"It's not your political future that's at stake here."

"Maybe not, but consider this a test. If you can't figure out a way to mitigate this little situation, how are you going to handle being in the White House?"

Moore scowled and glanced around.

"Watch it," he said sharply, in a hushed tone. "I don't want you starting any rumors."

"Of course not. But mull it over. Send her in another direction or give her a bigger story."

"A bigger story? Than this?"

"If you don't, I will."

"What are you talking about?" Moore asked.

Schwartz held out his phone with a fabricated IRS report showing how Moore had skimmed several million dollars off the top of his campaign funds.

Moore narrowed his eyes.

"What is this? Some blackmail attempt?"

"I consider this more of a strong motivation."

"It's bullshit and you know it."

"It's not about whether I know it, but whether the American public will believe it. And I'm betting they will. But, of course, this is just one example of a bigger story I could distract the press with until this all blows over. However, I'd rather you just handle Erica by some other method. Agree?"

Moore glared at Schwartz but said nothing.

Schwartz looked at his watch. "Great catching up with you, Mark, but I've gotta run to a meeting. Best of luck with all this. Let me know how things go, okay?"

Moore didn't blink, his eyes still locked on Schwartz before he hustled off.

Moore lingered on the Capitol steps, still stewing over Schwartz's distasteful attempt at persuasion. As the president's chief of staff, Schwartz had a reputation for being a bare-knuckled brawler when it came to addressing situations that were unsavory to the president. One profile piece likened him to early 20th century baseball star Ty Cobb, who used to sit in the dugout and sharpen the metal spikes on his shoes while staring at the shortstop or second baseman. Cobb's not-so-subtle warnings toward those players often resulted in them yielding their ground when Cobb came sliding into the base with his spikes knee-high. The only players who liked Cobb were his teammates. And Moore thought the comparison was perfect for Schwartz. He was the kind of son of a bitch you wanted on your team, but would hate him if you were going up against him.

Still, despite Schwartz's threat, Moore knew Erica's dogged pursuit of the real story about what happened in the Congo needed to be squelched. However, figuring out what buttons he could push in order to get her to stop digging was challenging. He'd learned long ago that making enemies with reporters wasn't the best way to get positive coverage in the news. Making an enemy out of Erica by strong-arming her would undoubtedly come back to haunt him. But what could slow her down, encourage her to let the story evaporate? That was the real key to achieving all of Moore's objectives, though the answer wasn't readily apparent.

Moore walked back down the steps and called his assistant, telling her that he wouldn't return to the office for another half-hour. Then he hung up and started scrolling through Erica's social media feeds in order to determine if she had any buttons to push. Most of Erica's posts were either shares of her recent articles or other colleagues' stories, sprinkled with a few personal pictures on excursions and trips with friends. Ten minutes of swiping up on Erica's timeline made Moore's eyes glaze over.

I'm never gonna find anything on here.

But just as he was about to give up, a post caught his eye. This was an article not written by any of her *Post* colleagues. With a headline of "When Journalism Goes Too Far", the article teaser asked a question: "In our world of reality TV shows and oversaturation of social media, are reporters guilty of trespassing into people's private lives just to gain readers?" Above the first few sentences visible, Erica added a comment: *I know I've been guilty of doing this, but I need to stop. We all need to stop.*

That was all the information Moore needed. He dialed Erica's number and waited for her to pick up.

"Senator Moore," she said. "I was planning on calling you at some point today, but I've been really busy."

"It's okay, Erica. I saw the news."

"Yeah," she said, "I've always been told that journalists should report the news and be careful not to become part of it. Unfortunately, the latter happened yesterday."

"Don't worry. It wasn't your fault."

"Of course not, but I should've known better than to try and talk to Joe Garber in such a private setting. He's got a reputation, though I didn't think he'd attempt anything like that on me."

"You and half the women in this town. Unfortunately, he's predictable in that regard, but usually discreet enough that his accusations are dismissed. Only this time, there's video evidence of it. And the Pentagon doesn't want to deal with a protracted scandal of someone who is, by and large, replaceable."

"I'm glad he's being held accountable, even if it was at my expense. However, that doesn't change what he told me about his trip to Africa. He denied giving Chase a gun."

Her last sentence didn't faze him. He'd fully expected that Garber would deny the accusation. But Moore decided this was the moment to pivot.

He sighed audibly and waited a beat before responding.

"Last night, I got some more information on Garber, including proof that he purchased a firearm at a gun show a couple of days before he left for Africa. It was the same one Chase used, a private investigator we hired learned."

"But why would he have given the gun to Chase? That's what I'm having a hard time figuring out."

"It's not that hard," Moore said. "It was dangerous. And without any other fellow Peace Corps members to stand with him, he needed some personal protection. And sadly, Chase decided to use the weapon on himself. Without that gun, we'd probably still have Chase with us today."

"Do you mind sharing with me the evidence of Garber purchasing that gun?" she asked.

"To be honest, my wife and I have had enough of this story. We were wanting confirmation from Garber, but we don't need it any more. We know what he did."

"But what about justice?"

"I think Garber losing his job is justice enough. Besides, we're just tired of reliving the pain of losing our son, again and again. And we'll have to do it all over another time if you publish this story. Joe Garber might be a public figure, but it's our private lives that we're talking about here."

"People need to know what he did," she countered.

"Do they? Because it's not going to bring back Chase. And then I'll just be asked about this for the next decade of my life every time I meet someone new or address members of the press. I'll forever be that sad senator whose son killed himself, all while the media tries to make me the poster child for gun control."

"I wouldn't do that to you."

"If you publish the story, you will whether you intend to or not," Moore said sharply. "The question is whether this article will open up an old wound and invite more questions, as our lives are placed in the proverbial fish bowl yet again. And for what? Likes and followers on social media? Is that the end game? If not for you, it will be for all your peers who pile on. Is that what you want? Shouldn't it matter that we're satisfied with the consequences for Garber?"

Erica was silent for a moment.

"I see what you're saying," she said. "And as much as I'd love to obliterate that bastard—not for what he did to me but for what he did to you—I'm willing to respect your wishes."

"Thank you," Moore said. "And for your willingness to drop it, I might be able to reward you with a big scoop in the very near future."

"I wouldn't want anyone to think this is a quid pro quo situation," she said.

"It's not. Think of it more along the lines of me showing my appreciation to a principled journalist. Can you live with that?"

"I think so," she said.

"Great," Moore said. "I'll be in touch."

He ended the call and then texted an update to Schwartz.

Then Moore sat down on a bench and started to dream up another scheme, the kind that was going to get him the true freedom—and power—that he craved.

CHAPTER TWENTY-TWO

Nadi, Fiji

Knox adjusted his prosthetic leg as he sat on the foot of the bed. He got dressed and grabbed his rucksack before heading downstairs to the hotel's breakfast buffet. Halfway into a second plate of over-cooked eggs and reheated bacon, he looked up to see Rico and Makenzie.

"I was wondering if you two were ever going to come downstairs and eat," Knox said, returning his focus to his meal.

"How long have you been here?" Makenzie asked.

"Ten minutes or so," Knox said. "I thought we were in agreement that we needed to get outta here."

"We were," Rico said. "But we're also not psychopaths who don't require sleep. Kinz has got to fly—and we were up kind of late last night, in case you don't remember."

"Oh, I remember," Knox said, his mouth half full. "I also remember that at one point in your life you were a Ranger. And sleep was always an elective exercise."

"I'm still a Ranger," Rico said. "Once a Ranger, always a Ranger."

Knox shrugged and grunted.

"Your sleep habits say otherwise."

"Let's settle this on the plane," Makenzie said. "We need to get moving, but I at least want to get a cup of coffee and something else to put in my stomach. How is it?"

"Egg-celent," Knox said, drawing an exaggerated eye roll from Makenzie.

Knox offered a wry smile, which vanished when he looked at the clock ticking loudly on the far wall.

"Apparently, I'm the only one who was serious about leaving early."

Makenzie punched him playfully in the arm.

"I'll be slinging comebacks at you as soon as I have some caffeine."

"I'm looking forward to it," Knox said.

After they wolfed down their food, the trio drove to the airport and filed into a short customs line for private air travelers. Makenzie went first, barely drawing a peek from the customs agent, who had her head down as she fumbled for a stamp to mark a departure. However, when she scanned Knox's passport, her eyes widened as the screen flashed red, the hue—and her expression—reflecting that something was wrong.

"I need you to wait right here," the agent said.

"What's the matter?" Knox asked.

"Just don't move."

She scurried away, disappearing down a short hallway behind her and emerging a minute later, with a beefy man shuffling behind her. He joined the agent in her cubicle as she pointed at Knox's passport and then the screen. He peered over the top of his reading glasses at the passport and then snapped it shut before pocketing it.

"Mr. Knox, I'm going to need you to wait over here for a moment," the supervisor said, before dabbing his brow with a hand-kerchief.

"Is there something wrong?" Knox asked.

"Just be patient and remain in the waiting area behind you."

Knox jammed his hands into his pocket and felt for his lucky coin. Whether rubbing it actually mattered, he wasn't sure. But he knew that it calmed him in anxious situations, also hiding his angst from others.

"What's going on?" Makenzie mouthed to Knox, who eased onto a wooden bench against the wall.

He shrugged and remained otherwise expressionless. The fact that he was being detained wasn't a good sign. He just hoped it was for a clerical error and not something else.

Rico sailed through the customs check without anything more than a cursory inspection. Once that was completed, the supervisor trudged over to Knox with his passport in hand.

The supervisor squinted as he stared at Knox's document.

"Mr. Knox?" the supervisor asked.

Knox nodded.

"That's me."

"We have someone who would like to speak with you, though this may take longer than you were expecting. I hope you didn't have any pressing matters to get to at your next destination."

"You mind telling me who you're detaining me for?"

"Inspector Villiame Nagata. He'd like to speak with you about an incident that occurred last night."

Before Knox could gather any more information, the supervisor left. Not that Knox needed to know more. More than anything, he wanted to make a run for it, fleeing the island, never to return. But that would create an incident that could land him on Ballard's radar, though Knox couldn't be sure he wasn't already there, if someone was monitoring his movements via his passport.

Moments later, the supervisor escorted Villiame Nagata into the room and pointed at Knox before leaving. Bespectacled and rail thin, Nagata marched toward Knox with the precision of a soldier standing watch outside his king's quarters. An expressionless stare, coupled with a suit and tie, gave Knox little to go on in determining what kind of man Nagata was. About all Knox could get out of Nagata's approach was that the man seemed professional.

Nagata stopped a few feet short of Knox and sat down on the other side of the bench.

"So a man walks into a bar—ouch," Nagata said.

Knox chuckled and shook his head, surprised by the inspector's dichotomy.

"I wasn't expecting that," Knox said.

A faint smile crept across Nagata's lips.

"Neither was the man."

Knox grinned.

"So, I'm not sure I've ever been part of an interview that started like this."

Nagata arched an eyebrow.

"You're regularly interviewed?"

"Not usually the police."

"So, who interviews you? Your CIA handler, before you target someone?"

Knox drew back.

"Whoa. You're good. Soften me up with some jokes and then get straight to the point."

"Mr. Knox, you're not going to get away with deflecting and then ignoring my question."

Knox held out his prosthetic leg and indicated toward it.

"Do you think the CIA would let someone with a leg like this enter the field?"

Knox was also skilled at this game, adept at leveraging sympathy for his plight when the situation called for it.

"The last time I checked, most assassins use their hands to shoot. And by the looks of it, you still have both of those along with all your fingers. And if you're any good, you won't need to run."

Knox furrowed his brow.

"I like how you think," he said. "Every good inspector plays his cards close to his vest. And if you really thought I was an assassin, you would've approached this conversation much more differently. Am I right?"

Nagata didn't blink, as he worked his tongue across his front teeth as if he were stalling in order to come up with a comeback. Knox had given the inspector a way to save face, even though it was quite clear that he believed Knox to be the prime suspect.

"What were you doing last night around ten o'clock at St. Paul's Catholic Church?" Nagata asked.

"Would you believe me if I told you I was there for confessions?" Knox asked.

"Absolutely not. You don't strike me as a man of faith."

"You would be very wrong about that. I have deep convictions, which is why I feel compelled to tell you the truth."

"That'd be refreshing," Nagata said. "I have a busy day."

"Well, it's going to get busier after what I tell you, because whoever killed Kevin Canfield is still out there."

"There's a little wrench in this story," Nagata said, as he stood and paced the floor. "Someone alerted us to the body last night. We took the dead man's fingerprints and entered them into an international database. This morning, it came back that he was a U.S. Army Ranger—and that he was already dead."

"That is curious, isn't it?" Knox said.

"So why don't you tell me what was going on last night?"

"And you have footage of me being there?"

"You just told me you were there, so I have all the proof I need."

"I never said that I was there."

"Then how would you know who was dead? I never mentioned the victim's name—or that there even was one."

"Touche," Knox said. "I'm trying to help you out, Inspector."

"Then you need to stop playing this game and get straight to it."

Knox took a deep breath and then stood, which ended Nagata's pacing.

"It's true that Kevin Canfield was a Ranger in the U.S. Army," Knox said. "He agreed to meet with me last night to discuss what he knew."

"What he knew? About what?"

"Inspector, this is not the kind of story you want to get tangled up in."

"Enlighten me."

"Doing so would put your life in danger. But what I can tell you is that I'm a journalist investigating a story of government corruption that goes far up the chain in the U.S. government. Canfield faked his own death and disappeared a year ago. But someone recently discovered that he was still alive. By entering Canfield's prints into your database, you're likely going to get a target put on your back, if you make this a full-scale investigation and try to discover the identity of the shooter. It's likely that he's already left your island and will never be found. So, my advice is, if you want to avoid an uninvited intrusion into your life, drop it. In fact, don't even mention it. Tell your superiors that the man was already dead and nobody is going to be looking for him, if you're worried about the narrative of a tourist getting shot on your peaceful island. And if anybody questions you, tell them that he was wanted by the U.S. government."

Nagata folded his arms and scanned Knox's face.

"The thing I find hard to believe in your whole story is how conveniently this works out for you," Nagata said.

"But you know I didn't do it," Knox said. "I suspect you have footage of the entire incident and know that I rushed up to the scene from a different direction after Canfield was shot. However, I must applaud you on your efforts. Your talents seem wasted on this island. A big fish in a little pond."

"I'm impervious to flattery."

"But not the truth," Knox said. "And that's what you're really after, though I'm not sure you'll want to find it."

"And is the truth what you're after?"

"It is. I'm uniquely positioned to expose it all. But I can't very well do that if you decide to detain me. In fact, the very people who murdered Kevin Canfield last night will soon put me in their crosshairs. And is that really something you want, to have the one man searching for the truth snuffed out?"

"I appreciate your candor, Mr. Knox," Nagata said. "You're free to go. And good luck with your quest."

Knox offered his hand, which Nagata shook, the two men looking each other in the eyes as they did.

"Thank you," Knox said.

Knox grabbed his rucksack and rejoined his companions. They hustled to the plane, none of them speaking until they were safely inside.

"What the hell was that all about?" Rico asked. "And how did you manage to talk your way out of that one?"

"Me and the inspector are kindred spirits, who both want the same thing," Knox said.

"And what's that?" Makenzie asked as she started her pre-flight check.

"The truth," Knox said. "The same thing we all want."

The engine spun up as Makenzie maneuvered the plane onto the tarmac.

"They're going to know we were here," Rico said.

"They're going to know that *I* was here," Knox said.

"And it's only a matter of time before they find out you didn't kill me," Rico said. "I need time to disappear again."

"Then we'll need to make sure they're looking for you in all the wrong places," Knox said.

"You're going to send them on a wild goose chase, aren't you?"

"I'm going to buy you some time and see an old friend," Knox said.

"So, where we going, boss?" Makenzie asked.

"How does some *aloha* sound?"

CHAPTER TWENTY-THREE

Washington, D.C

Erica Everhart exited the McPherson Square metro station and cut through Franklin Square as she hustled to her office at *The Washington Post*. Her editor had requested an in-person meeting, though Erica wasn't sure what for. She'd sent an email the night before explaining that she didn't feel like the story about Joe Garber was a viable one. With Garber resigning his post, there didn't seem to be much reason to pursue it.

Then there was her personal issue with Garber.

As she was getting ready for the day, she tuned in to her favorite news talk radio station and listened as the morning hosts discussed Garber's resignation. They shared how Garber's behavior was a secret to no one inside the Beltway, but he always managed to escape such stories coming to life, due to his position. One pundit joining the show suggested that Erica Everhart tried to set him up, in an effort to blackmail him for information on a story she was working on. Erica bristled at the mere notion that she would ever commit such a journalistic sin.

What she saw as she made her way through the park and set eyes on the front of *The Post* shouldn't have come as a surprise to her.

She'd been an advocate against harassment of women reporters in the nation's capital since she started working there, penning several pointed columns about the topic. Becoming a victim herself—and doing so in a way that became headline news—should've served as a warning that the story would grow legs quickly. Though she'd never been a victim until now, she'd always wondered why other victims were so reticent to recount the details of such incidents. But now she knew why. The last thing she wanted to do after this humiliating episode — one captured on video that everyone had seen on social media, no less — was talk about it. What was there to say? Joe Garber was a pig and everyone could see it for themselves. Why dwell on the obvious?

But that didn't stop a gaggle of reporters with video cameras and smartphones gathered outside the front doors of The Post to ambush her on her way inside the office. Once she realized a hornet's nest was buzzing across the street, she veered toward 13th Street and attempted to sneak in through the underground parking garage and get inside through an employee access door. However, someone spotted her and shouted her name, setting off a panicked sprint by the journalists to reach her before she could get into the garage.

Erica cursed under her breath, regretting her choice of heels instead of flats when she was deciding what to wear a few hours earlier.

Charles Ruggle, a veteran cameraman with enough girth for two or three reporters, got in front of her, holding her up just long enough for everyone else to surround her. Erica wanted to walk away more than anything, just wriggle her way through the crowd and vanish inside the safe confines of *The Post*. But she could already see the footage in her head that would be playing on cable news network stations later that day. A mousy version of Erica, head down in shame as she covered her face with her hands, struggling to get through a throng of reporters, all of it voiced over by a newscaster talking about her refusal to talk.

She stopped and sighed before slowly spinning around, looking at all the familiar faces. The reporters pelted her with questions, almost all wholly indistinguishable as they formed a headache-inducing cacophony.

Erica held her right hand in the air and shouted at the top of her lungs.

"Quiet!" she snapped. "If we're going to do this, we're going to do it my way. Maybe show one of your own a little professional courtesy. Everyone understand?"

The reporters' heads bobbed as a hush fell over everyone.

"Now, I'm going to give you a statement about what happened," she said. "And then I'm going to take five questions, and not one more. As I'm sure you can all appreciate, I've got a job to do myself, and a meeting with my editor in fifteen minutes. So, I'll give you enough for a story, but when I'm done, please respect what I'm asking you to do. If you want to text me later with a follow up, I may or may not respond—but whatever I do, I hope you'll understand. And just remember, I have dirt on all of you."

Her last comment drew a few chuckles and softened the tense atmosphere.

Erica got through her opening statement, recounting her version of the events, and then took questions. When she finished, she did as she promised, marching away from them, even as a few reporters who didn't get called on shouted their questions after her.

She checked her watch and swore softly.

Seven minutes until my meeting.

Erica wanted to settle into her office, get a feel for the day, find out what was buzzing among her colleagues, even though she had a good idea about the latter. There wouldn't be much time for any of that.

Then she saw another reporter leaning casually against the wall next to the underground employee entrance.

She swore again.

"Thomas, how did you get in here?" she asked.

Quinn, who was Erica's last serious relationship, wrote for *The Washington Times*. They had kept their romance a secret while working for competing news organizations, keeping Erica from being able to talk about it with some of her friends, all of whom were in the media. And she knew better than anyone that reporters were, by nature, the worst at keeping secrets.

But those eyes.

She got lost many nights staring into Quinn's eyes, which reminded her of Alpine lakes fed by glacial waters. So calm, so inviting. And here he was, fluttering those eyes at her, tempting her to do something she swore she'd never do again.

"I have my ways," Quinn said, with a wink.

"Did you pay off Albert?" she asked.

"It wouldn't be the first time."

Erica huffed as she pushed the button for the elevator.

"What are you doing here? You're not trying to get some exclusive out of me, are you? Please tell me you aren't that desperate—or delusional."

Quinn reached for her access badge and inspected her picture.

"New head shot?" he asked.

"Come on, Thomas. Why are you here?"

"I'm not here to get the scoop about your encounter with Joe Garber. Don't worry."

The elevator dinged and the doors slid open. She stepped inside.

"Thomas, it was good seeing you. But I'm calling security when I get to my office."

Quinn put his hand on the door, keeping it from closing.

"Really, Thomas. I've got a meeting."

"And I've got one question," he said. "What were you doing interviewing Joe Garber? I know you were there with a purpose, and it sure as hell wasn't to play golf. We both know how much you hate that game."

She glanced at her watch. Five minutes until her meeting.

"What does it matter to you?" she asked. "Jealous?"

"Of course not. Besides, you obviously weren't into Garber. But I'm curious as to why you were talking with him."

She tucked her golden locks behind her ears.

"You think I'm going to tell you anything? Dream on. Now, will you let go of the doors?"

The elevator alarm buzzed, signaling that the doors had been held open too long. Quinn didn't move his hand.

"You were talking to him about his interaction with the Peace Corps in the Congo last year, weren't you? Never mind. You don't have to say it. I know you were. But what if I told you that it was a smokescreen?"

"How would you know?" she asked.

Quinn removed his hands from door.

"Because I've been working on a story for the past year about some strange incidents happening in the field with the Peace Corps. And I think you may have stumbled onto one of them by accident."

The doors slid together. Erica swore softly as the elevator hummed and began its slow ascent.

She hit the button for the first floor and exited quickly, running back down the stairwell. Quinn hadn't left, still standing there but scribbling notes into his pad.

"Okay, I'll talk," she said.

Quinn looked up from his notes, his eyes twinkling. Erica recounted the story she learned about Chase Moore and the gun Garber had given him. When she finished, Quinn chuckled and shook his head.

"And you bought all that bullshit?" he asked.

"I haven't published any story to that effect yet."

"*Yet*," he said, "as in, you intend to."

"Well, probably not, because I made a promise to someone."

"Geez, what happened to the Erica I once knew? You'd shred a six-year-old kid for desecrating the environment. No one was safe from your crusades to tell a good story and expose the truth."

"This one's really complicated."

"I'll tell you what isn't complicated," Quinn said with a scowl. "Those bastards at the Pentagon are up to something, something very nefarious. It's the kind of thing that would fire you up for weeks, if you knew what was really going on."

Her eyes widened.

"I'm listening," she said.

"I think our military is covering up some massive crimes against humanity, for lack of a better word. I've been tracking two other incidents involving the Peace Corps and the U.S. military, intersections between the two that shouldn't ever happen. But they did. I have proof. And there's a third one I've been looking into, that I think happened around the same time Joe Garber visited the village where Chase Moore was. That little story they told you about Garber was something to throw you off the trail."

Erica sighed.

"I don't know about all that, Thomas. I know you. You're a little bit of a conspiracy nut. Once you sense there might be some potential Pulitzer Prize-winning story, you'd believe just about anything."

"I'm telling you, Erica. Something happened in the Congo. And I want you to come with me and figure out what. It'd be a story we could do together. What do you say?"

"It sounds exciting, but I'm not sold yet."

"Is your passport current?"

"Always," she said, her phone buzzing with a text message from her boss. "Look, I've gotta run. I'm supposed to meet my editor and—"

"Think about it, will ya?" he said. "I've got a flight scheduled for Friday morning at 7:30 a.m. for Kinshasa—and I've got a ticket for you, too. Meet me at Dulles at 6 a.m. I'll text you where exactly to find me."

"I don't know if I'll be there, Thomas," she said, as she strode into the elevator and spun around to face him.

"See you then," he said, with a wink.

When Erica arrived at her apartment complex, Ashley Moore was waiting for her in the lobby with a small box in her hand. Lines creased her forehead as she shifted her weight from side to side. She locked eyes with Erica.

"Mrs. Moore," Erica said. "I—"

"Please, call me Ashley."

"Okay, Ashley. What are you doing here? Is everything all right?"

Ashley drew in a deep breath, then exhaled slowly as she shook her head.

"I talked to Thomas Quinn today," she said.

Erica winced.

"I'm sorry," she said. "Is he harassing you?"

"Not at all. In fact, I've been the one harassing him."

"About what?"

Ashley glanced around the lobby, which was still empty.

"My husband doesn't like me doing this, so please don't tell him."

"Of course not. What's going on?"

"I stumbled across some of Mr. Quinn's reporting about the strange happenings at Peace Corps camps over the past few years. So, I reached out to him to see if he'd looked into what happened at Chase's camp."

"So, that's where he got all that information," Erica said, half mumbling to herself.

"I'm sorry. What did you say?"

"Never mind. It's just that—I'm friends with Thomas Quinn and—"

"I know," Ashley said. "He told me. And while I believe he's onto something, which might give me the truth about what really happened to Chase, I want you to be the one to tell it."

"Mrs. Moore—"

"*Ashley.*"

"Ashley, I'm sorry, but it's kind of complicated with Thomas."

"I know, I know. You used to be in a relationship. I get that. But this is a potentially ground-breaking story. What *is* going on with these Peace Corps camps? And maybe, just maybe, there's a better explanation as to why Chase killed himself. Because I'll tell you right now that Mark was lying to you. Chase wasn't a depressed kid.

He was happy, loved to help people, full of life. So, none of this made sense to me."

"But what you told me for the article ... ?"

"Look, I can't get into all that right now, but I really want you to go and find out. You know more about Chase and what he was doing than Mr. Quinn does. And it's a story I trust you would be able to handle better than anyone."

"I appreciate the vote of confidence, Ashley, but I can't just go to the Congo on such a short notice, chasing a story that may or may not be there."

"There's only one way to find out if it is," Ashley said. "I mean, isn't that what you do as a journalist?"

"Yes, but—"

"If you need me to help you in any way while you're gone—feed your dog or your cat or water your flowers—I'll do it. In fact, just for your own peace of mind, I bought you something that will maybe convince you to go."

Ashley handed a small box to Erica.

"What's this?" Erica asked, as she studied it.

"It's a personal GPS tracking device. I've set it up for you, so you don't have to do a thing. It will send me emails giving me your hourly locations over the past twelve hours."

"Ashley, I don't know. I—"

"Please, Erica. Don't make me beg."

"Okay, I'll consider it. And thank you for the tracker."

"Of course, and don't turn it on until you arrive in The Congo. I'm not trying to be a nosey mom. It's dangerous over there, and I want to make sure that if something happens to you, we can find you."

"It's a very thoughtful gift. I'll let you know what I decide."

"Thank you," Ashley said, before she gave Erica a quick hug and scurried out of the building.

Ashley looked at the device and shoved it into her bag. She still wasn't convinced a trip with Thomas was a wise decision, story or no story.

CHAPTER TWENTY-FOUR

Kauai, Hawaii

Knox watched the waves roll toward the shore before cascading onto the beach in a predictable rhythm. He found the view peaceful, calming, soothing. Amidst the consistent drumbeat of nature, he needed to organize his thoughts. He rolled his lucky coin through his fingers as he considered how he might expose a potential scandal within the U.S. military, one he'd fought and served in, one he'd sacrificed so much for. Knox didn't have any children, but he imagined what he had to do was what it would feel like if he had to turn his son in for a crime. No matter how much he loved his country and the men he served with, certain behavior couldn't be justified. Only one question remained: How bad was it? Given the lengths to which government officials were going to ensure this incident never reached the public, he could only assume it would spell disaster if the details were divulged.

Yet, Knox was about to embark on the second half of his mission, the part where he would be helping keep a secret. That's not what he wanted. Dead Rangers needed justice, and someone needed to be held accountable. But if he was going to get everything he wanted, Knox needed to navigate carefully, or else he would find himself in the crosshairs of another soldier being manipulated by some smooth-talking government agent. The cycle needed to stop with him. But that couldn't happen until he knew the full truth, and had a way to expose it that protected him and the people he loved.

He turned his attention to the sand and watched the water gush between and over his five toes, while his prosthetic foot held fast like a fortress on the rocks. It was the perfect picture for how he felt, at once both overwhelmed and defiant.

The sound of soft footsteps in the puddles left by the tide snapped him back to the present.

"Solve the world's problems out here?" Makenzie asked.

Knox pocketed his lucky coin as he turned toward her.

"The world will have to wait," Knox said. "I can barely solve my own."

"Want a little advice?" she asked, as she eased next to him.

"Can't hurt," he said.

"You don't have to shoulder this burden alone," she said. "I know Rico's wanting to go underground, but he's here for you. And so am I. We all want to expose the truth, so stop thinking like you're the only one. I'm more than just a pilot, though I'm sure you already know that."

Knox raked the wet stand with his toes and nodded.

"I appreciate that. It's just that I have a lot more riding on this. I had someone I—"

He paused before continuing.

"Someone I cared about very deeply experienced a threatening situation, all because of me. It's not something I want to happen again."

"We'll help you make sure it doesn't."

"The only way you can do that is to help me find the footage and deliver it to Colonel Ballard."

"That's what I'm here for," she said. "In fact, I just got off the phone with my boss and negotiated a week-long extension on my leave from work, as well as an extra week with the jet, so we're set.

We just need to figure out where to go next. You find the village where Chaos's brother is yet?"

"Still working on it," he said. "It's almost like he doesn't want to be found either."

"Whenever you know, just say the word," she said, before returning to the house on the beach.

Knox folded his arms and stared back out at the water, the sun beginning to rise higher on the horizon. A couple of minutes later, he was interrupted again, this time with the aroma of a fresh cup of coffee. He spun around to see his longtime friend offering a mug.

"It's Social Brews' Kona—your favorite," he said.

Knox took the mug and drew it up to his mouth, inhaling the rich aroma through his nose while closing his eyes.

"Does it smell better with your eyes closed?"

Knox smiled before taking a sip.

"Rooster, it's so good to see you," Knox said. "Sorry about the last-minute notice."

"You know my door is always open to you any time," Rooster said, as he gave Knox a quick hug.

Rooster, whose real name was Maleko Kanoa, had served in the Rangers. So had Rooster's father, functioning like an uncle to Knox when his father retired from the military. Rooster moved to an apartment down the street from Knox's home in Houston when his mother fell ill with cancer. With Knox's father dead, Rooster helped take care of Knox's mother, nursing her back to health as she beat the disease and recovered fully. Knox transferred from the University of Colorado to Texas A&M so he could be closer to home, complying with her wishes that he stay in school. Instead of indulging in the full college experience, Knox visited her every weekend and helped Rooster with her care. Knox and Rooster's time together forged a strong bond, and they stayed in touch after Rooster went back home to help work on his family's farm on the island of Kauai.

Knox took a sip of his coffee and commented about how good it tasted.

"I know you love the coffee here, Knox, but I have a feeling you came here for other reasons," Rooster said. "Want to tell me what's going on, and why there's also a pilot and another Ranger sleeping on my couches?"

"We were in the neighborhood and just thought we'd stop by," Knox said.

Rooster dropped his head and peered over his dark-rimmed glasses while stroking his scraggly salt-and-pepper beard.

"In the neighborhood?" he asked, his tone suggesting that he didn't believe Knox.

"Would Hawaiians consider Fiji neighbors?"

"L.A. is closer than Fiji. So if you considered Alaskans your neighbors while growing up in Texas, I suppose Fiji could be classified as neighbors."

Knox laughed, realizing his rationale was undergoing more scrutiny than he'd anticipated.

"What can I say? I tried."

"So, what's really going on?" Rooster asked, his expression serious. "You in some kind of trouble?"

"Not exactly, but I do need your help."

"You know, I promised your dad I would look after you, but he told me to make sure I spanked you when appropriate. Now, you're way too old for me to spank, but I will beat your ass if it needs it."

"Look, I didn't do anything wrong—at least not yet."

"But you're going to? And you need my help to do it?"

"When you say it like that, it sounds way worse," Knox said.

"Just spit it out."

"Okay, I don't entirely know what's going on, but I will tell you what I can," Knox said.

Knox recapped the events of the past few days, leaving out most of the names and poignant details to give Rooster a measure of plausible deniability. When Knox finished, Rooster stared at him, wide-eyed.

"I hate to tell you this, but you need more help than the kind I can provide," Rooster said.

"We just need a way to move around without anyone able to track us, or even knowing who we are," Knox said. "I know you're the best at getting passports, so I thought I'd start here with you. Can you help us?"

"Us?"

"Rico isn't coming with me, but he needs help resettling somewhere in the world. Makenzie and I need to travel without our government contact knowing where we are."

"I see," Rooster said, twirling a few strands of his goatee. "I'll tell you what. Get me mugs of you guys and wait twenty-four hours and I'll have them for you. But then you have to do me a favor."

"Anything," Knox said. "You name it."

"When this is all over, I want you to come back here and hike the Napali Coast with me."

"You do know that's a lifelong dream of mine, right?"

"Of course," Rooster said. "It's also my way of guaranteeing that you don't do something stupid."

"I can't guarantee that—"

"No, no, no," Rooster said. "You just told me *anything,* and then told me to name it."

Knox looked off in the distance as a large swell exploded against an outcropping of rocks a few hundred meters away.

"Looking pensively offshore isn't going to save you from having to look me in the eye and tell me that you understand what you're agreeing to if I help you," Rooster said. "No stupid decisions."

Rooster glanced down at Knox's leg.

"Hey," Knox said as he saw Rooster's eyes. "That's not fair."

"Maybe not, but I want you to act as if more is on the line when you leave here. You're not playing with house money any more. This is where everything gets real. You ready for that?"

"Of course I am," Knox said.

"No, I don't think you understand. If you're going to try and stare down a behemoth like the intelligence cabal in Washington, with their enormous budgets and never-ending ways they can put pressure on you, you're going to need to do this fast—and you're going to need lots of friends to pull this off, the kind of friends who would either take a bullet for you or sacrifice themselves for the truth. You think you know enough people like that?"

"I'm lookin' at one of them right now," Knox said.

"Find more, because you're going to need them. And, Knox?"

"Yeah?"

"I'm proud of you, kid. Your dad would be proud of the man you've become."

"Thanks," Knox said, before he took another long swig of his coffee.

"I'll leave you alone to figure it all out," Rooster said, before patting Knox on the shoulder and walking back to the house.

Knox remained alone on the shore for another fifteen minutes before his phone rang. It was Ballard.

"How's it going?" Ballard asked. "I was expecting to get an update from you, especially given how you've been jet-setting it the past few days. Brazil, Fiji, Hawaii—are you taking care of business or starting a vacation travel blog?"

"I go where the people are, where the evidence is," Knox said.

"So, how'd it go with Frederico?"

"He's dead," Knox said, as he swiped across the front of the phone and searched for the pictures he'd staged with Rico. "I'm sending you proof now."

"And what was Fiji all about?"

"Don't play coy, Colonel. I know you had one of your men there."

"What are you talking about?"

"Before I killed Rico, I tortured him until he told me about Kevin Canfield, the fifth Ranger."

"And?"

"Canfield was hiding in Fiji. He told me where the footage was before someone shot and killed him."

"He just volunteered that information to you?"

"Yeah," Knox said. "I may have told him I was going to use it to expose the government. You know, whatever it takes, right?"

"I knew you were the right man for the job," Ballard said. "So, am I right to assume that the footage is in Hawaii?"

"Not exactly. We needed to leave, since I was a suspect in Canfield's murder. Fortunately, I convinced the cops that I wasn't responsible, and left the country exonerated by the investigator working the case."

"So, where is the footage?"

"Still trying to determine that," Knox said. "But Canfield gave me a clue as to where he hid it."

"Anything I can help you with?"

"Probably, but I'd like to handle this myself. After all, I am a man of my word, and our agreement was to eliminate Rico *and* bring back the footage. I intend to complete this task."

There was a long pause and then a sigh from Ballard.

"Why don't you forget about the footage for now," Ballard said. "I'd rather you just come back. I've got another small errand you could run for me and we'll call it good. I'll send you a ticket, and I'll meet you at LAX tomorrow evening. How's that sound?"

"You're the boss," Knox said.

"Great. See you then."

Knox pocketed his phone as Makenzie sauntered up to him again.

"Who was that?" she asked.

"Ballard," Knox said. "He wants me to take a flight home tomorrow."

"You can't do that," she said. "Not yet anyway."

"I know. But I also know I don't want to get in Ballard's crosshairs."

"So, what are you gonna do?"

Knox bit his lip and stared at the large swell rolling toward the shore.

"I don't know," he said. "I'm sure I'll think of something. You got any news for me?"

"I found Chaos's brother Kyle."

"Where is he?"

"Where *was* he," she corrected.

Knox furrowed his brow.

"Was?"

"He was mugged and murdered, during a short trip to Johannesburg. But he was based out of the village of Bonjane."

"So another dead end, huh?"

"Maybe not," Makenzie said. "Kyle's wife still lives there with their family. I reached out over email, and she responded right away. She's willing to talk, but will only do so in person."

"Think she could help us decipher that note Chaos gave Rico?"

"That's a long way to go just to crack a code."

"Right now, that's all we've got," Knox said. "But first things first. I have to deal with Ballard."

CHAPTER TWENTY-FIVE

Los Angeles, California

Col. Ballard flashed his credentials to the Department of Homeland Security agents managing the steady stream of travelers itching to get to their departure gates at LAX. After a close inspection, the agent waved Ballard inside. The managing supervisor greeted the colonel and offered him a cup of coffee, which, after one sip, Ballard guessed had been sitting around in a pot for the most of the day.

He checked his watch as he sat down, calculating that he had about forty-five minutes before Knox's plane landed.

"What's your interest here at LAX, Colonel?" asked the supervisor, a gold plate with the name Simpson stamped on it affixed just above his right shirt pocket.

"I was in town for some other business, thought I'd pop by and see how things are going here," Ballard said. "After spending years of leading in the Army, I've always found it helpful to talk with the boots on the ground, if you want to know how things are really going."

"No disrespect, Colonel, but we've already got a lot of cooks in the kitchen here at DHS. Does the President of National Security Affairs really need to step in?"

Ballard eyed Simpson.

"You like your job, Mr. Simpson?"

The man nodded.

"That's a shame. Because I'm gonna make sure that today is your last day. I've been around long enough to know that when someone starts off a phrase with 'no disrespect,' they're about to completely disrespect you."

Simpson's face went ashen.

"Look, Colonel, I—I wasn't trying to offend you. It's just that, well, it's really hard to do our jobs consistently, not to mention do it well, when we've got people from every alphabet organization in Washington offering us advice on how we need to operate. It's exhausting."

"Perhaps you'll be able to find something else you're more comfortable with," Ballard said.

He marched over to the sink and dumped out the coffee.

"And another thing," Ballard said, as he grabbed the door knob. "If you manage things here anything like your coffee tastes, I know this airport will be better off with you out of the picture."

Simpson glared at Ballard and moved toward him.

"Why, you son of a—"

Ballard held up his index finger and wagged back and forth.

"Now, now. Let's calm down. No need to say things we'll later regret. You have yourself a good evening, sir."

Ballard grunted as he tugged on the door and exited the room. He needed to keep up the appearances that he was there in an advisory role, overlooking airport security for DHS. But he didn't care about any of that. Not Simpson. Not the coffee. Not even the way DHS was managed here. That was low-level stuff, assignments from hell with little room for advancement up the chain of command. If you were good at your job, you could expect to rise to the position of a managing supervisor—but nothing more. The real movement happened for those in Washington working at the DHS headquarters.

Ballard broke into a half-hearted smile as he strode away from the office. He knew he wasn't going to ask Simpson to be fired or even mention the visit to anyone. That'd be too much work. And Ballard didn't care enough to make the effort. It was all theater, a conversation Simpson wouldn't bring up ever again, unless he was placed under oath. And that was all Ballard needed to do—establish that he was there on business if anyone ever questioned why he was at LAX, and then let the details of that visit remain a mystery. After all, he was the President of National Security Affairs. Who was going to question him?

Ballard strolled along the concourse, no bag, no rush. He'd long since given up commercial flying, and he didn't miss it. Watching the frantic travelers rush from one gate to another reminded him why he hated airports so much. The 9/11 terrorists ruined what joy there was in the journey from one destination to the other. The arrival and return destinations were the only things to look forward to. And Ballard was very much looking forward to the arrival of Garrett Knox.

After checking his watch, Ballard paced the floor near gate 25B before finding a spot he could lean up against that also gave him a view of the passengers exiting the jetway. The final five minutes ticked by in painstaking fashion before people started to march into the airport. Ten minutes elapsed since the first passenger hustled by, but still no sign of Knox.

Ballard glanced at his phone again. The cell phone he'd given Knox was trackable. Surely he knew that.

Knox wouldn't try any stunts, would he?

After a few more minutes, the flight crew exited, signifying that the passengers were all gone.

Ballard approached the gate agent at the counter. He wore his work uniform along with a little red clown nose. Ballard couldn't get past how ridiculous the man at the counter appeared.

"You are aware of how silly that looks, right?" Ballard asks, his finger indicating toward the man's nose.

"It's Red Nose Day, sir," the man said, his head bobbing from side to side, his reply biting. "Don't you care about the future of our children?"

"Yeah, but do I have to wear a clown nose to show it?"

"Of course you do," the man snapped. "Now, unless you have a real question, I want to get going. My shift is about to end."

Ballard squinted, trying to read the man's nameplate, not something that he found easy to do without his reading glasses.

"Mr. Melvin, is it?" Ballard began. "I'm hoping you can tell me if there's anyone else on that plane."

"If the crew's gone, the passengers are gone."

"But I was tracking someone's phone. They were supposed to be on this flight."

"I suggest you go wait for them in the designated location. You must've missed them."

"That can't be," Ballard said. "I can track their phone. It says they're still onboard."

"Creeepyyyy," the clerk said, sneering.

"It's not like that," Ballard said. "It's just that—"

"Sir, please move along. Track whoever you want. I don't care. I just want to go home."

Before Ballard could move, the man's radio crackled to life.

"You still out there, Melvin?"

Melvin sighed and stared at the ceiling.

"What is it now?"

"This last passenger needs help."

"Ah-ha," Ballard said. "There is another passenger."

"Probably not who you're looking for," Melvin said, using the back of his hand to give Ballard a dismissive wave.

Melvin disappeared, re-emerging about two minutes later pushing a wheelchair with an elderly woman strapped in while she held an oxygen tank in her lap.

"Wasn't her, was it?" Melvin asked.

Ballard stared at the tank before noticing something secured to the side of it with clear packing tape.

Knox's cell phone.

Ballard swore softly.

"I beg your pardon," Melvin said. "What did you say?"

Ballard sneered at the gate agent before shuffling away. Knox had tricked Ballard. Instantly, he had questions about Knox's loyalty. Ballard concluded that maybe Knox had persuaded Canfield to give up the location of the footage by promising to expose a dirty little secret.

But if Knox is gathering evidence—

Ballard froze, processing what it would mean if Knox captured the footage and shared it with media outlets. Nothing good would come of it. And Ballard knew his political career—his military one, too—would all be over.

He watched the elderly woman for a few minutes so he could confirm that was where the phone's signal was coming from. Then he pocketed his cell phone and looked for a wall to punch.

You're in public, Ballard. Get a hold of yourself.

He fished his phone out of his pocket and dialed a number. It only rang once before a man answered.

"This is Ballard—Knox didn't get on the plane."

"Damnit," the man said. "I warned you."

"I know, I know."

"And now he's going to find that footage—and you're going to be exposed along with the rest of The Consortium."

Ballard swore again, trying to contain his rage.

"How could he do this to me?" he asked through clenched teeth.

"Don't say I didn't warn you about hiring Knox. It's a safe bet that he thinks you're lying—and he's going to do everything he can to pull the curtain back on you and reveal the truth. And if you don't like that, you better figure out a way to stop him."

Ballard had his ways.

After he ended the call, he made one more, punching in the digits of the man he needed to talk to, a man who could help him take care of the situation in a most discreet manner.

CHAPTER TWENTY-SIX

Washington, D.C

Erica Everhart struggled to keep her eyes open as the train clattered along the tracks, jostling her from side to side. The smell of hot coffee wafted through the carriage, rivaled only by the strong scent of perfume emanating from the woman sporting a tight-fitting v-neck t-shirt seated across from Erica. She'd smelled the woman when they were on the platform awaiting the train to arrive. It smelled like she took a bath in the flowery stuff, making Erica wonder just how long she could endure the aroma before she'd have to move to another car. But as the train slowed, the woman arose and exited, the cool underground air sweeping out the smell almost immediately.

Erica warmed herself with the steaming cup of coffee in her hands and then tilted her head back against the glass.

Am I doing the right thing? Is Thomas playing games with me again?

She wondered if she'd be the subject of one of his off-beat stories about love in the city. Or maybe he was just enticing her to go on a travel adventure story he was writing. But no matter how many reasons why she thought he'd invited her—other than the one Quinn claimed—one question remained: *Does Thomas still like me?*

Erica decided to join him because of the potential conspiracy —at least, that's what she told herself. But she couldn't deny the urge she felt to find out if she and Quinn could rekindle their lost love.

A faint smile spread across her lips as she imagined what it would be like, a dream she had since she was in college—she and her husband working together on stories that exposed big government corruption. Though she wasn't married yet, the idea of such a venture still appealed to her. And now that they worked for different news outlets, they could test it out, see if not only they had the chemistry for love, but also the chemistry to become a great reporting duo.

The intercom dinged, followed by a robotic voice announcing they had arrived at Dulles. She gathered her belongings and stood, clutching the pole in the middle of the car for support. Then the doors swung open. She waited for the flustered travelers scrambling for the line to clear out before she exited. Once she did, she strolled along toward the spot Quinn had told her to meet him.

The time wasn't something she was worried about, especially after arriving a half-hour before she was supposed be there. But she thought it was a good idea. The bigger the buffer, the better, she mused, glad she didn't have to say the tongue twister aloud.

She glided past the spot where Quinn had texted her to meet.

But he wasn't there.

She drifted along the concourse, back and forth, keeping an eye out for him while also trying not to appear like she was some desperate star-struck lover. But no Thomas.

Then came the time he'd told her to be there, his last words ringing in her ear.

"See you then."

But *then* was *now*—and he was nowhere to be seen.

Six o'clock came and went. And then a quarter after six. Still no Thomas Quinn.

She wondered if maybe she'd missed him and he'd gone ahead and checked in. But the woman at the counter shook her head when Erica asked if he'd checked in already. Then she asked her to reprint her ticket. The woman obliged, letting Erica know that he had indeed bought her a ticket and planned to go to Kinshasa.

Where is he?

She was about to leave when her phone buzzed with a call. Fumbling to get her phone out of her purse, Erica nearly dropped the device several times, anxiously hoping to see his name appear on the screen. Instead, it was the name of her editor, David Langston.

"David, do you know what time it is?" she asked.

"I know," he said, his tone somber. "I'm so sorry. I just didn't want you to hear from anywhere else."

"Hear what?"

Langston let out an audible breath.

"I know you and Thomas weren't still dating, but I figured you'd rather hear it from a friend than from the news."

"What are you talking about? What's happened to Thomas?"

"Metro police found him in his apartment this morning, dead in an an apparent suicide," he said.

"Suicide? Are you—"

Erica stopped to catch her breath. She crumpled to the floor before crawling to a nearby bench. Tears streamed down her face, but no sound came out of her mouth. The news sucked the life right out of her, like plunging into an Alpine lake in early spring.

"He—he did what? How?"

"I didn't get any details on how," Langston said. "But I wanted you to hear it from someone you knew rather than randomly while driving and listening to the radio."

She finally found her voice, albeit broken, cracked, despondent. Quiet sobs morphed into anguishing wails, mascara staining her face. Airport travelers barely gave her a second look as they hustled to their gates.

Erica eventually stopped and looked at her watch. It was six-thirty and she wanted to go home and climb under her covers and not resurface until the pain had subsided. Two days? Three days? A week? She wasn't sure how long it would take, nor did she care. Maybe never.

But then she glanced down at her hand, the one still clutching the ticket he'd bought for her. Thomas had been chasing down a story. And when he thought he was onto something, he wouldn't stop until he'd turned over every last stone, interviewed every last source, visited every last location.

There's no way Thomas killed himself.

Erica dried her face with her hands, carefully tending to the corners of eyes. She had a ticket for Kinshasa, a story that Quinn was chasing, a story that he wanted her to be a part of. For a moment, Erica considered her options—sob in bed for days on end, mourning his death ... or do the one thing that would honor him the most and uncover whatever it was that was going on with the Peace Corps.

She looked at the sliding doors that led from the airport to the Metro. Then she turned toward the security checkpoint leading to the gates.

Erica thumbed a quick text message to Langston, letting him know that she was still going to the Congo in pursuit of a story, a story Quinn believed to be promising. Then she dropped her phone into her pursue and marched toward the checkpoint, ticket and passport in hand.

It's what Thomas would've wanted.

CHAPTER TWENTY-SEVEN

Wheaton, Maryland

Ballard pulled his cap low across his brow as he entered Nick's Diner and found an empty table in the back corner of the restaurant. He picked up one of the four laminated menus on the table and scanned the offerings. Nick's had only been open for fifteen minutes, but was packed with what he guessed were regulars, every last one of them already with their coffee mugs telling stories or listening. The patrons were an even mix of retirees and blue collar workers, the latter wearing high visibility vests and hard hats. And not a single cell phone in sight. For a moment, Ballard wondered if he'd stepped into a place time forgot.

Where is he?

Ballard hadn't picked the place nearly a half-hour from downtown, though he understood the importance of getting outside of Washington where he wouldn't be recognized. He doubted anyone there even knew his office existed, let alone who he was. And that was the very reason he was there. To the regulars, Ballard would be a nameless, faceless drifter who happened by their place, a forgettable patron taking up a table in the back.

Moments later, the glass door swung open and then clattered shut as The Cleaner entered the establishment. He stopped and scanned the room before coming over to Ballard's table.

"Fancy place," Ballard said.

"You said you wanted to go where nobody knew who you were, didn't you?" The Cleaner said, as he sat down.

Ballard nodded. "Fair enough."

"I recommend the western omelet," The Cleaner said.

"You come here often?"

"Once or twice a year. Just infrequently enough that the wait staff doesn't remember me. But whenever I do eat here, I recognize almost all the same people every single time."

Their conversation was interrupted by Candy, a slender young waitress with her hair fixed in a messy bun, a pencil nestled inside. She slowly worked over a piece of gum as she placed two glasses of water on the table.

"You fellas know what you want to eat yet?" she asked.

Both men nodded before giving her their order. She collected the menus and went to the bar to read off the order to the cooks in the back.

"Good work on your latest assignment," Ballard said. "You should've already received your payment."

"I don't need to meet for breakfast just to get an 'atta boy' from you."

Ballard took a sip of water and then leaned forward in his seat.

"I've got another job for you."

"You could've just texted."

Ballard shook his head.

"Not this one. I don't want any trail that could lead back to me, digital or otherwise."

"So a high profile job? Got it. Who's the target?"

"I'd rather not say. Frankly, the less you know, the better."

"That's not how this works. I make my deaths look as natural as possible, eliminating possible suspicion before it starts."

"That'll be rather tricky on this one."

"How so?"

"Let's just say the target is a structure instead of a person."

The Cleaner shrugged.

"I can handle that. Just tell me where to go."

Ballard recited the address.

"Don't forget it. I wouldn't want the wrong people to end up dead."

"People? As in this will result in multiple deaths?"

Ballard nodded. "Is that a problem?"

"I know this is what I do, but I'm not a monster. I'm not too keen on innocent people getting swept up in something I do."

"Believe me when I say this," Ballard said, "but there are no innocent people in this group."

"*Group*? What the hell? How many people do you want to die?"

"Just one. But I'm sure you'll figure out who if you're there. This group will be checking in this weekend, a little guy's fishing trip. That's about all I know—and probably all you need to know to take care of business."

"Consider it done," The Cleaner said, "but just know that my fee goes up fifty percent for each *client*."

"That's not an issue for me."

"Fair enough."

Just as they finished their discussion, Candy returned with their food. She slid their omelettes in front of them and asked if they needed any other condiments before scurrying over to another table.

Ballard and The Cleaner finished their meal in silence before both men paid in cash. They left a moderate tip on the table, not so much or so little that either of them would be remembered,in case The Cleaner got caught.

But Ballard wasn't concerned. He knew The Cleaner never got caught, a consummate professional.

~

The Cleaner was walking to his car when his phone buzzed with a call. He expected it to be Ballard, who forgot to tell him something about the assignment. But it wasn't.

The Cleaner answered the phone.

"I wasn't expecting to hear from you so soon," he said.

"I have a job for you."

"I'm booked up at the moment. How quickly do you need this completed?"

"Maybe within a week or ten days."

"Are you aware of my expedited price?"

"I don't care. I just need this target gone."

The Cleaner stopped at the corner and waited for the light to change.

"Normally, I need a month to plan. But I'll do it for you. Send me the information about the hit."

The Cleaner's phone buzzed almost immediately.

"That was fast," he said.

"Like I said, I need this taken care of ASAP."

The Cleaner found the text message and opened it.

His eyes widened when he saw the name.

"Are you sure?" he asked.

"Absolutely. Will you do it?"

"Anything for you," The Cleaner said before he ended the call.

CHAPTER TWENTY-EIGHT

Bonjane, South Africa

Knox and Makenzie rumbled along the soggy dirt road, squinting as they tried to determine if they were in the right place. Bonjane, a small farming community nestled along the banks of the Nzhelele River, was an eight-hour drive from Johannesburg, located the northeast part of the country. Just outside small tin-roof houses, boys kicked soccer balls or ran around with sticks. Some of the girls played with the boys, while others watched, grooming baby dolls. Then there were some older girls carrying around their siblings on their hips. But when Knox and Makenzie drove past them, everyone stopped to stare at them.

"This looks like the one," Makenzie said, indicating toward a house at the end of the road.

She'd corresponded over email with Kyle Canfield's late wife Emily twice since their initial exchange to set up the details for their visit, and each time Emily seemed reticent about communicating much else, preferring to wait until they met in person. Knox parked the Land Rover in front of the house and he and Makenzie got out. Children rushed over to them, curious about what the two visitors were doing there.

Emily, a woman who appeared to be in her early thirties with curly auburn hair, smiled as she came out of the house to greet them. A young girl clung to Emily's chest in a child carrier, yet she offered to bring in their luggage.

"Nonsense," Knox said, waving dismissively at her. "We can handle it. Besides, you look like you've got your hands full."

Emily glanced down at the girl.

"Oh, this is just how I live. If I couldn't do anything else when she was asleep on my chest, I'd never get anything done."

Makenzie slung her backpack over her shoulder and grinned as she approached Emily. The two women shook hands before Makenzie's attention zeroed in on the little one.

"She's adorable," Makenzie said.

"Why don't you withhold judgment until she wakes up," Emily said, with a chuckle.

"I don't think it's possible for someone this sweet be anything but adorable."

"You don't have kids, do you?"

Makenzie shook her head. "Is it that obvious?"

Emily patted Makenzie on the back and laughed.

"I thought like you once, too. I'm only half kidding about Wendy. She really is a sweet girl, but there are times when she's inconsolable, mostly when she misses her daddy."

There was a short pause where everyone looked down, unsure of what to say.

"Can I show you to your room?" Emily asked.

They both nodded.

"Just be sure to watch your step," Emily said, lengthening her stride to avoid splashing into a mud puddle. "It's winter here, so it's our rainy season. There's been quite a bit of flooding along the coast, and I wish I could do something to help those people."

"Seems like you've got your hands full here," Knox said.

"The day I'm too busy to help others is the day I die," she said.

Knox and Makenzie followed Emily inside, where she led them to a cramped room with three sets of bunk beds.

"I know, I know," Emily said. "It's not the Ritz. It's not even Holiday Inn. But this is how we set this room up to help accommodate some of the mission teams that come to Bonjane and want to help with what we're doing here."

"And what exactly are you doing?" Knox asked.

"Aside from the traditional things missionaries do, we're teaching these people a lucrative skill so they can raise the standard of living, one that will help them not be so dependent on wealthy white farmers," Emily said. "Before Kyle died, we were helping set up a community hydroponics farm. The idea is that once everyone learns how to do this together, they can do it individually, either for personal use or for commercial use."

"That's an interesting approach," Makenzie said as she placed her backpack on one of the beds.

"Yeah, but it's been slow going lately without Kyle around. He was the real hydroponics expert. I helped some too, but I wasn't nearly as knowledgeable as Kyle. He'd started two commercial hydroponics farms before we met, so this was his baby."

Wendy made a cooing sound, followed by a grunt.

"And this is my baby," Emily said, patting Wendy on her bottom. "Now, I'll let you two get settled and then we can talk some more."

Knox sighed as he gave Makenzie a knowing look.

"This would be challenging for most single men," he said. "But now she's here as a single mom? She seems like she's Army Ranger material to me."

Makenzie nodded. "I'll help her make dinner tonight. I want to help as much as I can before we get outta here. I know just being here is putting a strain on her."

Knox nodded in agreement.

"Hopefully, we can crack this code and be gone tomorrow."

"Are you gonna tell her?"

"Tell her what?" Knox asked.

"The truth about her brother-in-law?"

"No need to dredge that up. If she'd already made peace with it, why make her do it all over again? Seems a bit cruel, don't ya think?"

"You're probably right."

After they finished settling in, Knox and Makenzie left the room and found Emily in the kitchen seasoning pork roast.

"Did you guys bring what I asked for?" Emily asked.

"Oh, yes," Makenzie said. "A dozen deflated soccer balls with an air pump and a bag of needles."

Emily rubbed spices over the meat.

"Perfect," she said. "Now, if you can get those inflated, they might just give you a key to the city."

Knox grabbed the pump and the bag of balls before easing into a chair at the kitchen table. He jammed the needle into the first ball and started pumping. After a few minutes of small talk, Knox cut to the chase.

"So, Emily, why did you agree to see us?" Knox asked, still inflating a ball. "What made you curious?"

She stopped peeling a potato and took a deep breath, staring out the window as she considered her response.

"I have a lot of questions," she said. "And I thought maybe you could help me get some answers."

"Such as?" Makenzie said.

"I don't know," Emily said. "Maybe I want to know why my brother-in-law and husband died a few months apart. What were they into? Was it random? Was it just God's timing? I don't know. My kids loved their uncle Kevin—and losing him devastated them. Then their dad? It all seems so cruel."

"But you wanted to talk in person," Knox said. "Why's that?"

"I know Kevin was in the Rangers, like you," Emily said, as she pointed with her peeler at Knox's tattoo. "Kyle told me that the last time he spoke with his brother, he was a little skittish. Then he wrote Kyle and told him that he'd hidden an important piece of evidence about something—he didn't say what—in Johannesburg. The mission agency we work for has a small apartment in Johannesburg for staff to stay overnight whenever we're doing business in Johannesburg. Kevin said the next time Kyle went to the apartment, he'd find a letter with instructions on how to retrieve the evidence."

"Did he ever get it?" Knox asked.

Emily shook her head. "That's what Kyle was going to get the night he was mugged and murdered."

"And detectives didn't find the note?" Makenzie asked.

"Nope. Not a thing. His wallet was gone, along with all his credit cards and cash. They said it looked like a simple mugging and that maybe Kyle tried to fight back. Whatever happened, it didn't go Kyle's way."

Emily teared up, dabbing just beneath her eyes with the back of her hand.

"I'm sorry," she said. "I still get emotional thinking about it."

Makenzie put her hand on Emily's back and rubbed her gently.

"That's understandable. I'd be the same way."

Knox finished pumping up the last ball.

"We really want to help you get some closure, or whatever else it is that you want," he said. "And I don't think we're going to get that until we get the truth. And Kevin hid that truth. We've just got to figure out this code he gave us."

"Why did he give it to you?" Emily asked.

"He hadn't heard from Kyle and wondered if he'd lost the information or didn't know what to do with it," Knox said. "So, he agreed to give it to us, if we promised to do something about it. Only problem is, it's in some code that we don't have the cipher for."

Emily laughed softly.

"That's Kevin—and Kyle. They both loved those types of puzzles. They used to send each other coded messages. After a while, I joined them, mostly because I wanted to know what they were saying. Can I see the code?"

Makenzie handed it to Emily, a smile spreading across her lips. "This is Kevin's handwriting for sure. But you said he gave this to you? When?"

Knox looked at Makenzie and winced. He'd forgotten about the timeline issue. If Emily caught him in a lie, she might not be willing to help.

He sighed.

"Look, Emily, there's something you need to know," Knox began. "Kevin wasn't really dead."

Her eyes bulged. "Come again?"

"I said, Kevin wasn't killed—at least, not when you initially thought he was. He faked his own death to have a chance at a new life. But somebody caught up with him."

"When?"

"A few days ago," Knox said. "We went to meet with him about this in Fiji, where he was living. And that's when he told us everything. As we were leaving, someone shot him and killed him."

Knox watched Emily crumple the note in her hand, nostrils flaring as her eyes narrowed.

"I'm not sure I trust you," Emily said. "How do I know it wasn't you who got this information from him and then shot him?"

"I swear I would never do anything like that, especially to a fellow Ranger," Knox said. "You gotta believe me."

"I need both of you out of here," Emily said. "Go give those balls to the kids outside and leave me alone. I need to think."

Knox slung the bag over his shoulder and trudged outside, Makenzie in tow.

"We may have screwed up our chance here," Knox said. "We should've just told her the truth from the start."

"It's easy to say that now," Makenzie said. "We were just trying to protect her emotionally. But, you're right—she has a right not to trust us, and I wouldn't blame her."

"But we need that footage—*I* need that footage," Knox said.

"Then now might be a good time to say a little prayer. Because we're going to need a little extra help to get her comply."

CHAPTER TWENTY-NINE

Kinshasa, Democratic Republic of the Congo

Erica Everhart strode through the N'djili International Airport, head held high, eyes scanning behind her aviator sunglasses. She'd been to third world countries before and was all too familiar with the bombardment she was sure to endure. Teenaged boys and young men hustled up to her, offering their services for a tip. One of the teens tried to yank her suitcase out of her hand and pull it for her. But Erica pulled back, catching him off guard and knocking him off balance. He toppled to the ground, drawing a chorus of laughter from his competitors.

Erica, realizing this swarm of enterprising beggars wasn't going away, stamped her foot and removed her sunglass, narrowing her eyes as she scanned her captive audience.

"No!" she barked. "I can do it myself."

With her forceful response, the crowd scattered in search of a new target.

Moments later, she found baggage claim and located her bag. Then she searched among the men holding small signs with the names of their passengers plastered on it. But she wasn't looking for her name.

A man wearing a pair of jeans and a lime green linen shirt hoisted a sign above his head that caught her eye: "Thomas Quinn."

She marched over to the man and introduced herself.

"I'm afraid my colleague had to cancel at the last minute," she said. "But he sent me in his place."

"You are Thomas Quinn?" the man asked.

She shook her head, frustrated at the man's inability to grasp the English language.

"Thomas Quinn is my friend," she said slowly, hoping the pacing of her speech might help the man understand more clearly. "He didn't fly here. But I did. He wanted me to take his place."

The man shrugged and then gestured for her to follow him. She wasn't sure he understood that she was his replacement. But Erica didn't care. As long as she could convince the man to take her to the same place as Quinn had scheduled the driver to take him, it wouldn't matter.

"Is your name Thomas Quinn?" the man asked.

"No," she said. "It's Erica. But he couldn't make it and sent me in his place."

The man squinted as he looked at her.

"Mr. Quinn isn't coming?"

She shook her head. "But he still wanted me to go."

The man paused for a moment, looked around the baggage claim area, and then tucked the sign under his armpit.

"It's a pre-paid trip. Need help with your luggage?" he asked, offering his hand.

"I've got it," she said. "Just take me to your car."

A few minutes later, Erica was in the backseat of a Toyota RAV-4, humming along Congo's sterling N1 highway, something she learned all about from her driver, Jacques.

For the next eight hours, Erica listened to Jacques' discuss the important of the N1 highway to the Congolese people. He shared how in the past, he required tires with mud grips to navigate the boggy section of the roads. But not today. The weather no longer mattered. He could make it across the country without having to stop for weeks at a time due to the rainy season.

She eventually fell asleep, and when she woke up, Jacques was pointing out the turnoff to Tango, the small village just a few miles south of a bumpy dirt road.

"If you ever get lost, come back here," the man said. "You will either be able to get back to the village or back to Kinshasa. You will have plenty of buses to choose from."

Erica thanked the man before exiting the vehicle, toting her luggage along the road.

He stopped and rolled down his window.

"Wasn't someone supposed to meet you?"

She shrugged.

"Not sure," she said.

"It can be a dangerous place for anyone, but especially a woman," Jacques said. "Are you sure you want me to leave?"

"Just stay here for a few minutes," she said. "I'll come back and let you know if you can go or not."

Jacques nodded as if he understood.

Erica turned in the opposite direction and began walking toward the village. She rounded a corner and came upon a tall 10-foot chain-link fence rolls of barbed wire affixed to the top of it, blocking her entry. She squinted as she drew closer, trying to read the message.

"Quarantined area. Do not enter."

The bottom corner of the sign was marked with The World Health Organization's logo. Erica looked to the left and right of the road entering Tango. Instead of seeing a way inside, she only saw the fence encircling the entire town.

Then she went to her right, hurdling branches and fallen trees. But the fence continued on, not a gap in sight. After a few minutes of exploring, she shimmied up a tree with a branch that hung some ten feet above the top of the fence. With a rough estimation of the height and some quick math, she figured she wouldn't fall more than thirteen feet off the ground if she dropped.

What's the worst that could happen? A broken leg? A sprained ankle?

It was a chance she had to take. Before she climbed up to the branch, she found a few sturdy vines. Weaving them together, she concocted a makeshift rope that she flung over the branch and used to lower herself closer to the ground. By the time she reached the end of her rope, she was only dangling about six feet off the jungle floor.

Once touched down, she somersaulted, avoiding the full brunt of a hard landing. She brushed herself off, pleased that she didn't suffer an injury. After navigating back to the heart of the village, she began her cursory investigation, still conscious of the internal clock running in her head for Jacques. She hadn't seen much of anything yet, but she didn't want to be stranded in Tango.

As Erica drifted from house to house, reticent to go inside and surprise someone, she realized why someone had cordoned off the village. Something had gone wrong there—terribly wrong.

She called out, hoping someone would answer her plea. But nothing. It was as if she'd stumbled onto a deserted movie set. No one was there to tell her the story and point her toward the directors or writers. All she had to figure out what had happened were empty huts.

Then she caught a whiff along the breeze. She nearly gagged, regained her composure, and continued along. That's when she saw it for the first time—a hut swarming with flies. She poked her head through the window in an effort to avoid the onslaught of the insects.

Sitting in a rocking chair was the gnarly flesh of a human. She couldn't even tell if it was a man or a woman, let alone how old the carcass was. Whomever it was, it been decomposing for a long while. And she couldn't discern if it was from a week ago or a month or more.

What the hell?

She moved closer, trying to get a better glimpse of the figure. What caused this? In an instant, her visit to Tango had created more questions than answers, questions she wondered if she could ever get answered. But she had to start somewhere. After all, this is where Thomas's investigation was taking him.

Then she ventured into another hut—same result. And another, and another. Some of the bodies looked they had decomposed naturally, while others looked like they had been torn apart by wild animals. Then she spotted a dead lion, sprawled on its side, which had been split open, though she couldn't tell by what.

Knife? Claw? Talons?

She wasn't sure what sliced through its side, but it was rotting. Erica pulled up her shirt to cover her nose, rushing from one dwelling to the next, searching for any clues about what had happened. But she didn't find anyone. It was like a living history museum, the type of park she'd visited many times in the U.S., where the workers mimicked the jobs and daily lives of people from a bygone era.

Except all the subjects were dead.

This is more like Mount Vesuvius.

She took pictures and video before finding a small opening beneath the fence.

But just as she was about to leave, the sun glinted off a shiny object that caught her eye. Hustling over in that direction, she stopped when she found a man in a bloodied hazmat suit with the name NocturaCorp stitched on the sleeve.

NocturaCorp?

The name was a new one for Erica. She made a note to look it up when she finished, clicking a quick picture of the suit. But what she really found curious was the fact that he'd looked like he'd been shot to death. Lying on his back, bullet holes riddled his chest. At least, she assumed it was a man. It was definitely larger, at least six feet tall. But she was going to remove the helmet to confirm.

With that, she rushed back over to the gap in the fence. Sliding underneath it, she rushed up the road where Jacques had left her. He was still there, windows down as he read a magazine.

"I was beginning to wonder if you were ever coming back," he said, a smile spreading across his face. "Did you find what you were looking for?"

"You could say that," she said.

"Good to hear that it wasn't wasted. Now, I'll take you to a hostel that Mr. Quinn had booked about two hours west of here toward Kishasa."

"Great," she said. "Do you get any cell reception here?"

Jacques shook his head. "We should in a few kilometers."

Erica leaned back in her seat, her mind buzzing, trying to process what she'd just seen.

What did that to those people? Who blocked it off? And why? Wouldn't someone want to study this?

"Do you know much about that village?" Erica asked, as Jacques spun his car around and headed toward the hostel.

"Not really," he said. "All I know is that it's cursed."

"Cursed?"

"Yes. No one goes there unless you have to. What did you find?"

"Not much," Erica said, not wanting to get into a protracted conversation about what she'd just witnessed. "Just a cursed land."

"Then what people say about Tango must be true."

A few minutes later, Erica noticed her phone signal went from a one to a five. She immediately dialed her editor's number.

"How are you?" Langston asked. "You holding up okay? What have you been doing?"

"Thomas and I were supposed to go on a trip to the Congo," she said.

"Again, I'm really sorry, Erica."

"Don't be," she said. "I decided that I wasn't going to waste the ticket he bought me."

"You're in the Congo? By yourself?"

"Calm down," she said. "You need to save your excitement for what I'm about to tell you."

"What's happened?"

"I know why he was coming here now."

"And why's that?" Langston asked.

"He didn't yet know it, but he was about to stumble on the story of a lifetime. And the best way for me to honor him is to write it and expose whoever was behind all this."

CHAPTER THIRTY

Shenandoah National Park | Virginia

Elliot Schwartz removed his rod and fishing tackle out of the back of his Range Rover, whistling his favorite Conway Twitty song, "Louisiana Woman, Mississippi Man." He stopped as he turned around and surveyed the house known as Summerhaven, an opulent log cabin nestled just above a riverbank just inside Shenandoah National Park. The scent of pine wafted through the small clearing around the house, which was otherwise surrounded by soaring trees that creaked as they swayed.

"Got a little Conway Twitty on your mind?" Jackson Miller asked.

"More like I've just got Conway on my mind—the Conway River," Schwartz said. "I just felt like it was the appropriate artist of choice."

"You're wife's from Louisiana, isn't she?" Randy Carmen asked.

"A born and bred bonafide Cajun."

"And she let you go fishing without taking her?" Miller asked.

"She was a little bit jealous, I'll say that much," Schwartz said.

Then Schwartz turned around and stared at the house where they would be staying over the weekend.

"If I didn't see it for myself, I wouldn't believe it," Schwartz said before he turned toward Miller. "The ultimate fishing cabin in the Shenandoah."

"Incredible, right?" Miller said as he glanced back at the sprawling two-story house.

"How did you get this place?" Schwartz asked. "I didn't even know you could build in national parks."

"You can't," Randy Carmen said, as he toted his gear and tackle box into the garage. "But some people know how to get special favors."

Miller clucked his tongue and waved dismissively at Carmen.

"Don't listen to him," Miller said. "I didn't get any special favors to build this house. Everything was on the up and up."

"Was it? Because I've never seen a place like this *in* a national park," Schwartz said. "Not that I'm complaining about it."

"I know some people who would complain about this if they knew that I owned it—maybe even do something to it," Miller said. "But this house is perfectly legal to be here, something known as an inholding, which is what they called deeds privately owned before national parks were established. My family had several of these in the Shenandoah Mountains before it received its national park status."

Carmen shuffled out of the garage.

"You say it so non-nonchalantly, Jackson," he said. "Like you come from some normal family."

Schwartz's eyes widened.

"You come from royalty?" he asked.

"American royalty," Carmen quipped. "Go ahead, Jackson. Tell him."

Miller looked down sheepishly, scratching at the dirt with his foot.

"Come on, man," Miller said. "You know I hate telling people about it."

"Okay, fine, I'll tell him," Carmen said. "He's a descendant of President Herbert Hoover."

"Damn," Schwartz said, with a wry grin.

Carmen pointed at Schwartz.

"Now that was good," Carmen said.

"You set me up," Schwartz said. "It's always my go-to respond when I hear the word *hoover*."

"So, Hoover built a big dam, and a couple of monstrous houses in Shenandoah," Carmen said, "one of which he donated to the park, which scored him some points with voters. They all thought he was a kind and generous man. But the truth is, ole Herbie was holding back some of that land for his family, so they could enjoy it after he was gone."

Miller frowned.

"That's not exactly how it was, but I'll let you believe whatever you want, Randy. You never listen to me."

"Oh, I'm listening, but your stories are dull. You gotta spice them up a little."

Schwartz put his gear in the garage with Carmen's before returning to the front steps.

"Well, I don't care who's responsible for what, if I can stay here while we fish this weekend," Schwartz said, hands on his hips as he studied the cabin. "Now, let's get inside. The sooner we get settled, the sooner we can get some lines in the water. I heard the trout are biting like starved madmen along the Conway River."

"And I'd like to confirm that," Miller said.

"And I'd like to drink to that," Carmen said, hoisting up two bottles of Johnnie Walker, one in each hand. "Let's do what we really came here to do."

Carmen unscrewed one of the bottles and took a long pull from it before letting out a boisterous whoop. He took another swig and then smacked his lips.

"Let's get this party started," he said.

Schwartz didn't need much time to put his overnight bag in his room and get a feel for the lay of the house. He tested out one of the leather couches facing the double-sided fireplace. The chimney was adorned with hunting conquests captured by a skilled taxidermist. A chandelier crafted out of deer antlers hung above him.

Carmen stomped upstairs, holding tightly to a glass of Johnnie Walker in one hand and his bag in the other. He moved his drink to his other hand and leaned over the railing to pet the nose of a moose head.

"Watch it," Miller said. "That's one Hoover took out himself."

"Ole Herbie, skilled with the fishing rod and the rifle," Carmen said. "So, Jackson, who do you think would win in a hunt-off between Hoover and Teddy Roosevelt?"

Miller growled.

"Hurry up and put your stuff away so we can get to fishing," he said.

"On it," Carmen said. The door to his room slammed shut.

Schwartz circled the room as he drank a glass of whiskey, inspecting the family photos of President Hoover captured in candid moments. He was amazed at how the place still looked so similar, aside from the updated interior.

When Carmen eventually returned downstairs, he poured himself another drink.

"Slow down," Schwartz said. "You need to pace yourself."

Carmen shook his head.

"Hell, no. I'm celebrating this weekend."

"What for?" Schwartz asked.

"Have you checked your stocks reports today?" Carmen asked.

The other two men furrowed their brows, unsure of where Carmen was going with the comment.

"Cell reception up here isn't that great," Miller said. "And even if it was—"

Carmen wagged his index finger at Miller.

"OK, I'm gonna have to stop you right there, Jackson. If you did what Schwartzie here told us to do last time we talked, you'd have a boatload of money."

"What—what did I tell you to do?" Schwartz asked.

"You said we were going to war soon, and to buy certain stocks in the military's preferred weapons manufacturers," Carmen said. "We're going to war now—and everyone knows it. Might as well get rich off of it, right?"

"That's not what I said," Schwartz said.

"You're right," Carmen said. "You were careful not to use those words, but I read between the lines. Nice move, King. Now, I'm ready to party."

Carmen exited the house, striding onto the porch.

Schwartz looked at Miller and gave him a half-hearted shrug.

"Forget about him," Schwartz said. "He's drunk. But let's not let him ruin it for us. Let's go catch some fish."

Miller stopped.

"We're gonna make a mint, aren't we?"

Schwartz smiled.

"Of course we are."

The Cleaner waited until the three men exited out the backdoor and tromped down to the Conway River to fish before climbing down from the branch he was sitting on in a pine tree about fifty meters away. He put on a full-body hazmat suit before entering the house. While he'd done this hundreds of times before, he knew that one strand of hair, one piece of DNA, could link him to the crime scene —and it would spell disaster for him.

Once he finished donning his gear, he entered the house with his bag.

He strode over to the counter and added a few more liquor bottles to the embarrassingly large stash, disappointed that full bottles would have to go to waste. One by one, The Cleaner checked the windows, ensuring that they were all secured. Once he was finished with that task, he descended the stairs into the basement to locate the gas line. After he found it, he cut it, sending the gas spewing into the room. He left the door to the basement open after hustling up the steps. After a quick inspection of the premises, he went through the front door and painted symbols of an extreme ecological group, one that had voiced its displeasure in some of the lobbying efforts put forth by Miller and Carmen.

Satisfied that everything was in order, The Cleaner returned to his perch and waited.

Dusk had settled over the forest before the trio returned. Carmen could barely walk, babbling incoherently about why he didn't catch as many fish as Miller and Schwartz.

Hope you enjoyed the fishing, boys.

"I'm starving," Schwartz said.

"That makes two of us," Miller said.

"Make that three of us," Carmen said before he slipped on the steps leading into the house.

Moments later, they were all inside.

And all The Cleaner needed was a spark.

Three ... two ... one ...

Boom!

A fireball shot skyward from the explosion, nearly igniting the overhanging pine trees.

There's no way anyone survived that.

The Cleaner scrambled down from the tree, smiling the entire way.

He rushed to his motorcycle and waited until he had driven about an hour outside of the park before texting Ballard.

It's done

He pocketed his phone and kicked started his engine.

But I'm not done. I'm only getting started.

CHAPTER THIRTY-ONE

Bonjane, South Africa

Knox trudged outside, the bag of soccer balls slung over his shoulder. Makenzie kept pace, walking next to him and trying to keep his spirits up.

"It could be worse," Makenzie said.

"Worse?" Knox asked. "What's worse than flying halfway across the world, only to have the one person who could help you refuse."

"She could've immediately thrown us out of her house."

Knox sighed.

"That's one way to look at it."

He stepped in a mud hole and swore softly. Then he stopped and picked up a stick, attempting to clean off the bottom of his shoe.

"That about sums up my day so far," he said.

Knox jammed the stick between the treads on his shoe and was continuing to clear out the mud when he heard squeals of glee.

"What is happening?" Makenzie asked.

Knox looked up to see about two dozen children sprinting toward him, shouting something he couldn't quite understand. In a matter of seconds, the kids surrounded them and chanted, their hands raised in the air as if they were expecting him to give them something.

"What are they saying?" Makenzie asked.

"Oh," Knox said. "The soccer balls."

He knelt among the children and loosened the drawstring. One by one, he dug out the freshly pumped balls and handed them to the closest child. Each delivery resulted in a triumphant shout before the kid wormed his way out of the pack and into an open space. This process repeated until Knox was down to one ball.

He looked around at the hands all reaching for him before one child caught his eyes. He was shorter than the rest, his shirt torn, quarter-sized holes in the end of both of his smooth-bottomed sneakers.

"What's your name, little man?" Knox asked.

"Jabari," the boy said pointing to his chest, his expression serious.

Knox rubbed Jabari's head and handed him the last ball. Jabari's face melted into a wide grin before tucking the ball under his armpit and running to join the other children. Then Jabari stopped and turned around.

"*Dankie*," the boy said.

"He said thank you," one of the older boys said to Knox.

"Tell him he's welcome," Knox said as he stood.

The older boy relayed the message to Jabari who smiled, flashed the peace sign, and then dart off again, this time the ball on the ground at his feet.

Makenzie patted Knox on the back.

"Even if Emily decides not to help us, I gotta say that moment right there made this trip," she said.

"I still want the evidence. No, I *need* the evidence. But that was pretty neat."

One of the other older girls approached Makenzie.

"Your hair is so pretty," the girl said.

"Thank you," Makenzie said. "Your hair is pretty too."

"It's not golden like yours though," the girl said. "It's hard to wash our hair now in the river, because of the flooding."

"Has it been raining a lot?" Knox asked.

The girl nodded and then pointed to the horizon.

"There's more rain coming this afternoon."

Knox turned his attention back to the children playing. A game had formed, as one of the boys let everyone use his ball. In a matter of minutes, rudimentary construction of goals comprised of sticks were staked into the ground about eighty meters apart. One boy whistled loudly signifying the beginning of their match.

Knox then scanned the area for Jabari. After a few seconds, Knox saw him standing with his hands up between two teens, who were tossing the ball back and forth in the air over his head as he tried to grab for it. Knox shouted at them to stop teasing Jabari, but they didn't pay him any attention. A few seconds later, Jabari ran at one of the boys and sank his teeth into his leg. The boy screamed and shoved Jabari aside with one arm, flinging him to the ground. Then the boy picked the ball up and booted it toward the river.

Jabari shook his fist at the boy, who gestured like he was going to run at the little guy before walking away. Once Jabari realized his ball was in danger of going into the water, he ran after it as fast as his chubby legs could carry him.

That's when Knox noticed danger.

He glanced at his leg and then back at Jabari before breaking into a sprint.

Knox struggled to reach his usual top speed, the mud slowing him down. He raced through the middle of the pickup game, dodging kids as he kept his main focus on Jabari.

He doesn't see it.

However, that's when everyone else noticed the danger Jabari was heading toward. Plodding up the shore was a Nile crocodile. And it was only a few feet away from Jabari's soccer ball.

Everyone began shouting at Jabari, but he ignored them, his mission clear.

Knox drew closer with each step, his lungs burning as he pumped his arms. Jabari ran down a small hill and then tried to climb up to reach his ball. The crocodile whipped its tail back and forth as it lumbered toward Jabari.

He slipped and then fell back down the hill, his feet getting stuck in the mud. He lifted one leg and then the other, slowly freeing himself.

Knox took in the scene, each moment playing as if in slow motion. The crocodile, mouth spread wide, appeared to be closing in on its meal. Jabari continued his quest to reach his ball as the children yelled frantically at him. As Knox drew within a few feet of Jabari, he stretched out his arms and grabbing the boy by his shirt. The crocodile snapped at Jabari's dangling leg, but Knox pulled him away from the reptile, missing its toothy bite by mere inches.

However, Knox knew danger still persisted.

He scooped up Jabari, who started crying, and placed him on his hip. Behind them, the crocodile broke into a sprint. Knox zigged to his left and then zagged to his right, the croc nipping at his heels. Then in a last-ditch effort, the animal clamped onto Knox's prosthetic leg, but its teeth couldn't get any traction on the smooth surface, leaving it with nothing more than a mouthful of fabric.

Knox didn't stop running, though, racing back toward the house. As soon as he reached the rest of the children, the surrounded Jabari, hugging him tightly and celebrating. Knox turned around to see the crocodile slither back into the water.

He collapsed to the ground before getting mobbed again by the children. After a minute or so, the kids stepped aside as Jabari walked toward him, tears in his eyes.

"Ball," Jabari said, pointing toward the water.

Knox, choking back tears, pulled Jabari in close and gave him a hug.

"I'll get you another one, buddy."

Once the excitement subsided, Knox rose to his feet to find Makenzie staring at him, her arms folded across her chest as she shook her head.

"You're crazy," she said.

"Crazy good, I hope," he said with a wink.

"I'd describe him a different way," Emily said.

Both Knox and Makenzie turned around and found the

missionary woman standing with the piece of paper in one hand and a key in the other.

"Rangers lead the way, right?" Emily said with a faint smile on her lips.

Knox turned away and bent over, hands resting on his knees. He didn't say a word as he replayed the harrowing scene in his mind.

"Knox, you all right?" Emily asked.

He sighed and stood upright again, waving dismissively at her.

"You sure?" she persisted.

"It's—it's nothing. At least, nothing I want to talk about."

"Well, I'm here if you do," Emily said.

"Look," he said, "about before—"

"It's water over the dam," she said. "What I just saw right there, it tells me everything I need to know about you. You were trying to protect my feelings, weren't you? You didn't want to dredge up old memories, right?"

Knox nodded.

"Yet I jumped to conclusions," Emily said. "And that's why I'm giving this to you."

She held out the paper and the key.

"What's this?" he asked as he took the two objects.

"I decoded the note. It's an address and a number," she said. "If I had to guess, it'd be to a safe deposit box at a bank in Johannesburg. And this is a key that one of the missionaries found in an unopened letter that apparently arrived after Kyle went to the city. I'm just trying to put two and two together here, but I think this will get you in."

"Not if I'm not on the list of people able to open the safe deposit box."

Emily dug into her back pocket and produced a driver's license.

"You're close enough to Kyle that I think you could pass for him using this," she said. "If I thought I could get away to help, I would. But after watching you a few minutes ago, I'm sure you can solve any problem you run into. Just keep me posted on what happens, will you?"

"Thank you for trusting us," Knox said.

"Do you think someone could've been targeting my husband?" Emily asked.

"I don't know. But if they were, we'll find them. And then we'll make them pay."

She thanked them again and told them dinner was ready.

"One more thing," Knox said.

"Yes?"

"Why are you still here? I mean, your husband died senselessly in this country and you're far away from your family, who could help you raise all your children. And then you want to help people on top of that? I just don't understand."

"This is my home now," Emily said. "And these people, these kids, the ones like Jabari—they're my family now, too. I couldn't even imagine leaving."

Knox sighed and shook his head.

"Seems like you lead the way too, Emily."

CHAPTER THIRTY-TWO

Auburn, Virginia

Mark Moore's black Lexus LS 500h rumbled over the dirt road leading to Dumfries Gun Range, marked by a dilapidated wooden sign with faded paint. A trail of dust followed his vehicle. Upon noticing the cloud behind him, Moore cursed under his breath, irked that he'd just washed his car a few days before and would need to do it again.

He squinted as he looked ahead at the trailer that served as the outdoor range's headquarters.

"You finding it all right?" Ballard's voice boomed over the car's internal speakers.

"Yeah, I've found it," Moore said, "but you're going to owe me a car wash."

"How about a drink instead?" Ballard said.

"That'll be two you owe me."

"How do you figure? Ballard asked.

"One for driving an hour out here to the boondocks and another one for getting my car dirty."

"Let's just make it three and call it all good."

Moore grunted.

"I won't call it all good until Joe agrees."

"Oh, don't worry about that," Ballard said. "What else is he going to do? The man's life is ruined. We're doing him a big favor."

Moore parked in front of the trailer next to a pair of pickup trucks. There was a red BMW parked in the corner, far away from all the other vehicles.

Joe's here.

Moore grabbed his gun case as he got out of the car. He ambled up the rickety steps and entered the room. An A/C window unit strained to keep the area cool, while the smell of tobacco permeated the room. He quickly figured out why when he spotted the man behind the counter spitting into a plastic red cup, his bottom lip stuffed with snuff.

"You lost, mister?" the man asked.

Moore scowled and then realized he was still wearing his suit. Then he held up his gun case.

"I'm here to blow some stuff up," he said. "Thought this was the place to do it."

"Aww, I'm just messin' with ya," the man said, before spewing a stream of juice into the cup. "What can I do ya fer?"

"I want to shoot for about a half hour, maybe more."

"Take stall seven out there," the man said. "She's all ready, with a fresh target and everything. We'll settle up after you're done."

"Sounds like a plan."

Moore left the trailer and walked to the designated stall. He put all his equipment there and searched for Joe Garber. After scanning the area, he found Garber in the first stall, far away from the other two men shooting on the opposite side of the range. Moore walked to meet him.

Garber sported safety goggles and ear muffs for protection as he sighted in his target. He took a deep breath before easing his finger onto the trigger and squeezing it. The gun barely recoiled. Garber set it aside and then pulled out a pair of binoculars to see where he hit.

"Nice shot," Moore said.

Garber turned around slowly and sneered in disgust once he saw who it was.

"You have a lot of nerve coming out here to find me," he said.

"We had to make the story go away," Moore said. "But you're the one who became the story. And you only have yourself to blame."

Garber stood up, his jaw set.

"You told me nobody would ever find out I went to that camp," Garber said, as he poked Moore in the chest. "But you were wrong. I'm the one who did you a favor, but I have to suffer all the consequences."

"I understand you're upset, but I'm here to try and make it right," Moore said.

"Make it right? Did you not hear that I was forced to resign?"

"I heard."

"This isn't something I can come back from."

"I'm not the one who made you get all grabby hands with Erica Everhart," Moore said. "You did that all on your own."

"But why was she even there in the first place? How did she know where to find me?"

Moore shrugged.

"No idea. But it all worked out. She agreed to just drop the story in exchange for a better one."

"One of your bullshit stories, I'm sure," Garber said, turning aside and kicking at the dirt. "Who's going to lose a job this time?"

"Actually, I'm here to talk with you about a job opportunity."

"Me?" Garber said, hooking a thumb at himself. "You have a job for me? The same man who got me fired wants to hire me?"

"Again, technically, I didn't fire you or even pressure you to resign. You did that all on your own, after the incident."

"But it served your purpose, didn't it?"

"More or less, but let's forget about that."

"Forget about it?" Garber asked, his voice rising an octave. "You want me to forget about that sweet government pension I lost and all the other awesome perks that accompanied it?"

Moore unloosened his tie and rolled up his sleeves before holding out his hands.

"May I?" he asked, gesturing toward the gun.

"Whatever," Garber said, as he handed the weapon to Moore.

The senator eased into a prone position, unbothered by how dirty it was going to make him. He sighted in the target and fired a shot. The bullet ripped through the target, hitting it just upper left of center.

"Sometimes, Joe, you have to make adjustments to get everything how you want them," Moore said.

Garber studied the target through a pair of binoculars.

Moore exhaled slowly before squeezing off another shot, this time hitting the target directly in the center. He stood and handed the gun back to Garber.

"Nice shot," Garber said, his tone begrudging.

"It's sometimes a painful process, but it's satisfying when everything comes together and you hit the bullseye."

"Okay, so, what's this job you have for me?" Garber asked.

"We want you to oversee the lab."

Garber's eyes bulged.

"Are you kidding me?"

"I'm dead serious."

"Have you forgotten that I've seen what that thing can do to people? I mean, I went there, saw it up close and personal."

Moore nodded.

"Making you the perfect person for the job. You've seen it, you aren't scared of it, and you might even be immune to it."

"Immune to it? You gave me something to protect me against it, didn't you?"

"Placebos," Moore said. "And apparently, it didn't matter, since you have some sort of natural immunity."

"I swear to god, if you—"

"We'll pay you triple what you were making at your old position," Moore said, cutting off Garber before he could finish his threat.

"Triple? From what I was making before?"

Moore nodded.

"That's what I said, isn't it?"

"Yeah, but I wanted to make sure I heard you right," Garber said, his mind still processing the offer. "So, let's say I take it, what exactly do you want me to do?"

"Keep it all a secret, and make sure everyone working for you doesn't breathe a word about it. Think you can do that?"

Garber nodded.

"Good," Moore said. "We want to get you up to speed right away. Because there's a lot you need to know about the latest generation. We were able to speed up the timetable, so we can get desired results within two weeks."

"Two weeks? Patience never was one of your virtues, was it?"

"I'm more of a man of vice than virtues," Moore said.

Garber drew in a deep breath and exhaled slowly.

"You drive a hard bargain, Mark. But what do I have to lose?"

"Not much," Moore said. "But you'll have everything to gain very soon, especially when I become president. I never forget those who help me."

"You're running for president? Since when?"

Moore looked around the range before putting a finger to his lips and looking at Garber.

"Not so loud," he said. "I want my announcement to be a surprise. And I have a grand way of making it."

"Whatever you say, boss," Garber said. "You pay me three times what I was making, and I'll keep a thousand secrets for you."

Moore smiled and put a hand on Garber's shoulder before giving it a squeeze.

"That's exactly what I wanted to hear."

CHAPTER THIRTY-THREE

Johannesburg, South Africa

Knox shifted in his seat and adjusted his tie as he sat across from the Standard Bank clerk, whose eyes shifted between Kyle Canfield's ID and the man in front of him. To Knox, the verification of his identity seemed to last several minutes, though it only took seconds—fifteen uncomfortable seconds. Knox fought the urge to scratch all over, the culprit being the cheap wool suit he and Makenzie had purchased at a second-hand haberdashery just hours earlier.

"So, you're a man of the cloth," the clerk said, as he mopped his brow with a handkerchief.

"More or less," Knox said, unsure of how to respond.

"That's what it says here on my form," the clerk said. "Has that changed?"

"I'm a missionary."

Knox felt a twinge in his conscience. Something about pretending to be a preacher or a missionary felt inherently wrong.

I'll definitely need to confess this to a priest at some point.

"I see," the man said, as he furrowed his brow. "Any other changes I need to know about? Is your address still the same?"

"No other changes to report."

"So, just to confirm, what's your address?"

Knox looked the man in the eye and recited the information he'd committed to memory in preparation for the encounter.

"Very well then," he said. "Let me get my key, and I'll get you access."

Makenzie's voice came through the earbud connected to his phone.

"You're doing great. Keep it up."

"Thank you," Knox said, responding to both the man and Makenzie at once.

After a few tense minutes, the man returned with a key and held it up.

"Shall we?" he said, gesturing toward the door.

Knox followed the man to the elevators before they descended two floors to an underground vault. A woman in a silver sequined dress greeted them with a tray containing a single glass of champagne.

"For you to relax while you're down here," she said.

Knox waved her off. "No thank you."

"We won't tell," the woman said, with an exaggerated wink. "Please, I insist."

"Complimentary champagne," the clerk said. "It's all part of our world class service here at Standard Bank."

Knox relented and accepted the glass, taking a short swig and forcing a smile.

"Happy?" Knox asked.

"I'm happy if you're happy," she said.

The clerk then gestured toward a room with an open vault. Inside, dozens of safe deposit boxes lined the outer wall. In the center of the room were four marble tables that clients could use to inspect and organize their belongings. The clerk walked over to Kyle's box, inserted his key, and waited for Knox to do the same. Once he did, the clerk excused himself and told Knox that he would be waiting outside until he was finished.

Knox opened his laptop on one of the tables, giving it time to wake up. Then he peered into the box.

The first thing he saw was a note. Knox immediately recognized the handwriting as Chaos's and scanned it.

Kyle,

If something happens to me, everything you need to know about the people who did this are contained on these files. It should be enough to expose them, but you need to make a copy of this, take it to someone you trust, and hopefully they'll be able to shut down whatever happened at this village in the Congo. Ever since we uncovered this village, I've had nightmares and am unable to sleep. So, beware. The footage is gruesome, but it shows who is behind it. Also, one of the men was adamant about giving me the piece of paper that's sealed in an envelope, even as our men shot him and he was dying. Whatever you do, don't get involved yourself. Just give it to the right people who can get justice for everyone in that village.

I love you, man!

Kev

Knox opened the envelope and took a picture of both sides before returning it. Then he removed the flash drive and inserted it into his laptop, creating a new folder and copying all the files from the device. When he was finished, he returned everything as he'd found it and notified the clerk. They relocked the box together and ascended to the main floor. Knox thanked the man for his help before walking back to the car where Makenzie was waiting.

"Did you get everything?" she asked.

"Got it all."

"But you didn't look at it?"

"I thought it was something we ought to do together."

Once they returned to their hotel room, Knox and Makenzie sat down at the desk and fired up the laptop. The files were organized by date with one labeled "village encounter" at the top.

"Guess we're starting here," Knox said.

He clicked on the file and a video opened on the screen, the date —just over a year ago to the day—affixed in the upper right corner. Chaos held the camera at arm's length and began narrating.

"This is First Lieutenant Kevin Canfield," he said, draped in head to toe in a hazmat suit, "and we're about to enter the village of Tango, in more or less the middle of the Congo. Our platoon was sent here today to address an outbreak of a contagion. Apparently, this partic-ular virus makes people go mad, subjecting them to wild hallucina-tions. We've been tasked with quarantining the area and ensuring that no one tries to escape. If anyone leaves here, they could spread this deadly virus to others—and we're going to make sure that doesn't happen, as unpleasant as it might be for us."

Chaos's first-person narration in real time captured his range of emotions, at first a determined can-do attitude before morphing into something else.

"Please remain calm, everyone," Chaos shouted, as images of a small dusty road leading into a primitive village rolled across the screen.

As he moved into the village, he panned the camera from side to side searching for any movement. Instead of finding resistant people —he found almost no one. At least, almost no one who was alive.

Dead bodies were strewn across the ground, some lying face down in the dirt, others sitting in chairs as if they had just been waiting to die. Chaos's platoon cleared the streets, dragging the bodies into huts. They rushed about, looking for any signs of life. Nothing.

Then a few minutes later, one of the other men called for Chaos. The camera shook as he ran to his fellow Ranger. Chaos ran around the side of the building and found a white man slumped against the wall. He looked like an American based on his clothing and appearance.

"Who are you?" Chaos asked. "And what happened here?"

The young man, who appeared to be no older than twenty-two or twenty-three, struggled to raise his hand up.

"Wa—ter," the man said."I—need—water."

"Get this man some water," Chaos barked.

One of the other soldiers handed the man a canteen. He barely had the strength to hold it up, requiring assistance from the other soldier to pour it into his mouth.

"Don't drink out of that again," Chaos said in a hushed tone to the soldier.

Then Chaos knelt next to the man.

"You look American. How'd you end up here? How'd you end up like this?"

The man nodded. "Get Senator Moore. Tell him—tell him I love him."

At that moment, another man approached them, also wearing a hazmat suit.

"Lieutenant Canfield, you got this under control?" the man asked.

"Of course, sir. But would you mind telling me what the hell happened here?"

"All you need to know is that there was an outbreak and we're working to contain it," the man said.

Then he handed the young man a pistol.

"What are you doing?" Chaos asked.

"This man's insides are nearly boiling. We'll never be able to save him, but he won't die for another three days or so. The compassionate thing to do is let him end it now."

The camera, which was focused on the man — who was indistinguishable with his helmet on —shook as a gunshot erupted. Chaos panned down to the young man, now lying on the ground, blood pooling around his head.

"Shit, man," Chaos said, his voice quaking. "Couldn't we have done something for him?"

The man shook his head.

"We did. We let him die with dignity—and also alleviated fears that he would spread this disease to someone else."

"Really? Is that what we're doing?"

"What were your instructions, lieutenant?"

"To make sure no one left, which is different than killing everyone."

The man cocked his head to one side.

"Not really. Now follow your orders."

Chaos seemed like he wasn't sure he was doing the right thing. But after a few minutes of gentle persuasion from the man, Chaos resumed scanning the village. They were almost done when they found another man in a hazmat suit running toward them with a piece of paper in his hand.

"Take this," the man said. "It's the formula for an antidote."

Chaos drew his weapon.

"Who are you?"

"I'm as good as dead—and you will be too, unless you take this antidote."

Chaos pocketed the paper. "I have so many questions."

"I'm sure you do."

Before Chaos could ask one, the man staggered backward, bullets peppering his chest. He fell backward, likely dead before he hit the ground.

"What was that for?" Chaos asked, as he turned, pointing his camera at the mystery man.

"The directive was clear, Lieutenant Canfield, was it not?"

"Yeah," Chaos said. "What's the harm in talking with him for a little bit? He seemed protected. I'm protected."

"As you can see, this isn't something to take lightly. Now, follow orders or I'll replace you with someone who will."

The camera glitched and then faded to black.

.   .   .

Knox pushed his chair away from the table and stood, huffing out a breath through puffed cheeks.

"What was *that*?" Makenzie asked.

"Hell if I know," Knox said. "But I can promise you that we're going to find out."

Then Knox closed his eyes, pinching the bridge of his nose as he grimaced in pain.

"Hey, man, you don't look so good," Makenzie said. "Are you all right?"

"I think I just need to sit down," Knox said.

He aimed to sit down on the end of the bed and missed, collapsing in a heap on the floor.

"Talk to me, Knox," Makenzie said, slapping his face.

Knox's eyes fluttered open before the closed shut again, the world fading to black.

CHAPTER THIRTY-FOUR

CDC Headquarters | Atlanta, Georgia

Violet Warren tapped her pen on her desk as she scanned the printout one of her research assistants had just handed her. As director of the Center for Forecasting and Outbreak Analytics—or the CFA, as it was known internally—Warren kept a sharp eye on new contagions and old ones alike. She had helped mitigate her share of contagions in Europe and the U.S., but she always held her breath when she saw numbers of a reported disease pouring in from African countries. Without as robust of a reporting system, she banked on the numbers always being four or five times as worse than what she was told they were.

After the global pandemic, she took over a beleaguered department and staffed it with some of the most conscientious scientists available, researchers who preferred to find solutions to medical problems rather than score political points for either side of the aisle. Almost overnight, she'd become one of the most trusted names in the virology field, expressing the tenets of her convictions to a reporter for *Time* magazine. Memes about her filled thousands of timelines on social media, though she remained oblivious, singularly focused on her work—preventing another global outbreak before it started.

As she scanned the report, she ticked off the usual suspects she always kept an eye on—dengue fever, malaria, measles. But then there was another one she watched closely. Every time she saw a zero next to weekly reported incidents, she breathed a sigh of relief. The Incaendium virus was one of the worst she'd ever see, both for the excruciating way in which the victims died as well as the sneaky way it spread.

Once a person contracted the virus, their digestive system began to heat up, pushing their internal temperature up one degree every couple of days. Victims contracted the virus through airborne particulates, expunged through normal breathing. However, it could take up to twenty-four hours before they became contagious. Most subjects admitted they didn't recognize they were sick for about forty-eight hours after coming in contact with another infected person. But even then, they said they didn't feel very sick, at least not sick enough to visit the hospital.

The Incaendium virus appeared to be problematic for Warren on many fronts, starting with the lack of funding for it. Her team had managed to isolate this virus, but the antidote her colleagues at the CDC developed wasn't as successful as they'd hoped it would be. Only about forty percent fully recovered, while another forty percent had long term effects. The other twenty percent succumbed to the disease.

What she also found puzzling was the lack of information regarding the virus's origins. And while the Incaendium virus hadn't been overly worrying to most high-level officials at the CDC, she foresaw an outbreak resulting in far more deaths than any global outbreaks in the past hundred and fifty years. Warren wanted to know where it came from and how it began infecting the first few subjects, if they could even trace that at this point. She was thankful that it hadn't resulted in anything serious, save a few articles in medical journals that warned a new outbreak could be on the horizon. But along with ineffectiveness of the antidote, what also worried her was the instability of a vaccine her team developed, though it had yet to be mass tested. Vaccines would spoil beneath the warm African sun if sent to doctors in primitive areas, rendering the cure useless, and only had a shelf-life of a couple of weeks. The titans of the pharmaceutical industry couldn't meet the potential demand if an outbreak swept across the globe.

These were the details that kept Warren up at night. They were also the details that made her the best in her field.

She kicked her feet up on her desk and squeezed a pink stress ball as she continued to scan the numbers.

I might just have a good week after all.

Just as she was about to go to lunch, her desk phone rang. She answered it and greeted one of her assistants, exchanging pleasantries.

"You asked me to contact you if we had any more of the Incaendium virus reports," he said.

"That's right," she said. "Did you find something?"

"Yeah, we've got one in Johannesburg, just a few hours ago. It didn't come in over the usual channels, which is kind of odd, but we still got it."

"Send over our protocol packet with recommendations on mitigation and isolation," Warren said. "The last thing anybody wants is an outbreak of Incaendium."

"Got it," he said,before he hung up.

She flung her stress ball at the wall and growled.

Just when I thought it was gonna be an easy week—

She snatched up her cell phone and dialed a number.

"Colonel Ballard?"

"Hi, Dr. Warren," Ballard said. "What've you got for me?"

"You told me to notify you immediately if we came across anyone contracting Incaendium virus in Africa."

"Well," he said. "Don't keep me waiting."

"We've got one," she said. "Just came through."

"Where at?"

"A hospital in Johannesburg," Warren said. "I'll send you all the details."

He thanked her and then hung up, leaving her wondering why he wanted all that information.

What's he *going to do with it?*

Warren picked up the report and kept reading before she quickly put it down again. She couldn't concentrate. She had a bad feeling about Incaendium—and she couldn't shake it. Or maybe it was about Col. Ballard. She couldn't quite tell the difference any more.

Warren just knew whatever was happening, it wasn't good.

CHAPTER THIRTY-FIVE

Kinshasa, Democratic Republic of Congo

Erica Everhart jammed her suitcase into the overhead bin above her seat and squeezed past two men dressed in suits to reach her window seat. She sat down and looked out the window before slipping in her earbuds and listening to some Steely Dan, which was one of Quinn's favorite bands. Although she understood the challenge ahead of her in uncovering the mystery of what she'd just observed in the Congolese village, she was ready to do whatever it took to write the story of a lifetime. It'd be the best way to honor Quinn, whose death was also something she planned to investigate.

Erica removed her earbuds to listen as the Brussels Airlines flight attendants went over the safety instructions before the plane started to taxi. They explained that once the jet reached three thousand kilometers, passengers would be able to use the inflight wi-fi.

"For a small fee, of course," the flight attendant said.

"*Of course*," grunted the man in the middle seat.

Erica offered a thin smile and re-inserted her earbuds.

As the jet lurched skyward, she closed her eyes and mentally organized all the things she'd gleaned in her short visit to the Congo. Without Quinn visiting her at *The Post*, she never would've even known about the troubling trend of Peace Corps teams being evacuated in hotspots that had viral outbreaks. If what she saw in the Congo had been repeated elsewhere, something nefarious was going on, though she didn't know by who or how.

NocturaCorp was a good place to start, a company she'd never heard of. Then there was the disease itself. *What* was it? How contagious was it? Had the whole village been quarantined, and it just didn't spread? Had it spread to animals, or were they shot before they could be infected and then devoured over time? The fact that it had yet to be cleaned up was also interesting. Why would they just leave dead bodies lying around—for over a year?

Erica couldn't wait to discuss this story with Langston. Even without him weighing in, she knew this had all the hallmarks of a Pulitzer Prize winner. International connections. Governments conspiring to suppress the details. A deadly virus. An obvious outbreak. A poor country with poor victims who had no voice. And a dead senator's son.

That last one really stumped her.

Of all the people who could do something about this, Senator Moore could. But why didn't he? Was he being lied to as well? Or, even more disturbing, was he involved in some way? Was it an experiment gone wrong? And if so, why hadn't he gotten his son out?

More questions abounded as she considered all the different elements to the story. It'd take her weeks to sort through them all. But it'd be worth it, if anything for the sake of the truth.

The plane continued its ascent to thirty thousand feet as the flight attendants began moving down the aisles of the cabin, taking drink orders and handing out tasteless snacks. The man in the seat next to her eyed her package of pretzels that had remained unopened for ten minutes as she thumbed out some notes to herself on her phone before finally asking her for them.

"Of course," she said. "I ate a big meal before I got on the plane."

The lie tumbled out of her mouth so easily. She wasn't sure why she made up a story. The truth was her stomach was grumbling, and her fellow passengers had to hear it. But she didn't want to hurt his feelings, as if her lack of hunger would make him feel better about eating a stranger's discarded snack. She considered correcting herself, but then decided that would be even more embarrassing.

Who lies about such a thing?

Erica posited the question to herself as she spent much of day going over the notes from her interview subjects.

Her mind drifted back to the story she had looming. In this one, there were no competing narratives, just a dominant one that nobody was sharing.

Once the flight attendants announced that the inflight wi-fi was working, she wrote a brief email to Langston, sharing her major discoveries in bullet-point fashion. While Langston was old school and never showed much emotion, she figured if it was possible to move his needle, this story would do it.

Ten minutes passed. Then twenty, thirty, an hour. But no reply from Langston.

Maybe he's not in the office yet.

Then she did some quick math, calculating what time it was in Washington. He should've been in at least two hours earlier. Erica considered all the other reasons why—a meeting, a doctor's appointment, a last-minute vacation day.

I know what will get his attention.

She selected one of the videos from her phone, edited it down, and sent it in a text message to Langston.

Another fifteen minutes, half-hour, hour—still no reply.

She decided not to worry about it anymore and pulled out her laptop to better organize her thoughts regarding the story. She'd finished just as the plane descended into Brussels for a layover and flight attendants issued warnings everyone to put away their large electronic devices. She complied and closed her eyes.

"You working on a novel?" the man next to her asked.

"Maybe," she said. "Though I'm not sure how plausible it all sounds."

"If I were you, I'd stick to writing non-fiction," he said. "There's no denying that the truth really is stranger than fiction."

If only you knew.

~

After an uneventful second leg of her flight, Brussels Airlines flight 9903 touched down at Dulles International Airport. Erica gathered her belongings and exited through the jetway. She couldn't wait to get started, despite the exhaustion that had set in over the last part of her flight.

However, that excitement all but vanished when she presented her customs form and passport to an agent at a kiosk. He examined her documents for a moment before picking up his phone and dialing a number. Seconds later, he spoke in a hushed tone, his glass encasement making it difficult for her to hear what he said.

"Just one moment, Miss Everhart," he said after hanging up.

"What's the matter?" she asked. "Did I do something wrong?"

"I'm not privy to the issue here," he said. "But I just have a note to contact my superiors once you returned to the U.S."

"This is ridiculous," she said. "I demand to know what's going on here."

"Demand all you want, but it's not going to change the fact that he's on his way over here to meet with you and get you squared away. He should be able to tell you what's wrong."

"*Should? Should?* He better answer every damn thing I ask him."

"Hey, okay, lady," the customs agent said. "That's enough. Please keep your cool. I'm sure we'll be able to sort this all out with a calm conversation. Agreed?"

Erica hoped that was the case, but she'd been trapped in a tin tube at thirty thousand feet above the earth for well over half of the last day, her mind gravitating toward worst-case scenarios. With lack of sleep and plenty of time to think, she'd concocted a slew of conspiracy theories, most of which she hoped wasn't true.

Before she could spiral any deeper, a portly man with a handlebar mustache waddled up to her. He pursed his lips as he looked her up and down.

"I didn't have 'dealing with a deranged hot woman' on my bingo card today, but it's Monday," he said.

"Sir," Erica said, her tone sharp, "would you mind explaining to me what's going on? Why am I being detained?"

"In a minute," he said. "Please follow me."

The man led her back to a small room off to the side of the agents' stations. He gestured toward a chair and suggested she take a seat.

"I'd rather stand," she said.

"Suit yourself," he said. "Be right back."

But there was something about how he said it that didn't give Erica any confidence she'd ever see the man again—or that he wanted to see her either.

A few minutes later, she heard a knock at the door. It slowly opened, not waiting for her reply. More of a courtesy knock announcing a new entrant.

She spun around and stared at the figure in the doorway. Her mouth fell agape as she sat down, unable to stand.

"Erica, we need to talk."

CHAPTER THIRTY-SIX

Johannesburg, South Africa

Knox opened his eyes, the smell of chlorine overwhelming his senses while the rhythmic beeping of a heart monitor pierced his ears. He glanced down at the crook in his right arm where an IV port pumped fluids into him. As he sat up, he searched for a familiar face, any face. But no windows to the outside world, no attending nurses, no signs of life anywhere.

Knox's head hurt, the pain both persistent and dull. He tried to remember what had happened. The bank, Makenzie, the footage at the hotel and then—he closed his eyes and tried to recall his steps, but he couldn't. Like a movie abruptly ending, his memories ended right there.

How did I end up here?

He decided to climb out of bed and get some answers. The only problem was he couldn't. His left arm was handcuffed to the bed.

What the hell is this?

He yanked on the cuffs, hoping to break free. But the chains clattered against the metal railing. A few moments later the door opened, revealing a man dressed in a hazmat suit. With a clipboard in hand, he shuffled into the room.

"Mr. Knox," the man began, his voice sounding almost robotic as it was relayed through a speaker on the outside of his helmet. "I'm sure you're wondering how you ended up here."

Knox didn't blink, eyeing the man closely and remaining silent.

"A few hours ago, you had an incident in your hospital room, and it appears that you've contracted the Incaendium virus. As a result, we've placed you in quarantine."

"I'm sorry," Knox said. "The *what* virus?"

"The Incaendium virus," the man said. "It's a relatively new virus that results in death in about twenty percent of the cases. It's also highly contagious. So, I'm sure you understand the extra precautions we're taking here."

"Are you my attending doctor?" Knox asked.

The man shook his head.

"My name is Dan Riffle, and I'm with the U.S. State Department," he said. "The CDC is monitoring reports of anyone contracting the Incaendium virus and being proactive about it. I've been instructed to transport you back to the U.S. as part of a medical evacuation. You'll be taken to Atlanta, where you'll be held under observation at a CDC research facility."

"Is there an antidote?"

Riffle nodded.

"There is, but unfortunately there isn't any here. It's only been produced in small quantities and is difficult to manufacture here. Since it's so rare and doesn't keep long, there aren't any available."

"So, my only option is to return home?" Knox asked.

"If you want to live," Riffle said. "Otherwise, you might very well die right here in this room."

"But I feel fine."

"That's why this virus is so deadly. Most people don't know they have it until it's too late, kind of like putting a frog in water and slowly boiling it."

"I don't like the sound of that."

"Exactly. Now, I have an emergency medical flight waiting to take you and your friend to Atlanta. I just have a few papers for you to sign, if you don't mind."

Knox looked at the documents, stalling as he searched the room for a way out. There was something about Riffle that he didn't trust.

"Why Atlanta?" Knox asked.

"The CDC is heading up this research in the disease's early stages."

"And my friend—does she have Incan—Incadium—In-"

"Incaendium," Riffle corrected. "But she appears to be fine. We just had to isolate her to make sure. So, she's also in quarantine. Her blood tests were negative, but we want to keep her under observation out of an abundance of caution. Now, would you mind signing these papers for me?"

Riffle held out a pen with the clipboard.

"The CDC is anxious to run some diagnostics on you," he said.

I bet they are.

Something felt off about Riffle. The explanation felt stiff, rehearsed even. Why was Riffle the first person to speak with him instead of a doctor? Then there was the fact that Knox had never heard anything about this virus. Not that he was that immersed in the world of virology, but Knox figured he would've heard about something this dangerous at least once.

The merchants of scaremongering would've been all over this story. It would've been on television for a week straight at least.

There also something about Riffle, the way he moved, the way he talked. He was trying to mask his anxiety. But why? Was he scared of getting the disease? Or was he afraid of something else? Maybe *someone* else?

Knox concluded that if his suspicions about Riffle weren't true, he needed some other viable explanation. What else would've caused him to pass out? Then he remembered.

The champagne at the bank.

Had Ballard been tracking him somehow, hoping that he would find the footage and get access to it?

Giving Ballard the footage was part of the deal—or was he worried that I might watch it and change my mind?

Knox couldn't be certain, but he knew one thing: if he caught the virus, there had to be an outbreak. And if there was an outbreak, everyone would've been talking about it.

"Mr. Knox," Riffle said again, tapping the clipboard with a pen, "your signature?"

Knox's left hand pulled against the railing, demonstrating how the handcuff restricted his movement.

"I'd love to help, but unless you can get me out of these handcuffs here, I can't sign anything," Knox said.

"You're a lefty?"

"Yeah, which is why it really sucked when I lost my left leg. Now I look like that uncoordinated kid wearing a headgear and glasses from gym class who couldn't ever get a ball in play during a game of kickball. But I've still got my left hand, which works a lot better when I'm not chained to the bed."

"I'm really sorry about that," Riffle said. "This is really for your safety as much as it is for ours."

Knox forced a smile and nodded.

"I get it," he said.

Riffle reached over and unlocked Knox before handing him a pen.

Knox clicked the pen a couple of times, casting furtive glances up at Riffle before looking down at the paper.

"Where do you want me to sign?" Knox asked.

"Right *there*," Riffle said, pointing to a blank line on the paper with an "x" next to it.

When he did, Knox grabbed Riffle's arm and yanked hard, catching the State Department official off guard. Pulled face-first toward the bed, Riffle didn't have enough time to react before his face was shoved deep into the mattress. Then Knox took the pen and drove it through the thin elastic band at the bottom of Riffle's helmet and into his neck. Riffle's hands instinctively reached for the wound, rendering him unable to fend off the attack. Knox scrambled to his feet and then drove his knee into the back of Riffle's right arm, pinning him to the bed. He screamed in agony. Knox slapped the handcuffs on Riffle and squeezed. Riffle yelped again, this time unable to effectively fight back.

"You can stop the charade," Knox said. "I'm not going to die— and I know it. And you're not going to die either. Maybe that's something you should've considered before you tried to kill me."

"Look, Mr. Knox," Riffle's eyes widening as he sought the words to explain what had happened. "You see, I was just—"

Knox wasn't interested. He detached the helmet from Riffle's hazmat suit before delivering a forearm shiver to his head and knocking him out. His body collapsed as he sank to the floor, only his arm remaining extended upward, still hitched to the bed frame.

"Sorry to do this to you, buddy," Knox said aloud before pausing. "Nah, who am I kidding? This was an absolute joy. And I'd do it again, if given the chance."

Knox quickly changed, putting himself in Riffle's suit before rolling the State Department lackey into the bed and arranging the sheets over him. For good measure, Knox rammed a needle into Riffle's arm and created a port. A few seconds later, morphine was coursing through Riffle's blood. Knox inspected the wound, which wasn't all that deep and had almost stopped bleeding.

You'll live.

Knox pocketed the certificate for the emergency medical flight before grabbing Riffle's security card and key fob. He poked his head out of the makeshift hospital room and looked in both directions down the hallway. It was nearly empty, a lone nurse marching down the hall in the opposite direction. He eased into the corridor and rushed over to the door across from his room.

Knox strode inside and found Makenzie.

"I don't know what's going on, but I want some—" she said before stopping and taking a breath.

Knox put a finger to his helmet in a gesture to silence her. She cocked her head to one side and wrinkled her nose.

"Knox?" she asked, in a hushed tone.

"We don't have a second to spare, Kinz. We need to go now."

"But how did you—"

"I'll explain everything later," he said, unlatching her cuffs.

"This ought to be good," she said, rubbing her wrists.

"Do you still have the flash drive?"

She patted her left pocket.

"Got it right here," she said.

"Good. Now just lay down and close your eyes—and follow my lead."

After she followed his instructions, Knox wheeled the bed out of the room and down the hallway. He kept thinking that each moment would be the time when everyone realized what was happening. But they didn't, carrying on business as usual.

On their way to the underground garage, Knox removed the suit in the elevator before stuffing it in a trashcan just outside. He held up the key fob and pressed a button, straining to hear a faint beep. After pushing it again, they identified the vehicle and sprinted to it. In a matter of minutes, they were driving to the airport in Riffle's car.

"What now?" she asked. "I thought you were infected."

"That's what they wanted me to think," he said. "And, evidently, you too. But I could see right through their ruse."

"So, what now?" she asked. "Do you have a plan?"

"Of course."

"You're not seriously thinking of going back to Washington, are you?"

Knox didn't say anything.

"Oh, come, Knox. You can't go back. As soon as you touch down in Washington, they're going to arrest you."

"They're sending me to Atlanta," he said. "And they'll *try* to arrest me. But I have a plan."

"Care to let me in on it?"

"Yeah," Knox said. "And it starts with getting Rico to Washington with you."

"You really have lost it," she said.

"No, this is how we're going to turn the tables on them and expose their plan, just as soon as we find out who *they* are."

"And who's going to help you expose them?"

"Remember the video?" he asked.

She nodded.

"We're going to start with Senator Moore," he said. "We're going to tell him what really happened to his son. I'm sure he'll want to help."

CHAPTER THIRTY-SEVEN

Atlanta, Georgia

With the glass inside Knox's helmet mostly fogged up, he could barely see the vast green canopy of trees blanketing the Atlanta landscape in between highways and interstates swirling around the city like concrete ribbons. Seeing anything challenged Knox, who couldn't wait to get off the plane and end the charade that he had contracted a virus. Even without an antidote, he felt fine, signaling that his hunch had been proven correct. But he knew there was some kind of virus. The video footage of the village in the Congo showed that much was true. But just how deadly it was and how it spread—and why an entire village was seemingly sacrificed—were all valid questions, with answers that wouldn't be surrendered easily.

The bigger concern Knox had was how he'd be greeted on the ground. By the time they touched down in just a matter of minutes, word about what Knox did would have reached Ballard's desk. Would he arrest Knox? Immediately take him to prison? Interrogate him? Torture him? Kill him?

Guess I'll find out soon enough.

The medical personnel attending to Knox during the flight told him to keep his helmet on until someone removed it for him. Then they opened the door.

Knox exited first and was greeted by two doctors and Col. Ballard, all dressed in hazmat suits. Ballard spoke first.

"Please accept my sincere apology about this," Ballard said. "If I would've thought for even a minute that completing the rest of your assignment would've resulted in this, I would've insisted that you come home immediately."

"Colonel, you can drop the act," Knox said. "I'm fine."

"I doubt that," one of the doctors said. "We've seen the results of your blood work."

"But I feel great," Knox said.

"That's because the virus doesn't show any effects until between twenty-four and forty-eight hours," Ballard said. "But you're about to experience some incredible pain if we don't get you the antidote soon."

Knox couldn't read Ballard's expression, but he sounded sincere.

"Look, about LAX—"

"Forget about it," Ballard said. "I know you were just trying to complete the assignment. I understand you have plenty of questions, so I'll fill you in once you get treated."

"And Johannesburg, too," Knox said. "I didn't exactly treat that State Department official with proper respect."

Ballard arched an eyebrow. "That's one way of putting it. But let's let bygones be bygones, okay. You're here, and we're going to get you all better, even if you think you feel fine right now."

Ballard ushered Knox into a van, which transported them to the CDC's headquarters. During the ride, Knox felt light-headed. He started wondering if he was wrong about the virus—and how he could've been so arrogant.

Did I infect Makenzie?

Knox didn't think he could live with himself if he had. But he couldn't communicate with her now anyway. His phone was with the rest of his belongings, secured in a bag before he left on his medical flight. He eyed it, but couldn't reach it. Even if he did, he wouldn't be able to text her, at least not without Ballard knowing what he wrote.

When did I get this? Where did I get this?

Knox could only figure that he got it while going through the materials stored in the safety deposit box. But wasn't this virus airborne? Or at least, that's what doctors believed? Could it be contracted in other ways, too?

How did I get this all so wrong?

An incident response team all outfitted in protective gear whisked Knox into a building and into a quarantine room. The door hissed as it opened, revealing a decontamination chamber that sprayed the outside of his suit with a mist before another door opened and led to the room. The CDC personnel all followed the same protocol, one by one, until everyone had reassembled inside with Knox.

A few personnel removed Knox's suit before hooking him up to a device that monitored his vitals. Once that was finished, everyone left the room except for one doctor.

"Mr. Knox," the woman said, "my name is Dr. Violet Warren. I want you to know first and foremost that I'm here to help you get better and make sure that you don't spread the Incaendium virus to anyone else. It's incredibly contagious, not to mention dangerous."

"But you'll be able to cure me?"

"I believe so," she said. "We have an antidote that I'll administer in just a moment. Then we can discuss what everything should look like. I just need to take some blood samples first. Are you okay with that?"

"I'm fine with anything that gets me better."

"Perfect," she said, before taking a tray off a nearby counter and prepping his arm for the simple procedure.

"So, where do you think you got this virus?" she asked.

"I don't know," he said. "One minute I was in a bank in Johannesburg, and maybe twenty minutes later I was in my hotel room, and just collapsed. I don't remember much of anything after that."

"And that was it?" she asked. "You didn't go anywhere?"

"I'd been in a small village before I went to Johannesburg, but that was well over forty-eight hours ago, maybe seventy-two. I don't know."

"But you didn't feel anything before you collapsed?"

"No. It was weird, though. Felt like I did when I didn't eat enough and was really exerting a lot of energy."

"What kind of work do you do?" she asked as she jammed a needle into his arm.

Knox wasn't sure what to tell her. He paused for a moment to consider how to respond while watching the blood travel through the rubber tube and into a vial.

"Anything to do with adventure," he said, hoping that would satisfy her curiosity.

She glanced at his leg.

"Were you chasing adventure when you lost your leg?"

Knox offered a thin smile. "You might say that."

"Well, you have to be careful out there. And make sure you eat enough, too. But we'll get you back out there in no time, once we confirm that you've cleared the virus."

"That's it?" he asked.

"You'll have to come back for periodic checkups as we monitor you for any type of internal damage," she said. "But based on what we've observed so far, in a limited number of cases, you should be fine."

"Are you going to give me the antidote now?" he asked.

"I'm going to look at your blood samples one final time before we do that. But since you aren't presenting yet, we have some time, although maybe not much of it."

She gathered all the needles and vials and other material before placing the trash in a hazardous waste bag.

"I'll be back to check on you as soon as I get these results back from the lab," she said. "In the meantime, just rest."

Knox thanked her before leaning back on the bed and relaxing, his fingers interlocked and behind his head. He stared at the ceiling and tried to make sense of everything.

Where did I contract the virus?

Then his thoughts drifted toward Makenzie. He wondered if she was okay, wanting to contact her and find out what she was doing, how she was doing. But if he reached out to her on his phone, it could put her at risk. She also could be starting a global pandemic, a twenty-first century Typhoid Mary. Before he could determine how to proceed, the door hissed as it opened. Ballard strode in wearing a hazmat suit and clutching a file folder.

"I understand you've received the antidote," Ballard said. "I'm sure you're relieved."

"Not yet," Knox said. "Just a little bit of preliminary blood testing first."

"But you will soon?"

"That's my understanding."

"Good," Ballard said. "In that case, we have something to discuss."

"Such as?"

"The whereabouts of your friend.?"

"My friend?"

"Your pilot friend who was with you," Ballard said. "We need to speak with her."

"Is she infected?"

Ballard shook his head.

"All her preliminary tests came back negative, but we still need to talk with her."

"She doesn't know anything. Just leave her out of it."

"If she was with you, she knows more than she should."

"And what do you think she knows?" Knox asked.

"Cut the bullshit, Knox. I told you to leave the evidence alone, but you refused. They warned me that you'd be like this, but I didn't listen."

"Who warned you about me?"

Ballard waved dismissively.

"Doesn't matter. The point is I told you to come back after you killed Rico, but you ignored me. You couldn't leave it alone."

"We made a deal," Knox said as he hopped off the bed and

walked over to his bag. "I wanted to make damn sure you didn't have a reason to go back on your word. Rico and the evidence, in exchange for you paying off my debt. That's what we agreed upon."

"Yeah, but I needed you to do something else."

"You something that wasn't part of our original terms?" Knox said, as he dug out the flash drive with the footage and held it up.

Ballard scowled as he thumped his file folder.

"I have the right to change the terms."

"Doesn't seem right to me," Knox said, placing the device in Ballard's hand. "I'm giving you what we decided upon—Rico and the footage. We should be done here."

Ballard glanced at the device before pocketing it.

"Did you look at it?"

Knox didn't say anything.

"You did, didn't you?" Ballard asked.

"I thought you said that the Ranger unit was investigating crimes committed against the people working in an Aspen mine."

"I know what you saw looked bad, but—"

"Looked bad?" Knox said, his eyes bulging. "It looked like they were killing people."

"It was a mercy killing," Ballard said. "Those people were already dying."

"From something that they contracted from the mine?"

"We're still trying to figure out what they contracted it from."

"Then why don't you explain to me what the hell Joe Garber was doing there."

Ballard shook his head. "I've probably told you a little more than I should have, based on the classified information regarding this incident. But I can assure you that it's not what it looks like."

Knox sighed, wanting out of the conversation as he realized he was pushing back a little too much.

"I did what you asked," he said. "Whatever you did in that village with those Rangers, it's none of my business, no matter how it looked."

"I'm sure during your time in the military, you understood there were times when you just had to follow orders. No questions. No explanations. You just did the job. Right?"

"You don't have to justify your actions to me," Knox said. "I just want to get on with my life, okay?"

"That's something we both want. But I still need to know where your pilot friend Makenzie, is because she's not back in Brazil, according to her boss."

"She won't say anything about what we saw. You don't need to worry about her."

Ballard shook his head.

"Doesn't work that way. I need to speak with her—and I need you to do one more thing for me."

"We're square?" Knox asked.

"Not until I say we are," Ballard said, tapping the file folder.

"What's your one more thing? Kill a whistleblower?"

Ballard shook his head.

"This man is far from a whistleblower. In fact, it's quite the opposite. This story has started leaking—and Aspen is doing all they can to keep it quiet, including hiring an accomplished assassin who goes by the name The Cleaner. I need you to take care of him for me. After that, I'll consider us square."

Ballard handed the file to Knox.

"All the details are in there. Call me when you're cleared by Dr. Warren, and I'll let you know where to find The Cleaner."

"After this, we're done," Knox said. "Understand?"

Ballard nodded.

"You have my word."

"Pardon me if I don't put much stock in that," Knox said. "Your *word* was to kill Rico and give you the footage, which I've done, in exchange for paying off my loan. But now you've changed the terms."

"The situation changed. Once you take care of The Cleaner, I don't foresee any other need to employ your services."

Ballard spun and walked toward the door. He pushed a button on the wall and the door opened. Then he turned around, waved lazily at Knox, and vanished from view as the door closed.

Knox opened the file folder and stared at the image of the target in the folder. Ballard had spun a good story, but Knox was convinced more than ever that the colonel was lying. Everything pointed to it being some kind of cover-up. And with Knox having seen all the footage, he was convinced the assignment to eliminate The Cleaner was a way for Ballard to finish the cleanup.

Knox shook his head in disgust.

Ballard is setting me up. The Cleaner's target is me.

Ballard could've actually infected Knox with the virus and let him die, but Knox knew that would've only created more questions, questions Ballard didn't want to answer. But a simple suicide would be easy to sweep under the rug — at least, that's how The Cleaner would likely make it appear. Or an accidental death, one where Knox was diving off a cliff into the river. It'd be believable to anyone who knew him.

Knox finished reading the file and stuffed it into his rucksack. Then he grabbed the remote control off his nightstand and flicked on the television. Skipping through the channels, he finally stopped on one of the news stations. A woman appeared somber as she shared about the death of a reporter.

"Thomas Quinn, a prominent reporter who recently worked for *The Washington Post* for over a decade before taking a position with crosstown rival *The Washington Times*, was found dead in his apartment late last week. He'd won several Pulitzers and had recently written a piece about The Peace Corps that resulted in sweeping changes to the organization."

Knox winced.

Suicide? I doubt that. I've got to get out of here.

CHAPTER THIRTY-EIGHT

Alexandria, Virginia

Ashley Moore stared at her sleeveless knee-length red dress. It was simple yet elegant, capturing the kind of persona she wanted to put forth if she became the nation's next First Lady. Her brown hair had been curled, and bounced just below her shoulders. She moved closer to the mirror to examine the wrinkles around her eyes.

Ashley couldn't deny the fact that she was getting older, though her aging appeared to have accelerated over the last year. Dealing with Chase's death had been tough on her, on her marriage with her politician husband, but they'd remained strong. A few months after the incident in the Congo, she struggled to get out of bed, weeping for hours daily. Meanwhile, Mark continued on with his duties on Capitol Hill, acting at times as if nothing had happened. They fought over the way he seemed almost indifferent to their son's death as well as her suffering. His comforting words consisted of trite phrases like "You never know what good might come out of this" or "Chase is in a better place now" or "You shouldn't agonize over the things you can't control." She wanted to punch him in the face, a violent act she almost followed through with one day when he said, "Maybe it's just part of God's plan."

Dealing with her son dying at twenty-two years old wasn't part of *her* plan. But nothing in her life resembled anything like she'd imagined when she first married Mark. Ashley had dreams of being a pilot, dreams that she forsook the first time she sat in the cockpit for her first flying lesson. She thought her fear of heights were just a phase and she'd get over it the moment she sat behind the control. But it didn't.

There were other areas of Ashley's life that hadn't panned out the way she'd envisioned either. She wanted grandchildren and lots of them. She even hoped for a household full of kids herself, but not long after giving birth to Chase, she had some medical issues that doctors said could only be solved with hysterectomy. That almost tore Ashley's marriage apart as she sank into a deep depression.

But she snapped out of it and decided to make lemonade out of the sour, rotten lemons life had given her. However, when Chase died, all those feelings came back. And just like last time, Mark was either oblivious or willfully ignorant of her suffering. She found neither response acceptable. Only she wasn't sure she could bounce back this time. The pain cut too deep.

Mark convinced Ashley to attend couples counseling, which helped pull her out of the doldrums again, this time stronger than ever. While his initial response had seemed lethargic, Mark fought hard to get her the help she needed, sacrificing his time and ambitions to find healing together. His effort endeared him to her. And it was what made his big news—the decision that he was about to announce that he was running for president—that much more special to her. Mark had quit virtually everything he could to support her recovery, and now she couldn't wait to return the favor.

While Mark shared his big dreams with Ashley early in their marriage, she never imagined it would result in a legitimate shot at the White House. Her father, Randall Collinsworth, one of most well-respected senators on Capitol Hill after serving for twelve terms, shared similar dreams, though they were never realized. But Mark was different. If there was one thing she knew about her husband, it's that he wouldn't do something unless he was confident he could win.

He didn't even ask her out until he'd asked three of her friends to see if she'd be interested in dating. But once he pursued something, he always got it.

She doubted this would be any different.

"First Lady Ashley Moore," she said aloud, as she inspected every aspect of her body in the mirror. "Almost perfect. It's missing something."

Then it came to her what she needed—a U.S. flag.

She thought for a moment, trying to remember the last time she'd worn her brooch with the U.S. flag on it. A few weeks ago, she wore it with a blue dress when they'd attended a two-thousand-dollar plate fundraiser for one of Mark's colleagues from the House who was gearing up for a senate run.

Where did I put it?

Then she remembered as a smile crept across her lips. She'd been a little frisky that night after they got home. Upon arriving home, they didn't even make it to the bedroom before she jumped him, leading to a wild escapade in his study. The next morning, she didn't even remember how she got back to their bedroom.

She padded down the hall and into her husband's study. After searching the top of his desk, she opened the drawers, going through them one by one. She found the brooch in the top middle drawer, and was about to close it when she noticed his bottom filing drawer was left unlocked.

That's odd.

It was almost always locked. She searched for the key and found it, inserting it into the lock. Just as she was about to close it, she caught a glimpse of a file folder labeled "The Consortium." The name seemed out of place. Most of the files had normal names one would expect—names of projects, names of bills, name of research topics. But "The Consortium"?

What is this?

Curiosity sank its teeth into Ashley and refused to let go. She reached for the file, her hands shaking as she did. While she was alone, she still feared Mark's wrath if he caught her looking at his files. He'd expressed on multiple occasions how she wasn't to touch his files, mostly because some of them contained national security information with details she wasn't cleared to know about. Mark claimed to keep hard copies because that way they couldn't be hacked. As a result, he rarely talked about his work on the intelligence committee.

Is there something he hasn't told me?

She didn't like him keeping secrets, though she understood that was part of his job. But the folder was right there.

Nobody's gonna know.

Ashley took a deep breath and retrieved the folder, committing to memory where it situated among all the other files. Then she placed it on his desk and opened it.

As her eyes fell on the page, she heard a noise from other room. She swallowed hard and slammed the folder shut. The garage door hadn't opened, at least, she hadn't heard it. Had her husband come home early, maybe to surprise her? He always parked in the garage, but had he decided to switch it up? Was he going to whisk her away for a shopping trip or a special dinner to celebrate?

She tucked the file into the top drawer and peered out into the hallway. Then she saw Boots, their Tabby cat creeping along.

"Silly Boots," she said. "You almost scared me to death."

Ashley returned to her husband's desk and pulled out the file again. She gasped as she started reading, blood rushing to her face. Rage filled her to the point that her vision took on a red tint. After each page, she grew more livid, furious over each new revelation. She pulled out her phone and snapped picture after picture of all the pages before putting everything back where she'd found it and locking the cabinet drawer.

As she marched out of his study and back down the hallway, her vision blurred from the tears welling up, her cheeks hot.

I can't believe he would do that. It's like I don't even know him.

Ashley took a deep breath and knew she should calm down. Acting impulsively never got her anywhere, but this was different. If she didn't do something now, the world might not know. And this was definitely something the entire world needed to know about, if anything to make sure that monster husband of hers—the soon-to-be ex-husband of hers—couldn't get away with this.

She returned to her bedroom, spent fifteen minutes crying, dried her eyes, and then thought about Erica Everhart. Rushing to check her email, Ashley hadn't realized she'd stopped receiving emails showing the reporter's location. The emails weren't all that interesting, merely showing the longitude and latitude of each place she'd visited. They meant nothing to Ashley—until they meant everything. After getting caught up in the dream of becoming First Lady, she'd forgotten about Erica. Then she checked her email and tapped in the final location into an online map program. It revealed she made it back to Washington at Dulles International Airport.

Maybe she just turned off the GPS.

Then Ashley searched for Erica Everhart's business card. She was the only reporter Ashley knew on more than just a surface level —and the only one she trusted. She found it on their dresser and dialed the number printed on the card.

The call rang several times before going to voicemail. She tried a second and third time. Same result.

Then Ashley tried *The Washington Post*. After getting sent from the desk of one reporter to the next, she finally reached Erica's editor.

"Mrs. Moore, this is David Langston," he said. "I'm a big fan of your husband's work on the Hill."

"Thank you," she said. "But I'm afraid I didn't call to talk politics."

"Then how can I help you?"

"I'm trying to find Erica Everhart. I have some information for her about a story I think she might be interested in, but I haven't been able to reach her."

Langston paused for a moment.

"Yeah, we're all kind of wondering where she's been, too," Langston said.

"She's gone missing?" Ashley said, trying to steady her voice.

"I'm not sure if I'd say she's missing," Langston said. "But she was working on a story that took her to the Congo. She sent me a message about some story she uncovered that she said was going to be huge, but I haven't heard from her since. She was supposedly on her way back, but that was only a couple of days ago."

"I happen to know she's back," Ashley said, "but don't ask me how."

"Okay," Langston said. "Sounds like you know more than me. Not sure why you decided to reach out."

"Because I know she's back, but that's all. You sure you don't know where she is?"

"Yes, though that's not entirely unusual when our reporters are out on big assignments."

"What kind of assignment was she working on?" Ashley asked, playing coy.

"I'm not really at liberty to say. I just know she believed it was going to be a huge story. Do you want me to pass along a message when we hear from her?"

"Please, if you don't mind," Ashley said. "Tell her I need to speak with her immediately."

Ashley gave Langston her cell number.

"I'm sure she probably got delayed somewhere, or is taking a few extra days to relax on her trip," Langston said before they ended the call.

But Ashley wasn't so sure, especially after what she'd just read in her husband's files. Why hadn't Erica reached out already? Did she think the truth would be too difficult to digest?

Ashley had one burning question, though: Where was Erica?

CHAPTER THIRTY-NINE

Atlanta, Georgia

Before seeing the report on television about the death of Thomas Quinn, Knox had never heard of the reporter. A dead journalist always grabbed Knox's attention, if for anything out of sheer morbid curiosity. And this time was no different, as he explored Quinn's work.

Knox found a plethora of tributes on social media to Quinn, most of them raving about his professionalism and his pit bull mentality when it came to squaring off with corporate and government goliaths alike. What Knox found most intriguing was the series Quinn penned about the strange link between the death of two Peace Corps volunteers in Africa about eighteen months apart. The bodies were cremated before they were returned to their families in the U.S., due to them allegedly contracting diseases. Local health officials were afraid the disease would spread from the bodies and dealt with it accordingly. However, fellow volunteers said they never saw any signs that the dead volunteers had a disease, and didn't find the dead bodies. In both instances, the bodies were discovered a few kilometers from their host family homes. According to volunteers that Quinn interviewed, such behavior was considered suspicious.

Ultimately, the series "Does the Peace Corps Have a Problem?" won the prestigious Pulitzer Prize for investigative reporting, catapulting Quinn into national prominence. The aftermath of his reporting led the Peace Corps to change some of their standards in determining host homes as well as introducing new health and safety protocols for the volunteers. But based on some of Quinn's cryptic social media posts in the time since then, Knox wondered if Quinn hadn't discovered something else. His final post hinted that he'd returned to an old case that he was going to investigate and promised to report more when he returned.

Certainly doesn't sound like a man hours away from killing himself.

Knox's deep dive session was interrupted with a knock at the door.

Dr. Violet Warren announced herself through an intercom system and then entered the room clutching a chart against her chest — notably without a hazmat suit. She removed her glasses and offered a warm smile.

"No suit?" Knox said, as he tucked his phone into his pocket. "This day is getting better already. I like that smile of yours, too."

"You're going to like the results from your latest bloodwork even better," she said. "Apparently, you never had the Incaendium virus, at least from what I'm seeing."

"So, I'm free to go?" he asked.

"Not quite yet," she said. "We've got to wrap up some paperwork, and we're going to have to do an exit interview with you, as well as schedule some follow-up interviews, just to make sure we didn't miss something. I know it might be a bit laborious for you, with all your adventure seeking, but it's important for us to gather as much information as possible, maybe even communicate with the hospital that misdiagnosed you and figure out why."

"Of course," Knox said. "Whatever you need."

"Excellent," she said. "I'll send one of my associates in to get you started on this right away."

Warren turned toward the door to exit when Knox called after her.

"Doc."

"Yeah?" she said, her hand about ready to push the button to engage the door to the decontamination chamber.

"Before you go, can you tell me how someone might contract the virus?" he asked. "Could you get it from an object that was near infected people?"

She shook her head.

"We don't have volumes of information about this virus yet, but we've studied it enough to know that its transmission is exclusively through airborne particulates."

"Like Covid?"

Warren groaned and shook her index finger.

"That's pretty much a four-letter word around here," she said. "But, yes, kind of like Covid."

Knox furrowed his brow.

"Very strange that they even thought I had it then, since I would've had to have caught it from another infected person."

"So true," Dr. Warren said. "Well, that should be enough to get you back out on your adventures in peace."

"Hope so."

"Well, what kind of adventure are you going on next?"

Knox shook his head and grinned.

"You have your secrets, Doc. I have mine."

"Fair enough," she said, as she walked back over to Knox and handed him her card. Her phone buzzed with a message. She swiped the screen to read the text before turning her attention back to Knox.

"Good luck, Mr. Knox."

Knox dropped the card, prompting Warren to bend over and reach for it. As she did, he went for the phone sticking out of her lab coat pocket. He touched the screen to prevent it from locking, then placed it on the bed behind him.

Knox thanked her again before she left the room. With Ballard likely monitoring Knox's phone, he didn't want to give away Makenzie's location, but needed to connect with her as soon as he could. He picked up Warren's phone, which was still unlocked. He sent her a text to let her know he would be calling and to answer. Then he dialed her number.

"Is this your burner phone?" she asked.

"It's my doc's here at the CDC," Knox said. "She doesn't know I have it and will be back for it in a minute, so I have to make this quick."

"Are you all right?"

"Yeah, I'm fine," she said. "How do you feel?"

"Normal."

"Okay, then there's probably nothing to worry about regarding the virus. And, frankly, I'm very suspicious right now. The Incaendium virus is supposedly airborne and highly contagious. And since you were with me virtually every minute you never could've-contracted anything, unless, of course, someone injected it into you directly."

Knox nodded.

"It is strange, isn't it?" she said.

"That's one word for it," he said. "But I'm convinced that Rico was right all along. Ballard is up to something here—and he was trying to use me to cover his tracks. He might have sent a military unit to the Congo to contain an outbreak, but I'm not sure it wasn't by his own doing."

"Then let's blow the whole thing wide open. What do ya say?"

"I wouldn't have it any other way."

Knox proceeded to catch her up on what he'd learned about Thomas Quinn and received an update about Rico, who she'd successfully sneaked into the country on one of her company's flights, as a flight attendant. She gave him a location to meet up in Washington when he'd left Atlanta. Before he left, he gave her Ballard's number and told her to call him.

Knox scribbled a note for Dr. Warren and left it on his bed with her cell phone. He grabbed his belongings and found a car in the parking lot. After smashing the window with the tactical flashlight from his rucksack, he hotwired the vehicle and headed north for Washington, the sun vanishing on the horizon just as the Atlanta skyline disappeared from his rearview mirror.

Knox didn't wait long to call Ballard, from a hastily-acquired burner phone, before asking for the final details of his assignment. When Ballard finished relaying all the information, he thanked Knox for all his great work and told him to give him a call when the job was completed.

"I'll be in touch soon," Knox said.

Ballard swirled the bourbon around in his glass and inspected it before taking a long pull. He stood on the balcony of his penthouse suite and stared out across the city. With a stifling heat wave sweeping across the Eastern seaboard, Ballard considered passing up his after-work routine, where he mentally replayed his day and considered what went right and what went wrong. The quick flight to and from Atlanta had worn him out.

After reviewing the footage Knox had given him, almost everything was going right for Ballard. There was just the thorny issue of Makenzie Hall, the pilot he'd hired to drop Knox in the middle of the Amazon. Their friendship was apparently rekindled during their harrowing escape from the jungle. And she'd remained with him ever since. Ballard had managed to break them apart, but he wasn't certain she wouldn't come back to haunt him. He needed to talk with her, to find out if she would need to be integrated into his erasure plan.

His phone buzzed with a call, a number he didn't recognize. Only a handful of people knew his number, and it certainly wasn't one that a telemarketer could ever get their hands on. Despite his reluctance, he answered the call.

"Col. Ballard?" a woman asked.

"Speaking," he said.

"This is Makenzie Hall. I understand you wanted to speak with me."

"Thank you for giving me a call, Miss Hall. I'm not one to beat around the bush, so I'm going to get straight to the point. I need to ask you a question, and I want an honest answer."

"That's the only kind of answer I give, sir."

"In that case, this ought to be a short conversation. Now, I understand you were with Garrett Knox when he retrieved the footage in Johannesburg."

"That's correct."

"Okay," he said, pausing to take another sip of his bourbon. "Did you happen to view anything on that flash drive?"

"Yes, sir," she said.

"And what did you see?" he asked.

"It looked like a military unit was trying to help contain a viral outbreak of some sort."

"Very keen observation."

"Thank you, sir. I've been a part of some disaster unit teams during my work in Brazil."

"And are you there now?"

"No, sir. I'm heading back in a couple of days, but I wanted to take advantage of my time back here in the States and visit my family in Charleston."

"I appreciate your candor, Miss Hall. I'd also appreciate it if you'd not mention this to anyone else. Footage like what you saw could easily be misconstrued and reflect very poorly on our troops."

"I wouldn't want that to happen, sir."

"Your discretion will be noted. And if you ever want a position in intelligence, you have my private number."

"Thank you, sir."

As soon as Ballard ended the call, he dialed one of his assistants.

"I need a trace on this number," Ballard said, reading off the number from Makenzie's phone. "Can you tell me where the location of that phone's most recent call? Just text me the results. Also, I need the address for the parents of Makenzie Hall in Charleston, S.C. You can text that to me as well."

Ballard ended the call and didn't go back inside until he finished his bourbon. After he sat down, sinking into his sofa and closing his eyes, his phone buzzed with a text message.

I have the info for you, sir. And interestingly enough, it's the same address.

The next text contained the address for the Bill and Lucy Hall.

Then he placed one final call to one of his operatives, requesting a small favor. Then he turned off his phone and, for the first time all day, relaxed.

This time tomorrow, no more loose ends.

Then he could really relax.

CHAPTER FORTY

Prince William Forest | Virginia

The Cleaner eased onto the front porch of the primitive cabin as the screen door rattled shut. Dusk blanketed the woods, shadows yielding to the fading muted light. In the surrounding woods, fireflies flickered and the chorus of crickets swelled. He leaned against a post supporting the porch stoop and drew in a deep breath, the pungent odor of the boggy terrain barely detectable to him now. The Cleaner had lived in isolation amidst the pines and the dogwoods long enough that it smelled like home now.

After a decade of working with Col. Ballard, The Cleaner was ready to retire and never leave his beloved spot in nature. He should've been more nervous as he pondered his future. After all, he knew where the bodies were buried, some of them in what he considered his backyard. It wasn't really *his* backyard, but living in isolation in the middle of a forest, nobody would ever contest the property line he'd established. Nor would they likely ever go digging, that is, not unless they found his cemetery map. To him, killing people was a job, but he never wanted to disrespect the dead. Even if his targets were supposed to disappear forever, The Cleaner felt they deserved a proper burial.

He glanced at the weathered leather Bible sitting on the rocking chair a few feet away. Years had passed since he'd been in a church and listened to someone else read from its pages. Yet with each person he killed, The Cleaner read a passage of scripture before eulogizing them. He'd developed his technique over time, often using the files that Col. Ballard provided to share interesting facts and details about the person's life. Even if it was only for the squirrels and the birds, he took the task seriously.

Resting beneath the Bible was a file folder, one for Garrett Knox. The eulogy would be an interesting one for sure, much like his life. The former Army Ranger had managed to escape over three dozen battles without sustaining any major injuries, waiting until after he left the military to lose his leg.

That story would be a fun one to tell. If he had a human audience, he might even get a few chuckles out of it, since most people assumed Knox lost his leg in combat. There would even be some touching moments, even some moments of empathy for his plight and the personal tragedy that drove him to pursue becoming a Ranger.

The Cleaner turned his gaze back toward the woods and the grave he'd dug about thirty yards away. Next to the pile of dirt sat a box made out of wood he'd hewn and milled from a fallen dogwood that had been struck by lightning. He considered it the perfect coffin for Knox, constructed to his exact measurements. The only question left for The Cleaner was whether or not he would bury Knox in his shoes.

The Cleaner checked his watch before retreating inside before the mosquitoes overtook the fireflies and sullied his memory of the moment. He sat down at his kitchen table and took his gun apart, inspecting every piece and cleaning them before reassembling it. In his line of work, there was little margin for error, and whatever he could do to reduce that gave him the best chance at being successful. And for his last kill, he didn't just want success—he wanted perfection.

Once he finished, he picked up his cell phone and texted Ballard.

Still no sign of the target. You sure he's coming tonight?

A few moments passed before Ballard replied.

He'll be there soon … just be ready

The Cleaner had bristled when Ballard first suggested letting Knox go to his house to finish him off. Nobody knew who he was now, let alone where he lived. That was the life he'd chosen years ago, the kind where the only satisfaction he derived from his existence was when he took the life of another. As many times as he faced death in tense struggles, The Cleaner had almost lost his fear of it. He always won. Always. After considering Ballard's suggestion a little bit longer, he decided, why not let Knox know where he lived? It wasn't like Knox was going to get the better of him. And if Knox happened to win, he'd be dead,so why would he care?

But The Cleaner was going to win. For the first time, he'd actually taken the time to write out his eulogy for Knox and couldn't wait to read it after putting the Ranger's body into the pre-dug hole in the woods behind his house. He checked his watch again and decided to sharpen his knives.

A week had passed since he last inspected his blades. He unfurled them from a microfiber cloth designed to keep them pristine. He polished each one after using it. He'd found remnants of blood were ill-advised when it came to forensics, as well as speeding up the oxidation process. The only thing worse than a difficult spot of blood to remove was rust. He picked up one of the serrated knives and examined his reflection in it. His tightly cropped goatee showed signs of gray, despite his best efforts to remove it with dye. He made a note to dye his beard after completing his assignment with Knox.

He'd almost finished when he heard something outside his house.

Has to be a deer or a opossum.

The Cleaner had a perimeter alarm that was infallible. With cameras stationed between every monitor, nobody could get around the invisible barrier the system deployed around his cabin. He clutched his blade tight as he got up and moved toward the door.

Then he froze, catching the whiff of a cigar.

Am I really smelling that or am I imagining things? If Knox is out there, he's being sloppy.

He put his hand on the doorknob and turned it before tugging gently.

~

If there was one thing Knox had learned during his time in the Rangers, it was how to create a perimeter, one nearly impenetrable, mostly because he valued his sleep. Rookie special ops agents used a single perimeter alarm. But not Knox. He believed you could never have enough. An outer perimeter, an inner perimeter, and as many as he felt necessary in between. As Knox stood at the end of a long dirt road leading to an isolated cabin, he assumed The Cleaner, who was clearly a professional, would subscribe to the same school of thought. Even if he didn't, proceeding with caution was always the smartest option.

Knox hated smoke, but he flicked his lighter, sparking a flame that danced for a moment. He eased the end of his cigar near the fire and puffed, igniting it. He puffed a few more times before spitting out some loose leaves of tobacco caught on his tongue. Then he pressed forward.

Using the smoke to expose the perimeter lasers, Knox held the cigar low to the ground. Once he found the first one positioned about shin level, he huffed out more smoke at waist level and then eye level before sending a plume of smoke higher. Nothing.

Knox wanted to believe that maneuvering through would be easy, but it would be a tedious process. At any point, The Cleaner could've switched up the pattern or placed higher lasers—and Knox knew he couldn't afford even the slightest of mistakes.

The process took nearly forty-five minutes as he navigated the woods in front of The Cleaner's cabin. However, before Knox approached the clearing surrounding the cabin, he moved around the outside and inspected the back porch. Just like in the front, the door was open, with only a screen door closed to keep the bugs from getting inside while allowing the breeze to blow through and cool down the interior.

Knox eased up to the front porch and set his cigar down on the railing before scrambling around to the back porch. With his back flush against the outside of the house, he waited until he heard the creaking of the screen door in the front. As soon as he did, he eased open the back door and crept to the front wall and waited.

"Think this is funny?" The Cleaner said, his accent surprisingly Southern. "I'm going to carve you up, Knox."

The Cleaner tossed the smoldering cigar onto the porch and ground it out. As soon as he opened the front door, Knox grabbed the man's arm and yanked him to the ground. The Cleaner spun onto his back and looked up at Knox before slashing at him with a knife.

Knox dodged to his left, the knife slicing his shirt. Without a weapon, Knox took a step back.

The Cleaner scrambled to his feet. He clutched the weapon in his right hand and shuffled from side to side, eyes locked on Knox. After a few seconds, The Cleaner glanced at Knox's hands and broke into a wry smile.

"I've heard of bringing a knife to a gun fight, but never bringing nothing to a knife fight," The Cleaner said.

"I've got everything I need to kill you," Knox said.

The Cleaner laughed.

"Good luck with that. I've been planning this for days now."

With that, The Cleaner lunged at Knox. He jumped back, leaving only his left leg exposed. And The Cleaner took the bait. He jabbed toward Knox's leg, only to have his blade slide off to the side. As soon as it did, Knox used his right leg to pin The Cleaner's arm to the floor. Instinctively, he dropped the weapon. Knox kicked it aside with his left.

"You want a fistfight?" The Cleaner asked.

"Whatever works," Knox said.

As the two men circled around the room, The Cleaner initiated again, this time diving for Knox's legs. Knox side-stepped his attacker, who was on all fours. Before he could get upright again, Knox jumped onto his back and rode him down to the floor. The Cleaner struggled, fighting to stand up. But Knox held fast, using his knees to pin down The Cleaner.

Knox wrapped his arms around The Cleaner's head, putting him in a sleeper hold.

After a few seconds, The Cleaner fell limp.

Knox grabbed the pre-made noose out of his bag and flung it over The Cleaner's head. Then he worked quickly to attach it to one of the beams running across the living room ceiling. After securing the rope, Knox yanked The Cleaner up to the appropriate height, waking the assassin.

The Cleaner flailed wildly, kicking at Knox while trying to create space between his neck and the rope. But his weight was too much, the struggling only tightening the rope.

Knox walked over to The Cleaner's desk and opened the top drawer. As he did, a light rain drummed on the tin roof as the house rattled with each rumble of thunder. He found a blank piece of paper before another document caught his eye. It was a sketch of The Cleaner's property, entitled Happyland Cemetery. Knox looked more closely and noticed small rectangular plots positioned around the perimeter of the house with names on them, a few that he recognized.

Knox scribbled out a suicide note, placing it on top of the cemetery map.

Meanwhile, The Cleaner continued kicking as he tried to say something, mumbling what Knox could only assume were threats. But it didn't take long before the struggling stopped. So did The Cleaner's breathing.

Knox picked up The Cleaner's cell phone and held it up to the now dead man's face to gain access to the device. Once open, Knox scrolled through text message to a number he recognized—Ballard.

What a bastard.

Then Knox took a picture of The Cleaner and texted it to Ballard with a message that the job was finished. He stopped at the front door and watched the rain, the biting aroma of peat bog muted by the scent of fresh rain. Knox enjoyed the brief respite, but his work was far from done. Then he texted one more message to Ballard:

You've got some explaining to do. Will call soon

CHAPTER FORTY-ONE

Potomac River | Washington, D.C

Col. Ballard stood on tip-toes, straining to see over the top of his boat's windshield. *The Gadfly*, his cabin cruiser, skimmed north across the water. A mixture of the boat's spray from the Potomac River and light summer rain pelted his face. Using the back of his sleeve, he wiped his face dry and then squinted, straining to see so he could to stay more central in the channel.

He slowed down as he approached the small strait between Roosevelt Island and Little Island. With the rain picking up, he navigated to a spot beneath the Roosevelt Bridge to wait out the storm. His radar showed the heavy rain would be gone in a few minutes, which would've been before his appointment was scheduled to arrive. The wind gusted, rocking The Gadfly and leaving Ballard nauseous.

There's a reason I never joined the Navy.

He staggered over to the edge and gripped the railing. Staring down at the water, he felt his stomach roil before it calmed down. He dropped an anchor and marched downstairs to get a bottle of water. Once he finished drinking it, he felt his phone buzz with the notification of a missed call as well as a text message. With all the jostling he'd just experienced, he wasn't surprised he'd missed something.

The call and the text were from the same person, the operative he'd sent to the address he'd received for Makenzie Hall. According to his contact, the house was an empty vacation rental. Though it was owned by her parents, she wasn't there. In fact, nobody had been there for days, according to the neighbor who the operative had spoken with.

Teeth clenched, Ballard cursed.

As if I need another problem to solve.

He made a note of it before his phone rang again. His face fell as he stared at the number.

Not now.

He couldn't ignore Garrett Knox, at least not forever. He pushed a button, sending the call directly to voicemail. He kicked himself, knowing Knox would understand he'd been dismissed. Seconds later, the phone buzzed again with another call from Knox. Then another and another. And each time Ballard sent the phone to voicemail. After the sixth call, Ballard gave up and answered.

"You sure are relentless."

"That's why you hired me," Knox said.

"Not exactly," Ballard said. "I mostly hired you because you were designated the toughest son of a bitch by your superiors, when I asked for a recommendation. I needed someone loyal and lethal, someone with experience. And, boy, did it pay off today."

Knox didn't say anything.

"What? No witty one-liner?"

Knox was silent a beat before responding.

"What? Did I defy your expectations?"

"There's the Garrett Knox we all love," Ballard said. "Now, you said you had some questions for me, right?"

"That's one way of putting it," Knox said. "I actually said you have some explaining to do."

"That's right, that's right. So, what do you want to know?"

"For starters, why'd you try to set me up with The Cleaner?"

"What are you talking about?" Ballard said. "I would never try to set you up."

Knox cleared his throat, suggesting that maybe Ballard wasn't being forthcoming.

"I read your texts with The Cleaner, so don't insult me by trying to play dumb. I know what you did."

Ballard walked over to the stairs leading up to the main deck and rested his leg on the second step. He picked a piece of lint off his shirt as he considered a way to assuage Knox's fears.

"Look, I—"

"Don't say you didn't care who won," Knox said, cutting off Ballard. "It's clear based on the details you gave him that you were hoping The Cleaner took care of me."

"Now, that's not—"

"Careful," Knox said. "When it comes to the list of things that make my blood boil, lying to me ranks near the top. That list also corresponds with how severely I deal with someone who commits one of those egregious mistakes against me."

"Okay, Knox, you got me. Maybe I wanted The Cleaner to win. But I can't say that I'm upset that you won. I know you don't believe me that I didn't care, but all I knew is that whoever won was going to be my guy moving forward."

"If you think I'm going to be *your* guy, you don't know me as well as you think you do," Knox said. "We're done. Well, *almost* done."

"Take a number," Ballard said. "But just remember that I own you now. I know what you've done and who you've done it to. Just think about that before you thump your chest and make bold threats. It's clear you don't have any idea how much power I have."

"I've played nice," Knox said. "But I'm out—just not before your little power trip is exposed. You need to remember, I know what happened in the Congo."

Knox ended the call.

Who does he think he is?

For all his bluster, Ballard understood the stakes. He knew his career as one of the intelligence community's top diplomats was in danger, if Knox really had a way to expose him. It would take more than just footage from the Congo. But if Knox could make a few links—something he wasn't convinced the former Ranger could do—the consequences would be dire and lasting, both for Ballard and U.S. intelligence.

"I warned you."

The voice echoed in Ballard's mind. He should've listened to his colleague regarding Knox's roguish tendencies. Ballard tried to convince himself that nobody else would've been motivated to do everything Knox did—to venture into the Amazon, kill an old friend, track down another Ranger, and retrieve the footage. Finding the combination of someone with the right motivation and the perfect skillset wasn't easy. And as vigorously as Ballard defended his position, the reality was, he didn't have a second viable option.

Or was it?

There was another way he'd considered before quickly dismissing it, another way to take control of The Consortium. It would require a big sacrifice, but Ballard was willing to make it. He'd already set up the infrastructure. He only wondered if he had the guts to do it.

By selecting Knox to tidy up the issue in the Congo, Ballard understood it was ride or die with the Army Ranger. The latter was looking more likely with each passing minute—unless he could pivot.

Ballard opened his catch-all drawer in the galley and fished out a pair of binoculars. After hustling up to the main deck, where the rain had all but dissipated, he scanned the horizon for any approaching boats.

Still nothing.

He returned to the kitchen and poured himself a drink before going back to the main deck. Checking the river again, he noticed a boat banking to the west. It straightened out, and then its nose dove downward before sitting upright, the roaring engines giving way to trolling speed. The boat puttered toward Ballard before pulling up alongside *The Gadfly*.

"That name's a little too on the nose, don't ya think?" the other man said, nodding toward the name inscribed across the side of the stern.

"You think most people today would even catch the meaning, let alone know it's a fantastic piece of literature?" Ballard asked.

"Probably the ones paying attention—and that's who you need to look out for."

"Tie off and join me over here for a drink."

Ballard watched Senator Mark Moore follow the instructions. With the two vessels tucked into a small cove, they retreated below deck on Ballard's cabin cruiser to discuss the recent events. Once Ballard finished catching up Moore, they topped off their glasses.

"So, how are you going to fix this?" Moore asked.

"Me?" Ballard said, hooking a thumb toward his chest. "This is a *we* problem now. We're all in this together. That's why it's called The Consortium. Words matter. Instead of someone dictating how things should go, we need to put our heads together to figure out a way to help us achieve our ultimate goal."

"Yeah—and a former Army Ranger with access to footage that exposes part of our darkest secret program is going to be a problem."

"That is, if he talks."

"What do you mean *if* he talks?" Moore said as he narrowed his eyes. "You set him up. He's not just going to shrug and say *screw it* before flying back to Montana. He's bound by his code to tell the truth about what he's seen. Even if he does go back to the hinterlands, all it takes is one person asking him the wrong question before half of Congress launches an inquisition, a witch hunt, if you will. How do you think that's going to go over?"

Ballard huffed and rolled his eyes before glancing at the floor, trying his best to make his displeasure for the diatribe know. But Moore continued.

"You think journalists are just going to drop it once they get a whiff of this story? No, we're going to have a legion of motivated people—some motivated by principle, some motivated by money, some motivated by fame—all doing their best to unleash a personal hell on all of us."

"You're too paranoid."

"Am I?" Moore asked. "What about that pilot woman? You deal with her yet?"

Ballard remained quiet.

"Didn't think so," Moore said. "You screwed that one up too, didn't you?"

"Are you done yet?" Ballard asked. "Because instead of sitting here and listening to you bitch about how things aren't going how you'd like for them to go, we need to get a solution and take it to the group."

"I've got a solution," Moore said. "And it's one I'm sure the group would ratify."

"Then let's hear it."

"We remove you as the head of counterintelligence."

Ballard drew back and scowled.

"Are you out of your mind?" he asked. "Who could possibly do this job better than me?"

"I'll rattle off a dozen names right now, if you want me to," Moore said. "The real question is, who *couldn't* possibly do this job better than you? That'd be a much shorter list."

"Without me, you wouldn't be able to deploy Incaendium. Without me, you wouldn't have access to half of the people in the intelligence community, who we need around the world to pull this off. Without me—"

"Would you listen to yourself, Colonel?" Moore said. "This wasn't your idea, but you make it sound like it was. We have to all work together, and that means everyone must be pulling their weight. If you're not pulling your weight, *you're* dead weight."

Ballard narrowed his eyes and pursed his lips.

"Look here, you little asshole. You're the one who screwed this whole thing up. If you would've just listened to me, we wouldn't be in this mess."

Moore slammed his glass on the side of the table. Shards flew about the cabin.

"You can't see it, can you? It's like you're blinded by your ego."

"My ego? You're the one who thinks none of this will fall into place unless you're in the Oval Office," Ballard said. "If you ask me, you've got the oversized ego. And for all I know, you're using the rest of us to win you the presidency."

"That's absurd and you know it. You're so replaceable, yet you don't even realize it."

Moore pulled his phone out of his pocket and held it up, the screen displaying that the conversation had been recorded.

"Wait until everyone hears this," he said.

"Delete that right now," Ballard said.

"Why? You scared how everyone will react once they hear how you really feel?"

Ballard opened his catch-all drawer again, this time rummaging through it until he found his pistol. He trained it on Moore.

"Delete it now."

Moore scowled and then shoved Ballard backward before darting up the steps. Ballard scrambled to his feet and chased Moore onto the deck. When Ballard reached the top, he found Moore rushing to remove the rope around the cleats affixed to the side of his boat.

"You can't run away from this," Ballard said. "You can't run away from *me*."

"And what are you going to do, Colonel? Shoot me?"

"If it comes to that. And don't forget, I'm very good at making people disappear."

"Even U.S. Senators?"

"Especially senators."

Moore sneered at Ballard.

"If you want this file deleted, you're gonna have to come and take it from me," Moore said, squatting on the ledge of the two boats as he loosened the slip knots.

"If that's what it takes."

Ballard used his foot to push Moore in the back and into his boat. As Moore got up and turned around, Ballard boarded the vessel. Moore felt the corner of his mouth, checking for blood. Realizing it was bleeding, he spat into the water and then locked eyes with Ballard.

"Delete the file," Ballard repeated deliberately.

Moore didn't move.

"And do it now," Ballard growled.

Instead of complying, Moore rushed Ballard, grabbing the Colonel's arm. The two men fell to the deck in a heap. The gun flew out of Ballard's hand before they started trading blows. Hits to the face, followed by body punches, resulted in a bruising fight. As soon as Ballard connected with a few combinations, Moore roared back, seemingly taking control. Back and forth they went, the altercation lasting longer than either man had anticipated.

The more the fight continued, the worse each man looked. Battered faces. Bruised egos. Demolished trust. After the beating they both dished out, the two men moved like heavyweights in the twelfth round of a title bout, neither fighter willing to surrender.

Then Ballard decided to end it. With a quick combination that sent Moore staggering backward and to the deck again, Ballard crawled toward the gun, still lying where he'd first dropped it.

"Don't do something stupid," Moore said, as he placed both hands in the air in a gesture of surrender.

"This is going to be the smartest thing I've ever done," Ballard said.

"You really think you're going to get away with this?" Moore asked, as he inched closer.

Ballard wiped the blood away from his mouth with the back of his hand and then inspected it.

"Got to say, Mark, I didn't think you had it in you. You earned some respect from me today. Hopefully you'll find some solace in that, as it's about to be the last thing you did with your life."

Moore, realizing that Ballard wasn't making an idle threat, charged the Colonel, eyes focused on the barrel. Before Ballard could get off a shot, Moore grabbed the end of the gun and aimed it into the water as the two men collided, a struggle ensuing to take control.

Then the weapon fired, the fight finally over.

CHAPTER FORTY-TWO

Washington, D.C

Knox pulled into a motel parking lot just off the Beltway, just beating the crush of morning commuters starting to clog the roadways. He squinted as he climbed out of the car, the sun peeking over the horizon. Used needles crunched beneath his feet as he walked toward the room at the far end of the building. Sirens wailed in the distance. A man wearing a tattered coat with a scraggly beard held up a plastic cup and rattled the change inside. Knox stopped and looked at the man, whose eyes were vacant. He mumbled something unintelligible before Knox continued walking.

He approached Room 116 and knocked on the door. Moments later, he heard a security chain slide across followed by the deadbolt clicking open.

Makenzie greeted him with a smile.

"Did you set the world land speed record?" she said.

"You can get places fast if you drive all night," he said, before giving her a hug.

She slid aside, revealing Rico, who had his hand out. Knox grabbed it and then pulled him close, giving him a hug, too.

"Thanks for being willing to come back," Knox said.

"I wouldn't miss this for the world," Rico said. "These bastards forced me out of my own country. I'd like to give them a taste of their own medicine."

Knox clapped his hands and then rubbed them together.

"So, where are we at with everything?" he asked.

"Based on our previous conversation," Makenzie said, gesturing toward the small table in the corner with a laptop, "I started searching for a way to connect with Senator Moore. If there's anyone who can help us take down Ballard, it'd be him."

"Parents will go scorched earth on someone if they think their kid was harmed intentionally," Rico said.

"Exactly," Knox said. "So, we've got to show him what happened to his son. That's the first step. But then we also have to be able to make the link that not only was Ballard responsible, but that this virus was intentionally created and deployed."

Knox looked at Rico.

"Have you seen the footage?"

Rico nodded.

"That was gruesome—and terrifying. Monstrous."

"Ballard insisted that it wasn't what it looked like, but I'm not buying it," Knox said.

"So you agree with me now?" Rico asked.

"A thousand percent," Knox said. "He had me drugged in South Africa. He wanted to get me back here, get me under control before I started figuring out what he's really doing."

"But do we know what he's really doing?" Makenzie asked. "I mean, obviously, he's up to something, but the Congo video aside, is whatever he's doing as nefarious as we think it is? Maybe he has a good reason for all this."

Knox shook his head.

"There's something else going on—I can just feel it," he said. "How else do you explain a Pentagon liaison pausing his diplomatic trip to just swing by an off-the-beaten-path village in the middle of the jungle to make sure Army Rangers are containing an outbreak? What about that screams 'normal'?"

"I agree," she said. "But we just need more information before we take this to anyone."

"Well, we don't need any more information before we take it to Senator Moore," Knox said. "If there's anyone who will help us without knowing everything, he will. The footage of his son's last few minutes alive should do the trick, if he wants to see it."

"Agreed," Makenzie said.

"So, have you made any progress on that front?" Knox asked.

"As a matter of fact, I have," she said. "I read online this morning that Moore is going to be at a fundraiser this evening. It's a couple thousand dollars a plate, but maybe we can figure out a way to get in and grab a few minutes with him."

"Sounds like a great plan," Knox said. "Rico and I will see what other information we can dig up, starting with Thomas Quinn. I'm really curious about that reporter, and if anything about his death is suspicious and could possibly be linked to Ballard."

"I'm on it," Rico said as he plunged his hand into his backpack and retrieved his computer.

An hour later, Makenzie was tapping on her keyboard when she let out an audible groan.

"I don't like the sound of that," Knox said.

"Or the sound of this breaking news either," she said. "Moore's fundraiser has been cancelled for tonight."

"What for?" Rico asked.

"Apparently he has some emergency business on the intelligence committee that requires his attention," she said.

Knox scowled.

"Emergency business?" he asked. "Wonder what's going on?"

"I know what's going on," Rico said as he pointed at his screen. "It's Ballard."

"Ballard?" Knox asked. "What he'd do?"

"He's missing. Found his boat *The Gadfly* floating adrift in the Potomac this morning."

"No body?" Knox asked.

"No body yet, but they found blood on the side of *The Gadfly*," Rico said.

"The President of National Security Affairs doesn't just go missing," Knox said.

Makenzie cocked her head to one side.

"So, if Ballard's dead—" she said, her words hanging.

"We don't know if he's dead yet," Knox said. "And if someone killed him, that means there's someone else likely pulling the strings."

"Who?" Rico asked. "The President?"

"Not sure. But we're going to find out. We've seen what that virus can do, so we can't let this go."

"And what if Ballard's still alive?" Rico asked.

"Then we have even more questions," Knox said.

"So where do we go now?" Makenzie asked.

"Same direction we were planning on going," Knox said. "We need to speak with Senator Moore."

CHAPTER FORTY-THREE

Washington, D.C

After a day full of speculation by pundits and the public alike over who what possibly happened to Ballard and who was responsible, the trio of Knox, Makenzie, and Rico huddled around a box of pizza and a six-pack of beer, sharing their favorite theories, some of them outlandish, others plausible ideas to consider. The fact that Ballard was so well-connected to so many different agencies in his role with the administration gave him access to any number of people who could order covert operations in the Congo. However, Knox was left wondering who Ballard ultimately answered to, if it wasn't President Lewis.

They gathered around Makenzie's computer and watched a few more video clips from social media with people speculating about Ballard's enemies and potential motives for killing him. But that was rote detective work. Knox was more interested in the *why* than the *who*. People confessed to murders all the time without explaining why they killed their victims. Whenever anyone died, the burning question was always *why*. What motivated the person to commit the crime? A crime of passion in the heat of the moment? A crime borne out of jealousy? A crime of necessity, one designed to cover up another crime? The possibilities weren't infinite, but they were numerous. And pinning down the most likely impetus for Ballard's possible murder would give Knox a place to start looking.

Knox couldn't help but feel a sense of disappointment over the news regarding Ballard. He wanted to be the one to enjoy the satisfaction of exposing the President of National Security Affairs, if for no other reason than because *that's what Rangers do*. He then felt a twinge of guilt over leaving his camp in Montana, over leaving Guy in charge, over leaving Allison.

That's where I should be right now.

But the call of duty, the sense of commitment to his country, that feeling superseded everything else in his life. And he couldn't shake just how important it was for him to shut down Ballard's operation and all those who were associated with it.

Knox had a restless night thinking about Ballard and what he could be doing, if he wasn't actually dead. Theory after theory flooded Knox's mind before he finally drifted off to sleep.

When he awoke the next morning, he didn't need a cup of coffee to get the blood flowing. Rico did that when he shouted and pumped his fist from the table in the corner.

"Rico, buddy, what the hell, man?" Knox said. "It's not even seven o'clock yet."

"I know," Rico said. "I couldn't sleep. But I've got us something."

Knox grunted as he sat up.

"Okay, I'm awake. Might as well tell me what it is."

"Us," corrected Makenzie.

"And a good morning to both of you," Rico said. "I've already had two cups of coffee. It's not Kona coffee, Knox, but it does the trick."

"What'd you find?" Knox said, trudging over to the coffee maker.

"I was in a 4Chan chatroom and—" Rico said.

"Wait. What?" Knox said. "4Chan? The site full of nutty conspiracy theorists?"

Rico held up his hands.

"Now, before you rush to judgment, I need you to put aside your preconceived ideas about that site. It might be the only way to get to the truth."

"What are you trying to say?" Knox asked.

"I don't want to leave any stone unturned. And that's something I thought you subscribed to as well."

"I do," Knox said, with a sigh. "Please continue."

"Okay," Rico said. "I found this one thread discussing Ballard's disappearance. But one of the users posted a link to another thread with a one-word comment: 'Related?' So, I clicked on it and found people discussing the disappearance of Erica Everhart."

"Erica Everhart," Knox said pensively. "Where do I know that name?"

"She's a reporter for *The Post*," Rico said. "At least she was before she went missing last week."

"Missing?" Makenzie said.

Rico nodded.

"According to what users are saying here, Erica was supposed to go to the Congo with Thomas Quinn before he committed suicide — on the night before he was scheduled to leave."

Knox snapped and pointed at Rico.

"Okay, I read all about Thomas Quinn. They were colleagues?"

"Former lovers and colleagues, if what people write on this thread is to be believed. But after he died, she decided to go anyway —and she hasn't been heard from since."

"Do we know where she was supposed to go in the Congo?" Knox asked.

Rico shook his head.

"But that's not the real juicy part," he said.

"Go on," Makenzie said, as she shuffled over to the coffee maker and poured herself a drink into the small styrofoam cup.

"What really caught my eye was a user, one named EyeNoThe-Truth, who insisted that he—or she—knew what happened to Erica and what she was looking for in the Congo."

Knox clasped his hands together and eyed Rico.

"This story better have a good ending," Knox said.

"The best," Rico said. "At least, the best it can have up until this point."

"Then get to it," Knox said.

"So, I started to wonder if it was a colleague posting all these details," Rico said. "I mean, how else would they know?"

"And?" Knox said, gesturing for Rico to continue.

"Long story short, I hacked into the 4Chan server and found the IP address of the user known as EyeNoTheTruth," Rico said. "Then I found exactly where the IP address was coming from—the home of none other than Senator Mark Moore."

"Wait a minute," Knox said, his eyes bulging. "Do you think the senator is the one posting all this information?"

Rico shook his head as he hammered on his keyboard. He spun the laptop around.

"No," he said. "Based on the fact that I checked Moore's schedule and found him at a Senate committee hearing when this was originally posted, I think it's his wife, Ashley Moore."

"Why would the—" Makenzie asked before stopping her question mid-sentence.

"Her motivation doesn't matter here," Knox said. "I'm more interested in *how* she knows."

"Well, we can find out the answer to both those questions later this afternoon, when I meet with her," Rico said.

Knox widened his eyes and drew back.

"You managed to get a meeting with Ashley Moore?"

Rico nodded.

"Told her I was a reporter—I know it's a lie, but I gotta do what I can—and told her I was interested in speaking with her about Erica Everhart's disappearance."

"And she agreed?" Knox asked.

Rico smiled.

"Here's the email," he said, clicking on his computer and displaying a message from Ashley Moore agreeing to meet. She gave

Rico her home address, which he explained that he'd quickly verified as one that matched Senator Moore's.

"So, you can meet with her today?" Knox asked.

Rico nodded.

"That's fantastic," Knox said.

"As a matter of fact, she texted me and asked if I could meet her at noon when she's home for lunch," Rico said.

"She wants to keep quiet whatever it is she want to tell you."

"That's what I was thinking," Rico said. "Must be big. I'll keep you posted.

A few hours later, Rico knocked on Moore's front door. He stared at his distorted reflection in the knocker while waiting for someone to answer to the door. A few minutes later, a woman dressed in a flowing white dress answered the door.

"Mrs. Moore?" Rico said. "I'm Robert Goodman. We chatted online about Erica Everhart."

"Of course," she said, pulling the door open wide. "Please, come on it. I've been looking forward to this all morning."

CHAPTER FORTY-FOUR

Washington, D.C

Mark Moore scanned the room and crossed his legs before taking a deep breath. In the background, faint dance music thumped through the restaurant's speakers. He eyed the man across the table, who furrowed his brow as he swiped up on his tablet.

J.C. Wellington stroked his chin as he stared at the screen. He squinted and moved closer to it, pursing his lips and then cocking his head to one side.

"What are you thinking?" Moore asked.

Wellington held up a hand and wagged his index finger as he continued reading. He leaned back and smiled.

"Well," Moore said, "what do you think?"

Wellington winced and put a finger to his lips, gesturing for Moore to be quiet.

Moore took a deep breath and then picked up his glass. He took a long pull on it, far too early in the morning for a Long Island Iced Tea, but he needed something to settle his nerves. Despite his best efforts to appear relaxed, Moore's stomach felt like a pretzel. Despite having done everything required of him, Moore felt like he needed the country's premier political strategist to run his campaign for the White House.

A few more minutes passed, with Wellington hammering on his keyboard, before he sighed and interlocked his fingers behind his head. He smiled faintly before looking at Moore.

"You got something for me?" Moore asked.

"Congratulations, Mr. President—future President," Wellington said.

"I like the sound of that."

"Who wouldn't? I mean, it looks really good, but it's not a done deal."

"It never is, until all the votes around counted."

Wellington wagged a finger.

"And even then, it's not always secured, but I digress."

Moore took another pull on his glass.

"So, talk to me. Tell me how things look from your perspective."

"You're in good shape as long as the voters focus solely on your experience and qualifications."

Moore chuckled.

"Well, what else is there?" he asked.

"That's just the starting point," Wellington said. "And if you have those, you're further ahead in the game than most."

"I've done everything required of me, of past politicians who've won the office," Moore said. "In fact, I went above and beyond, in an attempt to put myself in the best situation to win."

"So, essentially you're telling me that I've got everything I need to win—but you're not quite sure it's going to happen, because of the intangibles?

"Precisely," Wellington said. "There are a few things you're lacking, starting with a good campaign manager."

"What about you?" Moore suggested. "I mean, why do you think we're having this conversation?"

"That's not what I mean."

"I don't want anybody else. You're my guy."

Wellington looked down at the ground.

"I'm sorry, but I'm afraid I don't do that anymore. However, if your campaign is going wrong, I'm somewhat like a fixer for politicians."

"What's your fee?"

"Perhaps I wasn't clear enough," Wellington said. "My services aren't for sale."

"Nonsense," Moore said. "Everyone has a price."

Wellington shrugged and then stared off into space for a moment. "I don't."

"How about a base salary of three million dollars, plus a nice position within my administration once I win?" Moore suggested.

"Like I said, I'm not for sale, but you don't really need me."

"How come?" Moore asked.

"I'm not sure I could help you," Wellington said. "I've never seen a politician who checked off so many boxes. You're essentially the dream candidate I've been waiting for my entire life."

"So, what's the problem?" Moore asked. "Why are you so reticent to get involved?"

"I'm very busy, and I don't know if I want to be part of a campaign like yours."

"Like mine?" Moore asked. "What's that supposed to mean? Do you not agree with my platform?"

"I couldn't care less about any of that," Wellington said.

"Well, I'm paying you a lot of money just for this meeting," Moore said. "Will you at least tell me if there's anything I can do to improve my chance? Beggars can't be choosers, right? Give it to me straight."

Wellington sighed and smiled as he stared at his tablet again.

"Senator, you're going to have mass appeal. You're handsome. Your wife is a knockout. You're a former Army paratrooper, which means you've got appeal to veterans and members of the military. Your foreign policy experience is incredible. And your track record on passing legislation that is pro-business is impeccable. When it comes to qualifications, unmatched. Then there are the intangibles, those elements that none of your competitors possess. In fact, they couldn't get them now, even if they tried."

"That bad, huh?"

"I'd say it's most impressive, actually," Wellington said, glossing over Moore's sarcastic comment. "In fact, this might be the highest score I've ever ascribed to a national political candidate when considering a handful of these factors."

"Yet with all that, I'd expect to be leading in the polls with hypothetical matchups. But I'm not."

Wellington sucked in a breath through his teeth and then bit his lip.

"What is it?" Moore asked.

"There's one area you haven't exploited yet," Wellington said. "It's one that's a little sensitive, so I hesitate to bring it up. But it could be what you need to nudge you over the top, though I wouldn't presume to think you might consider this."

"Go ahead. I'm a big boy. If I couldn't handle tough conversations, I wouldn't even consider running for office, let alone the presidency."

Wellington's eyes widened and he drew back from his tablet before his gaze met Moore's.

"How would you feel about discussing your son's death?" Wellington asked.

Moore shrugged.

"I clearly don't have a problem with it," he said. "Did you see my recent press conference discussing it?"

Wellington nodded.

"But there's a difference between mentioning it and using it as leverage for political gain."

"Explain."

"Well, if you just mention it once as a way to bring awareness to suicide, then that's not very edgy, at least from a political standpoint. You're doing what most parents and friends do on social media when someone they love decides it's time to check out. But if you want to engender more sympathy, you must talk about it often, letting people know that you're a grieving father, that you had dreams for your kid, but now they're gone. You need to bring it up early and often in interviews and debates."

"And what good will that do?"

"It'll cement in every voter's mind that you deserve their sympathy and—more importantly—their vote," Wellington said. "When people think about you, they'll think about the enormous tragedy that you endured and how it's shaped you as a person."

Moore resisted the urge to grin. He knew every word out of the political strategist's mouth was true, proven over and over again through interviews and questionnaires. But Moore hadn't come this far, made this many sacrifices, worked this diligently all to have it fall apart by someone raising suspicion against him. Moore needed everyone privy to the details of his candidacy to believe that he was doing nothing more than taking advantage of the cards dealt to him, not that he was playing with a stacked deck, one he dealt to himself.

Stick to the script.

"Are you telling me that none of what I've done matters nearly as much as my personal tragedy?" Moore asked.

"All that other stuff allows you to legitimately throw your hat in the ring," Wellington said. "But it's something like tragedy that helps you win an election."

"Whatever it takes," Moore said. "I'll do whatever it takes."

Wellington grinned.

"In that case, my schedule might have opened up a bit," he said. "You have yourself a campaign manager."

"Excellent," Moore said, clapping and then rubbing his his hands together.

"You're going to do great in this town."

"I'm counting on it," Moore said, winking as he shook Wellington's hand. "With your help, of course. And before you go, I wanted to ask you about one more thing about the announcement that I'm running. I want to go big."

"The bigger the better," Wellington said. "And the sooner the better, too."

"I like how you think," Moore said.

CHAPTER FORTY-FIVE

Washington, D.C

Knox waited until Senator Moore was near his car before intercepting him. The senator accented his dark suit and tie with aviator sunglasses, walking purposefully while swinging his briefcase. His shoes scuffed against the parking garage floor as he stopped to avoid running into Knox.

"I'm sorry, senator," Knox said. "I didn't mean to startle you like that."

Moore cocked his head to one side and furrowed his brow.

"Do I know you?" he asked.

Knox shook his head. "I don't think so, but I know something about your son that I thought might be of interest to you."

Moore stepped back.

"Who are you?"

"That's not important," Knox said. "But what is important are some of the details regarding your son's death."

"What kind of sicko does this to a grieving father? Don't you know how difficult this is for me and my wife?"

"I can't imagine how tough this has been for you and your family, but I thought you'd want to know the truth."

Moore sighed.

"I doubt you're going to tell me anything I don't already know. But go ahead and try me."

"Joe Garber gave Chase the gun that he used to kill himself," Knox said.

"Again, that's not exactly a secret to anyone who's familiar with the details of this case."

Knox plunged his hands into his jeans' pockets.

"I wasn't aware those details had been made public yet."

"They haven't, which begs the question: How did you know about them?" Moore asked.

"I can't exactly reveal my source, but I doubt you know the conditions under which your son killed himself."

"What difference does it make? He was a depressed kid and didn't know how to get help. His mother and I tried to help him rediscover his joy for life. We knew it probably wasn't a good idea for him to enter the Peace Corps and go so far away from home, but he's like his old man—stubborn. Sadly, none of that matters now."

"With all due respect, sir, that's where you're wrong. It very much matters, because I wouldn't necessarily consider what Chase did to be suicide."

Moore scowled.

"What exactly are you talking about?"

"Garber gave Chase a gun, but only because Chase was suffering from an enormous amount of pain."

"How do you know that?"

"I've seen the body cam footage from one of the soldiers at the village in the Congo."

"Soldiers were there?" Moore asked. "What kind of soldiers?"

"Army Rangers," Knox said.

"What on earth for?"

"From all counts I've seen and heard, there was a dangerous viral outbreak in Tango, where your son was. Everyone started dying a painful death from a virus called Incaendium. You ever heard of it?"

"It's been mentioned before in some of our committee meetings, but I don't know much about it."

"To be honest, I don't either," Knox said. "I just know if you catch it, you've got a twenty percent chance of dying. At least, that's what I've been told. There are other horrible things that happen to you if you survive, too."

"And you could tell my son had this?"

Knox nodded.

"I know it might be difficult to watch, but would you like to see the footage?"

Knox dug from his pocket a small thumb drive and offered it to Moore.

"Who are you again?" Moore asked.

"My name's Garrett Knox, but I told you that doesn't matter. Just think of me as someone who's trying to help you. I know this might be tough for you, but I know I'd want someone to advocate for my son, if something like this happened to him."

Moore sighed. "I'm not interested."

"Not interested? How could you not want to know the truth?"

Moore held up the device.

"Is this your only copy?"

Knox reached for it, but Moore pulled it back.

"That answers my question," Moore said. "I'll be holding on to this—and whatever's on here, but it better not ever find its way to the internet, or else I'll find you and make you regret you ever spoke with me. Are we clear?"

Knox cocked his head to one side.

"I just don't understand."

"Have you ever lost a child?"

Knox shook his head.

"Then you don't know the world of pain that comes with such a tragedy. And so here you are, asking me to not only relive all those emotions and feelings, but you want me to witness it by watching my son kill himself? When it comes to reading the room, you're full-on illiterate."

"It's just that—"

"Thank you for the footage, Mr. Knox, but I have another appointment I need to get to."

Knox stepped aside and allowed Moore to get into his car.

Upon returning to their car, Knox asked Makenzie if she was getting a signal.

"Loud and clear," she said, turning up the volume on her laptop.

The high-pitched ringing of a phone came through followed by a man's deep voice.

"How was the meeting?" he asked.

"Couldn't have gone better," Moore said. "Wellington accepted."

"That's great news."

"It is, but we've got another problem—a big problem. Ever heard of a guy named Garrett Knox?"

"What about him?"

"He just handed me what he claims is footage of Chase killing himself."

"That's not good."

"Yeah, if this got out, it'd ruin all our plans."

Then static started to interfere with the signal.

"Damnit," Makenzie said. "We're losing them."

But Knox had heard enough.

"We need to call Rico."

CHAPTER FORTY-SIX

Washington, D.C

Rico scooted forward in his chair and clasped his hands together, setting them on the dining room table. He glanced around the room at the French country décor, and then looked back at Ashley Moore. The room, like the rest of the house Rico managed to see, was spotless. She pushed a folder across the table to him and then sat back while he opened the file and examined the documents inside.

"You have to tell me what I'm looking at," Rico said. "I'm not all that familiar with the world of political documents."

"This is a candidate prospectus, essentially a document for potential donors regarding a particular candidate that makes the pitch for supporting them," she said.

"Interesting," Rico said as he flipped to the second page.

"Before you go any further, check the date," she said, pointing to the right upper portion of the page displaying a date.

He squinted, examining the document for a second time, unsure if his eyes were playing tricks on him.

"Is this right?" Rico asked.

"No, it's accurate," she said. "This is part of a section I found in his desk drawer labeled 'The Consortium'. Now, I'm still trying to figure out more about what The Consortium is, but I think this document is one that you'll find interesting."

Rico knit his forehead, scanning the pages in front of him. After a minute or so, he looked back up at Ashley.

"I'm not sure I understand why this is all relevant," he said.

"Look on page twelve," she said.

He thumbed to page twelve and started reading. The document states, "The ideal candidate has experienced great loss in his life, and if he hasn't already, it should be fabricated."

"Sounds odd," Rico said.

"More than just odd," Ashley said. "I'm assuming you've read some of the articles online written about Chase, right?"

"I have, but, Mrs. Moore, I'm not sure I understand how this relates to the purpose of my visit, which is to figure out where Erica Everhart is. You said you knew where she is."

"I said I knew what *happened* to her," Ashley said. "Small difference, but big distinction."

"Again, how is this related?" Rico asked.

"Well, Erica Everhart met with Thomas Quinn before he was scheduled to leave for a flight to the Congo and investigate what happened in Tango where my son died. But something happened to her. She was scheduled to be back here, but no one has heard from her since. I left a message with her editor, but she hasn't let me know that she's all right."

"And you're sure she would return your call?" Rico asked.

"Without a doubt," Ashley said.

"So, where could she be? Is it possible she simply didn't make the return flight home."

"Here's the thing. I called one of my friends over at the State Department to see if she could find out if Erica was still out of the country, but—nope—she's returned."

"Really?"

Ashley nodded. "Her passport scanned not long after her flight arrived, which suggests she's definitely here. But she hasn't reported to her editor or let anyone know where she's gone. And in case you haven't noticed, there have been some really odd things happening in this town, even for Washington—unusual scandals, murders of high-ranking officials, strange disappearances."

"But why are you so concerned about Erica?"

"For one, she's been a friend to me and Mark. She wrote a moving piece about Chase and the importance of suicide prevention, an article that brought enough awareness to Mark's bill that it gained enough support to pass along bi-partisan lines, which, as you probably know, is a rarity on Capitol Hill these days."

"But you found out something else you wanted her to know?"

Ashley glanced furtively toward the entryway to Rico's left before answering in a hushed tone.

"I didn't give you everything because I want Erica to be the one to break this story."

"Okay," Rico said. "I can respect that."

"But I want you to understand what's going on here. And maybe it'll help you figure out what's going on."

"If you want to tell me something off the record so I won't print it, I can agree to that."

"Great," Ashley said, tucking her hair behind her ears as she leaned forward. "The truth is, I also found an addendum to Mark's political candidate prospectus. And in it, there are some details about me."

"Is that unusual?"

"It is when you consider that we hadn't even met."

Rico pursed his lips.

"What exactly are you implying?" he said.

"I'm not speaking in riddles here," she said. "I'm telling you as plainly as I can. There are several pages within that prospectus which say what kind of person he's supposed to marry. And while I took offense to some of the characterizations when I first read them, I know they're right."

"Can you give me an example?"

"For starters, he was supposed to marry someone with a certain standard of looks," she said. "I won beauty pageants."

"It's not all that unusual for a politician to want to marry a beautiful woman. Hell, that's what most men want."

"But there's more, a lot more. Like for example, he wanted a woman that had connections within Washington. My father was a former senator."

"Still not surprising," he said. "The elite tend to gravitate toward their own kind."

"Then he wanted someone with religious convictions, as well as someone who wasn't personally ambitious and would want to stay at home rather than pursue her own career. That's me all day long."

"Quite frankly, you sound like perfect wife material," Rico said.

"But then get this. If I met all these requirements, a committee would have to approve me. And I remember after we had been dating a while and were talking about marriage, we went on this lake retreat somewhere. I can't even remember the name of it. But while I was there, we went to a formal dinner and I met a bunch of well-dressed people I'd never seen before. And I haven't seen them since."

"I will concede that seems a little strange."

"The document I read said this, and, I quote, 'The woman must adhere to these standards as defined in this document. Any deviation requiring separation will be dealt with in a manner designed to assure the ultimate goals of the candidate are met.'"

"That's a little disconcerting."

"If you were to read everything about the kind of woman Mark needed to marry, you'd see how I met every pre-requisite, both tangible and intangible. I even met the really superficial requirements. There was even a footnote explaining how brunettes were perceived to be smarter than blondes by the American public. Now, I love Mark, but this makes me wonder if I even know the man I married."

"So, now you want to expose this?"

She nodded.

"I mean, sort of. Mark is announcing his intent to seek his party's nomination in a bid to win the White House in a couple of days—and becoming the First Lady seems like it'd be pretty cool. But not like this. This essentially proves I was groomed for this role. I auditioned to be his wife—and I'm not here because he actually loves me or even likes me. I'm here because I help sell a good narrative, an electable narrative."

"That's not a reflection of you—but it's very telling about the Senator."

"But that's not even the half of it," Ashley said, as she leaned back in her seat. "The worst part is the page about what it takes to separate himself from other candidates, the element that could set him apart."

"And what's that?" Rico asked.

"The one where his son died."

Rico's jaw fell slack.

"What did you say?"

"That's right," Ashley said. "I can see the disbelief in your eyes, too. I mean, what kind of father would do that to his son, right? Now, I can't be certain that's what happened, but I do know that the document—that one that he's adhered to, since everything else in there is reflected in his life—details how to maximize tragedy in the life of a politician. And he immediately took steps to follow that within days of Chase dying. It's almost like he didn't really love Chase, but just used him to advance his political career. It's sick, really."

"But you don't know anything else about The Consortium group?"

She shook her head.

"I haven't been able to find any other documents with details about them," she said. "I only found this by accident one night when I was in his study. He's got another safe that I don't know the combination to, so maybe there's more in there. I just don't know. But I wanted to give this to Erica and see what she could make of it. More than anything, I want her to be found."

"I promise you that I'll do everything within my power to find out where she is," he said. "And when I do, I'll get her everything she needs to either expose this story and what your husband is doing —or give you a rational explanation."

"I really hope it isn't true," she said. "But there are too many signs, too many coincidences."

"Thank you for trusting this information with me, Mrs. Moore," Rico said. "I won't betray your trust."

Rico took pictures of the documents before gathering his notes and leaving. As soon as he reached his car, his phone rang with a call from Knox.

"What'd she tell you about Erica Everhart's disappearance?" Knox asked.

"Enough to know she's truly missing—but not in the way you might think," Rico said. "She's gone missing since she returned from Africa."

"That's not good."

"But that's just the tip of the iceberg,," Rico said before recounting everything he'd learned about the prospectus and The Consortium.

"There's no doubt in my mind now that Senator Moore is dirty," Knox said. "And in order to stop him, we need to expose him in the most public way possible. Do you think she's ready to see the truth about her son?"

"If she's not already, she's close," Rico said. "But I can't be the one to show it to her. It's gotta be Erica. She knows Erica and trusts her. If she were to show a copy of the footage you found in Johannesburg, there's no doubt in my mind she'd turn on her husband."

"And does Mrs. Moore know where Erica is?" Knox asked.

"Not yet," Rico said.

Knox grunted.

"I've got an idea about how to find her," he said. "But I'm gonna need your help, Mr. Robert Goodman, Esquire."

CHAPTER FORTY-SEVEN

Washington, D.C

Knox called one of his former Ranger buddies working at the Pentagon in an attempt to find the whereabouts of Erica Everhart.

"Garrett Knox, as I live and breathe," said Randy Fortier, a strapping Cajun who was as adept at charming the ladies with his smooth talking as with his rugged good looks. "I never thought I'd hear from you again. How's Montana?"

"Cold and miserable—help spread the word, will ya?" Knox said. "We've got way too many Californians invading our precious state. They're overwhelming us like Mormon crickets."

"Well, I don't know what those are, but I'll just take your word for it that it's bad."

"In Cajun terms, it's like bullfrogs in the swamp."

"Now that I understand," Fortier said. "Speaking of the swamp, I heard you had an unfortunate incident in one."

"More like the jungle, but no need to be picky about it. I survived, and I'm grateful for it."

"So, I'm sure you didn't call me to talk about crickets and crocodiles, but, man, it's so good to hear your voice. Now, what can I do for you?"

"I need a big favor," Knox said.

"Anything for you, Knoxeaux, my honorary Cajun friend."

Knox chuckled, remembering the nickname Fortier had given him.

"I need you to find out where someone is being held, probably someone who intelligence officials wouldn't want anyone to know about."

"That's a tall order," Fortier said.

"But if anyone can do it, I know you can."

Knox texted Fortier the details and then ended the call. A half-hour later, he called back with the details. When he finished passing along the location of Erica Everhart, Fortier began humming the Cajun folk song, "La Belle et le Capitaine."

"You owe me one," Fortier said, after he stopped. "Maybe next time we meet in Lafayette, I take you Zydeco dancin' again and we pick up the ladies like we did last time."

"That wasn't anything special," Knox said, trying to downplay the event. "Just something in the air that night, if you ask me."

"Why you always gotta be so humble, Knoxeaux?"

"Sorry, Fortier. Would you rather me tell you they were attracted to me like skeeters to bare legs the swamp?"

"Now, that's more like it—and highly accurate."

Knox smiled.

"Well, either way, I owe you one. So, if you want to take me Zydeco dancing again, I'll have to acquiesce to your demands. But I'd say we'll be more than square after that."

"Then pencil it into your calendar. And I can't wait."

"You excited about dancin' or the ladies?"

"Can't a man be excited about both?"

Knox thanked Fortier again, before ending the call and then passing along the information to Rico.

"Think you can do this?" Knox asked.

"It's all about the swagger," Rico said. "And that's not in short supply around here."

~

Later that afternoon, Rico entered the Homeland Security holding facility in a gray suit, hair slicked back, rimless glasses, and a mustache. He was amazed at how such a simple change in appearance still couldn't strip him of his imposing presence. His broad shoulders, big biceps, and chiseled jaw line were enough to make anyone cower—at least, anyone who wasn't on the battlefield clutching a weapon. Rico had a way about him that was both imposing yet inviting. People wanted to tell him everything they knew before he pulverized them. But they also wanted to tell him everything because he listened like a friend. The unique combination made Rico tough to resist on several different fronts. And no matter what approach he settled on, he always figured out a way to make it work.

Rico decided charm was the way to go with the woman seated at the front desk when he walked in the building.

"Sign in here," the woman said, barely making eye contact with him before shoving a clipboard through the small opening beneath the glass window. "I'll need a form of identification, as well as the name of the person you're here to see."

"I'm here for Erica Everhart," he said.

"Everhart, Everhart, Everhart—sorry, but I got nobody here by that name," she said, tapping the name on her keyboard."

"Might want to check again," Rico said. "She's not listed for various reasons. Probably a protection issue. If the public found out she was here—"

Rico shuddered, his eyes bulging.

"Okay," the woman said. "Let me check one more place."

She opened up a drawer and pulled out a clipboard. Then she put it back and shook her head.

"Sorry, but there's no one being held here by that name."

Maybe charm was the wrong way to go.

"Then I need to speak to your supervisor," Rico said. "I doubt you want to be affiliated with a litany of crimes, chief among them holding my client for more than forty-eight hours without charging her and denying her right to legal counsel."

The woman huffed and stood up.

"Let me get my supervisor," she said.

About a minute later, a man wearing a white polo shirt waddled into the reception area. A few loose strands of his dark stringy hair were combed across his otherwise bald head. His glasses hung tenuously from the end of his gnarly nose as he looked over the top of them at Rico.

"Sir, I understand you're treating my administrative assistant poorly."

"If asking her where a client of mine is and informing her that you will be served with a lawsuit if you don't allow her to speak with me is considered treating her poorly, I must treat everyone poorly who doesn't comply with their legal obligations."

The man glared at Rico.

"Who are you?"

"Robert G. Goodman, Esquire," Rico said. "And I demand to see my client Erica Everhart immediately."

"That's not how it works, Mr. Goodman."

"Actually, it is. You charge her, and then she gets legal counsel. Or you don't charge her and you release her within forty-eight hours. This isn't that hard to understand—or to comply with."

"Sorry, Mr. Goodman, but your intimidation tactics won't work with me, especially when this woman, uh—" the man started snapping, "—what is her name again?"

"Erica Everhart," Rico said.

"Yeah, Erica Everhart. None of your schemes work when she isn't even here."

Rico pulled out his phone and started recording a video.

"I wonder what the judge will think when he sees how you denied Erica Everhart her due process," Rico said. "How you lied and said she wasn't here on this date?"

Rico directed the camera at an LCD clock on the wall behind the man, displaying the day's date and time.

"I've seen the footage of when she returned to the country through customs and was taken into custody by Homeland Security agents. It's time for you to let me speak with her, otherwise anything you try to do in a court of law will be dismissed."

"Sorry, Mr. Goodman, but I can't make her appear when she's not here."

Rico decided to get more aggressive. He reached across the counter and snatched the clipboard from the man, easily prying it from his chubby fingers. Rico ran his finger down the list but didn't see her name. Then he flipped to the second page and found Erica Everhart.

"Well, would you look at that?" Rico said, as he zoomed in on her name with his camera. "The judge will love all this evidence."

"Okay, okay," the supervisor said he scanned the office and then glanced at the clipboard. "I must've missed her name when I first looked at it. I'll let you see her."

He gestured for Rico to follow him.

Rico followed the man, who escorted him to Erica's cell. He unfolded a chair against the far wall and offered it to Rico.

"You've got ten minutes," the man said. "And I'm being generous. Visiting hours have been over for a while now."

Rico glared at the man.

"You'll give me as much time as I need," Rico said. "Or else I won't be so generous, and I'll still send this footage to a judge and file a formal lawsuit against you."

"Fine," the man said. "Take all the time you need. Erica, you have a visitor."

Erica, who'd been lying on her back in bed, groaned as she rolled over, sat up, and rubbed her eyes.

"Am I finally getting a lawyer?" she asked.

Rico nodded and put his index finger to his lips and pointed at the camera on the far wall. He gestured for her to come closer to him before instructing her to speak in a hushed tone.

"What's going on?" she asked. "Do you know why I'm in prison? Nobody's told me anything."

"You're in prison because you've picked a fight with the wrong people."

"Picked a fight?" she said.

Rico gestured for her to keep her voice down.

"Picked a fight?" she repeated, in a whisper. "I just went to the Congo following a lead from a friend of mine."

"And what'd you find?" Rico asked.

"I found plenty—and when I got back, I found out my editor is compromised."

Rico drew back.

"Compromised? What do you mean?"

"My editor, David Langston, met me at the airport in a DHS interview room. He tells me that he's super disappointed in me that I would attempt to smuggle secrets to foreign actors while I was in Africa and that he had to fire me. He knew damn well that I wouldn't do anything like that. And he said all that without a shred of evidence."

"Well, we've got the evidence," Rico said as he held out his phone. "Does this place look familiar?"

Rico held out his phone and showed her the footage of Tango.

She nodded, then gasped, covering her mouth with her hands. Tears streaked down her face as she recognized what was happening.

"Was that—"

Rico nodded. "Chase Moore. And we believe that's your buddy Joe Garber, in the suit there, who gave Chase the gun."

"Those bastards," she said. "What were they doing?"

"We believe it's a covert biological weapons program," he said. "We're not sure if it's sanctioned by the military, but we at least know a few of the people involved, including the senator himself."

Erica frowned.

"You mean to tell me that Senator Moore allowed his own son to be a part of this?"

"It appears that way. Now, can you tell me what you saw when you went there?"

She filled in Rico on everything she saw—the cordoned off

village, the rotting carcasses, the ghost town feel of Tango, her discovery of NocturaCorp.

"I don't know anything about NocturaCorp, so that might be something you could look into for me," she said. "I'm not sure just how culpable they are, but their logo was on everything."

"I'll find out what I can," Rico said.

Then she growled and punched her fist against an open hand.

"I want to expose that son of a bitch."

"You and me both," Rico said. "But first we need to get you out of here."

"And when is that going to happen?"

"Soon," Rico said. "I'll fill you in on all the details once you're out. Probably tomorrow sometime at the earliest."

Rico stood to leave.

"What's your name?" she asked.

"Officially?"

She nodded.

"Robert G. Goodman, Esquire," he said with a wink. "Unofficially, I'm officially dead. But we'll talk all about that tomorrow."

"Who told you about me, Mr. Goodman?"

"It's a long story," he said. "But oddly enough, you have Ashley Moore, the senator's wife, to thank for all this."

"Well, tell her thank you for me," she said. "I'm sure you'll speak with her before I do."

"Tomorrow, I'll let you tell her yourself."

Rico returned the folding chair to the wall. He marched down the hallway and got a guard's attention, who escorted Rico back to the front, where he told the supervisor that there'd better not be any more monkey business.

When Rico returned to his car, he dialed the number of a lawyer he knew and filled him in on Erica's situation. The man promised to secure Erica's release in the morning.

Rico sighed before he ignited the engine and headed back to the trio's temporary base.

CHAPTER FORTY-EIGHT

Washington, D.C

Senator Moore entered through the door leading from the garage and strode straight to his study. He flung his briefcase onto the chair next to his desk. After filing a few documents, he glanced at the blinking notification on his desktop. He clicked it and waited for the program to open.

Seconds later, Moore watched the footage from the motion-activated cameras he'd installed in his house. Set to record whenever there was more than one person in the room, Moore had his fair share of clips he'd saved whenever Ashley was feeling frisky and jumped him. He knew she wouldn't like the fact that he'd recorded them. But if there was one thing he'd learned about how to survive in Washington, it was that he could never have enough leverage. And that meant even on his wife. However, the file now playing on his computer screen wasn't of him and Ashley—it was of Ashley and another man.

Moore sped up the footage, which didn't contain any sound. They seemed to be doing nothing more than talking, but then there was a moment where they got up and moved to another room. The picture faded to black and didn't turn back on again until fifteen minutes later when they both re-entered the room. There was an awkward hug at the end and a nervous laugh, followed by a more professional handshake. Whoever that was at his house, and whatever had happened—Moore didn't like it.

What room did they go into? And why didn't any other camera begin recording?

Moore's system was supposed to capture any movement in the front of the house—the living room, the dining room, the sitting room, the solarium, his study. But where else had they gone? If Ashley had taken him to any other room, that showed a level of familiarity or intimacy, both of which Moore found disconcerting.

Was Ashley cheating on me?

Moore's paranoia consumed him. Even if she was just a trophy wife, a woman with the perfect backstory to make the media swoon and love him even more, he didn't want her cheating on him. If that kind of development went public, his campaign would be dead on arrival. He needed to keep everything looking perfect from the outside if he was going to have the best chance of winning his party's nomination. Despite meticulously following the plan for becoming president, Moore hadn't foreseen such a stumble this close to the finish line. His quest to ensure he was undeniably the best candidate had a hiccup. Over the past few months, he'd paid close attention to the details, but little attention to his wife.

He poured a drink and thought for a moment.

Maybe there's a way I could turn this into a positive, too.

But first he needed to know if his suspicions about Ashley were right. He walked over to the corner of the room, dragging a chair behind him. He eased onto the chair and stood up. Moore reached high and picked up the snow globe perched atop his bookshelf, the knick-knack he used to conceal one of his cameras. The light underneath was red instead of green, meaning that it had malfunctioned somehow and required a reset.

He swore softly as he held down the button, resetting the device. Once he saw the light had turned green again, he returned the snow globe to its spot and climbed down from the chair. After putting everything back in its place, he meandered into the kitchen in search of Ashley. When he found her, she was hunched over a pot of mine-strone soup, eyes closed as she inhaled the scent.

"Is that what I think it is?" he asked, a faint smile spreading across his lips.

"If you think it's minestrone, then it sure is," she said.

She returned her attention to the pot, stirring it without giving him a second look. Based on how she treated him most days upon coming home from work, Moore found her behavior odd.

She's probably just focused. Relax.

"How was your day?" he asked.

"Good. And you?"

"Fine," he said, growing more suspicious by the second. Her response hadn't been warm. She was distant, cold.

To Moore, she acted as if she were little more than part of the wait staff. A cook, a cleaner, an organizer—but nothing more. Something had happened; that much he was certain about. It was the *what* that had him bamboozled.

After dinner, he retreated to his study, where he worked on the details of his candidacy announcement. He stayed there for several hours before Ashley poked her head in the door.

"You coming to bed?" she asked. "It's getting late."

"I'll be there in about five minutes."

"Okay," she said. "See you then."

He offered a faint smile, which she returned.

Once he closed up his study for the night, Moore went back to his bedroom and began his nighttime rituals—brushing his teeth, floss-ing, washing his face. He took a few furtive glances at Ashley, who was busy with her bedtime routine as well.

Ashley beat him to bed by all of a half-minute, and she hadn't yet turned off the lamp on her nightstand.

"Ashley," he said, clutching his phone, "I have a question for you."

"Okay," she said, drawing out the word and narrowing her eyes.

"Are you having an affair?" he asked quickly.

"Whatever would make you think such a thing?" she fired back.

"You didn't answer my question."

"But I did," she said.

"Then please explain this to me," he said, as he held out his phone.

Moore had transferred the footage onto his phone, and pushed play before handing it to her.

Ashley's confused look melted into anger, her eyes narrowing.

"Are you spying on me, Mark? I mean, is this what our marriage has come to? You recording me when you're not here to make sure I don't go astray? You're unbelievable."

"Look, honey, I'm not trying to be belligerent here, but you're still not answering my question, which makes me think you are doing something behind my back."

"I'm not having an affair, Mark. The truth is, that's an image consultant. I figured that if I was about to become the First Lady, I better have all my i's dotted and t's crossed. I thought that's what you'd want?"

Her face softened.

"I'd never cheat on you," she said. "We're in this together, remember? For better or worse? Sickness and in health? Poverty and wealth?"

"I'm sorry, it's just that—"

"Forget about it," Ashley said.

He got up to get a glass of water when he noticed a business card of a political consultant company lying on the dresser. He picked up the card and studied the details.

"Is this the guy?" he asked.

She squinted as she tried to read the name.

"I think so," she said.

Moore committed the number to memory. When he reached the kitchen, he dialed the number on his cell phone. Instead of a simple voicemail, with the man saying his name and asking the caller to leave a message, it was a generic recording, the kind phone companies put on every account.

Instead of answers, Moore's questions about what happened that day increased.

Just as he finished filling up a glass with water and ice, his phone buzzed with a call. He thought it might be the consultant calling him back, but it wasn't. He recognized the voice right away, which was followed with more disturbing news.

"Just figure out a way to get it done," Moore said. "I don't care what it takes. Understand?"

Moore hung up and returned to his bedroom, where Ashley was sitting up in the bed, scrolling through her phone. Once he joined her under the covers, she swiped through several images of dresses, asking his opinion on each one. After he gave her his opinion, which she totally ignored, deciding on another dress, he turned the lights out and rolled over. He pulled up the covers and closed his eyes.

"I can't wait for your announcement," she said. "Two more days, right?"

"Uh huh," Moore said, his mind racing back toward the phone call.

"I can't wait," Ashley said. "I can't wait to be the First Lady."

"Me either," Moore said.

He knew a restless night of sleep awaited him. And while he couldn't wait to let the world know he was running for president, he also had some more details that needed to be taken care of before he could even begin to think about that.

An hour after he'd turned out the lights, he was still lying on his bed staring at the ceiling. He eased into a sitting position and looked at Ashley, who was sleeping soundly. Then he got out of bed and went back to his office to review the footage from earlier that day. He remembered seeing something that bugged him, something that terrified him more than her having an affair.

He found the location in the footage and enlarged it as much as he could, concentrating on Ashley's mouth as she spoke. Once he realized what she said, he clenched his fists, but resisted the urge to punch something. Then he slowed it down to watch it again, hoping that he was wrong.

He wasn't.

The words tumbled out of her mouth, obvious from studying her lips closely.

The Consortium.

He reached for his drawer and rifled through his files, praying that he hadn't forgotten to put the folder back in the safe. But he found it, and opened it up. Everything about his portion of the plan was there. If Ashley had read it, he doubted she'd ever trust him again.

He snapped the folder shut and placed it in the safe.

How could I have been so careless?

Then Moore returned to the footage and saw two other words that he recognized come out of his wife's mouth.

Erica Everhart.

He cursed and then dialed a phone number.

"Senator, what are you doing calling so late?" the man answered groggily.

"Ms. Everhart's visitor today—can you get me footage of him? I don't think he is who he said he is."

"Give me a few minutes."

Moore wanted to scream, mostly out of anger—at himself. With a couple of careless oversights, he'd jeopardized his future with the group, his prospects of becoming president, his lifelong dream. But as long as the details hadn't leaked out yet, there was still time to prevent disaster.

His phone buzzed with a text from his contact, along with a short clip of the man who'd visited Erica Everhart in the DHS holding facility. Moore's eyes narrowed as he recognized the man as the same one who'd visited Ashley.

Moore collected a screen capture of the man and entered it into a CIA facial recognition database. As he waited for a match, Moore contemplated how to proceed. He called his contact and told him that Everhart needed to be moved immediately to another facility. Then he placed another call with instructions for another man.

When the database program chirped, signaling it had found a

match, Moore read the words on the screen again, wondering if he'd made a mistake. But he couldn't deny it—or wish it away.

Frederico Garcia was supposed to be dead, killed at the hands of Garrett Knox. At least, that's what Ballard had told him. But Garcia was very much alive, evidenced by the fact that he'd paid a visit to Ashley and then Erica Everhart—all in the last twenty-four hours.

Moore recognized that he needed to be hyper-vigilant until he won the office of the president. No detail was too insignificant to be scrutinized. It wouldn't be easy, but his margin of error had vanished. And if he was going to succeed, he needed to control everything— including Frederico Garcia.

And the only way he was going to do that was to control Ashley.

Moore padded down the hallway before slipping back into bed without waking his wife. But he couldn't go to sleep. He needed to concoct a plan to silence them all. And after another half-hour, he figured out a way. He smiled before turning over and finally going to sleep.

CHAPTER FORTY-NINE

Washington, D.C

Erica Everhart woke with a start, a bright light shining in her face. She shielded her eyes as she tried to orient herself. But before she could get a word out, she felt a pair of strong hands wrap around her arms and lift her off her cot.

"What's going on?" she asked.

Without an answer, a pair of prison guards nudged her toward her cell door, which was wide open.

"Will someone please tell me what's happening?"

"You're being released," one of the guards said.

"Released? Is there any more explanation beyond that?"

The guard shook his head.

"But I'm being released right now? In the middle of the night?"

"That's right," the man said, with a grunt. "Better now than never."

"Yeah, but—"

She stopped herself, realizing that the men escorting her down the corridor had nothing to do with the decision. They were just following orders, likely enjoying the break from an otherwise monotonous overnight watch.

When Erica reached the front, a man shoved a clipboard in front of her and asked her to sign it. Once she did, he handed her a manila envelope with the belongings she had on her upon re-entering the country. The man also pointed toward her suitcase, which was next to a bench on the other side of the room.

"So, that's it?" she asked. "I can just walk out of here."

The man nodded.

"Need me to call someone for you?" he asked.

She tapped her phone repeatedly before realizing it was dead.

"Yeah, I guess so."

"I'll have them meet you out front."

As she stood there, she searched through her purse to see if they'd taken anything. Nothing appeared to have been touched except for the GPS tracker. It had been turned off. Or had it run out of batteries? Erica wasn't too concerned about it. She hadn't moved since she'd been detained for the past two days, though she wondered if that's how Ashley knew she'd arrived back in the U.S. She decided not to turn it on, and slid it back into her purse.

Moments later, a van appeared out front. She scowled as she looked at it.

"You called a van for me?" she asked.

"Lady, I just called a taxi service. Whatever vehicle they brought had nothing to do with me."

"Okay, just kind of odd, don't ya think?"

"Maybe that's all they had available. It *is* two o'clock in the morning."

Erica thanked the man, and then ventured outside, where a tall man was leaning against the passenger side door.

"Reginald," the man said, offering his hand to take her bags.

"Erica," she said, her bags close to her. "I'd rather just keep this with me, if it's all the same to you."

"No problem," Reginald said. "We've got plenty of room."

As soon as the door slid open, two men grabbed Erica and yanked her inside. She let out a scream, truncated when one of the men clamped a gloved hand over her mouth. Unable to fight off the stronger men, she plunged her hand into her purse and clicked the tracking device. A few seconds later, her body went limp.

CHAPTER FIFTY

Washington, D.C

Knox surveyed the motel room and then sipped a cup of Kona coffee. A grin spread across his face, eyes closed as he eased his face over the steaming mug.

"It's the little things, isn't it?" Makenzie asked, startling Knox.

He looked up at her sheepishly.

"I didn't know anyone was watching."

"That's okay," she said. "I belt out Whitney Houston's 'I'm Every Woman' in the shower most mornings."

"That's a fact I didn't know about you," he said. "But you need to give credit where credit is due. That's really Chaka Khan's song. It's got a much better disco vibe, if you're into that style."

"I have bellbottoms," Makenzie said.

"You *wear them naturally*, don't you?"

She rolled her eyes. "Bad dad jokes are back."

"No, no. They're Knox Knox jokes. And don't you forget it."

"A future generation of children have no idea how they're about to be tortured by you."

Knox held up his coffee cup toward Makenzie.

"And cheers to you too. I snuck out this morning and got us the good stuff for our cheap coffeemaker."

"Any ideas yet on how we're going to expose Senator Moore?" she asked, as she poured herself a cup of coffee and joined him at the kitchen table.

Knox nodded.

"As a matter of fact, I found an interesting article on the Beltway Confidential blog this morning," he said. "Some anonymous source in this article—meaning, Moore's press secretary—said that Senator Moore has a big upcoming announcement to make tomorrow. And I quote, 'The former paratrooper plans to drop the news tomorrow afternoon.' They might as well have just told us what they were going to do."

"They did," she said. "They said they're going to make a big announcement tomorrow."

"Come on, Makenzie. You gotta read between the lines. A former paratrooper is going to 'drop the news'? If that's not telegraphing what's going to happen, I don't know what is."

Makenzie squinted at him.

"I'm not sure I'm tracking with you."

"*Drop the news? Paratrooper?* Oh, come on, Makenzie. You got this one."

"Is this some sort of pun?"

"Maybe not a pun, but a play on words," he said.

"Sorry, my brain isn't hardwired for lame jokes the way yours is."

Knox sighed.

"A paratrooper drops in on a location. He's going to jump out of an airplane and land before announcing his run for presidency. It's as plain as the nose on your face."

"Yeah, that seems farfetched to me."

"We could get Rico to confirm it with the senator's wife."

"That could make her suspicious, if we start asking questions like that."

Knox took another long pull on his drink before smacking his lips as he set it down.

"At this point, should we really be worried about how suspicious we look?" he asked. "We need to stop this monster before he somehow generates support for his presidency, and then will have all the power he needs to unleash a virus on the world like Incaendium."

"But why? Why would he do that?"

"Those are the right questions," Knox said. "But we can worry about them later. It's the *what* we need to focus on stopping."

Rico groaned from the couch, rolling over and then squinting as he stared in Knox's direction.

"Would you two knock it off?" he said. "Can't you see I'm trying to sleep here?"

"It's almost seven-thirty, Rico. Or has your time away from the Rangers made you soft?"

"What a ridiculous question," Rico said.

Knox grabbed Rico's phone and tossed it at him.

"Give Mrs. Moore a call and see if she can confirm what's happening with her husband's big announcement tomorrow," Knox said.

"She's not going to trust me if she thinks I'm doing something shady," Rico said.

"Just call her and ask. Tell her we want to know because that's where we want to expose him. It won't seem like such an odd question, if you pose it that way."

Rico grunted and staggered to his feet. He made his way over to the coffeemaker and tipped it over, draining no more than a couple of sips out of the pot.

"Are you just trying to make me grumpy?" Rico asked.

"You do a good job of that without any help," Knox said, with a wink.

Rico narrowed his eyes and growled before tapping in Ashley Moore's number into his cell phone. He placed the call on speaker and waited for her to answer.

"This is Ashley," she said.

"Mrs. Moore, this is Robert Goodman. I apologize for calling you so early and—"

"I was already up, Robert. Now were you able to get Erica out of custody?"

"I think it's a little too early for that to happen, but I'll let you know as soon as I hear something."

"So, you're calling about something else?"

"As a matter of fact, I am," Rico said. "I was curious if you knew how and when your husband was going to announce his intention to run for his party's nomination for president."

"He's going to do it tomorrow, but he hasn't told me anything yet about how he plans on announcing it," she said. "He likes to surprise me."

"And the world, too, apparently."

"That's classic Mark."

"Well, if you don't mind, see if you can coax the details out of him. If you do, we should be able to expose him when he does it."

"I'll see what I can do," she said, in a hushed tone. "I need to get going. I'll call you later."

CHAPTER FIFTY-ONE

Washington, D.C

Ashley Moore stuffed her cell phone into her back pocket and continued stirring the eggs she was making for her husband. A few minutes later, the senator shuffled into the kitchen with a folder in his hand. He headed straight for the cupboard, selected a mug, and poured himself a cup of coffee.

"Good morning," he said, with a yawn.

"Did you sleep all right?" she asked.

"Not really," he said.

"Sleepless night?"

"I've got a lot on my mind lately, especially my novel."

Ashley glanced at him, her eyes widening.

"Your novel? Since when did you start writing a novel?"

"Well, I haven't technically started yet," he said. "But I've been in the planning stages for a long time. It's a political thriller."

"What's it called?"

"The Consortium," he said, as he tossed the folder on the countertop near her.

She peered at the folder, which was the same one she'd seen in his office.

"What's it about?" she asked.

"About a group that tries to take over the most powerful political positions in the world," he said. "The main character carefully selects his wife and everyone else around him in order to accomplish this mission. Similar to *The Manchurian Candidate*, but instead of others grooming him, he grooms himself."

"Sounds interesting," she said.

Have I gotten this all wrong?

She dished out a plate of eggs for her husband and joined him for breakfast. After a few minutes of small talk, she asked him about his big announcement.

"So, when are you going to tell me more about your big announcement?" she asked. "I want to be ready."

"Tomorrow, I'm going to skydive over the city."

"Can you do that?"

Moore smiled wryly.

"Not usually, but I happen to know a few people. It's all set up and ready to go. And I want you to come with me."

"Of course, honey. I wouldn't miss it for anything."

"With me in the plane," he said.

She cocked her to one side.

"Oh, Mark, you know how I hate heights. Would it be all right if I just watched it from the ground?"

"If you're going to be with me, I want you *with* me. We need to face our fears together, as a couple."

"I don't know."

"Come on. It'll be fun. You won't have to jump, unless you want to, which would be awesome."

"That's *definitely* not happening."

"Well, I want you there. And if you think it would help, you can bring along your image consultant, so he can get a behind-the-scenes feel for what you need to project that winning look."

"I'm not sure he'll want to."

"Really? That's surprising. Who wouldn't want to a front row seat to history? Just ask him for me, okay?"

"All right. I'll see what he wants to do."

"Great," he said, scraping his fork along his plate to gather his last bite of eggs. "It's going to be fun."

"And where's this happening?"

He gave her the name of the skydiving outfit that was handling his jump and scooped up his briefcase before heading off to work.

Ashley thought for a moment before her eyes fell on the folder sitting on the counter. She shuffled across the room and picked it up. Then she poured another cup of coffee before heading to the solarium and reading the document.

Thirty minutes passed before she decided she'd had it all wrong. The details surrounding Chase's death still made her question her husband, just not as much. If she'd gotten this wrong, she couldn't rule out that she'd concocted this entire thing in her head. She desperately wanted there to be an explanation for why Chase committed suicide—and she was searching for anything to piece together to help her understand. She mulled over everything she knew while finishing her coffee before reaching a conclusion.

She put the folder back on her husband's desk and then called Goodman.

"Mr. Goodman," she said, "I wanted to let you know that I've made a mistake in judgment."

"Pardon me," he said.

"I want to apologize to you for dragging you into this thing. I'm afraid I was terribly wrong about my husband."

"Ashley, are you being forced to say this?"

"No," she said. "Mark would never do something like that to me. He's on his way to work."

"So, you think you made a mistake? What about the document you found? The Consortium, remember?"

"Those were notes for a novel he's working on," she said. "He voluntarily told me that himself this morning. He has no idea I saw it."

"You never mentioned it?"

"No, not once," she said. "I think I was trying to see something that wasn't there. I'm so sorry that I dragged you into this. Please accept my sincerest apologies, and tell Erica I'll still talk to her, but I don't think this is the story she thinks it is."

Goodman paused a beat before answering her.

"You haven't heard from Erica?" he asked.

"No. Why?"

"I found out she was released last night," Goodman said. "I had an attorney friend go to the DHS holding facility and demand her release this morning. But when he got there, she was already gone. I thought she would've contacted you by now, especially after all that she told me."

"Hang on a second," Ashley said. "Let me check something."

She called up her email and had an automated message from the GPS device she'd given Erica.

"Well, she's definitely out—and her GSP tracker is reporting her location again," Ashley said.

"You have a GPS tracker on her?"

"I gave it to her before she left for the Congo as a safety precaution. I didn't want anything to happen to her."

"So, where does it say she is now?"

Ashley gave him the coordinates.

"And what about the announcement tomorrow?" Goodman asked. "Do you know where it's going to be?"

"He hasn't told me anything about it," Ashley lied.

"Okay," Goodman said. "Let us know once you hear something."

"Actually, I'm thinking what you're wanting to do probably isn't a good idea anymore."

"But you said—"

"I know what I said, but I was wrong. And I would appreciate it if you'd respect my wishes. I think I got some facts jumbled up. It's been a tough time for me, and I haven't always been thinking straight."

"But your son—"

"We're done," Ashley said. "Understand?"

"Understood," he said, before ending the call.

Ashley sighed, hoping her instincts about her husband were right this time. At least, she wanted them to be right. But she would think about it later. She had a dress to pick out.

Ashley practiced her beauty queen wave, one she'd perfected while winning pageants as a teenager. She'd almost forgotten what it was like to walk on stage in front of thousands of people gathered to admire you.

She smiled at the thought.

Ashley could already feel the intoxicating feeling of being America's First Lady. At least she could imagine it—and she couldn't wait.

CHAPTER FIFTY-TWO

Atlanta, Georgia

Violet Warren pursed her lips as she stared across her desk at Will Mitchell, her boss and director of the CDC. He leaned back in his chair, his left foot resting on his right knee while tapping a pencil on his hand. After a few seconds of silence, he arched an eyebrow.

"Violet, are you still with me?" he asked.

"Yes, sir," she said, stumbling over her words. "I'm just trying to understand why you would make this request. Protocol says we don't need to do this for another—"

"Protocol isn't set in stone," Mitchell said, as he waved dismissively. "It's only there as a guideline for how to handle the norm. But you have to admit that this isn't the norm."

"Sir, to be completely frank, it wasn't anything. None of the tests came back positive, so why would we even make this case a priority?"

"We could've always made a mistake."

Violet scowled. "Really? A mistake? We ran *two* tests on their blood samples, and they all came back negative."

"And you didn't consider running a third test?"

"Why would we?" she said. "Protocol says two tests are sufficient. The chances of us missing something like that on two tests are infinitesimal. A third test would surely be a waste of time and resources."

"I'm not asking for a third test," Mitchell said. "I'm asking for a follow-up test."

She eyed the pink stress ball on her desk before picking it up. She squeezed it several times and exhaled slowly, anything to keep herself from erupting at the stupidity of Mitchell's response.

Another clueless government bureaucrat.

"If you want me to reach out to them, I will," she said. "But I must warn you that this will in all likelihood be a colossal waste of time."

Mitchell slapped his knee and offered a thin smile before standing.

"We're a government-run entity—what do we know, if not how to spend money needlessly and create programs that waste everyone's time?"

Violet knit her brow.

"Is that a joke, sir? Because I take my job very seriously."

"Take my comment however you like—I don't care," he said, as he held out a piece of paper. "Just please call those two subjects, give them directions to this facility in Washington or one near wherever they might be, and have them report immediately for a blood test. Make it sound urgent, almost like you've found something."

"You want me to lie?" she asked, as she took the paper.

He shook his head.

"I'm thinking more along the lines of professional embellishment," he said. "You know good and well that if you don't create sufficient panic, the public will pay you no attention. And I think these two need some extra motivation to induce compliance. Think you can do that for me?"

She sighed.

"Sorry, sir, but I don't think I can."

Mitchell narrowed his eyes, his tone measured as he responded.

"If you can't perform a simple task like this, I'm not sure you're the right person for this job. I need someone who's not afraid of inconveniencing a few people, especially if it's for the good of the whole."

"But we know it's not," she said. "This is just unnecessary, like I said before."

"This isn't optional," he said. "Now, if you're going to dissent, perhaps I can help you find a job that's more suited for your dissent."

A guttural growl emanated from within Violet. She didn't try to hide it either. But she ultimately acquiesced, deciding that while it wasn't necessary, it also wasn't harmful. Mitchell just wanted the two patients to get a follow-up test.

Let it go, Violet. Let it go.

"Okay, I'll do it," she said, struggling to mask her reluctance.

"Good," Mitchell said, as he clapped his hands. "Tell them you found a strange mutation or something, anything to convince them to come back in. And then send me a report in an hour about how it went. I look forward to hearing good things."

He didn't wait for her response before he spun on his heels and headed toward the door.

"Good luck," he said, as he waved lazily, his back to her.

Violet waited until he was out of the room before muttering a few choice words to herself. Then she rifled through her contacts list and found the numbers for the two South African patients. It could be worse, she thought to herself, before coming to terms with the fact that getting to talk to Garrett Knox and his chiseled handsome self wouldn't be the worst thing she'd ever been asked to do—not by a long shot.

She called Knox and Makenzie Hall, leaving messages with them both, pleading for them to go to the CDC offices in Washington.

A half-hour later, Mitchell asked her if she'd reached out to them and, if so, what they said.

Violet fired back a quick cordial response, disguising how she truly felt.

Don't micromanage me.

She returned to her work, though thoroughly distracted, wondering how such a mistake could've initially been made by South African health officials. After a few minutes, she put it out of her mind.

CHAPTER FIFTY-THREE

Washington, D.C

As Knox paced around the motel room, refining his plans for how to expose Senator Moore, he stopped for a moment, inserted a battery into his phone, and turned it on. He was surprised to see a notification for a voicemail.

"There's only a handful of people who have this number," he said, holding up his phone. "Who could've left me a message?"

"Is that your burner?" Makenzie asked.

"One of several," he said. "You and Rico have the number. Ballard, too."

Her eyes widened.

"You think Ballard called you?"

He shrugged.

"Only one way to find out."

He tapped the access code into the phone and waited. Seconds later, he listened as Dr. Violet Warren left him a message about needing a follow-up blood sample.

"It was that CDC doc," he said. "She said there was a strange mutation she noticed in my blood samples after re-examining them, and they want us both to give samples."

"Think that's a good idea?" she asked. "What if it's a trap?"

"I'm more worried about it *not* being a trap," Knox said. "You saw what the virus can do to people. Besides, Ballard's out of the picture. Plus, Dr. Warren seemed like she was serious about her work, and definitely not one of Ballard's lackeys."

"Can we just look up the address to make sure it's legit?"

Knox nodded before he listened to the message again and jotted down the address. Then he searched for it on the internet. Seconds later, results returned on the screen displaying an official CDC facility. He pointed at the screen, showing it to Makenzie.

"There it is," he said, turning the screen around so she could see it. "I know Ballard is good, but he's not so good that he can create a fake address for a CDC facility with pictures of the sign and reviews from four years ago, *especially* when he's missing."

"I don't know, Knox."

"We can kill two birds with one stone," he said. "First, we make sure we're not about to be overwhelmed with Incaendium and die, much less spread it around to others. And we can grab those chemicals we need from a medical facility for our plan tomorrow."

"Or we could be walking into a trap."

"How are they going to trap us there?"

"Follow us after we leave? Inject us with something? I don't know."

"If they were going to do that with me, they would've already done it."

"You know they can actually do this, right?"

He furrowed his brow.

"You watch too much television."

"It's a thing, I swear."

"Come on, Makenzie. Let's go give them our blood samples—if anything, just to make sure they didn't miss something or there's some crazy mutation that we do have that's going to make me or you the infamous patient zero of the Incaendium virus. I mean, could you live with yourself if that was true?"

She sighed.

"If we do have it, we've infected so many people already, what would it matter?"

"Maybe, but for my sanity's sake—and maybe the opportunity to get those chemicals—can we just go?"

"I'm not going to win this argument, am I?"

He shook his head.

Makenzie grabbed the keys off the nightstand.

"Whatever," she said. "Let's go."

A half-hour later, Knox and Makenzie entered the CDC facility. Knox scanned the area and didn't notice anything suspicious. No extra feds. No fed vehicles sitting around in the parking lot. There wasn't anything to suggest that they were walking into a trap.

He told the receptionist at the front desk who they were and what they were there for. She pecked on her keyboard before she copied something off the screen.

"Just have a seat in the lobby and someone will call you in a moment," she said.

Makenzie eased into her seat and glanced around the room.

"Have I ever told you how much I hate hospitals?"

"This isn't a hospital," Knox said. "It's a research facility."

"No difference to me," Makenzie said. "It still smells the same."

"Is that your only beef with the place?"

"Probably," she said, with a shrug before falling quiet.

Knox leafed through a magazine before a woman called their names and beckoned them back. They followed her through a door that swung open automatically once they approached it. She led them down a long corridor near what Knox felt like had to be the back of the building. Then she gestured into a room at the end of a hall and closed the door.

Knox studied the room. It was painted stark white with tile

flooring that had been meticulously mopped. There were two examination tables in each corner of the room, though they both looked more comfortable than the ones Knox usually used for his yearly checkup. Other than that, the only other furniture in the room was a small table in the corner with three chairs.

"This is interesting," Makenzie said. "Never seen an exam room like this. Where are the cupboards to store things?"

Knox shrugged. "Maybe it's a new design or something."

A few minutes passed before someone knocked at the door. Knox beckoned the person inside. A man wearing a white lab coat strode inside with two young women. The man introduced himself as Dr. Boris Hoffmann, and instructed Knox and Makenzie to sit on the end of the exam tables. Within a minute, Hoffmann's assistants had plunged needles into Knox and Makenzie's arms, the blood quickly flowing into vials. Meanwhile, Hoffmann explained to them the dangers of Incaendium, and other symptoms that might indicate a viral infection.

"Sounds like every other virus out there," Knox said.

Hoffmann raised an eyebrow. "Trust me. Incaendium is *not* like every other virus. You don't want it."

"So I hear," Knox said.

Once the women finished, they both quickly injected Knox and Makenzie with something, before they had time to protest or ask questions.

"All done," Hoffmann said, clapping his hands and then gesturing for the women to exit the room. "I'll be back in just a minute to wrap up and get you on your way."

They scurried into the hallway with Hoffmann right behind them.

"See," Knox said, "that wasn't so difficult, now was it?"

"Why are we still here?" she asked.

"He said he's going to come back and wrap up with us."

Makenzie winced in pain, pinching the bridge of her nose.

"You all right?" Knox asked.

"Just a little lightheaded, that's all. It's how I usually react after getting my blood drawn."

Then Makenzie fell backward onto her exam table. Knox got up and rushed over to help her. Then he realized he didn't feel well, either. He took a couple of steps before he collapsed in a heap on the floor, his field of vision winnowing until everything went black.

CHAPTER FIFTY-FOUR

Washington, D.C

Rico shimmied up a drainage pipe as he worked his way onto a rooftop across the street from the GPS location for Erica Everhart. He scanned the area before easing into a prone position and studying the modern three-story home composed mostly of glass and white stucco. After watching the place for nearly ten minutes, Rico didn't see any movement inside. He began wondering if she'd already been moved again, and the GPS tracker had been left there. Or even intentionally placed there to throw off anyone searching for her.

The only portion of the house that was difficult to see was the top floor, which used frosted glass for privacy and contained what was likely the master suite, with a rooftop balcony. While Rico wanted to leave and report that it was a dead end to his partners, he didn't want to do so without making sure he'd performed due diligence. He slung his rucksack over his back and climbed down, then proceeded to approach the house.

To avoid the camera on the front porch, Rico walked past the house and entered a neighbor's backyard three houses away. He scrambled up and over fences until he reached the house, and then used a trellis on the side to scale the wall. Upon reaching the top, he eased onto the rooftop balcony and tried to see if he could detect any movement inside. He crouched behind a small outdoor couch on the balcony and waited.

Nothing.

After a few minutes, he was almost convinced no one was there. But then he thought he heard a noise coming from inside. He decided to try the door, but it was locked as he expected. Pulling out his pick set, he went to work on opening the door. After a couple of minutes, he succeeded.

Rico entered the house and gently closed the door behind him, listening carefully for any noises.

Still nothing.

He eased down the steps until he heard the faint sound of someone clearing his throat, followed by the sound of a glass clinking down onto a surface. Rico craned his neck to see around the corner and found a man in a suit lounging on the couch reading a book. When Rico was close enough that he was confident he could hit the man if he made any sudden movements, he spoke.

"Where is she?" Rico asked.

"Hey—what the—" the man said, as he scrambled to his feet.

"Easy," Rico said, as he moved closer, his gun trained on the man's chest. "Don't make a mistake you'll regret."

The man raised his hands in surrender.

"Look, I don't know who you are or who you think I am, but—"

"Where's the girl?" Rico asked again, in a measured tone, but with a growl.

"I—I—I don't know what you're talking about," he said. "There's no girl here."

Rico cocked his head to one side.

"Ever wonder what it would feel like to have your kneecap blown off?"

The man shook his head.

"Good," Rico said. "You won't have to wonder in about three seconds, if you don't tell me where she is."

He aimed the weapon at the man's knee.

"Okay, okay," he said. "She's in the basement. And, please, I'm just following orders."

Rico marched over toward the man and pistol whipped him, knocking him out. Then he dragged the man down the stairs into the basement. Once Rico flipped on the lights, he found Erica gagged and bound to a pole on one side of the room.

She squealed through her gag, eyes wide, as if she was trying to tell him something. He spun around in time to absorb a blow to the chest from a crowbar. The man wielding it glared at Rico and drew back to hit him again. But as Rico tried to avoid another hit, the crowbar snagged his gun and ripped it from his hands, flinging it across the room.

Rico rolled to his right and then jumped back to his feet, just in time to prepare for the onrushing attacker. With a wild swing, the man clipped Rico on the back of his leg, landing him flat on his back. The hostile straddled Rico, looming over him and drawing back the crowbar.

Rico pushed hard against the man's shins, causing him to lose his balance and topple onto Rico. Then Rico grabbed the man's wrists, neutralizing the threat of the crowbar. As Rico tried to get to his feet, he stepped on the bar and pinned it to the ground. The man released the weapon, and Rico kicked it aside.

Then the hostile shuffled from side to side and moved around the room. Rico moved with him until the man was closer to the gun. Just as he started to dive for it, Rico recognized what was happening and leaped in the same direction. The man wrapped his fingers around the grip but couldn't turn it on Rico, who belly-flopped onto the man's back. He groaned in pain, grimacing as he turned over. Rico ripped the gun from the man's hand before securing him in a sleeper hold. At first, the man fought hard, but then he resigned himself to his fate and went limp.

Rico tied both of Erica's guards to poles in the basement, all a significant distance from one another, making it impossible for them to touch. Then he confiscated the men's phones before opening them with facial recognition programs.

Next, he began freeing Erica, apologizing for not doing so first, but he explained that he didn't want to put her in danger again, by having them wake up and be mobile. She shrugged, still unable to talk.

Finally untied, Erica gave him a hug. Then she eyed him closely.

"You're not like any lawyer I've ever seen," she said, with a grin.

"I might not be a lawyer," he said.

"Then who are you?" she asked.

"A friend," he said. "And someone who wants to make sure you get the story of a lifetime."

"And how's that going to happen?"

"You're going to be the one to expose Senator Moore for who he really is, at his presidential announcement tomorrow," he said.

"How?" she said. "I told you my editor is compromised. In fact, this is his house."

"Don't worry," Rico said. "I already reached out to *The Washington Times*. As painful as this might be for you, I got you Thomas Quinn's old job."

"I'll deal with my emotions later," she said. "We need to nail these bastards while we have the chance."

"We will," Rico said. "But first, you've got a pit stop to make."

CHAPTER FIFTY-FIVE

Washington, D.C

Knox stared at his phone. The clock showed it was just before eight o'clock in the evening when he awoke with a headache. He groaned as he sat up, his face chilled after lying so long on the tile floor.

"Welcome back to the land of the living," Makenzie said. "I was beginning to wonder if you were still alive."

Knox sighed and closed his eyes.

"I know," he said. "You don't have to say it."

"What? That I told you so?"

He forced a smile and shook his head.

"I really thought Dr. Warren was someone I could trust," Knox said. "She seemed sincere, like someone who really cared about science."

"Maybe she didn't have a choice."

"I guess that's a valid reason, but I just didn't consider that possibility. And now I'm paying the price. This whole country might be paying the price, soon enough."

"No use sitting here second guessing your decision. You did what you thought was best at the time. Doesn't mean you can't correct course."

Knox jumped to his feet and tugged at the door handle. It didn't budge.

"Hard to correct course when we're imprisoned."

He dug his phone out of his pocket, but he couldn't get a signal, not even the smallest of ones. He held the screen so Makenzie could see it.

"What do you make of that? No bars? Where are we? The hills of Arkansas?"

"I've gotten cell coverage in the hills of Arkansas," she said. "But this is different. They're using something to jam all signals."

"Why would they let us keep our phones? We can document this stuff?"

"Document what?" she asked. "You in a room that you can't get out of. Not very compelling, if you ask me. Besides, if they let us keep our phones, if we want to bring this charge against the CDC, keeping our phones the whole time we're in here strikes against the narrative that we were held against our wills. People will ask why we didn't try to contact anyone. And when we tell them that our phones didn't work, it'll be difficult to believe us."

"I'll just take a screenshot of it."

"And that's about all the *evidence* you can get. Just face it— we're screwed."

A tap at the door ended their conversation. Before they could say anything, a small hatch near the bottom opened and two trays with food slid inside.

"Hey," Knox cried, "when are you going to let us outta here? We only came in for a blood draw, and it's been nearly twelve hours."

"Enjoy your meal," came the reply, from a man with a high-pitched voice.

Knox slapped the door and grabbed the door handle, shaking it vigorously.

"Come on," he shouted. "Let us out right now and we won't press charges."

He put his ear to the door, but all he could hear was a squeaky wheel on the cart and muffled footsteps. Then he pounded on the door again with his fist.

"So, what now?" Makenzie asked. "If there was an airplane lying around here, I could get us out. But that's not in the cards. This seems like your department."

"I know, I know. I'm thinking."

Makenzie and Knox grabbed the trays of food and dug in, Makenzie a little more cautious than Knox.

"What if this does something to us?" she asked, picking at the food on her tray. "I was right last time."

Knox grunted. "At this point, I'm halfway hoping it kills me. We're trying to fight our way up a mountain, where the four-hundred-pound monster at the top is hurling boulders at us like they're pebbles."

"You saying you're giving up?" she asked.

"No," he said. "But we need a miracle. Now are you going to eat that, or do I get two dinners tonight?"

She picked up her fork and stabbed a piece of chicken.

"Hope this doesn't kill me," she said.

She shoveled the food into her mouth and, after a few minutes, seemed fine.

Knox widened his eyes. "See, not everything is a conspiracy, is it?"

Makenzie glared at him.

"Too soon," she said. "Too soon."

CHAPTER FIFTY-SIX

Fairfax, Virginia

Erica Everhart stared out the window as Rico eased along the long drive leading to International Country Club. She drummed her fingers on her tennis racquet bag before adjusting her visor. When she first reported about Chase Moore's death, she never imagined it would lead her halfway around the world and back, with a story that would surely rock the nation. A committee that lurks in the shadows that grooms candidates to do its bidding?

Best to expose it now than after it's too late.

Erica sifted through the files on her phone and wondered how Ashley Moore would handle the images Rico had given her. Would it be too much for the senator's wife? Would she close ranks around her husband and deal with the grief another way? There was only one way to find out—and Erica was dreading the process.

Rico eased to a stop beneath the overhang and unlocked the doors.

"This is your stop, Miss Everhart," Rico said. "Good luck, and call me when you're ready for me to pick you up."

Erica headed straight for the clay tennis courts where Ashley Moore was working with her coach, a man who appeared to be in his thirties, cap turned around backwards and sporting a tight white polo that accentuated his buff upper body. He stopped hitting when he saw Erica walking toward them.

"Mrs. M, you didn't tell me that it was your sister who was joining us today," he said.

Ashley giggled.

"Oh, Kip, you just might be my new favorite person now," she said, as she feigned embarrassment. "Just stop it."

Erica rolled her eyes.

"Well, Mrs. M, you're good and warmed up," he said, as he started picking up the loose balls littering the court. "If you don't trounce this lovely young lady, I'll be disappointed."

"I'll find you in the clubhouse and let you know how it went," Ashley said, before sitting down on a bench near the center of the court.

Erica joined Ashley, who mopped sweat off her brow with a towel before standing up. The two women embraced.

"Sorry about the sweat," Ashley said, as they sat down.

Erica waved her off.

"Who's Prince Charming?" Erica asked.

"Oh, Kip?" she said, nodding in the direction of the coach. "He's just your typical tennis coach suck-up, always trying to feed your ego. Does it to all the women, whether you're a former beauty queen or a woman who decides at age sixty after sitting around and eating BonBons for the past thirty-five years that she needs to take her health seriously."

"Then he understands how his bread is buttered."

Ashley shrugged. "Guess that's one way of looking at it."

"Unfortunately, I'm not wired to operate that way."

"What do you mean?"

"After everything I went through, I'm just glad to be here, glad to be alive."

"I was beginning to wonder if I'd ever see you again," Ashley said. "And after all you did for our family, I just couldn't bear the thought of you losing your life over trying to help us."

"I was just trying to do my job—or at least my former job."

Ashley's eyes narrowed.

"*Former* job? Did you get fired over this?"

"Remember when I said I wasn't wired to operate like that, predisposed to take into consideration where my bread is buttered?"

Ashley nodded.

"Well, there's a lot more to this story that I don't want to get into right now," Erica said. "But that's pretty much the reason I don't work for *The Post* any more. Chalk it up to *creative differences*, if you want an elegant way to put it."

"What about an inelegant way?"

"My editor is a scumbag who's trying to suppress this story."

"So, there's a story?" Ashley asked.

Erica nodded.

"And it's a big one. Before I left, I found out something that your husband asked me to keep quiet, that thing about Joe Garber and your son."

Ashley knit her brow.

"What are you talking about?" she asked.

"I thought you knew," Erica said, with a sigh. "At least, your husband acted like you already knew, and didn't want to drag it into public view, where you'd have to answer more questions about it from the press and everyone else you know."

"I'm sorry," Ashley said, shaking her head slowly, "but I don't know anything about Joe Garber and Chase."

"The gun your son used to—well, you know—it was given to him by Joe Garber, who was in Africa at the time, accompanying the defense secretary on a diplomatic trip."

Ashley picked up a tennis ball and squeezed it, her eyes narrowing again.

"Are you serious?"

"Yes," Erica said. "But like I mentioned earlier, there's another story I came back with. And since I was freed in the last twenty-four hours, I've learned even more."

"What are you talking about?"

"As you know, I went to the Congo," Erica said, as she dug the GPS tracker out of her purse and handed it Ashley. "And I went to Tango, the village where Chase was."

Erica shared what she'd seen there.

"So, there was some kind of outbreak that caused him to do this?" Ashley asked.

"That's how it appeared at first, but then I just received this footage."

Erica swiped on her phone and played the video that Knox and Makenzie had retrieved. She paused it after the moment Garber handed a gun to Chase.

"You don't want to see the rest, trust me," Erica said.

"And Mark knew about this?"

"Not only did he know about it, but I learned that he's on the board of the company that ran these experiments on human beings."

"NocturaCorp?"

Erica nodded.

"Now, I need to confront the senator directly on this, since I've since learned his ties to NocturaCorp, but I found out that the Peace Corps requested that Chase remain behind during the transition from one team to the next. Yet that went against the organization's protocol."

"Why would they do that?"

"That's the question I had at the time," Erica said. "But the only thing that makes sense is that someone with a lot of weight pressured the Peace Corps into requesting Chase be left behind. And I believe that person was your husband."

"That doesn't make sense. He loved Chase. They were as tight as a father and son could be."

"It certainly doesn't make sense to us," Erica said. "But to someone with ambition, who might view the story as a way of making himself look more sympathetic …"

Erica let her words hang for effect. After a few seconds, Ashley stood and flung the tennis ball into the fence.

"That son of a bitch lied to me," she said. "Novel, my ass."

"What are you talking about?"

Ashley set her jaw.

"Nothing. It's nothing. But I'm gonna kill him."

"Whoa, whoa, whoa," Erica said. "Calm down. Don't do anything rash."

"Rash? Are you kidding me? That asshole deserves to die *right now*."

"Look, I'm on your side, but if you kill your husband, you're going to jail and the truth about what NocturaCorp was doing dies with him. That company has killed other people in the name of their experiments. But if you care about getting justice, not just revenge, we need him alive for leverage."

Ashley growled as she paced the court.

"Why would a company do those things? Why would Mark do those things? That's not the man I married."

"Let's make sure your husband—"

"Soon-to-be ex-husband," Ashley snapped.

"Let's make sure we get answers from both senator *and* NocturaCorp."

"How?"

"I have an idea," Erica said. "And it involves being in that airplane tomorrow for his big announcement tomorrow. Think you can get me on that plane?"

"How did you know about—"

"A good reporter never reveals her sources," Erica said, with a faint smile. "Just—can you get me on board?"

"Consider it done."

CHAPTER FIFTY-SEVEN

Washington, D.C

Knox awoke in the room, pitch black after they had turned off the lights earlier, too tired to stay awake any longer. He was confident that it was morning due to his hankering for a cup of coffee, but he glanced at his phone to prove it. He still didn't have a signal, but it had power, albeit fleeting.

Seven-thirty. I overslept.

"Makenzie," he whispered.

She stirred but didn't respond. He sat up and tilted his head back, looking into the darkness. With plenty of thoughts to sift through, he knew it was unhealthy to dwell on what had put him in this situation. But he couldn't help himself. He distilled his mistake down to one simple thing—trusting Dr. Warren and not listening to Makenzie. But the truth was he'd made other mistakes as well, starting with agreeing to help Ballard. Not that he could help himself.

Knox's pecking order of importance started with family, and then country. And while he didn't have much family left to speak of, Allison was the closest semblance of family he had, the one who was closest to him. But she didn't really know him. The version of Knox she'd known was the mountain man, the camp director, the veteran.

The military was a past life, one she didn't have to encounter except when he shared his memories.

But while Knox had left the military, he hadn't left behind the love for his country. It still remained near the top of things he cared about. He only retired early because he wanted more out of life. What he really wanted was a wife, a family, a legacy that wasn't reduced to killing terrorists in the desert.

However, if there was anything the past couple of weeks had shown him about himself, it was that he still loved his country. And for all those people out there who wanted the freedom to pursue their dreams—wives, husbands, sons, daughters, careers, community, deep and meaningful lives—they needed people like Knox. Americans needed warriors behind the curtain, those who stared down tyrants and rendered them powerless.

Who am I kidding? This is the only life for me. Too bad it's going to end early.

Sitting in the dark, he'd resigned himself to the fact that Moore wasn't going to allow him to live. It would be too dangerous.

A few minutes later, the lights turned on automatically, followed by a quick knock. Two trays with breakfast slid through the door's hatch. Makenzie groaned, pulling the covers over her head.

"Rise and shine," Knox said.

"What time is it?" she asked, her voice gravelly.

"Time for breakfast, according to our generous overlords," he said.

She grunted.

"Not funny."

"It's almost eight o'clock."

Makenzie sat up, her hair a matted mess, eyes squinting.

"We're going to miss it," she said.

"Miss what?"

"Senator Moore's announcement."

Knox chuckled.

"You think that's an option for us?" he asked. "You're not still dreaming, are you?"

"I'm wide awake—and furious. We were so close. And if you had just listened to me—"

Knox raised a hand.

"Go ahead. Say it. I deserve it."

"I don't want to. It goes without saying, and doesn't solve anything."

"Good," he said. "Now, let's see if we can figure out a way to get out of here."

"We wouldn't have to look for a way out if you'd just listened to me."

"Just say it and get it over with."

Makenzie set her jaw.

"I *told* you so."

"There. Feel better now?"

"Hardly. Nothing's changed. I'm still angry at you, at that CDC lady, at myself."

"So what should we do about it?"

"Figure a way out of here," she said.

The door opened and a stocky man strode into the room.

"I might be able to help you with that," he said, with a tinge of a German accent.

Knox studied the interloper for a moment, unsure of how to respond. He decided to be quiet and let the man speak.

"If you'll follow me," the man said, "I will escort you out of the building."

"You're just going to let us go?" Makenzie asked. "And we're not going to talk about the fact that you locked us in a room overnight and fed us like we were prisoners?"

"Who said anything about letting you go?" the man asked, cocking his head to one side. "I will help you get out of this room, though. Come, come."

He gestured toward the open door and the trio of armed guards standing outside.

"So, you're *not* letting us go," Makenzie said.

"Please," the man said, indicating toward the hallway, "we can talk about this on the way."

"On the way to where?" Knox asked.

"You'll see soon enough. Now let's get going."

The man and the guards escorted Knox and Makenzie down the hallway and to a flight of stairs that led them into an alley around the back of the building. A running SUV was parked by the door. Another set of armed guards got out, opening the door and gesturing with their weapons for Knox and Makenzie to get inside.

"You're not coming with us?" Makenzie asked.

"These gentlemen will get you where you're supposed to be."

"And where's that?" Makenzie said through clenched teeth.

"Get in and you'll find out soon enough."

Knox and Makenzie followed orders, though hesitantly. For a moment, Knox considered taking them on, but figured that wasn't the wisest approach, with Makenzie liable to be snatched up and used as leverage. If he was by himself, he wouldn't hesitate. But he couldn't risk her safety. He quickly concluded that there could be another opportunity to escape.

Be patient—and smart.

As angry as Makenzie was over the whole situation, Knox was just as upset, including at himself. Yet he still had to control his anger, bide his time, strike when they didn't expect it.

The SUV hummed along, leaving Washington before merging onto the Beltway. A few minutes later, the driver took an exit, leading them to an airfield in Virginia. When they pulled up to a hangar, Knox's mouth fell agape as he stared at the group of people gathered near the door of a Kodiak 100.

"Get out," the guard next to Knox said, nudging him with his gun barrel.

Knox slid across the seat and exited. Makenzie, who was sitting in the third row of the vehicle, also got out. The guard jumped back into the car and it drove off, leaving a cloud of dust in its wake.

Then Knox turned to see the last person he'd expected to be waiting for him at the end of his journey—Senator Mark Moore.

"Good morning, you two," Moore said, as he eyed Knox. "We've been anxiously expecting the two of you."

"Is that so?" Knox asked.

"Of course. It's a beautiful day for flying. Right, Miss Hall?"

Makenzie glared at him.

"Well, you can stand there and give me the evil eye, or you can go start your pre-flight checks," he said.

"You expect *me* to fly *you*?" she asked.

"Of course," Moore said. "Or I could always call my friends up and have them take you back to the CDC where you can become a test subject for Incaendium. I would never want to force you to do anything against your will."

She sneered before marching over to the plane. Knox didn't move, his eyes locked on Moore's.

"How's the leg?" Moore asked, nodding at Knox's prosthetic.

"It's good enough to kick your ass with," Knox said, with a growl. "What the hell do you think you're doing?"

"Calm down, cowboy. Why don't you hop aboard and find out? I promise to answer all your questions."

Knox looked past Moore and saw Rico chatting with the senator's wife and Erica Everhart.

Moore saw Knox's confused look and patted him on the shoulder.

"Come on, Mr. Knox," Moore said. "It'll be fun."

Knox made a move toward Moore, but three members of the senator's security detail moved closer, hands on their weapons, ready to draw.

Moore wagged his finger at Knox, who relented once he saw how outnumbered he'd be, again.

"You have the same choice as your colleague, Mr. Knox. Why don't you just play nice and see what the fuss is all about, okay?"

Knox narrowed his eyes as he studied Moore.

"You're going to regret this," Knox said.

"I doubt it," Moore said, pulling back the edge of his blazer and revealing his sidearm. "Now, hurry up and get moving. We've got a plane to catch."

CHAPTER FIFTY-EIGHT

Arlington, Virginia

Knox marched toward the plane, stopped at the steps to the door by one of Moore's security detail. The man held out his hand.

"Phone, please," he said.

"I don't think so," Knox said.

"No phone, no fly."

"Fine by me," Knox said, with a faint smile.

"If you don't fly, it's back to the CDC," Moore said, as he eased up behind Knox. "But of course, it's your choice."

Knox forked over his phone and trudged up the steps. He took the seat closest to the cockpit and shot a quick glance at Makenzie, who shook her head.

"I don't like this," she said.

"Just play it cool," Knox said. "I'll get us out of here."

Moore was the final person to board, and instructed everyone to put on their headsets so they could communicate more easily. Then he marched to the front and handed Makenzie the flight plan.

"Do you want us to get shot down?" she asked, as she stared at the map. "If we fly here, fighters will be scrambled in a matter of minutes."

"The Flight Restricted Zone can be breached with a waiver," he said, before producing one out of his pocket.

"You have a waiver to *skydive* over Washington?" she asked.

"As they say, it's all about who you know. Or in my case, it's all about who you *are*. I'm on the Senate intelligence committee. This wasn't difficult for me to get. Now, let's get going."

With the seating affixed along the cabin, the passengers sat across from one another. Knox put on his headset and locked eyes with Moore, who sat directly behind Makenzie and across from Knox. Ashley Moore buckled in next to her husband and sat across from Erica. Rico was seated to Erica's left.

"Time to go make history, gang," Moore said.

The engine spun up before it began rumbling across the tarmac.

Moore tightened his gloves and then looked again at Knox's leg.

"You know, I looked all throughout your service records and couldn't find any mention of how you lost your leg. It's quite unusual to have something like that expunged."

"That's because it happened after I got out of the Army," Knox said.

"I just always assumed you lost it to a roadside IED or some other accident, during battle. So, what happened?"

"I broke it off in some guy's ass," Knox said. "It'd be worth it to break off the other one in yours."

Moore laughed nervously.

"No, seriously, how did it happen?"

Knox sighed, unsure if he wanted to comply with Moore, before figuring it didn't matter.

"I was in the jungle, helping with a humanitarian mission," Knox said. "There were two kids playing near the edge of a riverbank when I noticed a crocodile swimming straight toward them. I dropped what I was doing and sprinted toward them, desperately trying to get their attention before they became a meal for the beast. I managed to get there in time to yank one of them to safety, but the other one didn't survive the bite. Then the crocodile came after me. I wasn't quick enough to escape the beast's powerful bite. He latched onto my leg and dragged me into the water. He performed a death roll and ripped my foot off before I managed to escape, and keep him from snacking on another appendage."

"You sound lucky to be alive," Moore said, his voice tinged with respect.

"We all are," Knox said. "Life is far more tenuous that most people think."

The plane continued its ascent, the engine whining as the nose pointed upward. Knox's mind had already drifted back to the murky waters in Africa. He wasn't sure he could've handled watching another child terrorized by a crocodile.

Thank God Jabari made it.

Knox hadn't had a chance to speak with Rico and didn't want to blow his cover. He certainly was surprised to see Rico there, and wondered why he'd been invited on board for this moment.

Moore checked his watch as they continued climbing. After a couple of more minutes, Makenzie leveled off the Kodiak and informed Moore that the plane had reached the altitude he was cleared to jump from. Then he stood and grabbed one of the handles attached to the top of the cabin. Slightly hunched over, he addressed his captive audience.

"I want to thank all of you for joining me here today as I unveil my intention to run for my party's nomination for President of the United States with an unprecedented announcement," he said. "I want this moment captured from every angle, all while shared by my beautiful wife."

Knox groaned as he shifted in his seat.

"Something wrong, Mr. Knox?" Moore asked, Knox's displeasure audible enough to be heard over everyone's headset.

"America's not going to vote for a man who murdered his own son," Knox said.

Moore pursed his lips, tilting his head to one side.

"That's a first," Moore said. "Never heard anyone make such a ridiculous claim, not to mention so hurtful."

"With all due respect, sir," Erica said, as she adjusted her sunglasses, "and by that, I mean you are due none—we know what happened in the Congo, and I mean *everyone*, including your wife."

"Of course you do," Moore said. "It was reported everywhere, specifically by you. Miss Everhart, you, of all people, know what happened in that village of Tango just over a year ago. It's not a secret."

"Not anymore, it's not," she said.

Knox scowled.

"It never was."

Ashley Moore eased to her feet, lips quivering, hands shaking.

"Honey, it's over," she said. "We have footage of what happened, including the very moment that Joe Garber handed Chase a gun before he—before he—"

She paused, tears pooling in her eyes.

Moore looked down and scratched his nose with the back of his hand, taking a moment before he spoke.

"I don't know what you think you saw, but I had nothing to do with it," he said. "This day was about us, about what we can do together."

"No," she said. "It's about your reckoning."

Erica held up her phone, recording the entire event.

"You think I care about what you're capturing right now?" Moore asked. "I couldn't care less, Miss Everhart. Whatever narrative you're trying to spin to take me down, it's not going to work. I didn't come this far to fail. And I certainly didn't come this far without a plan."

He grabbed a fistful of Erica's hair and slammed her head into the cabin wall, rendering her unconscious. Moore grunted with satisfaction as he tapped Erica's limp arm and watched it swing back and forth.

"When we get on the ground," Ashley said, "your plan is over. The world is gonna know what you've done. I'm gonna make sure they know what you've become. They're going to know that you sent your son into an area that was testing a weaponized virus. And let's not forget that it was a virus engineered by the same company that pays you handsomely to sit on their board."

"Paid," Moore corrected, as he held up his index finger. "I can't be on their board due to my position in the Senate."

"So, that's why we have the timeshare in the Caymans? And the offshore account that nobody else knows about -- that keeps growing, despite you claiming to never put any money into it?"

"Honey, I'm afraid you are a bit delusional, not to mention uninformed about our financial situation," Moore said. "There's an explanation for everything you've said."

"I'm calling bullshit," Knox said. "If there's one thing I've learned about politicians, it's that they couldn't tell the truth if someone was holding a gun to their head."

Moore unholstered his weapon and trained it on Knox.

"Good thing I'm the one holding the gun, then, isn't it?" Moore said.

He eased backward down the aisle away from Knox.

"Now, as much as it pains me to do this," Moore continued, "I'm going to have to switch things up a little bit. I don't have much time before I need to jump and make my grand entrance in front of the Jefferson Memorial. But I do want to tell all of you that I'm so sorry about Mr. Knox killing you all in a downed flight over the Potomac River."

Knox took a deep breath as he realized what was about to happen. Powerless to stop it, he understood his only chance was to disrupt it. He couldn't do that either.

"Senator," Makenzie said, as she turned around and faced Moore, "if you don't jump soon, you're going to miss your opportunity."

Moore whipped the barrel of his gun toward Makenzie and fired. The shot struck her in the stomach.

CHAPTER FIFTY-NINE

Washington, D.C

Knox glanced at Moore before lunging toward the flight controls. With Makenzie groaning in agony, Knox yanked back on the stick, causing the plane to pitch upward.

Moore reached up for a handle, but came up empty as he staggered toward the back of the plane and the open door. As he did, Rico stood and dove toward the senator. But Moore fired another shot, this one hitting Rico in the leg. He stumbled and fell into another seat, gripping its edge to keep from sliding all the way to the back. Then he applied pressure to his leg with his free hand while grunting through gritted teeth.

After Moore regained his balance, he steadied his weapon on Knox.

Knox then jerked the controller again, this time to the right. The plane rolled hard in the same direction, causing his shot to go low, lodging in the control panel.

"Mayday, mayday!" Makenzie shouted into the radio. "It's not working."

She let out a few expletives.

Moore laughed.

"How's this plan to *expose* me going, honey?" he said, as he looked at Ashley.

"You bastard," she said. "What makes you think you're going to get away with this?"

"For starters, Mr. Knox's prints are already all over this gun—not that it will matter, once you all crash and die."

Knox looked at the cargo net at the back of the plane. It was empty.

"That's right," Moore said. "I took out all the parachutes, except for the one on my back. Now, time for me to go make history and then play the role of the grieving widower, while Americans hear about the savage attack you made on my wife before you threatened me and I jumped."

"You're a sick bastard," Knox said.

Moore laughed again and shook his head before training his gun on Ashley.

"You were always just a prop, dear," he said. "But don't worry. I'll raise a glass in your memory tonight and celebrate the trivial life that you led."

Just before he shot, Knox jerked the control stick again. The gun fired and the bullet pierced Ashley's arm. She doubled over, clutching it as she screamed.

Knox glared at Moore.

"Good luck landing this bird," Moore said. "You'll need every bit of it to survive—and then there'll be the trial, the one where all the evidence will point toward you, showing you tried to kill everyone on board."

Moore put the barrel of the gun against his left bicep and pulled the trigger, the bullet ripping through his arm. He grimaced in pain and then smiled.

"Just do us all a favor and point this thing straight into the Potomac, Knox. Oh, and thanks for your service, Ranger. Now, just five minutes before I become a hero—five minutes before you die."

With that, Moore leaped out of the open door and hurtled toward the ground and a waiting press corps.

CHAPTER SIXTY

Washington, D.C

Knox scanned the plane and took stock of the situation. Makenzie was hemorrhaging while seated in the cockpit, clearly unable to fly. Rico wasn't in any condition to fly either, desperately needing to keep pressure on his wound. Erica was unconscious, and Knox was uncertain how long she would be out. That left Ashley, who sat upright, a wry grin on her face.

"What the hell," he mumbled to himself.

Ashley showed Knox where the bullet had just grazed her arm, her expression sly.

"There's hardly any blood," she said, as she inspected the spot. "I don't even feel it."

Ashley's health status had put a wrinkle in the plan he'd concocted. Knox wanted to get the plane on the ground and then figure out the rest. There was another way, a better way, though a far more dangerous one. And he didn't think it was possible, despite his desire to try.

Someone has to get this plane on the ground.

"Go," Ashley said, pointing toward the jump door. "Go now, if you dare. I'll get this plane down, but I'd rather die trying than to let that bastard husband of mine walk free."

"Are you sure you can fly?" he asked.

She nodded. "I've always wanted to try."

"Wait—" he said, freezing. "What?"

"I'll talk her through it," Makenzie said.

Knox's eyes widened. "But you're—"

"Just go!" Ashley said.

Knox couldn't be sure of anything. *Was Ashley goading me to jump to my death? Was she acting and it was all staged for his benefit?*

He paused for a second. *If Moore hits the ground before me, I'll never have a chance to prove otherwise.*

Knox took a deep breath, kissed his lucky coin, and dove out the door.

Speeding toward the ground, Knox felt the adrenaline surging through his body. If the senator pulled his chute, Knox was done. It'd be a death plunge, right in front of the media. If Ashley and Makenzie couldn't work to get the plane down, the only narrative that would be told was the one Moore concocted. He'd tell the story of how he jumped out, fearing for his life after Knox tried to murder everyone onboard—and Knox dove out to his death, in order to avoid suffering the consequences of his actions.

Knox kept his eyes on Moore, muttering a prayer that he would keep falling. The senator dropped, spread eagle, arms wide, the fate of the plane no longer his concern. He didn't even look back up. If he had, he would've seen Knox racing toward him.

Knox had practiced scenarios like this with the Rangers. A free fall, no parachute. The only person with a parachute was the target having jumped before him. But in those exercises, Knox actually had a parachute, in case he missed.

Missing wasn't an option now.

Knox squinted as his heart pounded. He estimated in his head how much longer he had before slamming into Moore and holding on for dear life.

Seven ... six ... five ... four ...

As Knox drew closer, Moore looked up for the first time since both men were free falling. The senator scrambled to pull his rip cord.

Knox swallowed hard. He stretched his arms wide and prepared for impact.

~

Ashley Moore worked her way toward the cockpit, using the overhead handles to maintain her balance as the plane pitched downward.

"Hurry," Makenzie said, over the headset. "I'm not sure how much longer I can stay ... conscious."

"Almost there," Ashley said.

Seconds later, she eased into the co-pilot's seat. She glanced at Makenzie's wound, her shirt soaked in blood. Ashley's eyes glazed over as the gravity of the situation hit her.

"You got this," Makenzie said. "Just stay focused. Now, have you ever flown one of these things before?"

"No, but I took a few flight lessons before my fear of heights kept me grounded."

"Let's just hope your fear of dying is greater than your fear of heights."

Ashley nodded and asked for instructions.

~

Before Moore could yank on the string, Knox collided with him. Knox grabbed part of Moore's harness as the two men tumbled together across the sky.

With the harness secured to him, Moore had more freedom to fight. He jabbed at Knox's midsection and then took aim at his face. Knox absorbed hit after hit, albeit weak punches. Moore screamed in his face before stopping the onslaught.

"I'll release myself from this harness and we'll both die," Moore said.

"Go ahead," Knox said. "I've made peace with my maker a long time ago."

Moore took no such action. Instead, he tried to head-butt Knox. But Knox anticipated the move and avoided a direct blow with Moore's forehead, only catching the left side of his face. Then Moore wrapped his hands around Knox's neck and squeezed. With only one free hand, Knox struggled to break Moore's grip. With each passing second, Knox gasped for air, already in short supply.

Desperate to get a breath, Knox kicked at Moore. But without enough traction, Knox's foot just glanced off the side of Moore's leg.

Knox felt his world going dim. If he blacked out, Moore wouldn't hold onto him.

Knox tightened his grip and turned to his last resort—pulling the cord.

He yanked it and held on.

The free fall ended abruptly as the chute opened. The jolt surprised Moore, causing him to lose his grip. That was all Knox needed to re-situate himself. He swung around behind Moore, able to get in that position for the first time since they'd made contact. It was ideal.

Moore reared back, trying to ram the back of his head into Knox, who moved his forearm just behind Moore's neck to prevent the tactic.

After a few more moments of struggling, Moore stopped, seemingly resigned to accept his fate.

"I can't believe you let all those people die," Moore said.

"Nobody's going to die today," Knox said. "We're all going to make sure you get what you deserve."

"You might survive today, but every day after this one is going to have you looking over your shoulder, wondering if this is your last," the senator said. "Besides, do you really think you're ever going to see the light of day again? Once your feet touch the ground, you're going to be swarmed. The FAA will sift through the wreckage of the plane and find the gun with only your prints on it. And it'll be my word against yours."

"There's not going to be any wreckage," Knox said. "Take a look to your left."

The Kodiak cruised through air, leveled out and flying smoothly.

"Want to know who's flying that thing?" Knox asked, continuing without waiting for an answer. "It's that beauty queen wife of yours. The one you hand-picked as arm candy for your political career, the one you chose because of her father and his connections in this town."

Moore laughed.

"If she's their hope, they're as good as dead," he said.

"You've severely underestimated your wife," Knox said. "And it's going to cost you everything."

"We'll see about that," Moore said.

Knox remained quiet as Moore navigated the chute toward its target in front of the Thomas Jefferson Memorial. But as he did, he didn't account for a large gust of wind that pushed them out over Tidal Basin, in front of the monument. Instead of landing on the ground, they sank into the water.

Moore released his harness and whirled around in the water to face Knox. Immediately, Moore went for Knox's throat, wrapping both hands around it and squeezing. Knox responded by applying pressure on Moore's wound. But it didn't shake his grip on Knox's neck.

The fear of being powerless in the water flooded Knox's mind. The memory of his foot being ripped off as the crocodile spun him around in the water almost paralyzed him.

Almost.

But then Knox remembered how he survived.

Stay calm. Keep your wits.

In the water, Knox couldn't create enough force to deliver a blow that would make Moore relinquish his grip. But there were other ways, such as the way he survived the death roll.

Instead of wasting time and valuable strength forcing Moore to remove his hands, Knox went for his eyes, gouging them with his thumbs. Instinctively, Moore released Knox and swam backward, eyes clenched shut. Knox swam behind Moore and wrapped his right arm around Moore's neck. With it nestled in the crook of Knox's arm, he started swimming for the shore. The murky waters of Tidal Basin made it difficult to determine which way to go. But once he surfaced, he spotted the throng of media members edging closer to the water, cameras focused on him and the senator.

"You son of a bitch," Moore said, with a growl. "You're gonna rot in prison."

Knox laughed as he slogged his way toward the press.

"You've got it all wrong, Senator. I'm gonna be a damn American hero."

Knox kicked against the water, slowly moving toward land. After a couple of minutes, he felt the soft mud against the soles of his feet. Then he dragged Moore up the bank and dumped him in front of the press corps.

Cameras clicked and flashed as photographers crowded around them. Knox eased out of the way, allowing everyone to get a clean look at Moore. Almost immediately, several reporters rushed over to him to ask what had happened.

"You'll have to ask the senator," Knox said. "It's his story to tell."

Moore coughed as he sat up, expunging water from his lungs. He pointed at Knox, fingers shaking.

"Arrest that man," Moore said. "He tried to kill me. Look at my arm."

No one moved. Every camera maintained its focus on the senator, blood oozing from the bullet hole.

"I said, *arrest that man,*" Moore said again.

None of the Capitol police officers even flinched.

"Senator Moore," one of the reporters said, "are you aware that Erica Everhart was live streaming the entire incident?"

"Whatever you saw was a lie," Moore said. "This man tried to kill me."

"No, he didn't, *sir*," one of the reporters said. "We all saw what happened. We all heard the story you planned to sell us. We're just not buying it."

"In the water! You saw it!" Moore said. "That man tried to kill me."

"No," another reporter shouted. "He saved you. But it's too late. The world knows the truth now."

"None of that is real," Moore shouted, his eyes searching for a sympathetic face. "You have to believe me. Whatever you saw, it was a lie generated by AI. I swear, this man tried to kill me."

Knox pushed his way through the crowd, fighting against the flow. He half-expected a dozen reporters to run after him, but they didn't. Except for one.

"Sir, would you mind tell us what your name is, and sharing your side of the story?" the woman asked.

Knox put his head down and shook it slowly.

"Sorry, but I don't really want to talk about it," he said, as he quickened his pace, his eye on a taxi cab idling near the parking lot.

She followed after him, and then several other reporters noticed him slipping away and rushed over to join her. But Knox broke into a sprint, opening the door to the cab and diving inside.

"Go, go, go!" Knox said.

The cab driver complied, stomping on the gas.

"Where to?" he asked.

"Just get me away from here, now."

"Whatever you say, boss."

The engine roared as the driver left the gaggle of reporters behind. Knox peeked over the back of the seat, hoping that they weren't watching. They continued to run after him, cameras and phones pointed in his direction, undoubtedly zooming in to get a closer look at the man who'd tussled in the sky with Moore.

The tires barked as the cab left the Jefferson Memorial parking lot and zoomed toward the Beltway.

"If you don't want to run up a fortune in a cab fare, I suggest you give me an address soon."

"Head to Arlington," Knox said. "There's an airfield there. I need to check on my friends."

CHAPTER SIXTY-ONE

Arlington, Virginia

Knox forked over the cab fare and some extra to cover the long ride from Washington. He hobbled out of the car, and over toward the Kodiak 100 parked in front of the hangar and surrounded by several ambulances. Emergency lights flashed and sirens chirped as ambulances began to leave the airfield.

He picked his way through the crowd, squeezing between curious onlookers and airport personnel. After a quick search, he found Makenzie on a gurney with a respiratory mask strapped to her face.

"Kinz," he said.

She opened her eyes and searched for his face.

"You made it," she said, before exhaling. "I wasn't sure—I didn't know—I was—"

Knox put an index finger to his lips and held her hand.

"It's okay," he said. "I made it. I'll tell you about it later. I'm just glad you're still alive."

She squeezed his hand.

"Ashley did great," she said. "If I didn't know better, I would've thought she had two thousand hours of flight time."

Knox raised an eyebrow. "That good, huh?"

"Smoothest landing I've had in a while, when I wasn't at the helm."

He smiled and pushed a few tendrils of her brown hair out of her face.

"You're going to be all right," he said.

"Don't lie to me. I know this is good-bye."

"Stop it," Knox said. "You're going to make it. I just know it."

"I've lost too much blood," she said, her voice fading as her eyes fluttered shut. "You're a good man, Garrett Knox."

The EMTs whisked Makenzie toward the open doors of another ambulance. Moments later, the vehicle roared toward the airfield exit.

Knox slumped to the ground, leaning against the side of the hangar. Everything seemed like a blur, almost surreal. He buried his head in his hands and sobbed.

By the time he regained his composure, the crowd had dissipated -- every ambulance, every emergency vehicle—all gone. He stood and looked around.

"You all right, mister?" a man asked, as he shuffled past pushing a dolly loaded down with a tall box.

Knox didn't respond.

"Sir, do you need help?" the man persisted.

Knox waved dismissively at the man before breaking into soft sobs again.

CHAPTER SIXTY-TWO

Washington, D.C

Knox's eyes fluttered open as sunlight streamed through the thin drapes over his motel window. He thought he'd heard something as he laid on his back staring at the ceiling. Then another noise. Someone was rapping on the door.

Knox rolled out of bed and stumbled toward the door. He removed the chain lock and then the deadbolt. After easing open the door, he squinted as he stared into the bright daylight and the figure of a woman in front of him.

"Mr. Knox," the woman said, as she offered her hand, "Camille Banks. I'd like a word with you."

Knox shook the woman's hand and then pulled back the door, nodding inside. Two guards flanked her and followed her inside Knox's room.

"Sorry about the mess," he said. "Guess the maids haven't made their rounds yet."

"Don't mind me," she said. "This won't take long."

"Is it about my friends?" he asked.

She indicated toward the small table in a corner of the room.

"Can we have a seat?"

Knox nodded and eased into one of the chairs.

"Do you know who I am?"

He shook his head.

"I'm not really up on the bureaucracy of Washington," he said. "Living in the mountains in Montana, I haven't been concerned with much of anything happening in this city for years now. Should I know you?"

She shrugged.

"Maybe. I'm the Director of National Intelligence, and I've been following you for the past few weeks."

"What on earth for?" he asked.

"We've suspected that there's a clandestine organization that's trying to usurp the federal government's authority, although in a most surreptitious way. We'd identified Senator Moore as one of the potential ringleaders. It wasn't until that stunt he tried to pull today that we realized just how embedded he was in the organization."

"Is it The Consortium?" he asked.

She leaned back in her chair and folded her arms.

"You know more than you're letting on."

"Not really," he said. "I've just come across a few things here and there, as I attempted to complete my assignment from Col. Ballard."

"You're still in contact with him?"

Knox shook his head. "I think it's safe to say that I'm at odds with Col. Ballard—that is, if he's still alive."

"I used to work in homicide for NYPD," she said. "We had a saying, with all due respect to Taylor Swift, that came out long before her song: 'No body, no crime.' So, until Ballard shows up, we're gonna assume he's alive."

"You don't think he's at the bottom of the Potomac?"

She shook her head.

"We would've found him by now," she said. "I think he's in the wind. And I need someone to catch him and bring him in."

Knox sighed and leaned back in his chair.

"I'm not exactly inclined to help another government intelligence agency, after what I just witnessed."

"I understand," she said. "But I'm the one trying to bring these criminals to justice. That's something I thought you'd appreciate."

"It's an honor, Director Banks. Truly, it is. But I have a camp to run in Montana. It's full of people depending upon me. Kids who've never experienced what it's like to roam the mountains and see Big Sky country, to fall asleep staring at a sea of twinkling stars. That's where my heart is."

"Is it, Mr. Knox? Are you hellbent on returning to Montana while letting these monsters roam free? You don't strike me as that type."

"Perhaps you've misjudged me," he said.

"It's possible," Banks said, as she stood. "But I want you to know that I want Ballard brought to justice. I want The Consortium shuttered. I want men and women who desire to see this country flourish leading us. And if we don't stop people like Col. Ballard, that'll never happen."

"Let me sleep on it," Knox said. "I want to help, but I want to make sure that this is the way."

"Take your time—just not too much time," she said. "I want to catch these assholes before they do any more damage."

Knox ushered Banks toward the door. She stopped and turned around.

"Your friends are okay," she said. "They're all gonna make it—at least that's what the doctors told me this morning."

"Even Makenzie?" he asked.

Banks nodded. "Her surgeon said she's very lucky. The bullet didn't pierce any of her vital organs, almost defying the laws of physics, according to the medical staff there. You should get dressed and go visit them as soon as you can. They're all anxious to speak with you. And then call me, once you've made a decision. Together, I believe we can be a strong team."

Knox didn't say a word as she walked away.

Montana's my home.

CHAPTER SIXTY-THREE

Hamilton, Montana

Two weeks later, the plane's wheels barked as they touched the tarmac. Knox unbuckled his seatbelt and snatched his bag from the cargo hold at the back of the plane.

"Please remain seated until the plane has come to a complete stop," a flight attendant admonished over the speaker.

Knox ignored the directive, heading toward the door. He checked behind him to see Makenzie, who didn't show any signs of recently being shot in the stomach. The engines wound down before finally stopping. Knox slung his rucksack over his shoulder and trudged down the steps. Once he exited the terminal, Allison Matthews awaited him. She rushed up to him and gave him a tight hug, before kissing him on the cheek.

"I'm so glad you're back," she said, as they started walking toward the exit, hand-in-hand.

Knox introduced Allison to Makenzie, who'd asked for a little more time off to see Knox's camp before returning to Brazil. Allison greeted the pilot warmly.

"You really missed me, didn't you?" Knox asked.

"More than you know, but maybe not as much as you'd like," she said.

Knox scowled.

"What do you mean?"

Allison nodded toward her car as the two trudged toward it.

"I'm not trying to send any mixed messages," she said. "I just want you to know where I stand."

"Where you stand on what?" he asked.

"On our future," she said. "I just don't see it being compatible."

"What do you mean?" he said, his eyes pleading.

"You're a good man, Garrett," she said. "But this isn't the life for me. I love the outdoors, but while you were gone, I realized that I'm a city girl at heart. The outdoors is a novelty, not a lifestyle for me."

"What are you trying to say?"

"I'm leaving," she said. "I'm going back to school to get my Master's degree in business administration. I want to run my own business, not work in the middle of the boondocks."

"I thought you loved this," he said, his hand waving toward the mountains.

"I do," she said, "but not as much as you. While you were gone, I had some time to reflect. And it's just not what I want for my future."

"But, Allison—"

She kissed him on the cheek.

"Good-bye, Garrett. And good luck. I'm sure you'll do fine without me. Guy has already found a replacement for me."

Knox stood and stared as Allison strode away. A few seconds later, he felt a firm hand on his shoulder. He turned around to see Makenzie standing there.

"Ah, unrequited love," she said. "What a terrible tragedy."

Knox took a deep breath, though he felt as if someone had knocked the wind out of him.

"You're gonna be fine," Makenzie said, patting him on the back. "This camp is gonna be fine."

Knox nodded in agreement. Then he dug his phone out of his pocket and placed a call.

"Director Banks," Knox said. "Count me in."

The story will continue in Terminal Threat.

THANK YOU FOR READING 5 MINUTES TO DIE

We hope you enjoyed it as much as we enjoyed bringing it to you. We just wanted to take a moment to encourage you to review the book. Follow this link: 5 Minutes to Die to be directed to the book's Amazon product page to leave your review.

Every review helps further the author's reach and, ultimately, helps them continue writing fantastic books for us all to enjoy.

~

Also in series:
5 Minutes to Die
Terminal Threat

Want to discuss our books with other readers and even the authors? Join our Discord server today and be a part of the Aethon community.

Facebook | Instagram | Twitter | Website

You can also join our non-spam mailing list by visiting www. subscribepage.com/AethonReadersGroup and never miss out on future releases. You'll also receive three full books completely Free as our thanks to you.

Looking for more great thrillers?

A home invasion ends in murder. Was it a burglary gone bad, or was it personal? Mild-mannered professor, James Harris, met his future wife, Rachel, when she was a student in his class. Despite her age, she was more an adventurous vixen than an innocent schoolgirl. They hid their illicit affair until Rachel graduated, and then James made her an honest woman. Rachel was the town *it* girl. The woman who all the men wanted and who all the women wanted to be. Even when she manipulated men for personal gain, they smiled and came back for more. But Rachel set aside her immature past to become a brilliant psychologist, who treated the most violent offenders. All that beauty. All that intelligence. All gone. Taken from the world during a brutal home invasion. James could've stopped the attack. He could've at least tried, but he froze. The police and Rachel's family suspect there's more to the story than James is telling. All James knows is what he heard while he hid. The conversation between Rachel and the home invader leaves more questions than answers. *Did Rachel know the home invader? Was it one of her psych patients? Was it an obsessed ex-boyfriend? Am I next?* **James must answer these questions before he joins his dearly departed**

wife in this unputdownable crime thriller full of twists from bestseller Phil M. Williams that will keep you guessing until the very end.

Get Death Do Us Part Now!

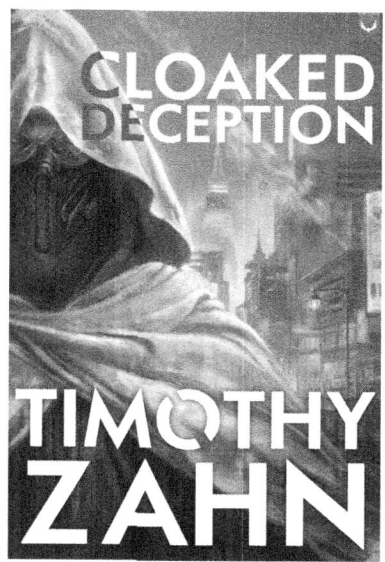

**From Timothy Zahn, Hugo Award winner and #1
New York Times bestselling author of *Star Wars:
Heir to the Empire,* comes this pulse-pounding
political thriller.** A tactical nuclear weapon is
stolen from an Indian research facility, setting off a
chain of events that spans the globe. Those behind
the heist plan to use it to take out thousands of
innocent people—all to assure death of a single
man who they believe is too dangerous to be left
alive. What are the lives of thousands compared to
the safety of the world? At the same time,
scientists have invented the world's first cloaking
device, able to render its user almost completely
invisible. It's the epitome of hidden-in-plain-sight—
a game changer for any military. At least until three
of the lead scientists are murdered and their work
is stolen the night before their first demonstration.
Authorities have no idea the two crimes are
connected. There are ten days before the bomb is
set to go off. Can they unravel the trail of red
herrings in time? The clock is ticking... **The
legendary Timothy Zahn, best-known for
creating the popular Thrawn character last seen
in *Star Wars: Ahsoka,* returns with this original,
unputdownable thriller. CLOAKED DECEPTION
is filled with twists and turns and a blistering**

conclusion you'll never see coming!

Get Cloaked Deception Now!

HE OPERATES IN THE SHADOWS SO WE DON'T HAVE TO. Soldier, spy, assassin, bodyguard. Chance Mock is an independent contractor who can be anything you need him to be—for a price. Unsanctioned by governments and unhindered by borders or laws, he's the last resort for those who demand results at all costs. Faced with an unknown enemy who threatens to undermine her family name, millionaire philanthropist Imogen Tolliver turns to the only man who can help her: Chance. He saved her life five years ago and now she needs him again. But she'll have to find him first, which isn't easy to do with a man who only exists in the shadows. Chance has problems of his own. One of the secret organizations he's crossed in the past has targeted him for removal. He needs to find out which one and why before they finish the job. Chance only has one person he can trust: Tarot, a voice on the phone who is as brilliant with a computer as Chance is with a gun. Chance Mock, the freelancer, is outmanned, outgunned, and running out of time. He has his enemies right where he wants them. **Don't miss this vigilante action thriller from Sam Sisavath, bestselling author of the Last Storm. Find out the fate of the Freelancer in this fast-paced, adrenaline-surging thrill ride. This gripping action thriller is perfect for fans of Lee Child, Jason Kasper, and David Archer.**

Get The Freelancer Now!

≈

For all our Thriller books, visit our website.

Printed in Great Britain
by Amazon